To

Wyoming Magic

Susan Hever

31/7/2021

Wyoming Magic

Published by The Conrad Press in the United Kingdom 2021

Tel: +44(0)1227 472 874

www.theconradpress.com

info@theconradpress.com

ISBN 978-1-913567-76-7

Typesetting and Cover Design by: Charlotte Mouncey, www.bookstyle.co.uk

The Conrad Press logo was designed by Maria Priestley.

Wyoming Magic

Susan Haven

Dedicated to the memory of my husband Les
and daughter Ann-Marie who always
encouraged me to write a book

Chapter One

Sandy Carson crested a rise in the rolling hills she'd been travelling through since leaving Cheyenne, bypassing the smaller town of Boulder before pulling her SUV over to the side of the road beside a grey rock formation that thrust up out of the greening grass like craggy fingers. She couldn't hold back the faint gasp of surprise that left her lips as she took in what at first looked like a wide flat valley spread out below her reaching all the way to a range of rocky hills in the far distance, streaked with pale creams, reds and grey.

It had taken two amazing days to drive from Phoenix and despite anxiously wanting to arrive at her destination of Sweetwater she'd tried not to be in too great a hurry to reach the end of her journey. The only time she'd ever left the State of Arizona had been to fly to Chicago to attend University there, and so far she had been enjoying the adventure, feeling triumph that she'd even managed to relax despite the disasters that she'd been told might happen to her.

Her whole life had been in the quiet town of Lone Tree. Fifty-five miles east of bustling Phoenix with all its malls and busy traffic, she usually only went into the city to meet up with her long-time friend, Mandy Romano for lunch and girl talk. She wasn't one for big cities, she felt uncomfortable with what she called the concrete jungle, preferring the more open fields around her home. That life had changed dramatically just a month ago.

Her day had started out as normal until she'd come home from working a new horse at her stables to discover a officious looking man sitting in the dining room with papers set out before him. With her mom Alice looking somewhat shocked, she'd immediately feared the worst.

'Mom, are you and dad okay?'

'We're fine, Sandy. This is Mister Amery. He's a lawyer and has some news for you.'

Indicating the man who'd risen from his seat at the dining table, Sandy was puzzled but as he held out his hand, she automatically took it.

'Miss Carson, Sandy Carson, I presume.'

'Yes.'

On being asked to sit, he had proceeded to inform her that Willard Thompson a distant uncle who she'd never really heard of before had sadly died in a tragic accident, that she'd been left his ranch in a place called Sweetwater, Wyoming and while it was at the present time being run by the foreman, it was a viable concern. In fact it had been doing very well for years. And she was now a wealthy woman.

She remembered the shock as she somehow managed to sift through a copy of the Will along with the deeds while Alice and Ken, her father having been called in from his work, seemed so surprised that they were almost as speechless as her. But the lawyer had assured them that it was totally legal.

'He left me a ranch. But why, and who is, or was, Willard Thompson?' she'd asked her mom once the lawyer had left but they didn't seem to know much themselves.

Discussing it several times with Mandy, she'd slowly been overcome by curiosity to go and find out about the place.

No, not curious, it was just something tugging at her heart to go and investigate until she'd finally come to the conclusion that she couldn't not. Perhaps she could sell it and then she would still be financially comfortable, to continue her work with horses.

With both Mandy and her parents finally won over, accepting her determination to go, they'd then been horrified to find out her intentions were to drive there, to have an adventure. It was too far, too dangerous, she'd be all alone they warned. But Sandy had slowly brushed all their worries aside. After all, she was curious as to what exactly she'd been given and for the first time in her life decided to do something completely out of the ordinary.

With her career of horse training, sometimes referred to by people as 'horse whispering' she preferred the term 'gentling' having slowed for the moment and no new horses in the pipeline at the present time, this would be the best time to leave her business. Blade Fuller who worked with her had assured her that he could cope with the few horses they had at the time, and would be quite happy to take on any extras if necessary.

When her parents, along with Mandy, finally realised that they couldn't talk her out of the journey they became more helpful, working out the roads she'd need to travel, motels she could stay at, gas stations, and even Sheriff's departments. Having rechecked she'd packed plenty of water and food for the journey, and her cell phone and laptop were fully charged, plus all the leads she needed, nearly nine hundred miles wasn't too far if she thought about it quickly!

The GPS would be her main guide but, as her parents warned her several times, it might just let her down if it ran out of signal somewhere and insisted on packing road maps, as might her cell which was something she also had to worry about. But despite their help she knew that they thought she was just taking too much of a chance.

Having packed a small suitcase as she didn't own much in the way of clothes, mostly dark coloured pants and shirts, with her straw hat and sunglasses on, she'd finally set out in her SUV. But despite her assurances to everyone that she'd be fine, she couldn't ignore the butterflies in her stomach.

Picking up the interstate for Flagstaff and setting the cruise she began to relax, enjoying the drive especially as on the way she was passing places with fascinating names. Horsethief Canyon and Bloody Canyon along with a town named Black Canyon City, let alone the amusing Bumblebee that made her giggle.

Navigating the big junction out of Flagstaff, she headed east for Winslow passing the site of the famous Meteor Crater before stopping at a gas station for fuel at Holbrook intending to keep her tank topped up. Not long after she spotted curiously shaped rocks scattered along the verges with the markings of bark and tree rings in varying shades of browns and blacks and a sign notified her that she was passing the Petrified Forest N.P. Somewhere she'd never visited but had heard about and would have loved to have stopped, but she didn't want to break her journey and add time to her drive.

Just before Gallop she was over the State Line into New Mexico leaving the interstate and onto Navajo land heading for Cortez, stopping for a rest at a diner to enjoy a light meal and a coffee before crossing another State Line into Colorado. Cortez and Monticello flew by until she reached Moab and the hotel where she had a room booked for the night. Across the road was a big diner its lights already glowing as dusk was creeping in and having taken her suitcase up to her third floor room, luckily they had an elevator, she was grateful to cross to the diner for a meal. Thankful to be able to stretch her legs even for that short a walk.

Having eaten, she returned to the room to set up her laptop to tell her mom and dad, and Mandy, where she was and that she was safe, with the distinct feeling she could hear their sighs of relief through the written replies. After a very quick shower, she tumbled into bed. She'd never driven so far before and with being excited at all the different and spectacular scenery, she'd been left feeling tired and drained.

Next day, re-invigorated from sleeping in a very comfortable bed, Sandy checked out of the hotel, pleased to give a good review on a form she was asked to fill in, crossing to the diner she found other early travellers already eating, and after a satisfying meal of bacon, scrambled eggs, biscuits and gravy, she was on the move again.

Driving to the next big junction and turning right, she was back on another Interstate towards the big city of Denver where the sight of the huge buildings nestled in a valley between snow tipped mountains even from a distance was a bit intimidating, and she was glad to find she could bypass the main town, picking up another Interstate, and crossing the State Line into Wyoming, aiming for Cheyenne.

Passing a large model of a buffalo adorning a ridge that had her smiling, a sign for a café encouraged her to stop for coffee and a snack. Built from hewn logs, she found herself the only single person there, just an elderly couple chatting at the back, hearing them say that last night had been a very cold one, and making her shiver at the thought as she slid into a window seat to take in the view. It had been so warm in the car. She was almost there, only a couple of hours from her destination and so immersed in her thoughts, she almost let her coffee go cold, forgetting it was in her hand until the man behind the counter came over to refresh her cup.

Cheyenne's long main street came and was left behind. More green rolling hills with rocky outcrops pushing up through the grass followed by red rocky canyons with green pines covering the slopes. Crossing the Laramie River and driving straight on through town, informed by the GPS to make a left for Laramie, she was more than a little worried about what she was doing the closer she got to her destination.

Having driven almost nine hundred miles to get here, and feeling more than a little jaded from the strain of the constant driving along what seemed to be never ending roads and only the occasional stop en-route for meals in diners or to refuel at gas stations to stretch her legs. Being alone, she'd felt more vulnerable than she'd imagined, only having short conversations with the people behind the counters but had never been even remotely 'hit on,' her parents' main worry.

Now, according to the GPS, the Boxed C ranch lay down in that valley close to the town of Sweetwater. Since crossing the state line into Wyoming, the sky had been a deeper blue than she'd ever seen it before while white fluffy clouds drifted lazily across leaving shadows rippling across the green plain. Mesmerising after the mostly dry Arizona desert region where she lived.

Opening a window, she took a deep breath to find that while

the air was sweet and fresh at first it had a noticeable bite to it and on an impulse pulled over onto the grass to look out over the country enjoying the tiny chipmunks darting across the rocks at a speed almost too fast to follow. Faint white flashes out in the distance turned out to be a small herd of Pronghorn as they fled from something either imaginary or threatening. Unlocking the back of her SUV, Sandy opened a bag looking for a warmer jacket beginning to realise that being this far north she should have taken note of the temperatures for Wyoming before she'd set out.

Immersed in the scenery she hadn't taken notice of a vehicle coming up from behind until realising from the sound that it was stopping and looked up nervously. A dark red, rugged pick-up had come to a halt and begun reversing towards her, stopped, and the driver's door opened. For the first time realising that she was alone and vulnerable, Sandy leapt into her vehicle, slamming the door shut as a tall man dressed in dusty well-worn cowboy clothing got out and began walking towards her holding his hands out in a friendly gesture. Her heart skipped a beat and tried to scoot up into her throat.

Wearing a beat-up dusty black Stetson, dark brown vest over a thick checked shirt, belted jeans with a huge shiny buckle and scuffed western boots he was breathtakingly masculine, and lethally handsome. Dark blonde hair curled from under his hat, he had a firm jaw and a strong face, his eyes hidden by dark glasses so she couldn't see them and as he strolled towards her, oozing sex appeal, she prayed that the wandering gaze taking in his wide shoulders and narrow hips, down to his western boots with all points in between, couldn't be seen. She flushed in embarrassment as she felt so unsettled, a slow heat building in her body. No man had ever affected her like this one.

After a few failed dates while she was at University, she'd thought by now she just wasn't into men in fact they hadn't been into her as she wouldn't put out and after word got round she was frigid she'd been basically snubbed. So she'd thrown herself into all the classes relating to working with horses including the veterinary ones so that she could at least look after some of the easier muscle and ligament damage along with minor cuts and scrapes before a vet would be needed.

'How do, Ma'am.' He stopped short of her window but she had no problem hearing his deep husky voice, it resonated down to her toes. 'Just checking you're okay. See you got Arizona tags, long way from home!' He grinned showing straight white teeth between firm lips that for a moment she couldn't take her eyes from, accompanied by the immediate thought of what would she do if he leant closer and pressed those lips to hers. A thought that made her pray she didn't just melt into a puddle in front of him. She gulped as her heart continued to beat erratically.

'I'm fine, thanks.' Sandy determined to keep her voice as normal as she could but would that be possible with him looking at her, even if she couldn't see his eyes? 'I just stopped to look at the view. I'm heading towards Sweetwater!'

'Bout fifteen minutes tops. You can't miss it.' He glanced back at the valley as if seeing it for the first time and as he smiled her stomach lurched with a feeling she couldn't, wouldn't try to identify. 'Unless you blink and then you'll be out the other side!'

Laughing at his own joke, he tipped the brim of his hat with his fingers, turned and walked back to his pick-up leaving her breathless with sensations she'd never felt before, tiny bolts of lightning pebbling her nipples, making her damp between her thighs. She blushed even more and not just her face, her whole body, glad that he couldn't see her any longer.

He had noted her interest in him, and where she'd been looking had quickened his libido for the first time in months. It hadn't taken much for him to be affected and not just revelling in the sight of the long blonde hair, the deep sapphire-blue eyes, or the light sprinkling of freckles over her nose. Her skin was a healthy golden tan, the same gold as her hands and forearms as if she spent a lot of time outdoors, but it was her flushed cheeks and those kissable lips only lightly adorned by pale pink lipstick that had fixed in his head.

He'd already noted her trim figure before she'd hot-footed it back into her car, curvy, not like those skinny modern girls whose hips he could have hung his hat on let alone rolling over in bed to find bones prodding his flesh, but full breasts and rounded buttocks that would fill his hands fine if he could just wrap them round her. That alone had made him interested enough to pull over to make conversation but noting the Arizona tags was a help although he'd have pulled over anyway whoever it had been, just to be neighbourly. He hoped that she would be staying in town for a while.

Busy looking after the ranch after his mentor had died from pneumonia brought about after a fall into an icy river which he'd been trying to cross to chase a cow back into the herd, he'd taken the death badly, had had to dig deep into his strength of will to carry on running the place, holding the ranch together as if his mentor was still there. From a youngster, the ranch hands of whom there'd been many for they were notorious for drifting from ranch to ranch had taught him riding, roping, and cattle work, while Sheb especially had attached himself to the boy having been at the ranch for many years. And as he'd grown up, he'd been taught the financial side of running the business as well.

But now he was worried about a new owner. He'd never heard of any family other than that the man's wife Mary had died a year before he had arrived at the ranch so he'd assumed that he would inherit the place some day. He was still in shock from when the Buffalo attorney had called him to say it had been given to someone else. Why hadn't he been told?

Sandy found she was having difficulty in taking her eyes from his firm rear in the tight fitting jeans, mentally trying to convince herself she wasn't interested despite the quivering of her nerves, but continuing to watch until he climbed back inside and drove off, giving him a ten minute start to prove to herself that she wasn't that interested. But her body was proving difficult to control. She wished she could have seen his eyes, suddenly grateful she hadn't, they could have been her downfall.

Driving between the walls of a canyon that blocked out everything, she emerged onto rolling hills and rocky outcrops only to have her breath taken by the sight of a magnificent white topped mountain range on the far horizon, its jagged peaks pointing into the clear sky. The winding road slowly descended to a plain passing several old buildings, and through fields of growing crops with huge metal wheels joined by pipes that she assumed would be used to water them.

Crossing the steel bridge over the Little Sandy Creek, to her it didn't resemble either little or sandy as the waters were a reddish colour and swollen with melt water, wide enough from bank to bank to have been called a river.

More single storey buildings lined the roadside mingling with older ones and then she'd reached Sweetwater. And yes, he'd been right, a blink and she'd have been through it, a lot smaller than she'd expected being used to Lone Tree and Phoenix but then she shouldn't have been surprised as most of the little towns she'd passed through on her way had appeared bigger on the maps.

Pausing at a crossroads, she spotted a sign for the Singletree Motel high on a post with another sign underneath announcing that, 'Everyone was welcome.'

A grassed area was centred on three sides by chalets painted in cream with blue shutters, pots of plants beginning to show signs of their spring potential. She swung into a space in front of the glass fronted reception and felt relief wash over her after the strain of travelling. With a grateful sigh, Sandy grabbed her purse and slid from the seat to the gravelled forecourt to enter the building. A stand with pamphlets showing the delights to be found in and around Sweetwater and Buffalo, including Yellowstone National Park, stood beside the counter. The sound of the door chime brought an attractive girl about her own age through a door at the rear, smiling brightly.

'Can I help you, Ma'am?'

'Sandy…!' she paused. She hadn't wanted anyone to know her name and therefore her business until she'd had the chance to go out to the ranch so she'd booked under the name of Sandy Reynolds. 'Reynolds. I booked a room.'

The girl didn't blink at the pause but ran her finger down the page of the book on the desk.

'Oh yes. You're booked for two nights, room 28 which is

eight doors down to your right. Can you fill in the card with your details?'

While Sandy filled in the sections asking for her car tag, name and address, the girl turned to pick out a key ring from the board behind her, she noticed that she was one of only five people staying here but then it wasn't anywhere near the height of the season when the crowds would be descending to see the famous geyser at the park, Old Faithful, about forty miles away.

'Thank you…' she looked at the girl's name tag, 'Doreen.'

'Hope you have a nice stay, Miss Reynolds, if there's anything we can do to make your stay more pleasant, please press 'O' on the desk phone in your room.'

Sandy smiled and returned to her car, driving down to the cabin and parking facing the door. Retrieving her purse and the suitcase from the trunk, locking the SUV, on opening the door to her cabin, she was pleasantly surprised by the freshly aired interior and how clean and neat it was. Two queen beds with prettily flowered quilts in bright colours, a small dark wood cupboard between them, wall lights above both, a standard lamp by the window, and a tan wood desk with a TV and just like the other hotel she'd stayed at there was a coffee machine with a choice of coffees, teabags, little containers of milk and foam drinking cups. A small fridge with a basic microwave on top stood close to the wash area.

Closing the door behind her, she tossed her hat on a chair, dropping the suitcase by the first bed with her purse. Leaving the drapes closed, the sun was now starting to drop behind the mountain range elongating the shadows creeping across the land, she switched the heater/air-con to warm, put water in the coffee maker, a sachet in the filter, and set it to percolate, slumping onto the bed to think. Now she was here, she was beginning to worry about how things were going to work out. By now her lawyer should have notified the foreman that she would be turning up today or tomorrow, later than she'd expected.

The machine bubbled and gurgled until it had finished brewing when she poured the coffee into a foam cup, added a container of milk and sat down at the desk with her laptop, gratefully sipping the hot drink. Quickly getting onto the internet, she emailed Mandy, Alice and Ken that she had arrived safely and was enjoying a much needed rest while she decided what next to do. That wasn't going to be too hard, it was too late to find her way to the ranch, it would be dark very soon so her main priority was to find somewhere to eat. She'd have to drive as the temperature had already started dropping.

Calling in at reception to ask for directions, Doreen told her to go left out of the car lot, left again and halfway along the street was Su Ann's diner where they had a good menu and she could recommend all the dishes.

Finding the wooden building, its lights already on, and nosing into a space, once out and standing on the sidewalk Sandy could make out a few other buildings in the gloom, some brick, some half brick and half wood, and people still strolling along the sidewalks. The signs she could make out indicated a drug store, Dana's Gifts, now that sounded interesting, a grocery store, and a Sheriff's office and what she thought might be a combined bank and post office up the street to her left.

Unfortunately, she became even more conscious that her clothes, more fitting for Arizona warmth, were just not up to Wyoming's cold wind especially now it was dark and with a shiver, the tantalising smell coming from the diner making her keenly aware that she was hungry, she gladly pushed through the door to stand for a moment to look about her.

The dark wood walls and low ceiling looked old and again, as she'd found in other towns along the way, felt as if she'd entered a film set for an old western movie. Padded bench seats with tables like cubicles ran along the wall to her left, wooden chairs and tables between her and the bar were more modern, the tables with washable plastic tablecloths, and as far as she could see only a couple were already occupied.

Heads turned to look as she crossed to the serving counter, aware of the interest she was causing, obviously standing out like a sore thumb not only being a stranger but her style of clothing would be shouting she was from out of town. Like from a big town like Denver. Settling onto a bar stool, the cook glanced out at her through the open serving hatch.

A neatly dressed woman behind the counter walked towards her from where she had been talking to a man at another stool, a beer in his hand, wiping her hands on a towel. Her silvery hair, plaited and held up in place by clips from which loose strands had escaped and curled round her neck topped warm and friendly eyes. The man looked across at Sandy, half smiled, and turned his head away as if embarrassed to be seen staring.

'Hi, I'm Su Ann, welcome to my diner. What can I get you?'

'Coffee, please and a look at the menu, everything seems to smell delicious.'

The woman deftly reached for the percolator behind her with one hand and neatly placed a clear plastic stand with the menu printed inside it in front of her at the same time.

'You've done that before!' Sandy smiled as the liquid was

poured into a tall mug and was immediately rewarded by dark brown eyes sparkling back, laughter lines creasing her tanned skin.

'You're not from around here!'

Sandy had noted the question several times after leaving the confines of the more open Phoenix city, the only way anyone could ask a stranger without causing offence.

'Arizona. Phoenix. How could you tell?' Sandy sipped at the hot drink, grinning.

'Your accent, plus you're not exactly dressed for Wyoming!'

Sandy grimaced. 'Yes, I've found that out the hard way.' She perused the menu and plumped for fried chicken and a salad with refried beans. Su Ann shouted the order through to Jonas and he nodded.

'Things will liven up later as folks start to come in.' Su Ann winked. 'You might have some fun with the local cowboys if they drop in. They're good guys, bashful but can get a little bit rowdy especially with a pretty girl like you.'

Sandy raised her eyebrows. 'I'm not looking for a date.'

'You might not but they sure as heck will. Just play along with them honey, I'll keep them in line!'

'Thanks.'

Retiring to one of the booths and removing her hat to shake her hair loose, she sat sipping her drink until Su Ann brought her meal and cutlery, refilling her mug.

Boots clattered on the sidewalk outside and three men came in chatting, sitting down at a table and ordering coffee and a meal, joshing with Su Ann. One nudged the other having spotted Sandy and they swung their heads to look over. Sandy gave them just a slight smile and then ignored them.

A couple of other younger men in range clothes wandered in, sitting at the bar and ordering their meal before Sandy spotted the man she'd seen out on the road passing the window, and her heart began to pound. Hoping he'd keep on going by, wanting him to come in, sliding back into the shadows in case he saw her, but he came in and she couldn't keep her eyes from drinking in the lithe whipcord body, the masculinity that seemed to cloak him as he crossed to the counter, striding as if he owned the world. It seeped across the room, setting her mind and body to his presence, and again she felt her pulse quicken, thoughts she'd never had before creeping into her. She closed her eyes and tried to think of other things until his voice slithered over her skin.

'Hey. Su Ann.'

Joining the two at the bar, requesting a cup of Java, they discussed cattle and the state of the range where it became apparent that the others were from a different ranch. But almost as if he was tuned in to her, he swung his head until he could just make her out in the shadows and his body tensed. Grabbing his coffee, he headed towards her and she fervently hoped he couldn't see her cheeks redden having noted that without his shades, his dark eyes showed interest, a lot of interest.

'Ma'am, see you got here okay. Mind if I join you?'

Before she could open her mouth to say no, however reluctantly, he slid into the seat opposite her as a faint groan from the bar made it obvious that the younger men felt they'd missed out on a golden opportunity. He laughed. The sound made her skin prickle with awareness, heated her body making her wonder why she would need warmer clothing, him just being there was heat enough. She froze for a nanosecond because she'd never experienced such feelings, they frightened yet enticed her and she had to gulp the mouthful of food before she choked.

'Name's Kyle.'

Sandy dropped her gaze back to her nearly finished meal at the unexpected name. Just her luck, he was the foreman of the Boxed C? She couldn't just blurt out who she was in here, she needed to see him on his own, in private, to make it easier to discuss, and for a second she hesitated hoping he wouldn't notice. So she said the first thing she could think of.

'Mandy.'

'Staying at the motel?'

'Just for a couple of days, it depends!'

Well, that was no lie. She finished the food on her plate and sat back, holding her cup in both hands to stop them from quivering. How would he take it when she revealed her true identity? The chemistry that seemed to zing between them was going to make talking to him even more difficult. She shut her eyes and tried not to imagine sharing the same space with him when she revealed who she was.

'Well, now the pleasantries are over, you want more coffee?'

His deep voice again sent a shiver down her back, and she made the mistake of looking at him, his admiring stare sending a strange sensation sweeping along her skin, through her body, and on down to her toes. She tried to avoid thinking about her nipples prickling and her inner core heating up. This was stupid. He was a total stranger, she shouldn't be affected this way but somehow he made her feel safe even if she was unused to interacting with men.

Kyle was even more intrigued than before, couldn't help but

stare at her. Even with her face in shadow she was very attractive, sexy even, her blue eyes now darkened in the dim light were like deep pools urging him to leap in, her lips needing to be thoroughly kissed, and by him, but he had a feeling that she was being cagey for a reason that he'd like to know. It was obvious that she had been attracted to him as much as he was to her but now she seemed a touch wary. Back on the road she'd been very nervous but then she had been alone.

Sandy was unsure, after all she didn't want him to discover who she was until she was ready, and with no experience of men, she could only go on instinct. But she liked the authorative sound of his voice, he was obviously used to being in charge and being the foreman of the ranch would have done that. She'd had to learn to deal with men who had been almost scornful of what she did in her line of work, trying to regain the confidence she used as a mantle against them. If she could just chat without making him suspicious she might understand a little about what she was in for.

'Thank you, I wouldn't mind.'

Her soft voice went straight through him and his blood headed down south making him very glad that he was behind the table as his manhood decided it liked it too and began to expand behind the zipper. He quickly indicated to Su Ann who came over to refill their mugs. She smiled at Kyle.

'Didn't take you long, did it, Kyle? You always did manage to find the prettiest girl in the place, but remember she's under my protection.'

'Coffees are on me.' He found some change in his pocket and handed it over before Sandy could refuse. Su Ann just smiled and picked it up as he added, 'Tip's for you.'

She waggled her finger at him as she turned to go, his cheeky smile lighting up his face and making Sandy stare at him almost in awe, her body charging with excitement, her breasts aching as a strange clenching of her thighs and lower muscles made her shift uncomfortably. What on earth was happening? She'd never felt anything like this before. She did not like men and up to now they'd never been interested in her. But then she'd never been anywhere before, just buried herself in her work so perhaps that was why she felt so attracted now. To try and hide her reaction, she carefully opened one of the little milk containers, pouring the contents into her cup before sipping it slowly, noticing that he took his black.

'Do you live round here?'

'Not far, about twenty miles as the crow flies!'

Her heart suddenly warmed to him as he gave another of those mischievous smiles that brought unknown sensations to her skin and her insides. She had to be careful here. Whatever spell he was weaving had to be disregarded. He was her employee.

'They fly in straight lines round here?' she teased, surprising herself by her boldness, sitting forward more, rewarded by another mesmerising smile, his eyes glinting.

No-one had ever looked at her like he did, but then such a sexy man like him would soon be turned off when he found out that at the grand old age of twenty-three she was naïve and innocent of life. She forced herself to appear cheerful, finding that that was made easier by his being unfamiliar. Well not really, she already knew something about him.

'Don't they where you come from?'

'That depends on where they're going! Are you a rancher?'

'Nope, I'm foreman of the Boxed C.'

There was pride in his voice, the voice of a natural leader, someone totally in control. She felt a touch of regret. That his life was about to change due to her made her feel very uncomfortable even though she'd been through the same thing when the attorney had suddenly turned up.

'Is it big? I've never been on a ranch.' Well that wasn't a lie.

'Perhaps I could show you if you're staying around here for a while.' He was flirting. Saw her cheeks pink up.

Now it was his turn to lean slightly forward. Did she tense slightly? Had he come on a little too strong? But he felt some sort of connection, a spark between them. He really would like her to come out to the ranch he was proud of. Not only that, somehow, perhaps he could get her to stay. He wanted her in his bed, could imagine their slick bodies skin on skin as he plunged into her eager body, as she clamped her wetness around his manhood, milking him until they both came. His body tensed with the thoughts as he took a deep breath, a silent gasp. They'd only just met and he was already planning on having sex? Even for him this was breathtakingly fast! What was it with her!

Sandy watched his expression change as he coolly looked her over, sending her senses into a spin, her body tensing with a need that made her burn deep down between her thighs but instead of putting up her usual barriers she found herself doing the same thing back to him. Despite knowing that she seriously needed to learn to put these new found emotions under restraint, was going to have to draw on all her strengths when she finally met up with him at the ranch. Wondered what it would be like to have his mouth on hers, his hands round her body. Lowered her gaze before he could read what was in them.

Even with his last girlfriend Kyle had never been as attracted to any other woman as he had been to her and with difficulty he had to shut his thoughts down of the girl in front of him. She intrigued him, her expression and her body outline one of confusion as well as interest.

Kyle hesitated, and as he leaned back, Sandy felt almost bereft which was stupid as she didn't want to know him as anyone but a business acquaintance. Her uncle had made both of them scapegoats in some weird plan because it was beginning to make her wonder if really he should have been given the place.

'I might.'

Did he do this to all women? One look back into those eyes and she knew that he probably did. She had to get away before she made a complete fool of herself and glanced at her watch. Despite the strong coffee she was feeling very tired and with what she was going to have to do tomorrow, she'd better turn in even if she would have liked to have continued talking to him. Really wanted to stay! But she needed to keep a clear head around him when they met officially.

'Leaving so soon?' he whispered regretfully. 'I do hope you stay around town for a while. It could be… interesting!'

'I'm afraid so. It's been a long day.'

Quivering, she shivered and grabbed her hat, eased out from behind the table, picking up her purse so she could go and pay for her meal. For the first time ever she'd have loved to have stayed and continued their conversation. She couldn't believe what was happening, that she had enjoyed his company, that he actually made her feel desirable. It was so, so unlike her.

'Thanks for the drink.'

'My pleasure, ma'am, hope to see you around.'

His rising erection agreed and he'd have liked to have followed her back to the motel for the rest of the evening but the smudge of dark skin under her eyes attested to the truth of being tired. Kyle remained seated so he could finish his coffee, appreciating the sway of her hips and the firm rounded buttocks outlined above long, long legs. Holding his breath at the way she filled those pants.

However, he couldn't help but be surprised at the way she was dressed, a black shirt covered by a dark jacket buttoned up the front, thin black pants, lightweight black trainers on her feet. She obviously hadn't considered the weather this far north judging by those. Totally unsuitable for Wyoming she looked more like a model with that long blonde hair falling down her back. Why had she come so far up country? She needed to get back to her room and get the heating on before she froze although his body had already decided that it wouldn't mind warming her up. Holding her close, peeling her out of those clothes to taste what he guessed were full round breasts before fitting himself deep inside her. They'd both warm up then.

The thought of those long legs wrapped round his waist nearly made him drop his drink. He shook his head. He had a feeling that he'd want more than a one night stand although in her case he wouldn't have minded just the one.

Aware of the appreciative interest shown by the other men in the room, he was surprised by his instant protective attitude towards her as she went to the door and passed out into the darkness, everyone listening for the beep of the alarm as she unlocked the door to get inside her SUV, the engine starting, and then the sound of the motor as she drove off, heading back to the edge of town for the motel. He was beginning to regret not trying to make her stay longer but she had looked tired.

Sandy was pleased to get inside her chalet for the engine hadn't had time to warm from standing outside the diner, gratefully turning the air-con to its warmest setting. Unpacking her PJs and robe, she was happy to climb under the hot shower, letting the water run down to take the chill off her skin. A quick soaping, a rinse off and a rub down to get herself dry before getting into her nightwear, checking again that the door was securely locked before gratefully climbing into bed.

She was surprised to have slept so well snuggled down underneath the sheet and warm quilt, glad for the heater and grateful for the robe thin as it was when she climbed out of bed to make a hot drink before needing to get dressed. Relaxing back against the pillows, she flicked through the TV channels before finally coming across an early morning programme to watch. She'd always skirted the news finding most of it depressing.

Energised after her caffeine fix, she sorted through her case for the folder containing the Will, the deeds to the ranch, her identification and her lawyer's details, double-checking that everything was in order for when she went to the bank. Her initial idea had been to just drive up to the ranch house and say who she was but her innate good manners made her realise that that could antagonise the foreman so decided to ring instead to warn them.

Washed and dressed in a grey shirt, black pants and a light-weight black jacket, she picked up the phone and rang the number the lawyer had given. After a couple of rings the phone was answered by a lady.

'Hello, Boxed C. Kate speaking.'

'Hi. Is Kyle Sherman about?'

'No, miss, he'll have gone to talk to the hands but if you want to come on over you're welcome to wait.'

'Thanks. I'll stop off at the diner for breakfast and come out.'

'Bless you, miss, Kyle will be wanting something to eat when he gets back, so you come and I'll have a breakfast here for you. There's always plenty.'

Sandy was intrigued by the woman's voice, she sounded older than the notes she'd read about the foreman, was she his wife, a girlfriend? Why did she suddenly feel oddly bereft about that!

'Thanks, I'll be about an hour.'

'You're more than welcome.'

Putting the phone back on its holder, she nervously picked up her purse and paperwork and headed out to her car, surprised to find how cold it was outside, the bodywork lightly covered in a faint layer of white frost. But it had just turned April! So different from Arizona! She rushed back in to put on a second lot of clothing before driving through town.

Already people were walking around or standing chatting. The town seemed surreal, like several others she'd passed through the more north she'd come, all reminding her of frontier towns from a western movie. After the hustle and bustle of Phoenix and the smaller Lone Tree the place seemed so relaxing, it practically oozed peace with no-one appearing to be in any hurry.

Her GPS, laughingly referred to as 'Jane' due to the voice she used, soon had her heading out on the road and into the open lands with occasional road signs warning to beware of cattle or antelope although she didn't see any, just one old pick-up heading in the other direction, when the disembodied voice of Jane advised her to make a left in half a mile. Her long drive here had only slightly accustomed her to wide open spaces, but through the windscreen before her stretched miles of grassland as far as the horizon, interspersed with the occasional rocks or boulders, and it was almost intimidating.

Driving under an iron arch bearing the words Boxed C and across a cattle grid, two mounds of stones appeared either side of the track each with a pair of upturned western boots sticking out that made her giggle. It was nice to know that someone here had a sense of humour. Following the dusty trail across the undulating plain, fenced either side with wire and with no sign of a building, after a couple of miles and just as she was beginning to wonder if she'd gone wrong somewhere, the house came in sight. And she had to stop to try and take it all in.

Far off,she could just make out a wide two storey log building. A veranda with a railed porch, touched with what looked like splashes of colour that she assumed from the distance were pots of flowers as well as hanging baskets, ran the length of the front. Another railed veranda ran the along the second storey below what she assumed would be bedrooms. Off to the right further along the trail showed the roof of at least one big barn. It was impressive but welcoming and she fell instantly in love with it and for what seemed a very long time but was probably not more than a few seconds she had to remember to breathe. This was all hers?

Starting to drive on, she headed for the house just making it before a pick-up came up from the barns driven by the cowboy she'd met on the road and in the diner. He stared at her in surprise but carried on going, obviously in a hurry. Parking up, feeling a little excited at coming across him yet again, wondering what he would do when he found out who she was, Sandy went to the front door and knocked.

Kyle had been bemused at the sight of Sandy in the yard, not that he'd mind seeing her again as a deep sensual pleasure spiked his senses and he felt his jeans tighten. Had she come specially to look him up? He preferred to do the chasing but there was no other reason that he could see for her turning up unexpectedly, and although he was not normally attracted to women so forthcoming, in her case he could easily change his mind. The last girlfriend he'd thought he liked had become too clingy after a couple of weeks and he'd had to tell her to go, and that had also helped his bank balance. With no time to waste, he had to get on but it would be nice to come back to the house to see if she'd stayed, and talk to her.

The door was opened by a motherly lady with a bright smile and laughter lines around her grey eyes, wearing an apron dusted with flour, obviously having been baking.

'Hi.' She hesitated. 'I'm Sandy. Sandy Carson.'

As the woman's eyes widened in surprise and then pleasure, she swept forward to clasp Sandy in a big hug before ushering her inside.

'Land sakes, this is such a pleasure. I'm Kate Barnes, the housekeeper. Come on into the kitchen. Nicest part of a house I always reckon. Coffee's on!'

More than a little anxious, feeling out of her depth, she followed Kate into the entrance hall. To the right were wide stairs with carved balustrades leading up to the second floor landing above an archway that disclosed a small lounge. A quick glance to her left showed a larger open lounge. She couldn't take it all in, it was just too overwhelming. It was big and showed the hand of a man who either wanted to show his status or just the love of his home. She'd ask Kate to show her around before she left. Sandy found herself being led into a large open kitchen smelling delightfully of baking and made her think longingly of home and her mom's cooking.

Lit by a large window to the left, on the far wall was a well-used cooking range with an aluminium cooker-hood over flanked by natural pine wood cupboards. Against a small wall on the right stood a tall metallic fridge-freezer, beside it an archway leading from the kitchen to a dining room, a quick glance showing a long wooden table and eight chairs. A counter in the centre had been built by stacking natural slabs of rock topped by dark grey granite and at the moment half covered by bowls, dishes and utensils. The same granite covered the work surface of the cupboards.

'Wow!' Sandy couldn't keep back the amazement in her voice.

'Sit yourself down, coffee's always on the go, you never know who will want to come in around lunchtime if they're not out on the range and I keep biscuits ready for a snack.'

As Sandy sat on a stool, tucking her knees under the overhang of the counter, Kate passed her a fork followed by a plate of bacon, eggs, and two biscuits covered in creamy sausage gravy taken from the top warming-oven, and her stomach almost growled at the delicious sight and smell. Smiling, filling two mugs, the housekeeper indicated for Sandy to eat.

'This is kind of you, Kate.'

'You're welcome. So you're Willard's niece. You look a little like him, same colour eyes, and same smile. I'm... we're all real

31

sorry about your uncle.' Her expression shone with sympathy as she sat down on her side of the counter while Sandy set too with a will.

'To be honest, I really didn't know him, only what my parents told me and that wasn't much. I'm somewhat confused that he left me this place, I know nothing about ranching.'

'We didn't know about you either, it came as rather a shock when the attorney notified Kyle. As to the ranch, that's no problem, as foreman Kyle can show you around. The ranch is his life, always has been since… But then I will let Kyle tell you whatever he wants to, I shouldn't gossip.'

Sandy grinned. 'Oh, but gossip keeps the world interesting doesn't it?' making the older woman laugh.

'You're someone after my own heart.'

'What was Willard like?' Sandy finished her meal, sipping at the coffee.

'He was honest, a straight talker, never let the men do anything he wouldn't tackle himself. They liked him a lot and no-one ever let him down. He took a great deal of pride in the ranch, he knew the history from when his great grandparents originally settled here, and then took over from his own parents. Kyle does know you're coming?'

'My lawyer should have informed him when I was coming, but doesn't exactly know who I am. Please don't mention who I am yet. We met outside of town when I stopped to admire the view and he stopped to check I was alright. I have Arizona tags. Then we met in the diner yesterday evening. He told me his name but I didn't want to talk there and told him my name was Mandy! I hope he's not too annoyed when I explain.' She grimaced. 'He did look a bit puzzled to see me just now. He was driving out.'

'Well, he's used to being chased by women even if he hates it.' Kate shrugged, standing up to take the empty plate. 'You were hungry and I like people with a good appetite. Kyle's going to have one heck of a shock when he finds out who you are. But I'm sure he won't mind me showing you round.'

Leading the way towards the front door she turned right into the long open lounge, drawing a faint gasp from Sandy as she saw inside for the first time. Stone and wood panelling round the walls should have made the place look gloomy but the big floor to ceiling windows facing the drive let in lots of light. She was immediately drawn to the big stone fireplace and could imagine sitting in front of a roaring log fire on cold evenings, the room only lit by that or wall and table lights. Right above it was a painting that she found fascinating, studying it, a man in a suit with his arm lovingly round the waist of a very pretty lady dressed in a pale blue gown.

'Willard and his wife, Mary,' said Kate, 'I never met up with Mary. She'd passed on before I came to the ranch.'

A couple of very large sofas along with several deep armchairs and a long glass topped table didn't even seem intimidating in such a huge room while thick rugs covered most of the stone floor. Turning slowly, she found several rows of bookshelves lining one of the inner walls beside the doorway.

'Oh.'

On a nearby table Sandy spotted several pictures and went over to look at them, surprised that they showed not only her, but one of her parents as well. She hadn't realised that they'd all kept in touch, Alice and Ken had only fleetingly mentioned Willard to her before the lawyer had arrived on their doorstep.

'You alright?' asked Kate coming to stand beside her. 'You are family.'

'My parents never mentioned Willard and I was wondering why.'

Turning back, Kate led her across the passageway and under the staircase into another smaller lounge lightened with the same big windows and a scaled down décor similar to the other room but with a table and chairs. Everything so far was so masculine, apart from a few potted plants, there was no sign of a woman's touch and she mentioned the woman in the painting to Kate.

'The plants in and outside are my way of brightening the place. As to Willard having a wife, all I know is that she'd died many years ago and he never remarried. I did ask once because of the painting but he clammed up so I never asked again. They must have been very much in love because I've been the only woman around here apart from one or two of Kyle's girlfriends that stayed for perhaps a weekend.'

Pointing to the left to a closed door, Kate told her it was Kyle's office and that he'd always lived in the house having one of the bedrooms upstairs. Heading up to the landing, Kate indicated that the first door was Kyle's, taking her along to show her the other two.

'All en-suite and both are ready made up so I'll let you choose which one you'd prefer, I assumed you would be staying. I do hope so. I'd enjoy some real girl talk time after being with all men although I do go into town for groceries or a snack at Su Ann's. I go into Buffalo for the main shopping.'

Further round she showed off a fully-fitted gym and a smaller room with an indoor hot-tub. Sandy rubbed her hands together.

'I'd like to have a go in that.'

'There's another outside which the men can use after a hard day.'

Back downstairs and in the kitchen, Kate resumed preparing the evening's meal.

'There's a pie in the oven already. The men eat over there.' She inclined her chin towards the big table, 'and if you don't mind chatting I'd like to hear about your mom, and Phoenix.' She sighed. 'Being this size I guess I won't be wearing anything fancy like you youngsters.'

'You're still catered for you know. Perhaps if I stay on, if Kyle doesn't think that I'm interfering, we could go into Buffalo or Cheyenne.'

'Oh I'd love that. My daughter lives in Chicago so I don't get to see her but once a year. She wanted the bright lights.'

'I'm sorry. My mom and I are very close. She and dad were both so worried when I said that I was going to drive up here to Wyoming.'

'You never did! Alone?' Kate sounded shocked, looking up from what she was doing.

'I wanted an adventure. Please let me help.'

Sandy got up to peel vegetables and they were gaily chatting away when the side door into the dining area opened and Kyle walked in. His eyebrows rose as he heard them, his gaze quickly taking in Sandy from head to toe in appreciation, and again she felt her body flush, her pulse jump. As he swept his hat off, he hooked it onto one of the row of pegs just inside the door. Realising that she was staring at him, more like gawking she told herself, she quickly looked away, unsettled.

'We've company I see,' he drawled in that throaty voice that sent chills down her back. 'I wouldn't mind a drink, if it's going.'

He stared at Sandy, a knowing smile on his lips that made her feel both annoyed yet somehow alive before sitting down at the counter effortlessly sliding his legs under. Mandy, she knew, would have called him eye candy.

'I'll do it,' she told Kate, reaching for the coffee.

Nervously she filled a mug and passed it to him, her hand trembling a little, her heart racing. He was so male he seemed to fill the entire room just by himself. Smelt of horses and the outdoors that mingled with his male scent sending shivers through her body. Somewhat taken aback by the appreciation that flickered in the hazel eyes as he lazily looked her up and down. She was glad to turn back to what she was doing before she made a complete idiot of herself.

Kyle watched her. He'd noticed the tremor, aware of the electricity that had shot through him, and that she was obviously feeling the same. Oh how he would have enjoyed taking hold of that hand, to pull her close into him, feel those round plump breasts against his chest, his growing erection pressed against her thigh… Kyle blinked and looked down at his mug, picking it up.

'Any biscuits, Kate?' he asked hopefully, trying not to look at the girl in front of him again.

'You know where they are.'

His smile was devastatingly sinful and it took a few seconds before Sandy could turn her attention away as Kyle pulled a big tin towards him, lifted the lid, and took out a biscuit before replacing the lid to take a bite.

'Delicious as usual,' he praised and Kate turned to look at

him as he finished the biscuit and smacked his lips.

'Don't go ruining your appetite.'

'I won't.' He contemplated Sandy thoughtfully. 'You come to see me?'

'Well, yes.' Sandy forced herself to look at him. 'I need to talk to you. Can we go somewhere?'

Kyle glanced at Kate's back suddenly feeling that things weren't what they'd first appeared, a strange atmosphere invading the normally peaceful kitchen, becoming aware of Sandy's nervousness since he'd come in. That made him curious because women didn't usually react that way to him, not that he was conceited. He waited for her to wash her hands before standing to allow her to pass him, instantly attracted by the faint smell of a light fragrance, perfume, soap or perhaps shampoo as she went by, his libido rising again as he thought of running his fingers through that long blonde hair. Last night it had been tied back, this time it was hanging loose almost to her waist. If she was coming onto him he needed to be somewhere private where he'd be more than willing to enjoy what she seemed to be offering, leading the way to the ranch office. Placing his mug on the desk top he spun to face her.

In the smaller area the effect of his maleness seemed to fill it and for a moment Sandy was almost daunted by his sheer masculinity. She was used to dealing with men but this was a totally different ball game. Looking into his face she wondered how on earth she was going to tell this man that she'd come to take over the ranch he'd thought was his. She hesitated and he smiled.

'I know why you're here,' he said seductively to break the silence, wondering why she was looking so nervous, enjoying his gaze to rove over her body, taking in the roundness of her breasts under her shirt as she curled her arms under as if to protect herself, but making her nipples stand out temptingly. Had she realised? Was this the come on he wanted? He leant his butt back against the edge of the table and folded his arms to wait.

'You do?' Sandy was unable to think clearly. Not only by what he'd said but the glint in his eyes, those hazel eyes that seemed to take her breath away when they landed on her and caused shivers along her spine. Her mouth went dry as she stared at his lips before forcing herself to look into his face.

'Oh yes.'

Reaching forward to take hold of her upper arms, he brought her up close, noting with curiosity how strong her muscles were, almost as if she worked hard, certainly nothing like the girls he usually dated. He quickly wrapped his arms round her waist, pulling her closer, her feminine scent swirling into his nose and enticing him. Sandy gasped, suddenly finding herself trapped between his hard thighs. Her heart skipped a beat, blood pulsing in her ears at strange sensations that slithered down to pool in her lower belly as she gazed up in bewilderment into his eyes, so close that she could make out tiny flecks of gold in them. His warm breath shimmied across her lips and cheek while the flare of want in his eyes sent a searing aching need she'd never felt before deep inside, a warmth pooling between her legs as she realised that he was staring at her mouth as she ran her tongue over the bottom one to moisten it. That he intended to kiss her unless she backed off, tried to stop herself from being pulled closer, slamming her palms against his hard warm chest. Felt his heart racing like hers.

'I don't think you do,' Sandy stammered.

Kyle looked at her with a knowing smile, sure she was trying to make him think that she was an innocent at this game and before he could stop himself, he so wanted to taste those lips, his mouth had swooped down to hers. His lips gently tantalised and when she gasped, trying to draw breath, he flicked his tongue into her mouth, pulling her tight into him, his erection thickening behind his zipper.

Sandy had never been kissed like this before, her senses reeled as she tried to pull away but it only made him hold her tighter. This wasn't a kiss it was something far more dangerous making her feel giddy and her legs weaken. Before she knew what was happening, her tongue was entangled with his as he explored inside. It was so sensuous that for a moment she couldn't pull away, found herself melting into his arms, hypnotised by the chemistry as her hands revelled in the warm hardness of his chest.

Kyle clasped the back of her head, holding her to him, inviting her tongue to tangle with his as he devoured her, shockingly aware that he'd never felt so strongly about a woman before. As if an electric current had shot through them, he knew that she'd felt the same when her blue eyes darkened, then closed. Only slowly did Sandy become aware of what was happening when his palm cupped her breast, fingers brushing over a sensitised nipple and sending an intense hot pleasure shooting down through her body. For a moment she melted against him, feeling heat and wetness between her thighs. And then her senses snapped to what was happening, somehow she fought against this new pleasure and managed to jerk back, saw him smile knowingly.

'Please, no,' she whispered. 'I can't.'

'Why not, isn't that what you followed me out here for?'

So she thought she could come here and tease him? He stared intently at her expression, something was wrong here, she'd sounded as if she was distressed, certainly shaken. And that kiss. It had felt as if she hadn't known how to do it, that it had been him guiding her. Now, that was odd.

'No. I didn't.'

She tore herself free, shaking like a leaf, torn between stopping herself before things went too far, leaving her wanting more. What had come over her to react like this! Kyle scowled. For a moment she'd responded to him, so why had she suddenly retreated?

'Then what are you here for!'

He stared at her in frustration, noted the confusion on her face and feeling the same, whirled round the desk to slam himself into his chair, mainly to hide his obvious reaction to her that at the present was trapped painfully behind his zipper.

Sandy was taken aback that he could turn so fast from sensuousness to anger unaware of why as she didn't know anything about adult males or their raging desires. What she read about in books hardly made her world wise!

'I'm... ...I'm not Mandy. I'm Sandy, Sandy Carson!'

Chapter Two

In a nanosecond the atmosphere in the room changed as he stared at her, trying to grasp what she had just told him. Sandy Carson was supposed to have arrived last week, he'd assumed she wasn't coming after the first initial shocking letter from her lawyer to say that Willard had left the ranch to some unknown niece he'd never heard of. He ran his hands through his thick hair and tried hard not to feel sick. This slip of a girl had been handed what he had considered to be his ranch, his land.

'Willard's niece!' he blurted, his mind going every direction at once.

She'd finally turned up? He was mortified, he'd wanted, would have taken Willard's niece to bed, Willard, his mentor, guardian, friend. Elbows on the desk he put his head in his hands. 'Good God.'

'You were in the diner. You said your name was Mandy,' he grated out through tight lips. 'You lied. Why?'

'You didn't tell me exactly who you were either!' Sandy came back at him sharply, nervous about being the brunt of his aggression but in no way scared. For some reason like when he'd stopped to help her out on the road, she'd felt safe with him then and even now she didn't feel threatened.

'Oh? And why didn't you?' he accused.

'Oh yes, you think I would have blurted personal stuff like that out in front of someone I didn't know and the towns people while in the diner? I didn't know exactly who you were,' she snapped before she looked at him in sympathy. 'I wanted to talk to you somewhere quiet.'

'I guess not.' He had to admit at least that. 'That still doesn't make it right. No-one told me you were turning up a week late!'

Sandy swallowed hard. 'My lawyer was supposed to have been in touch. My travel here was taking longer than I expected since I was driving.'

'Driving?'

She met his look full on, lifting her chin in defence, and he had to admire her strength in standing up for herself, as if he'd hit a nerve. A bobcat sprang to mind.

'Oh, you don't think a woman could do it, I suppose!'

Kyle stilled. 'Who said anything about that, it's just the danger.'

'Well, for your information I had no problems at all in fact Colorado was stunning and Wyoming turned out to be lovely.'

'I stopped to help and could have been just anyone, who could have taken advantage…'

'Oh, you mean, like in here,' she interrupted, her cheeks pinking, clutching at her shirt buttons.

Kyle had the grace to look disconcerted. 'I thought you were here for a different reason.'

'So I noticed. It's obvious that women throw themselves at you so you immediately thought that of me. Well, tough!'

Sandy made herself turnabout, her whole demeanour stiff, to walk out the door heading back for the kitchen, trying to take the time to get her breath back. What had just happened? She'd almost lost her head when her body had betrayed her, responding so shamelessly at his touch, the total opposite of who she was, who she had been. Suddenly she'd been craving what he had been offering, hadn't wanted it to end.

Unconsciously, she found herself licking her lips to remember his taste before she became aware of what she was doing. How could he make her forget who she was, that she never let herself go around men. The thought of running into him anywhere around the ranch now put her on edge, felt totally out of her depth. Back at the kitchen Kate turned to speak, realised that something was wrong, and stopped.

'Didn't go too well,' Sandy murmured to her unsaid question. 'He assumed I'd chased him from town. Is he always this big headed?'

'Give him time. It must have been quite a shock!' She laughed, delighted. 'I hope he met his match with you! Women come here with all sorts of excuses but very few he'd go out with and they've never stayed for long. He's too involved with the ranch and they want the high life.'

'Going to make life somewhat interesting round here,' Sandy replied, remembered how her body had tingled at his touch. They heard the front door open and then slam shut.

Kyle was frustrated and angry, angry at Willard and angry that this slip of a girl could just turn up without even knowing anything about a ranch. How could he have come on to her like that! Deep down he knew why, she was like a breath of fresh air. He'd wanted to know her better when he'd first seen her, had felt the chemistry between them that had shaken him, had known from her expression that she'd felt it too.

She'd been nothing like the women he usually dated. He could still feel the roundness of her breast in his hand, throbbing with her fast heart beats as he'd teased the hard little

43

nipple through her clothes, had felt the tremble, letting him know that she'd wanted him as much as he had. She'd found it pleasurable, until she'd suddenly backed off, nervous, and that had thrown him.

Why'd you do it, Willard, he asked the sky as he saddled up his favourite horse, riding out, needing to let off steam. Given a loose rein, Ranger was more than willing to take full advantage and stretched out into a gallop until they were both ready to stop. Pulling the horse to a walk to cool off until they'd reached the river, Kyle stepped out of the saddle to walk to the water's edge to let him drink and as if knowing his master was unhappy, Ranger pushed his head against his arm as if trying to help.

Staring out across the range, all Kyle could remember was how he'd felt with Sandy's mouth under his, her tentative reaction to the kiss, felt the taste of her on his lips, under his hands. Knew he wanted to do it again but now hounded by the thought of her being Willard's niece. How he would stop himself was another matter because judging by his libido firing up just thinking of her, he was already in deep trouble!

Settled in the saddle, he headed across the range to join Sheb and Buck in checking on the stock, hoping that a day's hard work would clear his mind.

Midday, Kate did a small salad, she and Sandy chatting until it was time to prepare the meal for dinner. Sandy helped by laying the table with the filled dishes, thick steaks waiting to be covered in the creamy white sauce, mash and corn along with salad greens when voices were heard outside the back door.

Having been placed at the table in the small lounge so that she wouldn't be disturbed by Kyle or the interest of the other two ranch hands on her first evening, Sandy was joined by Kate who brought her own meal along with a small bottle of wine and glasses. They ate in silence, Sandy mulling over how she was going to cope when she met up with Kyle again.

The thought of his male scent, of his mouth on hers, his hands exciting her, was disturbing. She had to stop thinking of him as anything other than her foreman, a man who worked for her!

'That meal was delicious, thanks, Kate.' Sandy patted her stomach. 'How is it in there?'

'He'll cool down,' Kate assured her as they sat back to drink a glass of wine. 'The boys know to tiptoe round him when he's upset about something, but it's usually the ranch accounts or the stock.'

'Hmm, I think it might take just a little bit longer over me. I've appeared out of the blue and taken what he obviously cares a lot about.'

'Not your fault, he needs a challenge. I'll put everything in the dishwasher and come back and sit with you.'

'Oh no, that's fine. I've paid for another night at the motel and I think it would be better if I left. I really need to think things out a bit more before our next meeting. But I'll see you sometime in the morning with my things.'

Sandy finished her wine, stood up, grabbed her jacket, made her way to the front door, picking up her hat, then noting that dusk was already falling, and as she made her way to her car, that the temperature had dropped considerably. Kate watched as she got into her car, waved cheerfully, reversed and headed away down the drive.

'Where's she going?'

Kate jumped not having heard Kyle come up behind her, and frowned at him. 'Don't you go upsetting that girl, Kyle she's really nice, but totally out of her depth. She's paid for a room at the motel and is going to stay there tonight before moving in here.'

Kyle ruffled her hair playfully knowing she hated him doing it.

'Well, I guess she'll have to come back. Thanks for dinner, I'm going to see to the paperwork,' turning to stride into the small lounge, trying unsuccessfully not to remember Sandy's lips on his, her taste as his tongue tangling with hers, her firm breasts pressing against his chest. The way she had started to reciprocate. Just what was it with him, it wasn't as if he'd had no other girlfriends, he had, but it was just her. She was pretty, but more than that it was about the way she moved, the brilliant blue eyes that made him want to keep reaching for her. He wanted to know more about her.

Sandy had been everything he wanted, but now he fully intended not to do it again even if it was going to be hard. She had to be off limits as Willard's niece, and yes he could do it! He knew he could. But the more he relived the moment when he'd first touched her, held her in his arms, the more sure he was that she had responded before pushing him away, leaving him wondering what sort of game she was playing. Well, he had every intention of finding out!

Sandy made her way along the ranch track back to the road and now it was dark, her headlights picked up the glow of several pairs of eyes that fast disappeared when the herd of antelope on the far side of the fencing, fled before her. Turning at the gate to drive back to town, headlights of cars on the highway revealed that there were more people about now than when she'd first arrived.

Reaching town, she nearly overshot the turn into the motel car lot, distracted by the memory replaying over and over of Kyle, trying to rationalise it. Unable to because her experience of men was basically zilch! And then there was that intensity that had made waves of emotions race through her, heating her body. What was that all about!

Parking up, shivering in the night air as she left the warmth of the car, she was glad to get inside her room and more so that she'd left the heater on, even if it had been by accident. Setting up her laptop to answer the two emails in reply to hers earlier, she was able to assure both Mandy and her parents that she was safely back in her motel room and would be moving into the ranch house in the morning.

Sliding into bed with nothing to distract her, she found that her thoughts kept returning to what had been her first real heady kiss. Nothing like the boys at the University who'd tried hard to kiss her and she'd always turned down, this had been a full blown kiss from a sexy attractive male who knew what he wanted, totally confusing her emotions. It had been almost frightening knowing how much she had enjoyed it, that her body had been demanding something more than she knew how to cope with. Almost, but not quite she had to admit to herself. But then became nervous. How would he treat her if he found out how inexperienced she was? Turn away and leave her alone? But deep down she knew that her body was awakening, she knew she wanted more of his kisses, wanted to experience again being held in a man's arms especially by someone like Kyle. No! Not just someone. Him!

Spending another restless night, Sandy had finally drifted to sleep, waking later than she was used to, the alarm on her cell luckily on repeat because she obviously hadn't heard it the first time. A faint light through the curtains showed that the sun had already risen.

Taking a quick shower followed by a coffee to settle her nerves, Sandy sat on the bed to put on the light make-up she sometimes wore, just to cheer herself up, she told herself. Not for anyone else. It didn't take long to finish re-packing her suitcase, but she really should go into Buffalo and get warmer clothes as the thin ones she'd brought with her were proving to be totally inadequate without some sort of heating. The car would be chilly until the engine warmed, she could run it like a lot of people did, but fundamentally it was against her principles in the face of saving the environment.

Deep inside, her muscles were clenching, excited at actually going out to live on the ranch and oh, so not thinking of meeting up with the good looking foreman again! No. But with her heart already fluttering at the thought of seeing him again, she was nervous because he might still be mad at her for not saying who she was at the diner. But then she was mad at him for assuming that she was chasing him. And as she was the owner, he'd have to be careful where he trod now, wouldn't he! Her spirits soared, just like at home with her business, she was in charge of the ranch and him!

Signing out in reception, Doreen attempted to hide her curiosity as to where she might be going next, but Sandy was evasive, just leaving the impression that she wanted to tour around to see the local sights.

Driving to Su Ann's to get some breakfast, she suddenly

remembered that she hadn't confirmed with Kate about what time she'd be arriving and hoped that she wasn't expected to eat there this morning. Nosing into a space in front of the sidewalk wasn't a problem as there were only a couple of cars and a battered truck already outside as well as across the street where a few people were walking along the sidewalks or going into the shops.

Walking inside, she was warmly greeted by Su Ann who ushered her to a booth assuming from the evening before that that was the seating she preferred, fetching over the coffee and a mug.

'What do you fancy this morning?'

'Biscuits, gravy and bacon would go down well, thanks.'

As Su Ann swung away Sandy glanced round the room noticing two men already eating while a single man on the far side of the room stared at her thoughtfully before looking away, almost guiltily, putting his head down before she got a clear look at his face. Su Ann called out the order to the cook and walked back behind the counter, leaving her to sip her drink. Would she ever get to like how strong they brewed it up here? The further up-country she'd driven the stronger it had become.

The food arrived and she set to with a will, she didn't often have the chance to have her favourite meal, but then she was on a sort of holiday and she might as well make the most of it. Fortification before bearding the dragon in his den! Stifling a giggle at the thought of Kyle as a dragon breathing fire and smoke! Very apt after what had happened yesterday.

But that made her stomach tighten as she thought of him, his tall broad shoulders and narrow hips, the easy rider's grace as he walked, his firm chin and those dazzling eyes. And then that smile of his. How would he feel today when she'd just walked into his life as the owner of the ranch? She knew how most men had trouble accepting her in her own profession. Would he be very unfriendly, angry after the mistake yesterday?

Collecting her purse she paid for the meal and walked outside, looking for the bank, she needed to inform them she'd arrived, to show all her documentation. As she paused looking up and down the street, two men in overalls walked round her to get to the door, both removing their hats.

'Help you, ma'am?' asked the older, while the young one, about her age she thought, stood and looked embarrassed, turning his head away with a shy smile on his face.

'I'm looking for the bank.'

'Cross the street, end of the block.' He pointed over to the left.

'Thanks.'

'You're welcome.' He shoved the younger towards the door of the diner. 'Time's wasting!'

Arriving at the bank, Sandy found the big wooden door already open for customers and walked in, to be faced by a middle aged lady sitting behind a wired counter who looked up to see who had arrived. After the size of her bank in Lone Tree let alone any in Phoenix it was very small and took her totally by surprise, but then this was a tiny town. Stepping up, she asked for the manager.

'Can I tell him your name?'

The woman, dark hair drawn back in a bun, smiled, her brown eyes looking her over, obviously curious but trying not to be.

'Sandy Carson.'

'Oh! Miz Carson. It's good to meet you. Welcome to Sweetwater. I'm Wanda.'

She let herself out of the cage and went to knock on a door behind her, opening it. Sandy heard a murmur of voices before she backed up as a rotund, bald headed man bustled out almost wringing his hands and Sandy had to suppress a giggle. He looked like Humpty Dumpty from the children's book she'd read as a child.

'Miz Carson, please come in.' He ushered her through to his musty smelling room, files on shelves, books on others, showed her to a seat in front of his big wood desk. 'I'm Charles Greenham. Welcome to Sweetwater, I'm sorry we meet under such sad circumstances. What can I do for you?'

Sandy produced her paperwork and slid it across the desk towards him.

'I believe I need to show proof of my ownership of the Boxed C and to arrange to manage the finances with you.'

'Yes, yes,' he picked up the papers and studied them very carefully. 'They're all in order, thank you,' sliding them back to her. 'I will take care of the necessary forms for you to officially take the reins regarding all payments and the running of the ranch. You do know that the foreman, Kyle... Kyle Sherman has been doing all that until you arrived.'

Sandy nodded. Willard had fortunately had that written into the terms of the Will.

'Are you going out there now?'

'Yes. I need to look over the whole enterprise!' She managed a firm smile as if this sort of thing happened every day and that she wasn't fazed by inheriting a huge ranch. Obviously surprising the manager with her attitude.

'Would you like me to get Scott Scully over in Buffalo to come out to the ranch with the forms for you to sign or you could go to his offices there. He dealt with Willard.'

'If you, or he, could let me know when they're ready, I can arrange to meet him. Thank you. I passed through Buffalo on my way here so I know where it is.'

Standing up first, she held out her hand making him hurriedly get up, embarrassed at being so lax, but then she'd intended that he understood that despite being a woman, she knew what she was doing. Having had problems when she'd first set up working in Lone Tree, she well knew how to stake her position in financial circles, had had to fight with an establishment that still thought women needed to be overseen in case they failed.

It hadn't helped in the beginning that she was slim and blonde. But she hadn't failed, had ended up impressing the bankers when she began to finally make a profit after paying off the initial loan. As the owner of a large ranch she needed to reinforce this. He met hers with his, a podgy damp palm that almost made her flinch but she took care to hide anything but a polite smile.

'Thank you, Mr Greenham. It is good to do business with you.'

Sandy allowed him to go past and open the door to usher her out, relieved to get into the fresh air, heading for her car. And Kyle!

Driving out of town, it was still somewhat daunting, but exciting all at the same time, trying to take in such a vast empty area the further she went, and now that she knew where she was going, turned onto the trail leading to the ranch house.

As she parked beside the small car she assumed belonged to Kate, her attention seemed to be magnetically drawn to two riders near the barns, her heart beating faster as they looked up to see who had arrived, noticed by his body language that Kyle had turned his attention to her. Was she wrong or did he look angry? He waved away the other rider and rode over fast pulling his horse to a stop startling her, waves of annoyance emanating from his taut body as he leaned down from the saddle just as she stepped out of her SUV.

He looked her up and down disapprovingly. Even though she so had the wrong sort of clothing for Wyoming, she still looked phenomenal and as an unexpected heat spiked through his body at the thought of having held her in the office yesterday, that only made him even more annoyed with her.

'I don't know what type of world you come from but out here we inform people if we are not going to arrive when they've specially waited breakfast for them,' he snapped sharply his eyes glinting and Sandy backed up, shocked.

'What… What do you mean?' she finally managed to ask, her legs feeling boneless.

'Kate kept breakfast for you. Don't act as if you didn't know! We eat early, at sunrise so we can get out and work the ranch, we don't have the time to wait for a townie!'

Sandy flushed. 'Oh, no I didn't arrange… I had to… !'

'Next time make sure you have the decency to tell someone!'

Tearing his gaze from her enticing lips, he swung his horse round sharply and loped off towards the other men, passing through the barn before they all reappeared, taking a trail up a rise beyond which they were out of view, leaving her unexpectedly ashamed. But even worse, aware that he'd turned her on so much that her body was hot, her heart thudding in her chest and, for the first time in her life, her breasts ached as unexpected warmth spread from them down to her thighs. If he'd swept her into in his arms she knew he would have been able to do almost anything he wanted with her.

Scornful at herself for feeling so wanton, taking a few minutes to draw deep shuddering breaths to get herself under control, she made it to the front door and went inside, mentally chastising her thoughtlessness towards Kate before heading for the kitchen. Calling out to let the housekeeper know she was there.

Kyle was calling himself all sorts of uncomplimentary things during the day. He shouldn't have been mad at the woman. That was no way a man should treat a woman let alone someone who was now his boss. Trouble was she'd got under his skin and half of being mad was because she so turned him on but he couldn't afford to let his feelings get away from him. There should be nothing more than a working relationship between them.

'Why, Sandy, are you alright?' Kate paused in the doorway and immediately looked concerned, coming forward to take Sandy's hands in hers. 'Come in and have a drink.'

'Kate, I'm so sorry, I should have let you know when I would be turning up, I didn't think about you doing breakfast,' she blurted out.

'Land sakes, Sandy, that wasn't a problem.'

'But you made breakfast for me… !'

'Good Lord, I make enough for all the men so if you'd come it would have been okay.'

'But Kyle was furious I didn't let you know.'

Kate stared at her as if baffled. 'He was? He didn't say anything to me.'

Sandy put a smile on her face that she didn't feel. 'Oh well, he must have got the wrong end of the stick.'

In fact she was now growing angry herself. Time was coming when she'd make him fully aware that this was now her ranch and he got used to her issuing her own reprimands.

'I need to go into Buffalo for a more appropriate outfit,' looking down at herself reprovingly. 'So if you could, would you have time to show me around the town.'

The older woman immediately looked pleased. 'I'd love to do that, thank you for asking. When did you want to go?'

'Whenever it's convenient to you, I can make do with what I've got at the minute. I'll wear two sets of clothes when I go out!'

'I usually do all my baking tomorrow for the weekend so how about the day after, Saturday.'

'Fine by me, I'll go get my things and unpack. Which room is mine?'

'Either two at the end,' smiling at the sudden thought that obviously showed on Sandy's face. 'Bless you, Kyle's moved out to the smaller cabin beside the bunkhouse. That reminds me. Do you want me to stay here with you? I have a place out back.'

'I'm sure I'll be fine, what time do you start in the morning? Can I do anything for you?'

'I'm normally in around daybreak to get the men fed before they go out, I have a key for the back door, but as I have a steady routine there's no need for you to get up until you want to.' She smiled when Sandy assured her that she was used to getting up early and usually only needed a hot drink first thing.

'I'll have breakfast warming for you, and you can either eat at the same time or after the men have gone.'

'Thanks Kate, I don't want to be a nuisance, I've got a lot to find out about.'

'Honey it's no problem, you just take the time to take it all in, it has to have been a shock.'

Finishing her coffee Sandy went out to get her suitcase and purse, taking them up the stairs, and for some unknown reason decided to take the middle bedroom, her blood tingling knowing that she would be next door to where Kyle had been sleeping. Mentally telling herself off for being childish, she pushed the door open and went inside.

Not having been able to take much notice of the rooms when Kate had first shown her round, she was totally overawed by the size of the room, the comfort and luxury. The Queen sized bed with its spectacularly carved headboard was covered by a multicoloured quilt and matching pillows making her want to jump straight on and sink down into it. Tan wood cupboards either side of the bed matched the big leather armchairs, as did the legs of the glass covered table. All the furniture had been carefully built from natural wood and it was utterly perfect.

But what blew her away was the huge window and dropping her case, she rushed over to look out at the range of mountains in the distance their tops covered in sparkling snow, the lower slopes with dark green pines. Closer was the open range with dots she thought could have been either cattle or horses, on down to the barns one of which included stabling from what little she could just make out through the big open door, and the main bunkhouse. Beside the bunkhouse stood what she took to be the cabin where Kyle would be living while she was here, and she couldn't help the thought that it would serve him right to have to slum it.

Turning back, two slim slatted doors opened up to show her a big closet with a chest of drawers at the far end. Pulling open two more slightly bigger doors revealed a bathroom with shower unit, sink with a glass fronted cabinet above for toiletries, and a rack with fluffy white towels. Wow, she had trouble getting her head round it all, it was fantastic. But studying the big unit she found her thoughts wandering, could imagine it was big enough for two, and for a moment lost herself in a daydream, Kyle stepping in with her, closing the door, taking her in his arms and… ! She quivered with shock, this had to stop! She'd never had a boyfriend and had nothing to relate to a man's physique except imagination. Anyway, a closer look at her slight boyish body and he'd run away. She smiled sadly to herself.

Unpacking her case, sliding it under the bed out of sight, she arranged her toothbrush, toothpaste, what little makeup she had and a hairbrush in the bathroom, hanging the few shirts and the two lightweight jackets she'd brought with her in the closet. The chest of draws soon contained her pants and underwear, PJs and the thin robe, the bottom one she reserved for her laptop and chargers. Opening up her emails, she got straight in to inform everyone that she was now on the ranch and in her bedroom, giving them a good description of her accommodation as well as what she could see from the window.

Wandering downstairs, she made her way outdoors, pausing on the veranda to look out over the greening grassland dotted with a few bushes and trees, the sun shining from a clear blue sky and just a few wispy clouds. The wind was fresh and she shivered but was determined to walk down to the barn and see what she could. Apart from horses milling in a corral, the place was deserted but she was glad to get to the barn and hide inside away from the chill. Even so she didn't stay long and quickly returned to the house and the warmth of her room.

Deciding to try the bed out, she collapsed onto her back, arms outstretched, gazing up at the ceiling. What had she got herself into? It had all seemed so easy back in Lone Tree, here she was like a fish out of water and it was now being made even worse by having the hots for the good looking, sexy foreman who apparently now disliked her!

The next thing she knew was a voice shouting up the stairs. Groggily she stirred, wondering where she was as the voice came nearer. Kyle? There was a tap at the door and she swung her feet over the edge of the bed to the floor, rubbing her face to clear the fog from her thoughts.

'Yes?'

'Kate said dinner's on the table.'

'Oh, okay, thanks.'

'You okay?' He sounded gruff. 'You didn't hear me shouting.'

Was he worried about her? About what he'd said to her? No way!

'I dozed off. I'll be down in a moment.'

She heard his humph then feet descending the stairs before swiftly heading into the bathroom to comb her hair and tidy her rumpled clothes. Downstairs and turning towards the kitchen, Kate met her at the door as she heard the clatter of cutlery against plates, surprised that otherwise it was quiet, no voices.

'I've put dinner in the small lounge again for you along with a glass of wine.'

'Thanks, Kate but there's no need after today, I'm more than happy to eat with you in the kitchen.'

'It's no trouble but if you'd prefer to be in here that's fine.'

'Will you join me? I'm not used to being alone.'

Sandy was glad when Kate nodded, her face wreathed in smiles on returning with her meal to sit at the table. It was obvious that she was happy for somebody other than the men to talk to.

'You'll have to give me a hint as to what I need to buy when we go out, if you don't mind.'

'Not at all, but Torrey over at McNades will show you everything. I've lived here all my life, met my husband here, he became the sheriff about twenty years ago, and I've remained ever since. Never had the chance to see the rest of the country although my daughter, Amy, lives in Chicago now. She's working towards becoming a consultant in paediatrics there.'

'Is she with her dad?'

'He was killed in a shootout when kids tried to rob the store in Sweetwater ten years ago.'

'Oh my God, I'm so sorry.' Sandy put her wine glass down and stared in horror at the housekeeper. 'I can't imagine what that was like.'

Kate shrugged. 'Something you have to try and live with when your man is policing an area, but it was the first and last time anything like that happened round here. Right, I'd better get back and sort out the kitchen, the men will probably be gone by now.'

'I think I'll turn in, it's been a long day.' Sandy took up her plate and glass to follow the older woman, not sure if she was happy the dining room was now empty or a strange emptiness that Kyle wasn't. Whatever is the matter with you, she chided herself.

Clearing the big table Kate shushed her away when she tried to help load the dishwasher, reminding her to make sure the house was well secured after she'd gone. Then she was out the back door, Sandy heard the door lock and she was alone, feeling slightly lost on being left in such a huge place but deciding to leave any further exploration of the rooms until another time.

Reaching her room to take a warm bath, having dried herself off with one of the big fluffy towels on the rack and pulled on her PJs, she sat down at the desk to email Mandy who much preferred to use Skype with everyone but Sandy who disliked people either looking at her or her seeing them. Mandy came straight back almost as if sitting and eagerly waiting her news. Yeh, she would be Sandy knew.

Any hunky good looking cowboys I should know about?

You are a confirmed romantic but no, no-one worth mentioning.

She denied herself the sliver of excitement that shot through her as she remembering those hazel eyes of Kyle's. And then the moment when his expression had turned to dismay as he'd backed away having found out who she was.

What's the foreman like?

A bit confused, it's a lot for him to take in and he's been out working most of the day but there are two more cowboys on the place, haven't met them yet.

I want to know all!

I'll be able to tell you more after we've met up to discuss the situation. So anything happening there? I feel so far, far away.

That's cos you are Sandy like a million miles away. Must be scary, what's it like?

Haven't seen much of course, I'll take photos and email them but the housekeeper Kate is really nice she's going to take me shopping. I should have Googled the weather up here everything I brought isn't nearly warm enough it's freezing when the sun's not out.

Find yourself a nice hunky eye wateringly gorgeous man. Have an adventure, you needed to get out more. Just remember to flutter those baby blues.

Sandy couldn't help her body from shivering, remembering Kyle wrapping her in his strong arms, their bodies blending and the hard feel of his body pressing against her thigh warming everything inside her. She'd never allowed anyone to get that close before. Mentally she shook herself free of her thoughts and back to typing.

Ok. Off to bed now I suspect it's going to be a very long day tomorrow.

You're not telling me everything, are you?

Sandy knew her friend was quick at picking up on her vibes but not even being face to face with Mandy she was still apparently intuitive.

Night friend

A quick email to her mom before closing down, she climbed into bed, snuggling under the sheet and quilt to quickly enjoy the luxury, falling asleep almost instantly.

Chapter Three

Woken by the faint sounds of horses calling from the corrals even through the double glazed windows, Sandy yawned, puzzled, wondering for a moment where she was. It had already been slightly disorientating to wake up in two strange rooms on her way here not quite knowing where she was until she could collect her thoughts, so being on the ranch was the same. She just allowed herself time to lie still and let her brain kick in.

This was her new home, she owned all this. It made her apprehensive, gave a jolt to her insides, and for a moment felt very nervous. What was she really doing here? She had no idea how to run a huge ranch or manage the everyday things that needed doing, and especially nothing about the cattle business. She knew how to deal with men and horses through her own professional place, but they were customers not employees.

Climbing out from under the bedcovers, she noted that it was dawn, only seven o'clock, and crossing to the window she could see Kyle and the two hands discussing something, sorting out what would be done during the day obviously before they finally climbed into their saddles. As the two cowboys started off, Sandy was somewhat startled to see that Kyle had lifted his head to stare up toward the house, to her window, almost as if he knew she was peering through the curtains. He rode off and Sandy couldn't stop the flicker of excitement that he might also have been recalling what had happened, nearly happened in the office the day before. Without thinking, she ran her fingers over her lips, her body hot as she remembered the feel of his toned body against hers, wheeling quickly away from the window.

Kyle had stiffened as he'd turned to follow his riders towards the range, dismayed that the part of him most influenced by the awareness of a beautiful woman had been affected by just a glance in the direction of the house, shifting in the saddle to ease into a better position. Wondering what Sandy looked like lying on her bed. Did she sleep naked? What would that long blonde hair look like as it cascaded over the pillow and curled across the full breasts that he'd felt against his chest? What would those long legs feel like wrapped around his waist as she cried out his name, as he drove himself into her wet tight body.

Had he thought he'd seen a flicker of movement by the curtains? He wasn't sure but she'd have been disturbed by all the activity at the barns wouldn't she? So would look out the window? Damn it to hell! He'd got a ranch to run. When had he been so turned on by a woman? He hardly knew her, worse she was Willard's niece! He needed the occasional night out to go and have some fun in Cheyenne or Buffalo to cure an itch, always glad to leave his willing one night stand to come home. But since Willard's illness and death, he'd been starved of female company. That's what was wrong with him, he decided. Spinning Ranger round, he got out of there fast, a day's hard work helping to move one part of his herd to higher ground for fresh graze would clear his mind and cool his blood.

Having washed and dressed, heading downstairs drawn by the delicious smell of cooking, on reaching the kitchen Sandy was greeted with a big smile by the housekeeper, her hands already covered in flour making pastry for the evening's meal.

'Hello, Sandy. Sleep well?'

'Lovely. Please, don't stop, I can see to myself. I take it that the men have eaten and already gone out?'

'Yes they eat very early. Your plate's in the warmer and the coffee is hot. Willard didn't want me living alone and had a warm cabin built at the back of the house so it doesn't take me any time to get in here.'

'He sounds like he was a nice man. I wish I'd known him. Perhaps that would have explained why he left me the ranch when he never knew me… Or, I didn't think he did. He had to have known something or why the pictures in the lounge!'

Using a towel to retrieve the plate, bacon, scrambled eggs, and pancakes, picking up a fork and filling a mug, stronger than she had been used to but she'd already found that she was actually beginning to like it, she settled herself at the big table where the men usually sat. She tucked into the meal, finishing it off in quick time.

'That was great but any more like that and I will have to treat myself to clothes bigger than I'm used to,' she laughed, taking her plate and mug round to stack them into the dishwasher. 'I'll have a look round outside while there's no-one about.'

Kate looked at her. 'You sure you're going to be alright dressed like that? It doesn't get warmer till about ten and even then a sudden chill can come at any time.'

Sandy grimaced. 'I should have checked up on weather conditions before I left home. I'll put on extra clothes but if I get too cold I'll come straight back,' she promised.

Having made her bed and put on two layers of clothing, she couldn't help but glance out the window towards the barns and corrals, accidentally she told herself, not really wanting to see if Kyle was still there but disappointed to find that he wasn't. Unable to keep back the tingle that ran over her skin as she remembered his arms round her, his lips on hers, how she'd nearly failed to tear herself away. What was it about this man, this virtual stranger who she'd only met twice and at that fleetingly, that he'd made her react in a way she never had before. The tremble inside as it began to slowly dawn on her that she would like him to do it again, but knew that it shouldn't!

Heading out the front door to stand on the veranda, the shimmer of the sun on the meandering river in the distance caught her eye before it disappeared behind a rise in the grassland, re-appearing like magic nowhere near where expecting it to. The landscape was not as flat as she'd first thought when looking down at it from her vantage point on the way into Sweetwater. Drawing a deep breath of fresh sweet air, she found it was far colder than she'd expected, chilling the back of her throat, her senses invaded by the smell of the blue sage and other plants still damp from the night's dew. The air was so clear she had no idea of distance whichever way she looked.

Following the sandy track towards the barns, she headed for the corrals to the right of the main barn, one with several horses kicking up their heels as if unhappy at being left behind by their friends. Stopping beside another, two animals trotted over. The buckskin appeared friendly, enjoying having his neck scratched until the blue roan paint with him nipped his flank and they thundered off bucking and squealing. As they did she made note of the fresh smelling hay in the hay racks and the clean water tanks, approving of the care the animals were receiving.

Peering through the wide doorway into the bigger barn,

feeling like an intruder, she half expected someone to jump out and ask just who she was and what she was doing there, she stepped inside out of the sunlight waiting until her eyes adjusted to the gloom. Through an opening to the left was a big room where saddles were stacked on wooden burros, assorted bridles and other tack hung on hooks along the walls, and big metal containers against the back that she assumed held hard feed. Breathed in the smell of leather and felt a pang as it brought back memories of her stables back in Lone Tree.

A set of steps far against the back wall seemed to lead up to a small balcony where another door obviously opened into some sort of a storeroom, although it was so dark up in the roof area that it was difficult to really make out anything. Further into the barn was a row of four roomy pens and at the end, a big stack of baled hay. A noted tidiness freak at home, she was pleased to see various halters and ropes hung on stable doors off the ground and, lifting the lid of a metal box, found it contained equipment for shoeing and brushes to clean the horses. Not what she'd really expected on a working ranch and was becoming more impressed by how Kyle was running it the more she looked.

Outside, wire fencing was strung out onto the range in both directions leaving a wide pathway to the other huge barn from where came the smell of hay, still sweet even after the winter months. She leaned over the big gate to look up the trail along which the riders had gone to where it breasted the long rise, finally disappearing from sight. With the sun now having warmed the air plus being on the move, Sandy couldn't help but decide to follow the pebbled trail, well used to walking and only slipping occasionally on a particularly loose stone if she didn't watch where she was going, but enjoying herself. It was the first real exercise she'd had in days.

Even being fit she found herself breathing heavily when she finally reached the top of the ridge, sitting down on a big boulder to rest, automatically checking for signs of snakes although it was probably still too cold for them to be out and about. The view was breathtaking. To the left in the distance, striped with a mixture of pastel blues, greys, reds and cream rose what she guessed were the Big Horn Mountains, dark green vegetation covering some of the slopes and the tops of the ridges.

Out on the plains, one or two single story dark wood houses showed up alongside the road and almost hidden among the multi coloured bands of horses and cattle scattered over the vast area. Off to her right she could just make out the little town of Sweetwater and the road she'd come in on winding its way through the rocky outcrops. Far off she could see a herd of cattle being chivvied along, just close enough that she could hear the faint sound of the cattle and the cowboys' whistles whenever the wind carried the sound towards her. Kyle would be there. Her breathing grew ragged and she shut her eyes to the memory of his lips on hers.

Forcing herself to look back down towards the ranch she was astonished at how small and far away the buildings were, she'd been so into climbing the hill she'd not realised how far she had come and it was no wonder she'd been out of breath. A quick glance at her watch, and to her amazement she discovered she'd been so lost in a daydream, it was past midday. How long had it been since she'd actually relaxed, even back home she was usually too busy, and she felt quite lazy almost unwilling to actually move but finally standing to make her way back down.

Startled to hear the faint jingle of spurs followed by the thud of hooves behind her, she turned and quickly moved off the trail as a big blue roan horse appeared from behind the rock she'd been sitting on snorting its fright at her unexpected figure, and was reined in. She found herself staring into Kyle's almost incredulous expression. He looked around with a slight frown that almost made his eyebrows meet in the middle.

'How did you get up here?'

'I walked!'

'Walked?'

He was astounded, no-one walked round a ranch. He was amused even more when with a sharp tone to her voice Sandy put her hands on her hips and without thinking said, 'I do have legs, you know!'

'Yes ma'am, I've noticed,' and with a blatant stare looked her up and down causing her body to react with a rush of something sensual that tightened her nipples and sent warmth spiralling downward to tighten her inner muscles. She forcefully clamped down on her emotions, angry with herself, knowing that he must have seen her tense. Was he aware of what he did to her? The smug grin showed her that he did.

'You shouldn't be roaming about in those clothes, they're not suitable. You need a warmer hat, a warm waterproof coat, jeans and boots,' he grumbled, annoyed that she'd been so stupid. At least western boots could have protected her against a snake bite even if the chances were slim to nothing of there being any about. The property might belong to her now but she had no right to put herself in danger while he was in charge. Well, she hadn't sacked him so far so he assumed he was!

'Wyoming weather can change without warning. And you

need gloves as well.' The horse shifted, anxious to get going but Kyle curbed it gently, more than willing just to sit and take in her figure, loving the blush rising up her neck to her cheeks, painting them pink, those slightly pouting lips after her quick response to him. She was probably stubborn. Well, she could do that in Arizona just not here. But as he looked at her he began to feel that same need he'd felt earlier and had to shift in the saddle unsettling his mount.

'Do you ride?' he asked before things got further out of hand. 'I'll take you back down. Unless your legs need more exercise.' Yes, please, wrapped round me went through his mind, his imagination running wild! He tamped the unbidden thought down, becoming amused when she seemed unable to make up her mind obviously not used to taking orders. Perhaps he should have been less sharp with her but anything could have happened out here.

Sandy found herself in a cleft stick. To either ignore him when she really needed to keep him sweet and talk to her about the ranch, or get up behind him, and that would mean leaning against that broad muscular back with her arms round his waist. No contest. She knew her cheeks had gone even redder, what on earth made her think such a thing?

'Yes, I can ride.'

Taking one foot out of the stirrup, Kyle leaned down to clasp her hand, effortlessly swinging her up behind him but as the gelding moved forward suddenly, anxious to go, she felt like a beginner as she grabbed him round the waist, her body heating in embarrassment. She gritted her teeth as he started down the trail at a walk, putting one gloved hand over hers to hold her on, as if I need that, she muttered to herself. Trying not to feel the hard muscles of his body under her palms as he moved in time with the horse despite the jacket he was wearing. And held back a flinch as she realised his jacket was open and she was actually feeling his sculpted chest through the thick checked shirt.

As the trail tipped downward, she found herself leaning against his back self-consciously aware that her thighs were hard against his, the wind swirling back carrying the intoxicating smell of sandalwood and a hint of musk all mixed with his own personal man smell that set every nerve ending alight. Angry at her body as it perked up. Trying to remove her hands from under his, he just clamped down harder as if he thought she'd fall.

It was over all too soon for her as they arrived at the gate. He didn't offer to let her off but instead, wanted her to stay behind him a little longer as her hands still clung to him stirring his blood as the warmth from her body continued to affect him even through his coat. Kyle leaned over to unlatch it and rode through, replacing the latch and heading into the gloom of the barn. Sandy blinked to get her eyes adjusted still enjoying the feel of his body before flushing awkwardly as she realised that the horse had come to a halt while her mind had drifted. Kyle swung round to look at her, a curve of a smile tweaking his lips. He'd really liked too well the feel of her palms holding onto him.

'You can get down now. If you want,' he told her pointedly, holding his hand out to help her.

Sandy tried not to take any notice but did need his help, unwilling to slip and end up on her butt in front of him so allowed him to lower her to the floor, her hand tingling from his touch. Electricity seemed to pulse between them, lighting intimate parts of her body with a warm glow, her heart looping the loop. She couldn't help glancing upward into his eyes and from the look on his face, even though he was trying to hide it, she knew that he was feeling the same sensations. Sandy kept her expression bland in case it showed too much that she'd been wishing the ride had lasted longer, a lot longer, backing off to smooth her rumpled clothes.

Tossing her head, the pin holding her hair away from her neck fell free and he watched spellbound as the blonde lengths cascaded down her back, some falling forward of her shoulders, unaware that he immediately had a vision of flicking the locks aside to expose perfect full naked breasts and pebbled nipples for him to feast on. Kyle's libido intensified and he tried to tamp it down.

'Thanks.'

'You're welcome.'

Shaking the mental images of her naked body away with difficulty he swung out of the saddle, trying to hold back a wince brought on by his hardening erection, but the movement of his horse nudged him against her and he had to grasp her waist to keep her from stumbling backward. Already suffering tight jeans from her hands clasped round him and her body pressed against his back, Kyle reluctantly pushed her away turning to see to his horse, disconcerted by the effect she was having on him.

'I need to meet up with you to discuss the ranch when you have time!' Sandy kept her voice calm.

'I've got to go back out again after Ranger's re shod, perhaps tomorrow.'

He kept his back to her, picking up Ranger's foot as a down draught through the barn brought the faint scent of something flowery mixed with her warm body, making his nerves twitch. He really should have a night in town, Buffalo might be far enough away from her and he grimaced, still making the pretence of studying the bare hoof. But Cheyenne would probably be better as it was even further away!

'I'm going with Kate to get new clothes tomorrow. It could wait till Monday morning.'

She didn't want to see him this evening, or any evening. It would be dusk and the thought of being inside that office again with just the soft glow from a light bulb, so close to him, almost touching, made her stomach clench. No, she really didn't.

'Monday's fine.'

Kyle released Ranger's foot and went to the equipment box fetching a hammer and nails, along with a ready-made, and became aware that she was rubbing his horse's nose. His eyebrows went up as he went to warn her of the danger she was in, Ranger never took to strangers and was prone to bite even an unwary cowboy, but he seemed totally at ease with her. Kyle caught the faint sound of her whispering while she rubbed his face gently until Ranger's ears began to ease back a little as if he had been caught unawares and Sandy stepped away, giving him space. So she did know horses, wondered how.

What seemed to concern him was her choice of clothes. Brown and now black? Why was she hiding herself under such boring colours? It came as a surprise given she was very attractive and from what little he'd felt against him, twice now, a stunning body. None of your concern, he told himself sternly. She was his employer and Willard's niece.

'You know horses!' Kyle couldn't stop himself from saying as he picked up Ranger's hoof and started to rasp it. Once satisfied it was ready, settling the shoe in place he began hammering in the nails. Any cowboy worth his salt knew how to replace shoes and while no expert he could certainly deal with any normal problems that arose. But you don't want to look at her do you he told himself, denying the pleasure of a glance in her direction. If he did, those blue eyes would be his downfall, those and the kissable lips that dared him to plunder them again, and with no-one around he'd have needed more than his iron will not to pull her close into his body.

'By the way,' she snapped, watching his head jerk up and his eyes narrow at such a change in her manner. 'I was late arriving yesterday because I had to go to the bank first. Thanks for asking why!'

Sandy glared at him, felt the tension rising as he dropped the hoof and stood up, spun on her heel and walked off, her back rigid. She had to get out of there fast before her resolve gave way, even though she wanted him to hold her again. Before he could bring himself to apologise Kyle was left staring after her, gone so suddenly she left him feeling as if the light had gone out of his body.

Finishing the shoeing, with a sigh he put the tools back in the bin and led Ranger outside the gate, mounting and heading back out onto the range more comfortable in the saddle now Sandy was out of sight. And touch. He could keep his hands to himself from now on! Yeah, when bulls produced calves!

The kitchen smelt heavenly and Sandy sniffed in appreciation as she entered making Kate laugh as she tipped a pie out onto the cooling tray.

'Well now Sandy, how'd you get on outside?'

Pouring herself a coffee Sandy sat on one of the stools sipping gently at the hot liquid.

'I enjoyed it. I climbed the hill to see over the countryside.'

'Climbed?' Kate's eyes widened.

'You look just like Kyle did.' She gave a quiet giggle. 'But he did bring me back down on his horse. Ranger had lost a shoe and he was going back to the barn otherwise I'd have walked.' She continued to sip at her drink, blowing on it to try and cool it. 'I hadn't realised I'd gone so far or that the hill was so tiring. I thought I was fitter than that.'

'The air's thinner this high and will take some getting used to. You really shouldn't have gone without the proper clothing if you're planning on tramping round the countryside, the weather can be very unpredictable.'

Sandy laughed. 'Yes. Kyle also suggested warmer clothing.'

Kate looked at her. 'Kyle will have been worried about you, you being a stranger and unused to the area. As foreman, he is responsible for everyone's safety while on the ranch and he takes that very seriously!'

'Oh, I never thought of that!' Sandy was instantly remorseful, Kate was right. 'I suppose it was a bit silly, but the view from up there was wonderful. Hopefully the next time I do it I will be on a horse.'

'You ride? You wouldn't get me near one of them dangerous things, the cowboys can get hurt on the uneven range if a horse slips or spooks and I've doctored them a couple of times over the years. But it doesn't happen very often,' she assured Sandy on seeing the look of worry cross her face. 'I'll stick to my nice safe oven, thanks.'

'I train horses back home, have my own small business. I might think of doing the same thing here, but I won't tell Kyle yet. He thinks I don't ride very well. Ranger moved as he swung me up and I had to cling on like a beginner so he has a surprise coming!'

She paused, finishing her drink, placing the mug in the sink. 'Kate, where… Where was Willard buried, I'd like to go and pay my respects.'

The woman turned in a fluster. 'I'm so sorry, I should have told you but it's all been so sudden. I can take you, or if you go out the back door and follow a little path up the rise you'll see the fence around the family plot. I usually go most Sunday's.'

'Thanks.'

Once outside Sandy had no trouble following a thin path worn in the grass as it gently sloped upwards until, rounding some rocks, she spotted a square of iron railings surrounding both headstones and some old weather beaten wooden crosses. Through the gate she stopped and took a deep breath before standing beside two graves, both with a bunch of wild flowers, one very recent mound of earth announcing the resting place of her uncle, Willard. Beside it, with the name Mary chiselled into the granite, the headstone announced that it was in loving memory of a beloved wife and mother. A mother? no-one had mentioned a baby or a child so far. Behind them were two more headstones turning green with algae and bearing names for who she presumed were his parents while beyond that were three aged wooden crosses for their parents along with a son. So many generations of her family tree that she'd never heard about, including a child?

Wondering why she hadn't seen the graves from where she'd

walked that morning, looking up she could see that they had been hidden by another fold in the landscape. The wind here was warmer than when she'd walked earlier now with the full sun, and again she could almost taste the freshness of the air, tinged with sage and faintly of pine from trees far away and she stood for a while allowing herself time to appreciate the views, totally different from her home in Lone Tree.

Back indoors, she dashed upstairs to see if her mom had replied to her earlier email and instead of emailing her back, decided to call and spent an enjoyable hour just chatting, letting them know how much she was enjoying herself.

Closing her cell phone, she lay back on her bed and shut her eyes so that she could let all the happy times at home drift into her mind, her mom baking for the diner on Main Street, mostly pies and pastries, being coerced into making the occasional cake for birthdays or anniversaries for families and friends. Happy memories of growing up, coming in from playing to find her mom's hands covered in flour, a smile on her face, and how she'd pretended to be mad if Sandy had tried to sneak a biscuit or cupcake from the table.

And then her dad would come in for dinner smelling of wood dust, picking her up to give her a quick peck on the cheek before kissing his wife, having shaken any remaining wood chips from his work clothes outside on the porch. He loved his work making anything from shelving to cupboards and tables. Once, he'd even made a rocking horse when she'd been about six, had allowed her to ride it until it went to its new owner, saw her disappointment and made another.

Was that when she'd fallen in love with horses, or was it because she used to avidly watch them interacting from her bedroom window, their manes and tails flying in the wind. To her they had been magical beings. Then the shock of finding out that not all people were kind when she'd spent hours crying over a neglected or sickly animal that the owner had not wanted to spend money on, just left it to die alone in a field. Memories of her mom coming into her room to cuddle her not saying anything just being there.

Even when she was very young they had always told her that she'd been adopted at just a year old because, as they said, she was special and they had chosen her themselves. It had never upset her when she was little but as she grew older and began to think about it, it had. Eventually even the thought of who her real parents had been finally ebbed away and now she never thought about it. Some day she wanted to find the kind of love like her now mom and dad shared but after her experiences at University she'd shut herself down to concentrate on her work with horses. They gave unconditional trust and friendship, and she'd even managed to tame the most frightened with her patience and special training as she took the time to get to know and understand them.

How complicated things had got. She still had no real idea how to talk to Kyle who was obviously used to taking charge over the ranch and getting his own way. And then there was this chemistry between them. The thought of sitting in such close proximity made her both nervous and confused, yet her body yearned for more. Why on earth did he look at her like he did? She was ordinary, not his type at all with a snub nose and faint freckles, hadn't been interested in wearing cosmetics although she did use a touch of pale lipstick to keep her lips moisturised while outdoors. She didn't even dress up, hated gatherings. When she went to her first party at University it hadn't gone well. Keeping to just one drink, she hadn't liked the coarse jokes and smutty remarks. Nor had she liked being touched when the boys tried to get over friendly so she'd turned down any further invites.

Anticipating dinner, she showered and went downstairs, breathing in the delightful aroma rising from the kitchen reminding her again of her mom's cooking. And just for a moment feeling lost and homesick. Kate beamed at her having already placed dishes of food on the table just as the men came in the door at the far end of the kitchen. Hats were torn from heads as Sandy came under scrutiny.

'Ma'am,' stuttered the youngest. He had a shock of red hair, his face turning almost red in embarrassment when he couldn't keep back his interested look. 'Name's Buck an I shore am pleased to meet yuh.'

'Hi, Buck.'

She nodded back and looking across at Kyle, noted he was looking somewhat annoyed. At the attention she was receiving from Buck? Looking at the older man beside him, she became aware of his scrutiny of her face. Did she know him? He smiled pleasantly and inclining his head, said, 'Sheb Willett, ma'am.'

He'd already removed his hat revealing greying hair cut very short, bushy eyebrows above his pale blue eyes appearing thicker than his hair while his darkly tanned face had the well-worn craggy look of years of being outdoors in the saddle, but again she felt that strange feeling that he was studying her as if he thought he knew her. They waited until Kate cheerfully called out, 'Sit boys and help yourselves.'

Self-consciously, Sandy sat on a stool opposite Kate,

conscious of the men taking their seats only after she was seated, admitting to herself that she could get used to this Wyoming politeness, although the further north she'd driven the more she'd noticed other men doing the same thing. Yes, it was done back home, but compared to here it had appeared forced. Her body quivered as she caught Kyle's eye and he nodded politely, his face devoid of any expression. But his eyes showed something else that made her feel very warm! Very warm all over!

Trying to ignore the admiring glances from Buck, there was a sharp cough from Kyle and he turned his attention to what he was eating. For a moment Sandy resented the man's interference, he had no right to run her life, she'd talk to anyone she liked, but then as foreman he was in charge of the men and she said nothing. She was in a new place that obviously had different standards and would have to learn their rules.

The meal was delicious, steak pie with thick pastry, roasted potatoes and greens covered in gravy, followed by apple tart and ice cream.

'Why did no-one talk at the table?' Sandy asked Kate after the men had gone, clearing the table, having decided on the old adage when in Rome do as the Roman's do, one of many sayings her mom used to trot out when it was warranted. Not that she would have felt comfortable about discussing anything in front of people who were virtual strangers, but she had expected small talk.

'Never have,' she replied, placing the rinsed plates and dishes into the washer. 'It's just one of those unwritten things. Years ago men had very little time to eat out on the range, they had jobs to do. Do they talk where you live?'

'I don't know about ranchers I only sometimes deal with their horses but in restaurants and diners everyone seems to chat.'

'I'd think they'd get indigestion,' Kate laughed.

'I've never found it a problem but then I only meet up with my friend Mandy, either in Lone Tree or Phoenix, mainly we go to diners for girl talk. Thanks for dinner. Are we still on for tomorrow?'

'I'm looking forward to it. What time do you want to go?'

'Anytime that's convenient to you, you're my guide.'

'OK. About ten, then I can get back to prepare dinner.'

'Thanks. See you for breakfast.'

Waiting until Kate left, locking the back door behind her, Sandy hurried through to the front to check that it too was securely locked, and once back in her room, shutting the thick curtains, she couldn't help but peer around to glance at the barns. Lights were still on in the stable area as well as the bunkhouse. As she watched, the barn light went out followed by lights coming on in the cabin. She ducked quickly back behind the curtains despite knowing that she couldn't possibly have been seen but blushing all the same.

Somewhat bewildered that her thoughts kept straying to Kyle, she couldn't help but recall the movement of his body under her hands, of leaning against his hard back as he'd moved with the horse, the outline of his muscles, the manly smell that had had her feeling needy and hot. She looked critically at herself in the long mirror on the door of the closet and grimaced as she went to put on her PJs.

With all the hard work with her horses, she had developed what she considered unbecoming boyish muscles, certainly didn't look feminine, not curvy and rounded like other women even if men were immediately attracted by her long blonde hair. Now why would she hope that Kyle would like her the way she was? Would he run his fingers through her hair, take tight hold of it in his fist so he could tip her head as his lips took hers in another blistering kiss that her senses wanted even as her mind tried to deny it. Totally shocked she watched her nipples harden as her breasts ached to be touched, damp pooling between her thighs. Mortified, she crawled into bed with her body burning from her thoughts, reprimanding herself about reading too many romance books, tossing and turning most of the night. Trying hard not to remember his scent, the looks he gave her before she finally fell into a deep sleep.

She awoke moody, hair untidy, the PJs feeling tight across her breasts as even the silky material was rubbing against her sensitised nipples. Did other women feel this way? The same way her core ached, craving something she'd never known! For a moment she wished she knew how to act with such a virile man. What would he want of her, better still, what did she want herself?

Leaping out of bed she shot into the shower lowering the temperature in an attempt to cool her skin before towelling off and combing her hair, easing the tangles out gently before dressing. Today she'd go and get some of those cowboy clothes and look more part of Wyoming just as an unwanted thought warmed her, wondering if Kyle would notice. He was her employee, she should be telling him what to do! And unbidden, a shocking thought rocketed through her mind at the idea she could order him to hold her to his hard body, and kiss her again.

Furious with herself, she remade her bed, untangling the bed sheets and yanking them straight, almost stomping round the big bed until both sheets and quilt were as straight as they would ever be before taking a deep breath and going downstairs. Only to find that the kitchen was empty but for Kate who turned and smiled before tilting her head to one side, a slight frown wrinkling her forehead.

'You didn't sleep very well!' She looked at Sandy with motherly concern, filling a plate with thick pieces of ham, two eggs, and hash browns. 'Sit yourself down and I'll get you a hot drink.'

'Probably too much fresh Wyoming air,' Sandy laughed. She was very hungry now she was up, hoping that her neutral expression would convey peace with the world. 'Especially after that lovely walk I took.'

'But not back!' Kate eyed her with tiny laughter lines appearing beside her eyes.

Sandy shrugged. 'I'd rather have walked but I need to keep on Kyle's right side if I want to talk to him and learn about how the ranch works.' She quickly finished off her meal before rinsing the empty plate, putting it and the cutlery in the dishwasher, leaving Kate to switch it on. It began chugging away.

'Give me a little while and I'll be ready to go.'

'OK.' Sandy wandered into the big lounge for something to do still trying to work out about the pictures of her.

The room was fascinating, overpowering and all masculine with Native American rugs on the floor, a couple of thin colourful ones on the walls along with what appeared to be old antique ropes, chaps that she thought might be batwings due to their size, and several pairs of rusty spurs. Statues of cowboys and a bucking bull adorned the cabinets and she'd already admired the paintings of Native American chiefs hanging on the walls in the hall.

'Miz Carson!'

She jumped at the sound of Kyle's deep voice, slowly turning, trying to maintain a straight face and at the same time slow her heart rate.

'Sorry, didn't mean to startle you. I thought you might have some time to have a quick look at the books before you go out.'

His gaze roamed her body and she tensed when they rested rather too long for her on her breasts, especially aware that they showed all too well that under her shirt she was suddenly breathing heavily. A fleeting faint smile showed for a second on his lips and then disappeared. He'd been awake half the night just thinking of her, of how her breasts had pressed against his back, her arms wound round him, how he'd held her hands to keep her safe on Ranger, well that had been his excuse. Wondering if he shouldn't get up and take cold showers to stop the erection that kept him aware of her bedroom being so close to his old one, imagining her lying in her bed, or in his, under him as he plundered her lips and her body!

'I... I'm sorry, but I'm waiting for Kate to come, we're going shopping,' Sandy almost stammered, embarrassed at being flustered. Because she wanted to take all of him in, the way his presence let alone his size seemed to fill the doorway. She was so out of her depth around men, his maleness just kept taking her breath away.

'That's okay, just thought I'd ask.' His eyes twinkled. 'Anytime you need me.'

He smiled again, fully aware of what he was doing to her let alone what she was doing to him, glad he'd kept his hat in his hands to hide his response to her behind it, unwilling to adjust his jeans while she was looking at him. Reluctant to back out of the room as all his senses had picked up on her body language, their eyes meeting and holding, wanting to see how far she'd let him go. Was she really as innocent as she was making out?

'I'm ready, Sandy,' called Kate appearing behind Kyle.

She frowned slightly making both Sandy and Kyle wonder if she'd picked up on the tension between them. He spun on his heel, muttered something about going to do some work and disappeared into the other room while Sandy quickly put the small picture she'd been looking at of Willard and Mary back on the mantle above the open fireplace.

'I think he's not really come to grips with some strange girl sweeping in and taking over what should have been his place,' Sandy said to clear the air. 'It's early days yet. I hope he accepts me while I get over the shock as well.'

'You're right.' Kate sighed. 'He and Willard were very close and it's been a shock to me let alone Kyle.' Kate seemed to have been skilfully diverted and Sandy picked up her purse from where she'd laid it on one of the big chairs when she'd come into the room.

'Right, one very welcome shopping expedition coming up, I feel so out of place in these clothes. You want to use my car?'

'If you don't mind we can take mine, I need to pick up some more supplies while I'm in town. I like to give the men a surprise occasionally but I warn you it's usually something very sweet and calorie filled.'

'I could do with a little bit of weight,' Sandy sighed, getting in beside Kate and fastening her seatbelt. 'I feel positively skinny up against other women in town.'

'Nothing wrong with you my girl,' her companion huffed as she drove out of the ranch entrance and set off for Buffalo. 'Girls these days don't do enough work, just sit about with their computers and Smartphones and don't get enough exercise.'

Sandy laughed. 'You'd enjoy meeting my mom, she'd agree with you there.'

Chapter Four

As Kate turned onto the road and drove through Sweetwater heading for Buffalo, Sandy chatted to her about Alice and Ken, never mentioning that she was adopted. As far as she was concerned whoever her real parents had been they'd obviously not wanted her. It didn't bother her any more because who she called her now mom and dad, had given her everything she'd ever wanted, their unconditional love and support.

The sixty miles to Buffalo seemed to speed past, the road winding through trees and grasslands that she'd traversed on her way to the ranch before houses and buildings began to appear and then they were entering the outskirts of the town, passing between a church meeting hall and an impressive town hall that made up part of the town square. Kate parked up on one side in front of a big store, Timbrol's, their sign showing her they sold tack and animal feeds. Next to it was a bank, and a Reality office.

On the opposite side of the grassed square stood a Walmart store while sandwiched between that and a clothing store called McNades was a diner called, appropriately, The Eat and Greet. A bandstand took pride of place in the centre of the green, some of the bench seats already occupied, the green shingled roof held up by white iron pillars that matched the iron railings. People were strolling about the square passing in and out of shops or standing chatting and as they got out of the car, several women called out to Kate who was quick to take Sandy over to meet them.

'This is Sandy Carson, she's Willard's niece come up from Phoenix to look at the ranch.' She sounded quite excited to be able to show Sandy off.

Sandy soon discovered that people here were more open and friendly, really pleased to meet her and to find out what had made her come to visit Wyoming so quickly, even more astonished that she'd actually driven all the way. She began to feel like a celebrity but was happy when Kate finally led her away.

'I'll take you to McNades and leave you to shop, unless you want me to stay with you. I don't mind, really.'

She'd driven all the way here alone but had never shopped without Mandy so this could be yet another challenge for her to overcome. Could she do it? She'd never been interested in clothes or fashion but she did want to show everyone that she could fit in especially if she was going to ride or work round the ranch. It was safe to say that appropriate clothing did not include fashion so that should make it much easier to cope with, everyone was wearing jeans, shirts and coats along with either western or work boots, and hats. She was feeling a little out of place as she was. She needed to blend in.

Noticing the questioning look on Kate's face, she took a deep breath reassuring her that she was wanted and quickly adding why she'd decided to try doing it by herself. Having arranged to meet up at the Eat and Greet diner for coffee and before she could back out, she found herself heading for McNades, crossing the square to stand outside the store feeling more than a little daunted.

Taking a moment to collect her thoughts she walked through the glass doors and inside, her sight slowly adjusting to the gloom after the bright sunlight outside, a little intimidated by the rows of clothing, shelves with shirts, jeans and accessories, glass topped counters with belt buckles and bolo ties, and one with hand guns of all shapes and sizes.

'Can I help you, ma'am?'

She started, so intrigued by all the clothing and what on earth she was doing trying to buy without Mandy in tow and she should have brought Kate after all, that she hadn't heard the young man arrive at her side. For an instant she almost changed her mind but managed to force a smile and decided to throw herself on his mercy.

'I've only just arrived in Wyoming from down south and seem to have brought the wrong clothing.'

'No problem. My name's Torrey, I'm sure I can get you kitted out real fine.'

He was a little taller than her with an easy smile showing slightly uneven white teeth and was quite good looking. About her age she estimated, putting her at ease, he had ebony eyes, tanned skin, and black hair curling from under his western hat and Sandy began to wonder if every man in Wyoming was good looking, recalling Buck as well. Or perhaps her senses were being seduced by being in a different lovely part of the country. She couldn't remember anyone back in Arizona having made her feel as if she was the perfect woman. If she wasn't careful it could all go to her head.

'I'm Sandy.'

'So what exactly are you looking for? Working, casual or hey I'm gorgeous!'

Sandy began to smile. Hit on three times in as many days? Wow, Mandy would have been stunned at her even taking notice knowing her background.

'Hmm, casual I think. Outdoor waterproofs, warm clothes as I only brought lightweight with me. I forgot to Google the weather up here and it came as such a shock.'

'Come with me. Where are you from that you don't know about Wyoming weather?' He led the way to the shelves. 'We've got plain or checked shirts, warm or lightweight, although I think the blue with the white fringes would suit you!'

She couldn't help the giggle that rose in her throat. 'No, I don't think so unless I was going to a rodeo, that is. I'm from near Phoenix!'

'Wow, you must find it a real change, up from Navajo country!' He smiled. 'Okay.' He showed her some in various colours, laying one of each on the counter including two made of warmer wool. 'The days can still be chilly, and especially the nights,' he grinned.

'Umm, one brown and the dark blue, I think and I'd better have those two warmer ones.'

'Ok, jeans, we've several types, hard wearing or a softer line and fitted.' He grinned. 'Fitted?'

Sandy had to laugh. 'I know which you would suggest but I'll go with hard wearing as I'll be riding, and they have to stack.'

'Ah, I see we have a cowgirl here.' He dug out three different ones for her to choose. 'The fitting rooms are over in the back, and you can try the shirts too if you wish. If you need anyone to show them to I could help you out there.'

'Torrey, do you hit on all your customers?' Sandy asked with a smile, actually beginning to enjoy herself.

'Not all, only the pretty ones!'

'Waterproofs next, I think.' Becoming slightly embarrassed,

way out of her depth now, she changed the subject.

Led over to the racks of both jacket and long slickers mostly blacks and browns, her eye was taken by a warm shower-proof woollen jacket and tried it on, then had to choose a long slicker because she'd forgotten to pack her one. If she did continue walking she'd have to check for local forecasts before venturing out.

Torrey took the items to the counter, and on a whim, Sandy asked for the fringed one as well. His eyebrows raised, he chuckled. Picking up the shirts and jeans, he left her at the fitting rooms to try things on. Everything looked fine and taking everything back to where Torrey was waiting, decided on some black fitted jeans to go with the shirt.

Torrey turned out to be a good salesman and she ended up looking at gloves as well as belts and buckles, 'no cowgirl should be without a big shiny buckle,' choosing a beautiful silver one with Wyoming in big letters, a couple of neckerchiefs and some working boots.

'Oh. And a better hat than I've got!' Sandy removed her straw hat, starting to get a bit worried about spending so much, but after the past couple of years saving almost all of the monies earned from training horses, she deserved to treat herself, in fact she was actually enjoying herself for a change, helped in no small manner by Torrey who was delighted in guiding her.

She finally plumped for a dark brown Resistol that fitted her like a glove, firmly but not tight, and was then encouraged to have it steamed and shaped. He seemed not to want to stop, carefully bending the brim and refitting it on her head, standing back to study it until she laughingly told him that it was good enough just to stop him. For the first time ever she was actually relaxing and enjoying herself.

'I can sew a storm strap on for you while you wait!'

'I've got to meet with a friend in ten minutes,' she giggled as he brought out a brown and white, plaited horse hair braid with matching fancy tassels.

'No problem if you want to leave it with me,' he assured her.

'Now frighten me with the cost or are you still on commission?' Torrey grinned and began totalling everything as he carefully packed the clothes into two strong bags and two smaller separate ones for her hat and the boots.

'Um, I'm afraid that comes to $2,395 with tax.'

'Oh well, easy come, easy go.' Sandy handed over her card and paid, reaching for her bags to leave.

'Is your car close by, I can help you with your bags,' he offered.

'I came with my friend. I don't suppose that I could leave the bags here and pick them up when we leave.'

'Sure that's no problem and your hat will be ready.' Going ahead, he opened the door for her then hesitated. 'Next weekend there's a dance. At the meeting hall! I don't suppose you'd like to come into town and go with me!'

For a couple of seconds Sandy hesitated as she felt her stomach lurch then as if her mouth took over before her brain could kick in, found herself saying, 'Ok, I'd love to. What time and where?'

'Half six, I can meet you next to the bandstand!'

'OK, see you shortly.'

He grinned, touching and slightly tipping his hat. 'Yes ma'am.'

Making her way to the diner, Sandy pushed through the door

and entered the steamy interior, the smell of cooking making her realise how hungry she was. Lots of people were already there some sitting on bar stools at the counter most everyone looking up to see who had come in, the chatter quietening for a moment before carrying on. She finally spotted Kate waving from one of the rows of bench seating and alongside a window.

'Did you get what you wanted although from the look on your face you've actually had fun. But where is your shopping?'

Sandy slipped into the seat opposite her. 'I left it in store for when we leave. I think I got encouraged to buy out the whole place.' Kate's eyebrows rose. 'Torrey served me. I think he knew that he'd come across a goldmine!'

The waitress came over for their order bringing two mugs and a coffee.

'He's a nice lad,' Kate continued, 'I know his mother, Tania although her real name is Dancing Wind.'

'He's Native American!'

'Half, Tania is Sioux, his father a travelling salesman from a fancy store out of Denver about eighteen years ago. Tania had to bring him up alone and done a darn good job, too.'

'He invited me to the dance next Saturday.'

Kate smiled. 'He's a nice lad. I'm not surprised he asked you, you're such an attractive girl. Have you left a boyfriend back home?'

'No, no-one. I've been too busy.'

She always used the excuse of working with horses, but lacking in confidence after her experiences at University, she'd never wanted to go out with any men, closing down any feelings so that she never got hurt. Until Kyle that was! Confused she thought of Torrey. Now why had she done that! Was it the old world charm of Buffalo or that she felt much more relaxed here! Neither man had put pressure on her.

After eating, they made their way back to Kate's car, pulling up outside the clothing store but almost before Sandy could get out, having obviously been waiting for her, Torrey came out with the bags and put them in the trunk.

'See you Saturday.'

'Okay.' Her stomach contracted at what she'd promised but, she told herself, she could always pull out at the last moment if her nerve failed her. Wyoming was certainly playing havoc with her normal life.

Back at the ranch, while Kate went to start dinner, Sandy dragged the heavy bags up the stairs and into her room spending an hour trying everything on but she'd really fallen for the blue shirt. She'd never worn anything so colourful, if she could call dark blue colourful, preferring to hide in the background and not be noticed by wearing dark clothes, or sometimes a deep grey. Ended up deciding to wear it with jeans, taking the coats and boots down to the hallway.

As she turned to head for the kitchen, Kyle appeared from the small lounge and she couldn't help the sheer quiver that raced through her body when he stood stock still, his eyes widening as he looked her up and down, trying unsuccessfully to veil his pleasure.

'I've been shopping,' she faltered blushing, annoyed with herself for being embarrassed.

'So I see. Nice!' Kyle was almost lost for words.

With the fitted shirt along with the figure hugging jeans he had to acknowledge his attraction for her yet again. He'd tried to stop thinking about her by attending to paperwork but once again he was aware of his body's immediate reaction, his heart pounding in his chest. She looked stunning. But even more noticeable was his affect on her as her breathing deepened and he could see the pulse in her neck flickering. Interesting! Damn it, he had to remember that she was Willard's niece and should be totally off limits.

Sandy tried to turn her gaze away from his but she seemed to be pulled into his appreciative gaze, his eyes holding hers in its intensity, her legs threatening to buckle under her. Taking a deep breath, she finally managed to look away and headed for the kitchen while he stayed tied to the spot, unwilling to take his eyes from her very curvy butt as he wondered what it would feel like in his hands. Mentally trying to claw his way back to some sort of normality, Kyle followed her, turning away to the table where Sheb and Buck were seating themselves, his body fully aware of her presence. He hoped the others wouldn't pick up on his body language during the meal, glad when they'd finished eating and he could return to the barn, and his cabin.

Sandy fetched her laptop down and retired to the lounge to contact her friend, relaxing back into the cushions on the big sofa.

Anybody there.

Only me what gives friend.

Been shopping!

Alone who are you and what have you done with my friend LOL.

No went with the housekeeper Kate. She is so nice.

What did you buy?

Warmer shirts, jeans, pair of western boots, a new slicker because I forgot to bring mine, a warm coat, and a new hat.

No way take a pic and send it I gotta see this.

It was kind of interesting! And... I've been asked to a dance next Saturday.

Sandra Carson I'm shocked, by the foreman?

No, the salesman, his name is Torrey and I didn't mean to say yes, it kind of popped out. I swear on my life it's the fresh clean air round here. Everyone seems so laid back and friendly nothing like Phoenix.

Please, please don't tell me you aren't coming back.

Sandy could almost hear a wail in her friend's voice.

Early days yet don't worry things could always go pear shaped I haven't got into the office yet. If not you can come visit whenever you like stay as long as you like. There's a nice cowboy here too his name's Buck.

You're such a temptress. So how you getting on with this ranch foreman, Kyle?

Not sure.

Sandy's fingers hesitated while she tried to sort out what to say, or how much.

No way Sandy! You haven't fallen for him!

Yeah a little very little but you know how I feel about men, not interested. I'm bound to upset him not wanting to be touched so no chance of him liking me. Anyway, I'm off to bed, they get up at the crack of dawn here. Take care of you LOL.

Go you Sandy :)

Sandy took the time to quickly email her parents before checking all the doors were shut and locked, changing into her PJs and climbing into bed. Too tired to shower she'd do it in the morning, falling asleep snuggled under the quilt to dream of a sensual cowboy with dark blonde hair, glittering hazel eyes and a hard muscular body. She could almost feel him there, touching her.

Sandy woke next morning tangled up in her bed sheet, the quilt tossed sometime to one side in the night, a thin sheen of damp on her body, heart pounding. If she hadn't sat up with a start and looked she could have sworn Kyle was actually in the room. Angry with herself, she climbed out of bed to find she'd overslept while a glance through the curtains showed the yard empty. Washed and dressed she finally went downstairs.

Male voices rang out along the hallway from the kitchen and she hesitated until the scrape of chairs on the floor attested to the men leaving and she drew a deep breath. But her relief was short lived as a familiar shape loomed up and walked towards her, his expression blank despite realising that she was obviously hovering. His eyebrows raised but he said nothing.

'Hi!' Sandy managed to get out as normally as she could but feeling that she'd been caught out doing something she shouldn't have, before the full force of his smile left her with a fluttering, unsettled feeling inside.

'Hi.' Again he raked his gaze from the top of her head to her toes that as usual made her blood rush downward pooling in her belly with the sheer magnetism that seemed to radiate from him. Even her knees began to tremble. How could he do this to her with just a look? Surely she could have got used to him by now! Fat chance, said her body. She steeled herself and walked past as if nothing had happened, leaving him feeling disappointed at the thought of her going, and trying to think of some way he could get her to stop and talk to him.

'Miz Carson.' His tongue suddenly related to his brain, grasping at a straw. 'If you have time this afternoon, I could go over the ranch details with you.' Two could play at this game of cat and mouse, Miss Carson. He made his voice sound sharper than usual, watched her long pony tail swing behind her as she turned to face him, trying not to smile at the steely stare she gave. How could she turn him on so? Just a glance at her lips and he could imagine tasting them.

'That would be fine,' and then she gave him the sucker punch she'd been waiting for, asking him to take her riding when she'd show him that she could ride as well as him. 'I was hoping that before I went into the paperwork that you, or one of the hands, could find a horse and take me to see more of the ranch than I did the other day.'

Kyle hesitated for a moment remembering that she'd not seemed that competent climbing on behind him although his libido quickened to remind him how nice it had been to have her arms wrapped round him, his hand on hers to steady her. Quickly he assessed which of the horses he could put her on safely before deciding that the Palomino, despite his name being Satan, bestowed on him by the hands as a joke because he was the quietest, would be best. A slow ramble round the gentlest slopes would probably test her limits. But what about yours, he asked himself wanting to resent that he'd have to keep taking time off from working to chaperone her everywhere for her own safety, but unable to. A few hours out in her company would be nice.

There could be benefits by taking her out alone, he could find somewhere quiet to rest a while. Perhaps she'd need his help, wouldn't she, getting down from the saddle. He would need to put his hands round her waist as she slid down the length of his body. He could hold her against him, she'd look up and he would devour those lips while he wrapped his hands under those delectable buttocks. Pull her against his body, show her how much he needed her. To undress her and suckle those luscious breasts!

'When do you want to go?' He'd somehow managed to divert his thoughts and keep his voice calm although he hoped she wouldn't notice the slight hoarseness. He coughed to disguise it. Her voice broke him out of his wandering thoughts and for a moment they stared at each other. He wondered if she knew what he was thinking because her eyes had become wider staring up into his face and perhaps she had an idea because he could see the pulse in her neck throbbing, her breathing increasing.

'I'll have breakfast and come down to the corrals if anyone can take me.' He had a fleeting impression of her mouth crinkling slightly on one side as if she was trying to hide a grin, as if she held some sort of secret from him as she quickly turned and almost cagily walked into the kitchen. Something about her attitude instantly made him wary, putting him on his guard. Oh Miss Carson what are you up to!

Sandy was ready with a 'sorry, I'm a bit late' to Kate when she realised that somebody else was behind the island.

A young girl stood there wearing an apron and wielding a spatula, scrambling eggs and frying bacon. For what seemed a while they both stared at each other, Sandy finally finding her voice and saying, 'Hi.'

'Hello. You must be Miss Carson.'

The girl, in mid-teens Sandy judged, chubby with brown hair cut almost as if she'd hacked at it herself, several rings in each ear and tattoos on her neck, was close to scowling, sounding put-out as she looked at Sandy.

'You're late.' Then, in a less sulky voice as she obviously realised that Sandy was staring at her, and also employed her, 'It will be ready in a minute.'

'Thanks. And you are.'

'Jilly. I work here on Sunday's, sometimes a Saturday. Didn't Kyle tell you?' She tried a sweet but very insincere voice and Sandy got the impression that she'd said Kyle's name just a little too forcefully. Staking a claim? Although Sandy knew she was far too young for him.

'No, I'm afraid he didn't.'

Seating herself at the counter, she waited on her breakfast and when it came, the plate wasn't slammed down but it did go down hard. Sandy decided to ignore her and just said, 'Thanks! And what exactly do you do on weekends?'

'Kyle had me come to help Kate out a few months back when she wasn't well. Cooking and cleaning, making beds, tidying the bunkhouse!'

Hands on hips she almost dared Sandy to tell her that Kyle was off limits, but well used to recalcitrant young horses, Sandy was non-confrontational and almost felt the wind leave Jilly's sails when she didn't respond. She also began to see the light. Jilly was taking her as competition, and as a teenager, had immediately taken a dislike to someone usurping what she considered her place with Kyle, so having eaten, she allowed to girl to get on with cleaning the kitchen.

Grabbing her hat, coat and gloves, shoving her feet into the new boots that she knew would pinch her feet, made a mental note to ask Sheb for some leather oil that would help to make them supple and keep them waterproof. Walking down to the yard she was immediately aware that while Kyle was standing holding Ranger and a Palomino, Sheb and Buck were hovering in the background pretending to be working but not doing a very good job of it.

'Miz Carson, this is Satan. Despite his name he's fairly quiet and should suit you.'

He ducked his head so she couldn't see his expression and handed her the reins. Sandy heard what she thought was a snigger from the barn and decided not to show she'd had, but inside she was laughing. She was well aware of cowboy jokes. Taking the reins and patting the horse, she eased its head down and whispered in its ear, glancing up at Kyle who couldn't hold back his curiosity.

'I asked him to go gentle with me,' she murmured before attempting to clamber up into the saddle, making it on the third go. Sticking her feet forward, and holding onto the horn, shaking inside with laughter, she gathered the reins but left quite a curve in them, looking round at Kyle who was trying to hold back a grin. The other two were almost bursting, struggling not to laugh out loud.

'I'm ready, where are we going?'

'Just follow, Satan will take care of you.'

Kyle mounted with the usual lithe grace of a seasoned cowboy and she noted he wasn't wearing his fringed chaps this time. Possibly expecting a very gentle walk ride! Even hidden by his coat just the sight of his supple body moving with the horse sent a shock of desire that ripped through her body as he reined Ranger towards the gate through which she'd walked yesterday. She forced herself to concentrate on Satan.

The Palomino dutifully following Ranger gave Sandy a problem pretending she'd never ridden before because the horse had the smoothest stride, and once through the gate he was quite content to just plod. But every time Kyle faced forward after checking how she was doing, she began to jiggle the reins and nudge him with her legs until even he began to get slightly agitated, tossing his head at this irritation. Mentally Sandy apologised to him for what she was doing. Surmounting the rise where Sandy had sat two days before, Kyle began telling her about the range, how many cattle they ran, available feed and finally the best prices they could hope to get after roundup in the fall, and she heard the pride in his voice.

Following the gently sloping trail with Kyle keeping an eye on her, they headed towards what had at first seemed to be a flat plain but turned out to be deceptive because as they got closer she found the grassland lay in gentle folds, the trail rising and falling like a gentle roller coaster while skirting rocky outcrops. Pointing out obvious landmarks, he motioned towards Finger Rock, a tall stone monolith far in the distance, to the right of it a grey rocky mesa rose up, the sides streaked in shades of grey, blue and pale orange stripes and with white snow on the top that she'd seen from her window. To the left rose a mountain range with softer shades of pastels and lines of pine trees covering the lower flanks. It was glorious.

Trying to note everything and having a rider's flair for terrain, she felt certain that if she ever got lost she could always manage to find her way back to the ranch. Reaching a flat plain scattered with small boulders where a line of green trees showed the course of the creek, the blue grey of the sage tinged the air with the scent of lavender, and small clumps of once shrivelled prickly pear were starting to fatten with the wetter weather.

Several times Kyle had begun to look back curiously at poor Satan who was starting to get wound up over Sandy's prodding. And then, what Sandy was looking for, a long straight track. She let Satan come alongside Ranger who looked almost affronted, as stunned as his rider at the temerity of his companion.

'Can we try a little faster?' she asked, breathlessly.

'Are you sure you can?' Kyle looked at her face, concerned.

'Oh yes.' She smiled at him, shook the reins, kicked Satan in the ribs and sat into the saddle as the Palomino took the chance to run away from his irritating rider, leaving Ranger plunging.

With the wind in her face and a good mount under her, with a wild laugh and a wave of her hand, Sandy was some distance away before Kyle got Ranger under control and as he tried to get to grips with what he was seeing, he automatically set out after her. For the split second he'd thought the unthinkable, that Satan had been bitten by a horsefly or scared by a rattler, but with the laugh and the wave, he began to realise that this girl was toying with him, in fact had been.

Trying not to get too close, he didn't want a real runaway, he followed behind admiring the sway of her lithe body in the saddle, her long hair flying out behind her. She was a great rider so why the pretence? A light came on in his brain. She was getting her own back for earlier comments. He gritted his teeth. He'd make her pay for this, preferably on her back and under him, naked, writhing, screaming his name with the intense orgasms he'd give her.

After a couple of miles and when he knew that the lake was coming close, just as he was preparing to shout out for her to stop, she reined in, face flushed, grinning like a Cheshire Cat.

'Slow coach!' she teased him, laughing.

Swinging down from the saddle, she patted a heavily breathing Satan before loosening the cinch a little and starting to walk him, caring for her horse first Kyle was quick to note. That still wouldn't stop him from doing what he wanted to do to her, and how about out here? In the sun, on the grass, the cool wind would pucker those tempting nipples, would tighten her body around his swollen shaft as he sank into her!

He stared at her until the smile slipped from her face and Sandy for a moment wondered if she'd gone too far, made nervous by the look that seemed to see through her clothes to her very skin, the lust in his eyes that he only finally managed to control. He stepped out of the saddle throwing the reins wondering whether to take her in his arms or just stand and appreciate her animated face with those attractive freckles standing out even more as her skin grew pinker under his scrutiny, the shining blue of her eyes now hooded as he became aware of how tense she had become.

'Well, you got me good,' he finally managed to get out, again

aware of what she did to him, the tightening of his appreciative growing erection at her curvy body only held in place by
the tightness of his jeans. He smiled his face lightening and
reassured she let her reins drop to the ground turning to face
the vast expanse of the lake, the sky reflected in it all the way
from the beach where tiny waves rippled and far away to what
she assumed was the Rockies with their white tops.

'Oh, it's so beautiful,' she whispered, awestruck before turning to face him. 'Hope you forgive me for having some fun,' she
asked softly still not sure of his attitude at her deception. Would
he accept her joke or get mad. And then he was laughing, the
two horses tossing their heads as his voice seemed to echo across
the lake, moving slightly away from this strange noise.

'Poor Satan, he's never moved like that since he was a youngster! What did you do to get him so worked up, and why didn't
you tell me you could ride!' He folded his arms across his chest
as if to hold his beating heart from leaping out.

'I did but when Ranger moved suddenly I became unbal-
anced so you assumed I couldn't.'

'And you decided to keep up the pretence,' walking closer,
eyes glinting with fun, lowering his voice to a whisper. 'And you
so wanted to hang on to me! You know, you only had to ask.'

Sandy stood still, shocked for an instant that she'd been
caught out, paling as her brain tried to get back into gear.
Having unbuttoned his coat, she became highly aware of the
heat from his body as he stood in front of her forcing her to
look up into his face, as he watched the way she swallowed, his
calculating smile. She should have felt intimidated shouldn't
she? Then why wasn't she?

His eyes were on the pulsing vein in her neck giving the

game away as to what she was feeling. One glance at his lips and she knew she'd be begging him for another kiss as a bolt of searing need speared her whole body. She mustn't. But it was too late. He'd caught her stare, stepped up until their bodies were so close she thought they could hear each other's heartbeats. Found his glittering hazel eyes engulfing her, unable to tear her gaze away from them.

'You think too much of yourself,' she tried to snap back but could only manage a throaty whisper, saw his body tense as he smiled.

His hands were so quickly on her shoulders she was hardly aware until he had pulled her into his tense body, bending his head to lightly touch his lips to hers. She shuddered slamming her hands against his chest to half-heartedly stop him, absorbing the warmth through her palms, heard his breath quicken as he pressed harder. She tried to tell him no but as her lips opened, he instantly slid his tongue into her mouth to tangle with hers, a faint groan caught in his throat as with one hand he angled her head to demand more, devouring her. Felt her firm breasts pressing against his torso as with his other hand at her back, pulled her tight into him, heard her breath quicken.

Sandy couldn't help herself, raising her arms to run her fingers through his hair, could taste a hint of mint and coffee as he plundered her mouth, trying to draw in breath, her body craving what he was promising and as he became more forceful, her legs threatened to give way. She wanted him, needed him in a way she'd never experienced before as he held her tighter, his mouth demanding more, crushing their lips together. Holding her on her feet, he palmed her jean clad buttocks, the blood pounding in his veins, pressing her tight so his erection was hard against her sex, where he wanted to be. Felt her try to struggle but refused to let her, needed her to know what she was doing to him.

Sliding his hand from her neck, he felt for and found a warm firm breast through her shirt and bra, and Sandy couldn't help it, moaning softly into his mouth as he teased the hard nipple between finger and thumb, white hot flames skittering down her entire body from the tip of her head to the soles of her feet, frightening her even though she wanted it. Trembling with want, drawn by his fervour, her body responded before she could stop it and she began to kiss him back, to mould herself to him. Kyle let her mouth go reluctantly, the charge between them so strong he was on fire, his lips tracing her jaw line, nibbling, lowering his mouth to taste the fluttering pulse at her neck.

'Kyle,' Sandy whispered, almost overpowered by his animal magnetism, by his firm arms winding round her. Suddenly aware of his obvious desire, she tried to pull away, unable to stop the cry that was torn from her throat as she finally made herself wrench free, seeing his confused expression as she stepped back, astounded by how far she'd let things go.

Taken aback, Kyle stepped away from her, crossing his arms in front, walking away a few paces until he could get his breath back, his emotions inflamed, both confused and a little embarrassed. Had he misread the situation? She had seemed willing at first, until he began recalling her hands pushing at his chest like she had that day in the office. Both times now she'd called his name, both times trying to stop him? He hadn't listened, just acted like a teenager on heat and on his first date!

Angrily he turned back to find her standing beside Satan

about to put her foot in the stirrup. Without a word, he leapt up on Ranger and led the way back down the trail at a steady jog until the chill breeze had cooled his hot face. Slowing until she was almost alongside him, he looked at her, almost amused by a glare that should have set him alight, her face set, shoulders stiff.

'Sandy, I apologise,' he found himself saying although why he was he wasn't sure. He'd done nothing to apologise for! 'It was unforgivable.'

Got nothing in reply and continued, trying to relieve the awkwardness that was there between them like a dark chasm. 'I can only apologise again. I find you very attractive, and I lost my head.'

Sandy was still wondering how on earth she'd lost control herself, her body still aware of his touch, confused at what he'd made her feel, what she still felt, apprehensive that put in the same position she'd probably do the same thing. But to get so carried away that she might have succumbed to more, leading into something more dangerous, had been nothing short of idiotic. She could only put it down to the excitement of the ride and the breathtaking scenery. She used to think, imagined, of finding that special person one day who would find her alluring, of being asked out on dates, falling in love, swept off her feet like in the romance books she liked to read when she had the time. But out in the open, however much she was attracted to him. No way.

His words finally began to penetrate, momentarily stunned at his calling her attractive, found she could only manage a nod in acceptance, worried that if she spoke her voice would tremble, totally unaware that by licking the dry lips that still tasted of him, still swollen from his kisses, was turning him on again. Kyle turned away sharply, accepting her silence as a sudden dread hit him.

My God, she'd seemed so innocent, so naïve when he'd kissed her, as if she hadn't really known what to do. Never had a boyfriend? At her age could she possibly still be a virgin? What the hell was wrong with Arizona men, to him she was beautiful and sassy with an amazing sense of humour. He was so wrapped up in his thoughts that the ranch appearing ahead made him conscious of the silence standing between them like a dead weight, finally dismounting with a quiet sigh of relief when they reached the gate. He felt guilty for neglecting her. Technically she was the ranch owner, she could tell him to leave, dismiss him. He drew a deep breath.

'I'll take you out again and show you more of the ranch, you probably know from the deeds that we have around ninety thousand acres and run cattle including two breeding herds. It will be spring round up soon when we check out the cattle and then they'll be driven up into the higher country for the summer.'

He felt like he was rambling, sounded like a breathless school kid on a first date, threw her a light smile and was relieved to see a slight smile on her face almost as if she'd known what he'd been thinking before he'd said it.

Climbing down from the saddle, Sandy kept her face turned from him while she loosened Satan's cinch, somehow managing to get herself under control, unwilling to do or say anything to make things more awkward, hardening her heart and her emotions. This had to stop and if he couldn't, she would!

'I'd like that. But tomorrow morning I want to discuss the

records. If you're not too busy, that is.' She patted Satan, and in a clearly audible whisper, thanked him for a nice ride. Lost for words, Kyle let her through the gate first before latching it behind them. Sheb appeared from the gloom of the barn and took the reins from her leaving Kyle seeing to Ranger.

'Can you let me have some oil for my new boots?' she asked Sheb with a big smile attempting to convey that all was well. 'They're a bit stiff.'

'Sure Miz Carson, I'll leave you a bottle on the front porch by the door.'

'See you at dinner!'

The remark, carelessly tossed over her shoulder to show Kyle that what had happened between them, that she didn't care about it, Sandy was through the barn and out into the light, her back straight. That would tell him she wasn't taken in by his kissing her! Removing her hat, she rubbed the mark that she could feel left by the sweatband before slamming it back on, the new harder hat bumping down on her before she remembered it wasn't her lighter one. But her heart was still thundering in her chest, could still feel the chemistry between them, still feel his arms wrapped round her, his mouth on hers. Not taken in by her strange surrender? She could try to lie to herself for as long as she liked, but it was still a lie. Wasn't it!

'How'd she like the ranch?' Sheb asked while Kyle removed his saddle, slinging it onto the wooden horse outside the stable before brushing Ranger, the loose hair flying as he began to moult his winter hair.

'After her home, it's a bit of a shock. Don't think she'd been used to such wide open spaces. There's a lot more to that girl than meets the eye!' Sheb waited, brushing down Satan.

'She can ride! Miz Carson was putting us on that she couldn't, must've deliberately irritated Satan when I wasn't looking till he was ready to buck or run, then lit out for Elk Lake like the devil after a yearling.'

Sheb grunted but stayed silent, not one much for conversation, went to get a scoop of feed, giving half to each horse. With a short glance he looked at Kyle as if silently asking another question but was ignored, turned and left leaving Kyle wondering if the older man had sensed that something had happened. Or was it because he felt guilty?

Angrily he threw the brush into the tack box, slammed the lid down and decided to go to his cabin for a cold shower. But as he crossed the yard he couldn't help but glance at the house wondering what Sandy was doing! How was he going to cope when they were both in the same room tomorrow? Oh yeah, he'd have himself under control by tomorrow and could manage. Couldn't he!

Back indoors, headed upstairs to put her cell phone on charge and get washed and changed, for the first time Sandy found herself bemused, staring into the closet, trying to decide what to wear, flushing because she knew why and because this was all so new for her, her brain seized for a few moments. She never dressed for anyone else but herself. Finally, she decided on a pair of black pants and the green shirt. Now all she had to do before going downstairs and finding him in the dining area was to stop her body reacting. She'd behaved wantonly with him, had managed somehow to push him away before things got out of hand, but how had he taken it? Angry and confused! And how was it going to affect their working relationship? Oh how she wished she could speak to

Mandy but there was no way she could involve anyone else, she'd just have to take things as they fell and hope she could cope with her lack of expertise.

Putting a smile on her face she went down and into the kitchen, only to be met with a sulky expression on Jilly's face who had obviously found out that Kyle had taken Sandy riding from Buck. Sandy just smiled and seated herself at the island while Sheb and Kyle entered, removing their hats, hanging them on the hooks by the door. Kyle, she noted, came in last, discussing work for tomorrow to Sheb, and to her relief totally ignoring her, apart from a slight nod of the head.

Jilly who had already put heaped dishes on the table for the men, placed a plate of food in front of Sandy before smiling towards Kyle, her face hardening when she returned to eat her own meal, glancing at Sandy with a, stay away he's mine look, even though Sandy totally ignored her. She ate in silence like everyone did before pushing her plate away.

'Do you want dessert?' Jilly asked as Sandy thanked her for the meal.

Sandy nodded with a smile, there was no way she was going to allow the girl to intimidate her but it only made Jilly more intense until even the men noticed the interplay. Kyle looked annoyed making Jilly more agitated, unhappy that Kyle wasn't amused by her antics, so she changed tack and smiled at Sandy as she spooned peach cobbler onto a plate and handed it over. A saccharin sweet smile accompanied it but at least it was one, and having taken some for herself, she took the rest of the dessert over to the men.

'I'll drop you off home when you've finished, Jilly,' came from Kyle and the girl looked unhappy, suspecting that she was going to get a telling off from him on the way.

Finished, Sandy thanked her and left the kitchen for the lounge and load up the emails she hadn't had a chance to read earlier, one from her parents, two from Mandy, deciding to reply to her friend first. She only had to wait a few minutes before she came online.

How's it going there in cowboy land? And how's Buck?

Oh, we're interested in Buck are we?

It's the only interesting thing you've told me about Wyoming so far! Have you got those pictures of you yet, I got to see.

I will. How's mom and dad, I'm going to ring them shortly.

They're doing ok, Ken still working away and your mum cooking like there's no tomorrow, nothing changes although I still try to catch a guy's eye. Have you ridden yet?

Yes, went for a walk, don't think that's the done thing out here and got a lift back!

Back? A lift?

Sort of, by the foreman, on the back of his horse, first day I was here, he was totally shocked that I'd walked up a hill to see the view. But today he took me riding out onto part of the ranch and it was nice. I still can't believe that I own all this. I pretended I couldn't ride well, he gave me a very quiet horse, but I managed to get a gallop out of it. You should have seen Kyle's face!

Oh, oh, Kyle!

Well, that's his name. You don't think I should keep referring to him as my foreman, do you!

I guess not. But I want to know any juicy details.

A vision from this morning made Sandy flush, the kiss that had curled her toes and made her want more!

Sandy? You still there?

Yes, was just trying to think of something else to say. Nothing, but I will keep in touch.

Okay friend. Yippee as they say out west or is it Yeehah? Bye.

Bye.

Sandy closed down, checking the house was secure now there was only her in it before she rang her parents spending nearly an hour just chatting easily to them, assuring them that all was well and that she was starting to get used to being here, well, sort of, as it was so different. They had such an amazing marriage compared to a lot of people around them but she'd never really heard them say a cross word. Perhaps because they both did different things so that when they got home they could talk about what they had been doing. Whatever it was made her slightly jealous wanting the same for herself.

Staring out the window into the dark yard there was a light on in the bunkhouse, and she wondered where Kyle was, imagining him sprawled out on his bed. Did he wear anything under the sheets? Or was his hard muscular body naked? She could almost imagine running her fingers across his chest, what would his abs feel like without his shirt on? Remembered the feel of his fingers rubbing against her breast, causing her nipples to pebble and her sex to dampen and ache. It was so bewildering, she'd never been so attracted to a man before, had no idea how to keep him at a safe distance. Every time he was near her defences seemed to fail.

What was sex like, would it hurt? Anything she thought she knew had only been gained from the romance books she read, and that hardly made her experienced. Would he take the time to go slowly until she'd learned all she needed to know? With a start, astounded at her wayward thoughts, she spun away and headed for the bathroom to take a shower, turning the heat down until it was so cool it made her skin tingle. It did help, a bit, and she finally climbed into bed to get warm, feeling sinful and slightly self-conscious, and had another very restless night!

Next morning, with dawn showing through the slight gap where the curtains didn't quite meet, she climbed out of bed with a yawn to watch Sheb and Buck disappearing over the rise and out of sight. A sudden unsettled feeling made her feel edgy and for a moment she was puzzled. Oh no, she was going to have to talk to Kyle in the office! Her resolve from yesterday was beginning to crumble already. What was she? A weak willed mouse, or his boss! Apparently, a weak willed mouse where he was concerned. She had to get a grip!

Hurriedly making sure her hair was combed, she hesitated as to what to wear before finally deciding that either her usual black or brown made her look more business-like and would hopefully put him off of whatever he might be thinking. Heading downstairs to the wonderful smell of biscuits and gravy, happy to see that Kate was back in charge, pretending all was well and she didn't have a care in the world. That fell flat when she realised that Kyle wasn't there and she immediately felt like a deflated balloon. But then she had to practice not noticing when he was around, hide her feelings from everyone.

'Mm, that smells nice. Nice to see you back, Kate!' She was greeted with a big smile although the housekeeper's face looked slightly taken aback.

'Hello, Sandy. My you look a bit like you're off to a funeral! What happened to your new clothes?'

'Board meeting today, this is looking professional.'

Kate's face was a picture, as if she didn't know what to say, dishing up a plateful of food with a raised eyebrow as if something didn't sound quite right but kept quiet. Even so Sandy tried to do justice to her breakfast, hampered by becoming slightly uneasy about what was going to happen when she met up with Kyle in the office. A couple of cups of strong coffee helped to bolster her confidence and with a thank you to Kate, she made her way to the big lounge, sitting down to riffle through a magazine until she heard footfalls in the hallway and glanced up. The doorway seemed to have shrunk with Kyle's body filling it, and to get her pulse under control, she looked back at the article she'd been reading before climbing to her feet.

'Morning, Miz Carson.'

He was determined to be polite, to quash every memory of her lips and her body but he knew it was going to be difficult especially when he noticed her cheeks becoming faintly tinted with pink and he felt even more attracted. Being together was obviously going to be a strain for her too, even though she was obviously trying to show she was as unaffected as he was pretending to be, the dark clothes a good indication of how she was feeling. Professional, and totally hands off! Now that was going to be a shame. He turned and headed into the smaller lounge while she followed, opening the office door to stand back and let her through.

'Please make it Sandy. I'm not that old,' she told him tartly, determined to lay down the rules from the start, missing out on his grin as she had her back to him.

'Yes ma'am.'

Once inside she was impressed at how the shelves were neatly lined with files, and the desk, while cluttered, still looked as it was in some sort of order and she couldn't help but be pleased. Blade had always called her a neatness freak. Heading over she scanned the labels informing her exactly of what was inside. Went to pull one out, hesitated and turned to him. He anticipated.

'No problem, go ahead.'

Her heart slipped up into her throat and back again seeing him lounging against the wall, big and imposing. How could one man just stand there and ooze such potent sexuality? Did he always have to do that? Make her so aware of his presence. But strangely for her, he wasn't making her feel intimidated as she normally did back home when ranchers or reps came into her office to discuss cases or the financial costs she charged. She'd learned to put up a barrier towards men that had the immediate effect of putting things strictly on a business level.

Waiting for a second while she made up her mind which to look at first before pulling out the one headed household accounts, sitting on the chair to open it, scouring through some of the contents. Wow, everything had been neatly noted in big bold handwriting and while she suspected every other file would look the same, couldn't help replacing it on the shelf and picking another. Well, she was the owner here, and then the power of actually owning everything suddenly hit her making her stomach lurch.

'Are you okay?' Kyle watched her expression freeze as if something, a memory or a thought had shaken her for a moment, then surprised at how quickly she seemed to regain control. Concerned, he continued, 'Everything's on the computer and backed up on a memory stick, that's held in the safe.'

'Yes, I'm fine. It's all just a bit bewildering and if I feel like this, how on earth must you be?'

He shrugged and as he came round the desk beside her, the waft of his scent seemed to fill the whole room making her determination not to be affected by him fly straight out the window. Turning the computer towards himself and switching on as if he hadn't noticed, he deftly started pushing buttons and typing in information, scrolling down through the charts to show her and Sandy became immersed as he explained everything, from buying animal feeds and equipment, to wages, the household items that she'd already seen in the file, ranch taxes, and vet bills both for the cattle and the horses.

Sandy blinked, it was almost too much to take in, the scale of the commercial side of the ranch was too overpowering and there was a heavy silence as her brain seized up. For her, luckily, there was a knock on the door and, looking up, found it was Kate with two mugs on a tray. A rush of relief slithered along her veins.

'Thought you two would like a drink.'

'Lovely, thanks Kate.'

'Thanks.' They both spoke together and Kate smiled, looking

in concern at Sandy.

'You okay there?'

'It's a bit overwhelming. It makes my business look so minute.'

Kyle stared at her. 'You have your own business?'

'Yes, but nothing on this scale.'

He seemed to be lost for words obviously taken aback before pulling himself together to ask, 'Have you got the copy of the bank withdrawal, it needs to be entered into the accounts.'

Sandy stared at him, confused. 'What withdrawal?'

'The money you spent, to pay for your new clothes.'

'Oh.' She looked blank. 'I used my own money!'

Kyle frowned. 'You do know you can draw on the ranch accounts!'

'Er, no,' her brain seemed to shut down while she tried to get to grips with what he was saying, 'No, I never thought, never assumed.'

For the moment she was unsettled, tried to compose herself, to regain her confidence. She could spend the money in the bank? For a second it was almost freakish as she again tried to come to grips with her circumstances. She owned a huge ranch, owned everything on it, wouldn't have to touch her own hard won bank savings anymore! Her life would be comfortable from now on even if she was still struggling to take it all in. But then the confidence that she'd built up most of her adult life began to kick in. She could do this. She could show another man that she could take on the challenge and win.

Having left University at only nineteen, with the support of her parents behind her that they'd always given, she'd insisted on making it on her own, negotiating a loan with the bank herself to buy a small farm close to home, supplying a spread sheet with proposed incoming and outgoing finances that would take her through until she'd made enough to start repaying it. Having impressed the bank manager to invest in her, she'd turned the old farm into a horse facility, to take on the challenge to make life better for her horses. She smiled at that thought. Any animal that came to her for whatever reason became hers while under her wing!

She'd taken Blade on when more people heard about her and came asking for help, and he'd wanted to learn her skills. And now, four years later, she was determined to at least try to learn everything she could to run this place. With Kyle's help, of course!

Suddenly becoming aware that Kate had left and that Kyle was still staring at her, she immersed herself in scrolling through the information on screen until he pushed her coffee across the table top, taking her by surprise just as she went to reach for it and their fingers met. The powerful connection she'd had before swept through her body and she could hardly breathe. Glancing at him, as their eyes met, she saw that he'd been affected the same way and for what felt like minutes, he held her gaze with his. Looked as flustered as she felt, until his hazel eyes turned molten. She felt his presence even more as her feminine parts decided to sit up and take notice.

Kyle so wanted to taste those lips again and it took a great deal of self-control not to drag her up, to see if she wanted him as much as he did her. Kiss her until she melted in his arms, to strip her clothes, lay her over the desk, to work his fingers inside her until she came with an orgasm before plunging himself deep into her warm wet depths. He mentally shook himself to try and tamp down the ache in his growing erection.

'It's getting cold.'

'Thanks.' They both spoke at the same time.

Picking up the mug to stop her hands from trembling, Sandy tried to carry on, taking a sip while she unscrambled her brain followed by a bigger gulp as the liquid had cooled. Wishing he'd leave. Hoping he wouldn't.

'I think that I'm going to have to take a lot more time trying to get to grips with all this.' She avoided looking at him, she'd been so involved in looking at the records that she'd almost forgotten yesterday completely, but now the sense of his body near to her was distracting. Had he moved closer!

'What do you do? Back home!'

'I train and rehabilitate horses.'

'You train? Train for what exactly?' He'd started to look at her in a new light especially after seeing how well she'd ridden Satan.

'Whatever people want to do, competition or just general horsemanship, teach people how to make their horse their best friend. Get them to trust each other. Personally I prefer doing Trail but everything in between like Showmanship or Pleasure classes. Just the basics so the horses are ready to move on with their owners.'

'And rehabilitate?'

Sandy hesitated, her cheeks pinking as she looked at him defiantly, anticipating the usual reaction. Over the years she'd realised that some people didn't understand what or even why she did what she did.

'I take in horses that have been ill-treated or traumatised through thoughtlessness. I try to regain their confidence until

121

whatever has hurt or frightened them is overcome. Make them trust humans again and then, when it's time, I find them the appropriate home, somebody who will love and respect them.'

'No wonder you looked so good on a horse yesterday.' Kyle ran his fingers through his hair and looked at her with a respect that hadn't really been there before. It shamed him to think that of course there hadn't been as all he'd been doing up to now was lusting after her body. 'What made you want to do it? Or is that too personal?'

Sandy sat back in her seat keeping her eyes on the screen in front of her while she decided how much to tell, how much to open herself to him, and found that she wanted his approval. Now why did his understanding mean so much to her!

'It's always been horses, I loved to see them run, free, inter-acting with each other, learning what made them what they are.' She clasped her hands together and looked down at them in contemplation, seeing the animals in her mind, the scars, mental and physical, the lack of care and worse, the desperate look in their eyes as they begged for help. Tears welled into her eyes before she could stop them, brushed them away in embarrassment.

'My mom used to come up to my room and hold me tight while I cried, feeling so helpless about the cruelty, so I went to University, learned everything I could, including studying other people who were perfecting or had perfected the art of what people call horse whispering although I prefer to call it gentling.'

Chapter Five

She trembled slightly as she felt his strong hand cover hers, his fingers curling round. Looking up into his face, she saw the same type of compassion for her as she had for horses but was now tinged with admiration.

'So, you set up your own venture?' He smiled. 'Forget the paperwork, I'll give you the password to get in and you can look any time. I think that we should explore a bit more of the ranch, properly this time.' He pulled her to her feet.

'Oh, before we go, I really should have your cell number, and Sheb's, in case of an emergency.'

'Good idea, I'll take yours as well.'

Having swapped numbers, once they were both warmly clothed they were out of the door and walking down to the stables. Sandy took a deep breath of fresh air to clear her brain, as if a weight had fallen from her shoulders. She could learn about the working of the ranch, try to run it with Kyle's advice or, she could leave the cattle to him while she incorporated her work with horses here.

She frowned. She'd either have to close down in Lone Tree or pass her business on to someone who had her same values and commitment. Blade would probably jump at the chance, he'd been talking about owning his own yard one day as his knowledge and skills had begun to equal hers. Reaching the stables, when Kyle suddenly stopped, she ran into his muscular back. It was hitting a brick wall. Embarrassed, she flushed.

'Sorry, I was thinking.'

'Lot to take in I guess. Would you like Satan again, or another horse although I suspect you could get the best out of anything. Satan's very safe!' He turned, his eyes twinkling.

'Oh, you don't need to get me something quieter. I think Satan and I will be able to get along just fine.'

'Saddle's there.' He swung his hand in its direction determined to find out if what she'd told him had been true, then pointed to Satan. 'He's all yours.'

Finding a brush, Sandy went into the stall letting Satan snuffle over her outstretched palm before rubbing his neck in little circles allowing him to get used to her before she started brushing him down.

Aware of her presence, as Kyle saddled Ranger trying to keep low key and watch covertly to make sure she knew what she was doing, still unsure after her seeming insecurity behind him the other day. He could just about make out a soothing constant murmur as she slid the blanket onto Satan's back, smoothing it down before swinging the saddle over, reaching under to cinch it. Noticed Satan's ears flickering back and forth as she moved about, he discovered that Ranger too was being affected the same way, as if both horses were mesmerised by the sound. As with the saddle, she was just as careful not to let the bit bang on the Palomino's teeth instead letting him take it up almost by himself before re-tightening the cinch. Kyle was pleased to see how much care she was taking to make sure he was comfortable.

A strange feeling shot through him. Not his usual, I'm going to take you to bed for an unbridled night of passion, nor imagining what she would look like naked, but more appropriate thoughts after having learned more about her this morning. That she was not only sensitive and kind, but had a backbone most women didn't have, certainly none that he'd known. And that thing about spending her own money! She hadn't come to take advantage of the ranch, but had been prepared to spend her own money instead of taking anything from the accounts. How many women would do that? After several grasping girlfriends, women who had been more than willing to take everything they could get out of him money-wise, she was proving to be novel.

Once outside the gate, they both mounted and with Satan happily falling back into his usual routine of following Ranger, they set off up the rise and down the other side, but this time instead of heading for the trail to the lake, Kyle led her to the right and through another gate.

'We've moved the herd closer north, towards the summer pastures. But not like they do on the TV films.' He began to enjoy himself, he loved this ranch as his own and even if Sandy wasn't to stay here, perhaps she would let him run it for her.

'We move cattle fairly gently, the cowboy is there to keep them going together in the right direction, pushing stragglers who're determined to head back home. Haze them, go slow, don't want to run the weight off them or you end up getting less money. Like any viable business, we're here to make money not lose profits. Moving them usually takes a few days.'

'You camp out, with a chuck wagon?'

Kyle chuckled, sending a thrill through Sandy's body. 'Oh yes. No chance of a McDonalds where we go. And we sleep on the ground, in bedrolls!'

As Sandy looked askance, he grinned at her expression. 'No,

no bedrolls. Tents with put-you-up beds that are transported in an old rough terrain 4x4 to our usual campsites, and sadly no chuck wagon, just food cooked over an open fire.'

From out of the blue, taken aback by an impulse and having no idea where it had come from, before he could stop himself, he asked, 'You want to go?'

He held his breath. Days out on a cattle drive with Sandy close by. Oh, yes please! Normally he took point but he could always come back and watch over her, couldn't he? To watch her perfect butt in the saddle in front of him he'd try and make sure she was ahead, and then sleeping in a tent next to his.

'I'll think on it.' Despite her slight hesitation he had a feeling that she liked the idea of such an adventure, and it lightened his mood. She was certainly game. None of his former girlfriends had wanted anything to do with the ranch, just how much they could spend on looking good. Sandy was a breath of fresh air and his mood lightened.

'Come on.'

He heeled Ranger into a lope and they followed a winding track, made by the cattle she imagined, relaxing into Satan's gentle lope that needed no skill to stay in the saddle, and no steering either as he followed his friend. Far ahead were soft rolling hills and set high on a reddish sandy soil slope covered with clumps of the blue and grey sages was a large red finger of rugged sandstone. Chimney Rock, Kyle informed her over the soft sound of hooves and the creak of leather.

After a few miles they were slowing down and Sandy caught glimpses of the wide creek just ahead, a gap splitting the bank leading into the murky water. To her surprise, it was moving faster than she'd thought but started to walk Satan into it to let him drink. He baulked, trying to turn back, and as she went to apply her legs, Kyle grabbed the reins. Sandy bit back a sharp retort, she wasn't a novice rider.

'Quicksand,' he warned her before she could say anything. 'Satan, being range bred, knows it. He'd never have allowed you in,' and seeing her frown explained that the saturated loose sand, when agitated by fast flowing water, became treacherous.

'Oh, can you sink and drown?' She looked at him quizzically. Saw him trying hard not to smile.

'Unlikely. Not like in films, but a heavy animal can sink far enough that their legs get bogged, although potentially you could drown if the water rose while you were trapped which is why we have to ride the range every day, looking for any mired cattle. If they're not in too deep we can rope them and haul them out.' He laughed. 'They don't appreciate help and can turn so quick you need a horse with cow sense to get you out of the way.'

'Cow sense? I've heard of that!'

'Ever watched a cutting event?'

'Only in a documentary about rodeos and the different cowboy skills, although I don't like to watch the bucking horses, or the bull riding.'

'I'll try and get Sheb to show you. It's amazing what his horse can do. Come on!'

Kyle led the way to the left and alongside the river ducking under the lower tree branches and thicker bushes, increasing their speed and as they headed into the wind, Sandy was glad she'd put on her coat before setting out.

'Does it ever get hot round here?' she shouted above the sound of the hooves. Kyle turned and her breath caught at the ease his body moved in the saddle as he looked back at her.

'We're waiting on summer to arrive!'

'When's that?'

'Around May through September normally.'

His voice came floating back to her on the wind as he gave Ranger a longer rein and his horse began to increase speed, Satan keeping up. Exhilarated, she went with his swinging gait, loving the freedom she always felt when riding, the sun and wind in her face. Kyle began to rein in, stopping beside a bend in the river where the water ran faster between high banks, swirling round old log jams caught up on the bends. From the look of it, Sandy could see the water had been a lot higher at some time.

'Wow that was fun.'

Kyle looked at Sandy as she drew up beside him, her cheeks rosy from both excitement and the wind, her bottom lip slightly swollen from her teeth pinching it with the exhilaration of the ride, making him want to bite it himself, to devour those pink lips. Her eyes met his and for a minute that electricity they both felt for each other drew sparks but Sandy looked down and patted the Palomino, her heart racing from something other than the galloping, her nerves tingling at his appreciative gaze.

'Where is the ranch from here?' she asked, trying to move away from the danger of wanting him to take her in his arms and kiss her, reddening when she realised that he was looking at her with a quirk at the corner of his mouth as if he knew exactly what she'd been thinking. He seemed so in tune with her thoughts, and it disturbed her. Kyle waited until he could make sure that his voice was level before pointing back and to the left.

'About ten miles, follow me.'

Turning away from the river, he set off through the long grass along another cow trail at a ground covering lope letting the horses get their breath back, aiming towards what Sandy had thought in the distance was the rise above the ranch but when the trail bore off to the right around it to head for another, she realised that she'd misjudged. Her legs began to ache, she'd never ridden this far before, there not being much open space now with all the building going on around Lone Tree, and finally she had to call out to Kyle. He stopped and swung Ranger to face her looking concerned.

'You okay?'

'I'm not used to riding this long a distance. Can we walk for a while?'

He glanced about as if for any danger then nodded, dismounting with no sign of muscle fatigue while Sandy groaned inwardly as her feet hit the ground making her thighs and ankles throb. Taking the reins to lead Satan, she was amused to notice that Kyle wasn't quite as steady on the rough ground in his higher heeled boots as he was in the saddle. She, luckily, had bought lower heeled ones and couldn't hold back the soft giggle that had Kyle looking back over his shoulder.

'What's so funny?'

'It's nothing!' The man must have had the ears of a bat! She wouldn't be so wicked as to tell him, would she!

He stopped, forcing her to draw alongside, a slight frown of puzzlement on his face, and she couldn't stop the slight grin despite wondering if she'd overstepped the mark on their, so far, pleasant day out. She shrugged, kept her voice light.

'You, err, don't look so comfortable on this rough ground.'

'I can say the same of you, you know.' His eyebrows rose while a glint of mischief flashed in his eyes.

'I'm not used to it while you look as if you've ridden all your life. I didn't mean it rudely. Most cowboys look the same on the ground.'

He studied her for a moment, thoughtfully then sadly. 'You've hurt my feelings!'

Sandy immediately felt guilty. 'I'm really sorry, especially as it's been such a lovely day, learning about the ranch.'

'You'll have to pay a price or I won't show you the way home.'

Sandy went red, she had an idea what he was about to say and her body lit up like a candle flame, warmth heating her breasts, everything south of her stomach feeling hot, then and wet. Embarrassed, she quivered. Would he demand a kiss? She bit at her lower lip sending Kyle's body into a spin as he imagined nibbling at it himself while their tongues danced crazily together.

'You wouldn't!'

'Trust me, I would.' He dared her, his eyes darkening, the flecks of gold in the hazel more noticeable, but he also looked hot and slightly uncomfortable as if he'd said something he almost wished he hadn't. So, he could dish it out but he couldn't take it himself.

'Oh,' she whispered, trying to avoid showing any emotion, determined that if he wanted his pound of flesh he'd have to come and get it himself. 'Alright, if you have to!' daring him back. Closing her eyes she found herself nervously flushing with anticipation, turning her face towards his, her heart jumping into double time.

Kyle's blood pounded through his body, ending up in his

lower region and into the part that wanted to be inside her so much, already thickening, knowing that kissing her could be the biggest mistake of his life. Suppose he couldn't stop. Deep hidden embers began to race through his veins like flame, just the thought of her tempting lips on his making him perspire. She was so innocent and yet she was willing to play along with him.

'Oh no,' he finally said, and she heard the effort he was making to take up the dare in his voice. 'You have to pay me.'

Her eyes opened to find that he'd moved closer until only a couple of inches lay between them, staring at her lips as if he was ready to consume her. Her heart lurched, but she had been rude, hadn't she. Just a quick peck and that would be it. Only to apologise! They could laugh about it and ride on. Taking a deep breath, she pressed her lips to his but the sizzle of hot pleasure it brought was only intensified as his hand reached up to the back of her head, pulling her mouth harder against his, an iron arm enclosing her waist, pressing her body hard against him.

And Kyle devoured her, encouraging her lips open with his tongue, tasting her as they tangled in a sensuous dance, felt her melt into him as she moaned, reciprocated, her hands grasping at his shoulders. Blood pounding in his ears, his jeans became too tight as his erection threatened to burst through his zipper, his hand slipping lower to grip a firm buttock, to squeeze her into his hardness, hearing the breath catch in her throat.

Undoing the top of her jeans, he slid his fingers down inside, into her panties, into the slick wetness between her legs, sliding between the soft folds, hearing her breathing deepen as he caressed and played, held her tighter as she arched into him, pressing against his hand, demanding. He slid a finger up inside to find her hot and wet, heard her whimper as her fingers slid around his neck gripping him tight while his mouth continued to stoked the fires for them both. Until she thought she couldn't take it any more when a wave of exquisite pleasure at his touch overpowered her. As her body exploded in a mind blowing orgasm that left her reeling.

A slither of common sense began trying to edge into her brain as she began to be aware of what they were doing, and then another heady explosion tore through her as he pressed harder to the part of her that was so sensitive, leaving her trembling. And despite the desire to let him go on stimulating her, she was almost grateful that he was the one to stop. Even so, her body felt abandoned as he withdrew his fingers leaving her drained, legs limp, her core throbbing.

'Sandy!' His throaty voice shaking with agitation, Kyle eased his fingers out, making her pull back to stare at him, bewildered at what she had let happen. 'We have to stop!'

He had to now, before he laid her on the ground, pulled her jeans off and did what he wanted to do every time he saw her. Thrust his hot swollen erection deep into what he now knew was a warm, wet delectable body. Panting, he forced himself to hold her arms until he knew she was able to stand before moving away, turning to gulp in deep breaths. Frustrated, knowing that she deserved better, she needed to be made love to slowly whatever his body thought otherwise. He mustn't destroy her first time. If he was guessing right and he would be her first.

Sandy was shaking. She'd allowed things to get too far again. She had to stop this hot need that ravaged her body every time their lips met. It was obvious that he was experienced, for a fleeting second wondered how many women he'd been with. Was he seeing anyone? He hadn't said, and she couldn't just blurt out the question on her lips. And if he was, how could she explain the chemistry between them!

'I'm sorry,' she blurted out seeing how hurting he was, grateful to be released from the hold he had over her. 'I should never have played along. I'm so sorry.'

Doing up her jeans her body felt desperate, wanting him even more than it had before. He'd woken a simmering volcano deep inside her depths that she was afraid might not be put out until they'd taken this thing between them to its inevitable end.

'It's not your fault.' Kyle turned back. 'I just seem to lose my head whenever you're around. I'd be better off playing with lit matches,' watching a slow smile twitch the corners of her mouth at his attempt to joke, lips swollen from his fervour. She began to relax even though she'd obviously been shaken by what had just happened. 'We'd better get back before they send out a search party.'

As she swung back up into the saddle, he mounted Ranger and for a while they rode in silence while he tried to damp down the still raging lust coursing through his body, made harder as his fingers replayed the feel of being inside her. Her hot kisses when she'd responded. While his throb of need that was taking a fair time in slowing down. It hadn't been easy to pull back in time. But Kyle wasn't prepared to go through another long embarrassed ride like the other day, pulling Ranger back until he was alongside Satan to make small talk, anything that he could think of until finally they were in sight of the ranch.

'Sheb's watching over the gate so you good to go?'

'Yes.' Sandy met his gaze and straightened her back seeing the admiration in his brooding hazel eyes that turned her inside out again. 'Just stop looking at me like that.'

He chuckled, for a moment curbing Ranger's eagerness to start off and she brought Satan to a halt to look at him, puzzled. 'I really enjoyed the ride, to show you a bit more of the ranch.'

'So did I.' Sandy was relieved to find that her voice sounded normal. Drew a breath and went on, 'Perhaps you could take me out again sometime, when you're not busy with the ranch work. There is so much to see and back home I don't get a real chance to travel any distance. Just give me a couple of days to get my muscles working again.' Smiling as they halted by the gate, she gave a soft laugh for Sheb's benefit.

'Wow, that was some ride but could we make it a little shorter next time, Kyle, my legs are aching, I didn't realise how far we would go.'

'No problem, Miz Carson,' caught her stare and floundered. 'Er, Miz Sandy. Hope you're okay, I forget sometimes just how big this ranch is.' He turned his face away from her as his imagination swirled. 'Perhaps a hot soak would help!'

He looked at Sheb as if embarrassed at even mentioning such a thing in front of them all but Sandy pretended not to be affected by his remark and slid out of the saddle gratefully handing the reins to Sheb.

'Please could you take care of Satan just this once, I do need to get into the hot tub.'

She made her way slowly through the barn and towards the house, trying to hide the fact that she was uncomfortable, grateful to reach the door, knowing that taking the stairs was going to be somewhat of an effort. Once upstairs she went to switch on the hot tub, stripping off in her bedroom to put on a robe, waiting for the water to heat.

'Worried bout where you'd both got to!' Sheb took Satan into his stall and began unsaddling while Kyle took care of Ranger.

'My fault, she was really interested in the ranch. Asking all the right questions for someone not used to all this, and then tried to ride into the ford. Never heard of quicksand but Satan was having none of that. Guess I just got carried away telling her everything.'

Sheb grunted. He well knew how Kyle felt about the ranch, the same as he did.

'She say what she's wantin' to do?'

'No!' Kyle's guts wrenched as he wondered what had been going through her head since she'd arrived. Would she want to go back home, and if she did, what would she do with the ranch? It was the only real family home he'd ever had and the thought of moving away was like a boulder settling in his guts. 'I'm hoping she keeps on liking it here.'

They finished off in silence before Kyle headed to his cabin for a shower, a cold one, because once on his own he couldn't help remembering coercing Sandy into what would have been a quick daring kiss. He should have known better that even a quick kiss with her wasn't likely to stay that way feeling like he did about her. How close had he been to taking her there and then, it worried him that he always lost control when she was around.

And as the water poured down his body he recalled how she'd responded to him again even if she didn't seem to have any experience of kissing, other than just a quick peck as friends. As if she really couldn't stop herself from putting her arms round his neck and kissing him back, her response to his petting. He had to stop getting up close and personal with her and remember that she was the owner, and the only way to do that was going to be to throw himself into his work.

Getting everything ready for the drive into the hills should give him enough time away from her to curb his desires, until he remembered he'd invited her to join him. That gave a further jolt to his nerves and despite trying to tamp down his feelings with the cold water, according to the reaction of the favourite part of his anatomy he'd already lost the battle! Frustrated at his thoughts, he had no option but to take immediate action to relieve himself, pumping out his frustration, but even that failed to sate him because all he could think about was her!

Sandy decided to shower quickly before heading for the hot tub, but just a touch to her breasts pebbled her nipples and sent pleasure splintering through her body, down to the yearning between her thighs, reliving Kyle's sensual kiss. To remember her body's response to him, and without thinking began to rub gently where she ached, where his fingers had been, pretending that he was caressing her again, lost in her thoughts until she stopped with an embarrassed lurch. What was she thinking of? Oh yes her brain told her, you know what or rather who! She'd never felt this way, it was making her too aware of things she knew she wanted but she'd never been out of control, ever! It had to stop.

Wrapping up in a towel and heading to the hot tub, she gently and slowly lowered herself into the bubbling water, feeling the jets pummelling her achy muscles, lost in her thoughts until the timer pinged, letting her know her fifteen minutes were up. Climbing out she dried herself off, returning to her room to stare critically at herself in the long mirror hanging on the inside of the closet door while she tried to decide what to wear. Once again, turning slightly sideways, she stared gloomily at her overall outline. She was too skinny and very unladylike. What on earth did Kyle see in her when there were many prettier women around! Was there an ulterior motive in his coming on to her, was he trying to lull her into giving the ranch to him, yet she couldn't deny the hold they both seemed to have over each other. Horses she could read, but people?

Everyone but Kate seemed to be comfortable in jeans and although she preferred her thinner pants, especially indoors where it was warmer, she finally decided to pick the dark blue shirt that would go with jeans. Seeing the clothes she'd disposed of on the bathroom floor, she must find out where to do her washing.

Heading slowly downstairs, her legs not aching quite so much, hopefully due to her fitness and the hot soak, she entered the kitchen to find Kate serving the meal, thick steaks covered in delicious smelling gravy, roast potatoes, chunks of home-made bread, and salad greens. Greeting everyone with a, 'hi,' the men rising from their chairs until she was seated at the centre counter, Buck kept looking at her with evident approval whenever he thought Kyle wasn't looking but was eventually caught out and spent the rest of the meal trying to take more interest in his meal. Sandy smiled, ignoring Kyle's displeasure and not looking at him.

The meal was deliciously filling, and she had to reluctantly refuse a piece of apple pie, managing just a cup of coffee while she waited for the men to finish up. As they tramped out with their thanks to Kate, she cleared the plates and mugs from the table, wiped it down and sat keeping the housekeeper company.

'Who exactly is Jilly?'

'Sorry, Sandy, I forgot to tell you about her, she comes in at weekends or whenever she's needed for pocket money really as she's still at school.'

'Is she local?'

'Her mom died when she was young, her father brought her up. He brings her over usually on a Sunday when he's not working at the saw mill outside of town. They have a small shack and she does the cooking and cleaning for him during the week. I know she looks unconventional but she's of the age when she's rebelling a bit.'

'She was a bit of a shock at first. Poor girl, it must be rough without a mom. My mom and dad live back in Lone Tree, been there all their lives, and oh so happily married. She cooks for our local diner, pies and pastries mostly, and occasionally, if she can find the time, which is every time because she can't resist turning friends down, cakes for special occasions. Our house always seems to smell of baking. Dad's a carpenter, a really good one. He can make almost anything from a set of shelves to a table or a cupboard, does them to order, or just to sell from outside his store.'

Kate smiled with her, enjoying the younger girl's pleasant thoughts. 'That's nice, do you have any siblings?'

'My brother, Carlton, he's five years older than me and sales manager for a big electronics store in Dallas. I only really see him unless it's for mom and dad's wedding anniversaries or Christmas, when he can get the time to come visit.'

Carlton had always been her best friend and champion when she was very young, had always played big brother, picking her up when she fell or reading stories to her at bedtime, playing in the backyard with her until he got in with older boys and drifted away but by then she could stand on her own two feet. Until she'd left home to go to the University when he would listen stoically over the phone when she needed to talk, trying to give her long range support.

She reciprocated whenever he'd called to say he'd fallen out with a girlfriend or lost one to somebody else. So she'd been thrilled when his latest, Dana sounded as if she was there to stay, he always sounded so happy these days. She really should phone him tonight even though her mom would have been straight on to him to say she'd left Arizona to come here.

When they'd both finished a glass of wine, Kate left to go to her place, locking up behind her, leaving Sandy to check the front door was also secure, going to the small lounge to set up her laptop.

Mandy didn't reply to her email, she assumed that her friend had gone out for the evening, so called her mom instead before Carlton. Alice was relieved all was going well so far and slipped in a quiet question as to what Sandy intended doing.

'I've no idea, mom. It's really stunning out here. I went out with Kyle again to see some of the ranch and it's so vast. I haven't really had a chance to look through the books but Kyle seems to have kept very good and complete records, and when Willard was here it made money. I suppose the profits are mine but I can't get my head around it all. I didn't think about spending anything but my own money for the new clothes and it came as a shock when Kyle told me he needed a receipt for the records. He seemed very surprised that I'd used my own funds.'

Alice laughed. 'Now that I can understand of you, so independent, I can only advise you to do what you think best but don't let all that money go to your head.'

'Oh mom, you know me. You brought me up to respect money and it's going to take a while to even think about using what I still consider to be someone else's, it's so difficult to get to grips with it.'

'You know where we are love, whatever you want to do.'

'I know mom, thanks for letting me out from under your wing to come all this way to see it without flipping out,' and heard her mom give a faint sigh.

'All children leave the nest eventually. Love you.'

'Love you too, mom. Give dad a big hug and a kiss for me.'

'I will even though I know where that will lead. Goodnight.'

Sandy giggled, and her mom's echoed with hers. Even after all these years, the love between her parents was as strong as ever. Perhaps that was what she was looking for. Someone she could love and would love her back. What about Kyle, her rebellious self asked. Could she see him in her life, a forever love just like the books? Well, they seemed to be off to a good start, she thought with a wry smile. But perhaps she would just be a fling to him. Finishing her call, she closed and rang Carlton who answered after a delay, sounding breathless.

'Hi Sis, how you doing up there? Like being a lady millionaire?' he teased. 'Getting to boss the staff about?'

'Carlton that's not funny, and no I'm not a millionaire. And no I haven't bossed anyone about yet because the place is being run well by the foreman.' She sighed. 'I thought I had a lot of work in Lone Tree but this is way beyond that and very intimidating.'

'I've got every confidence you'll keep everything and every-one on the ranch whipped into shape.'

'How's you?' she asked, on tenterhooks for the reply, and heard him chuckle.

'You're worse than mom. I'm great, in fact I'm going out to dinner with Dana, you only just caught me as I headed for the door.'

'I'm so happy for you, Carlton. I wish you luck. You take care and say hi to Dana for me. Perhaps we will all meet up sometime soon.'

'Will call you about the next anniversary party for the folks, it will be special, forty years. Anyway, take care, and make sure the guys know you're in charge. Gotta go, you gals are always impatient once you're ready. Bye, Sis,' and the line went dead.

Making her way upstairs, Sandy had a quick wash before diving into bed and snuggling under the covers, drifting towards sleep but wondering if it hadn't been for her treacher-ous body deciding to overrule her head several times, just how far she'd have let Kyle go. Sadly a lot further, remembering how he'd sent her body into meltdown. Lucky for her he'd pulled back, even if reluctantly!

Waking to the surprising thought that she'd been here nearly a whole week already, the time had gone so fast she'd hardly noticed although she was feeling more confident with each passing day. Oh yes, her inner voice prodded her, and you know why, that foreman is getting to you! Big time!

Shaking her head to clear it, climbing out of bed she quickly showered, dressed and ran down the stairs towards the kitchen, curious because it was quiet, no sound of men's voices, just Kate moving about.

'Have I missed something?'

Kate took a plate from the warming shelf and placed it in front of her as she sat down.

'Kyle wanted to get going early today, they've gone. Why?' She'd noticed the small frown on Sandy's face.

'I wanted to have a look through the records but I don't like to do it without asking his permission, it wouldn't sit right with me and anyway I need the password to get into the computer.' She wasn't going to admit to herself that she'd prefer to do it without him around distracting her.

'Can't help you there, I'm not expecting them back till late.' She poured Sandy a cup of coffee and one for herself sitting down so they were face to face.

'Thanks Kate, but please let me get my own drinks, you have enough to do.'

'I wanted one anyway. Glad you've settled a bit now, you look like you're feeling less overwhelmed.'

'I am, much better. I don't think I've eaten so much before I came here, must be the fresh air and the exercise yesterday, I don't usually ride such distances.' Kate blossomed with her praise while Sandy picked up her empty plate and took it to the dishwasher, placing it on a rack.

'I need to do some washing…!'

'Out here.' Kate led her through the dining area and outside to a small wooden shack, and when the door was opened Sandy could see two machines. 'One for the men's working clothes, the one on the right for us, they both wash and dry, so much easier. Powder's in the waterproof bin on the shelf, just help yourself.'

Up in her room, Sandy sorted her clothes taking the pile of

coloureds downstairs and putting them into the top loading machine, opening the bin to scoop out the amount of powder. Reading the instructions, she pushed the start button. For a moment when nothing happened, she thought she'd got them wrong but with a click it finally started the cycle.

Putting on her warm coat, hat and boots, Sandy started down the trail towards the corrals and barns still trying to decide what to do about staying or leaving, but meanwhile she'd look over what was here to see if she could put in a round pen and continue her work with horses.

She thought at first the corrals were empty and the place deserted but without warning what she thought was the faint shadow of a man flitted across the opening at the far end of the barn, so fast that for a moment she thought she'd imagined it. Even so she stopped dead in her tracks.

'Who's there?'

Silence greeted her query. She knew it couldn't have been Sheb or Buck, and would have recognised Kyle, hesitating to go further until she felt a touch of anger that a stranger could be on her land and so close to the barns. Who was it? Clenching her fists, calling out again, she approached the barn but could only hear the sound of horses moving inside. Satan whinnied softly, recognising her voice, his head swinging over the door to his pen as another horse did the same thing next door. Sandy moved closer into the gloom and was reassured from the horses' ears pointing towards her that they were not listening to anything else, seemingly at ease. Half deciding that she had been mistaken, that something must have moved in the wind, she approached Satan to rub his nose, as much for his comfort as her own before returning to the corrals.

Looking over at the large grassy paddock dotted with trees coming into leaf after the winter, as she began to assess its potential, where she could site a round pen, another look at the smaller corral made her wonder if it would do to start with even if the corners looked a little tight. If that would work, the paddock could be turned immediately into a Trail course while keeping to the edge would be good both for ground-work and for ironing out paces.

With the warm sun on her back and the chilly but refreshing air, she lost herself in thought before returning to the house, stopping to sit out on the porch in the warming sun, undoing her coat, taking in the sight of all the land stretching out before her, the mountains in the distance, tiny flashes of light from cars on the road as their windows were caught by the sunlight. She still couldn't begin to understand that this piece of heaven was actually hers. That someone wouldn't come and demand it all back, tell her that it had all been a horrible mix up with the paperwork. She was brought back to reality with the opening of the front door.

'Coffee, Sandy?' Kate approached and she leapt to her feet to take the hot mug from her hand. 'You looked far away.' The housekeeper took the other seat.

'I was just thinking if I could start up my project here in Wyoming. I was looking over the pasture next to the corrals. But that would mean either selling up there to move here or to leave it with the guy who helps me at the moment. Or, I could return home and leave Kyle to run the ranch. He and Willard have done so well I just couldn't sell it out of the family.'

'You need to talk to Kyle about that. You've been left with a bit of a problem when you put it that way and I doubt Kyle has even thought about it, I certainly didn't. I was pleased that Willard left it to family although Kyle has been his family since he was about eight or nine I think.' She looked at Kate quizzically. 'Now, don't you take no notice of me, my mouth sometimes runs away. If Kyle wants to tell you anything it's up to him.'

'Kate, is there anyone on the ranch besides Kyle, Buck and Sheb?'

'No, not until new hands are taken on to drive the cattle to the higher pastures. Why?'

'Oh nothing, just my imagination playing tricks. Thanks for the drink.'

'You're more than welcome, does me good to have somebody here who I can sit and chat with. You want some lunch?' She smiled, 'Home-made soup and fresh bread?'

Sandy's eyes lit up. 'That sounds good,' following the house-keeper indoors.

Having filled up with lunch and leaving Kate to carry on fixing dinner, she rescued her now dry washing and took it upstairs to sort out before returning to the office, slowly taking one file at a time and perusing the paperwork so absorbed that it wasn't until the light into the office was suddenly blotted out that she found Kyle slouched against the door frame.

She felt her cheeks bloom as her body went into sensual overload, every nerve ending tingling, trying not to drink in the sight of his shirt half undone, revealing a smattering of dark hair on his chest, wondering what it would feel like under her fingers, coarse or soft, before forcing her eyes back to look at the figures on the page.

'Enjoying yourself?'

'I wouldn't… couldn't get into the computer without your permission so I thought I'd look through the records instead.'

She was immediately alert, confused yet strangely annoyed that this man kept having such an effect on her, kept putting her mind and body in turmoil. Kyle came to the side of the desk to turn the computer to face him, switched it on and typed in the password before writing it on a slip of paper.

'There you go.'

'ridetherange? Neat, thanks. I have to say that you're a good bookkeeper, I've found it easy to get a hold on what it is to run this place.'

'High praise from such a young business woman,' Kyle grinned, hitching a buttock cheek onto the edge of the table to gently swing his leg. Enjoying how flustered Sandy became in his presence however she tried to hide it.

'Are you mocking me, Mister Sherman?'

Sandy smiled to let him know she was teasing and made the mistake of looking up at him, noticing the dark shadow of stubble round his jaw, the laughter lines crinkling the side of his eyes, drowning in the intensity of his eyes. He was seriously eye candy! Get a grip, Sandy. You don't like men she tried to remind herself! Bit too late to remember that!

'I wouldn't presume.' His wide grin lit up his face and she forced herself to look away.

'Miz Carson!'

Startled, they both looked up as boot heels clumped across towards them and with stunning quickness, Kyle was up and facing Sheb as he came in, hat in hand.

'Buck's sin buzzards circling over by Finger Rock close tuh the line shack, an with them spy glasses, think I sin a rider. I

146

figgered could be someone rustled a steer!'

'Okay. We'll ride out first thing in the morning.'

'How far is that away?' Sandy asked, standing up suddenly, and both men looked round at her.

'About forty, forty five miles, some of it rough country.'

'I guess it's too far for me at the moment, I'd have gone with you otherwise. How long will it take you, there and back?'

Kyle frowned. 'Day and a half if the weather holds out. We could get us a stray blizzard this time of year because of the higher ground.'

'Okay, but be careful, I don't want dead heroes. I want a full report when you get back.'

Both men stood regarding her warily as if suddenly being approached by a bear with cubs and as she stared from one to the other intently, while Sheb had a strange look on his face which she couldn't decipher, Kyle looked taken aback, almost annoyed. He was! She was interfering with his job and he wasn't going to take that.

'Dinner,' shouted Kate breaking the spell and while Sandy turned to replace the file she'd been looking at, both men left heading for the kitchen. She hoped she'd hidden her nervousness from them both, but she was so out of her depth here. Were they just going to ride out all that way? It could be dangerous if it was a murderer or someone violent.

Buck was already seated when she arrived, standing up as she appeared, Kyle and Sheb waiting, but with a nod and a smile from her they sat and began filling their plates as if everything was normal. Kate placed a full plate in front of her as Sandy poured them both a mug of coffee, sitting down opposite with her own meal, and apart from the clinking of cutlery on plates, there was silence.

At the end of the meal, Kyle told her and Kate that Buck would be staying behind to keep an eye on the ranch while he and Sheb were gone leaving Sandy perturbed, this was getting a bit nerve racking for her, being right out in the wilds and so far from of town, from civilisation, but bit her lip. Kyle had taken charge and while the others were willing to let him give the orders, overall it was now her responsibility. Should she allow just the two of them to go!

'Kyle!'

He looked at her, sensing her uncertainty, then followed her through to the lounge where she swung round to face him.

'I'm not sure I like the idea of you two going that far away. Do you think it could be dangerous? Should you call the sheriff?'

'Won't know till we get there, but it's probably just a drifter down on his luck and hungry. Ranchers do lose a beef that way from time to time.'

'This is way out of my comfort zone.' She folded her arms as if to put up a shield. 'This country is so open and unpopulated compared to what I'm used to.'

'Sandy, out here it's no big deal. A lot of the time we ranchers have to police the range ourselves, and we're used to it,' he tried to assure her, feeling an urge to pull her into his arms, but refusing to do it. He knew where that would lead! 'As foreman it's my responsibility and my job to check things out. It's only a day and a half at most and we'll be back.'

He could see apprehension in her expression before she drew a deep breath, reluctantly nodding. He was right. She was usurping his authority if she kept interfering and he and Sheb

would only be doing their job. Rightly she should be supporting him for protecting the ranch especially as she felt sure he
should have inherited it, not her.

'Okay, but if you get hurt, either of you, I'll never talk to
you again!'

Kyle grinned. 'If I do, you can kiss it better, but only me!'
And before she could say anything, he was gone and she heard
the front door closing behind him. Sandy returned to the
kitchen and told Kate what she'd said to Kyle, taken by surprise
when the housekeeper also shrugged it off.

'That's what it's always been like out here, honey. We women
keep house, the men do the protecting. I'm sure, like Kyle said
it's just a drifter and he'll be gone when they get there, so don't
worry,' and hugged her. 'Well, I'm away. The men will be in
early tomorrow and want to get away as quickly as possible.
Goodnight.'

'Night, Kate.'

She locked the door, checked the front door and opened up
her laptop, relieved when Mandy answered quickly.

Hi friend, how's things?

Worrying! Kyle and Sheb are going to a line shack because
some squatter's been there these guys think nothing of
riding out like the Lone Ranger and Tonto while the ranchers apparently police their own properties.

Sounds good to me, you're out where men are men and
that's how us gals like 'em.

Well I don't like it, it could be dangerous.

You've watched too many cowboy films chill my friend.

Easy for you to say but I guess you're right. So what you been doing? Night clubbing with some poor sucker who buys you drinks and then gets sent home on his own?

How did you know? :] actually I met up with Sam.

I know how you operate, so Sam again that's got to be what, five or six times you've been out with him and that's serious for you! But I'm still going to try and go out Saturday with Torrey. I guess everyone dresses in jeans and fancy shirts.

Go you Sandy sounds like fun to me wish I could be there with you.

Wish you could be with me, too. Sort out holiday time and come up and stay if I'm still here.

You need an adventure my friend to live life and if you're not planning on staying go have a fling with that foreman!

What?

Seriously Sandy you need to get laid at least once you can't be a virgin the rest of your life you have no idea what you're missing you've let those idiots in Chicago get to you it's not healthy.

Mandy Romano! I'm shocked.

Come on Sandy you're over twenty live a little doesn't he like you even a little bit?

I don't know. Anyway that's it I'm off to bed my friend and alone.

Bye Sandy, you take care of you.

I will. Say hello to Sam for me.

Closing the lid with a snap, blushing madly, Sandy rushed to her bedroom and slept restlessly worrying about Kyle and Sheb. This was turning into a nightmare, and even Mandy saying, chill out, wasn't helping. It was alright for her, she was way down the country not out in the wilds of Wyoming, wondering if she was overreacting because she was in a strange place, where the rules for policing were so different to cities. Kyle and Sheb, and even Buck seemed to be taking it all in their stride as if it was normal. Perhaps it was just she wasn't used to men being macho. Or, a tiny voice at the back of her mind whispered, are you worried about Kyle?

Chapter Six

Somehow she must have slept, waking with the dawn. Leaping out of bed and glancing out the window her stomach gave a lurch to see that all was quiet by the barns, no sign of any riders. Had she missed them? After a quick shower and dressing even faster, she shot down the stairs heading for the kitchen, her worst fears realised when she found only Kate who, having heard her coming, was putting her breakfast on the counter. The older woman frowned slightly at Sandy as she came into the room, smiled knowingly.

'Bless you child, they'll be fine. I know you're not used to this sort of thing happening where you live.'

'Well no, we normally call the local sheriff and leave it to them. But it's so open here. I just hope that they're safe.'

'The other ranchers in the area will have been told what's going on and to keep a look out for any strangers. We all stick together out here, rely on each other. Don't let it put you off.'

'That would be a bit difficult because I really love it here,' she assured the other woman and meant it. Did that mean her being determined to stay on to help run the ranch, to start up another business here? After all she had to do something, there was no way she was willing to sit around doing nothing while the men were out working. That wasn't her.

Kate left to do her normal house cleaning and despite still being anxious, Sandy surprised herself by finishing the whole meal. Once the plate was rinsed off and in the washer, she decided to get into the computer, typing in the password Kyle had given her but before opening up the accounts, she went into her emails to contact Blade.

Despite no immediate reply, which was to be expected, he'd be working one of the horses, she gave him a quick rundown of what she'd been doing since she'd got here and that she needed to speak to him sometime, preferably on Skype. Now that would surprise but hopefully not worry him because he knew she was very uncomfortable about using the face to face screen. To her it distorted faces and didn't like to think about how she appeared, or how her expressions came over, but he deserved to know that she was contemplating the possible change to her life.

She flushed. Was it really that she'd fallen in love with the land or her strong attraction to Kyle urging her to stay, knowing he was attracted to her too? Although why he would want her was bewildering. It must have been obvious the day before when he'd touched her, to a man who'd been with other women, that she was inexperienced. She should be embarrassed, mortified shouldn't she! She'd never had such thoughts before and for a moment her hands trembled until she forced herself to stare at the screen while she finally got herself back under control.

For a couple of hours she was absorbed by the bookkeeping, monies coming in and going out, and where, until her brain seemed so overloaded it felt fried. Signing out, feeling a bit guilty as if she was being invasive, she had a look through the desk draws, finding mainly stationary, pens and pencils, and a thick cheque book. Closing it, she decided to go and see how Buck was doing on his own, unplugging her laptop before she went.

Glancing out the window at the yard she could see him working by the corrals and went to dress for the cold but surprisingly, having bundled up in a coat, the sun was a lot warmer and she felt overdressed, immediately unbuttoning it. No wonder she'd been warned the weather could be unpredictable. Buck was just coming through the corral from one further away where she could see horses moving about, tipping his hat to her, a shy smile on his face.

'Hi Buck. Just wanted to check that everything's okay, and thought I might saddle Satan to go for a ride.'

He looked serious. 'Can't let you do it on your own, ma'am or Kyle'd have my hide.'

Sandy frowned. 'And why not, Satan's quite safe.'

Buck coloured up. 'Never know what might happen, ma'am. Some cattle can be plain ornery, there's bears, and cougars, an' places plumb bad. You bein' new here in these parts, Kyle said can't let you out alone.'

Kyle had expected her to want to go out alone? Sandy stared at the barn suddenly recalling that the first time she'd gone out she'd been rescued from making a mistake at the river when she hadn't known about quicksand, reluctantly admitting Buck could be right.

'Yes, you're right. Everything fine here?'

'Yes, ma'am, done it before an' probably do it again.'

'Let me know if you have any problems!'

Buck tried to hide his astonishment, obviously only being used to taking Kyle or Sheb's orders. But even as a woman they had to know that she was the one in charge now. Obviously coming to the same conclusion, Buck tipped his hat again, 'Yes, ma'am.'

Turning away Sandy couldn't help but feel a warm glow at being treated with such deference, a far cry from when she dealt with men back home who usually told her what they expected from her and her training methods. That had taught her to stand on her own two feet. It was her way or not at all and most crumbled. They needed her more than she needed them.

Returning to the house she found Kate watering the outdoor plants and sat down in one of the chairs, staring thoughtfully out along the drive towards the highway while the housekeeper eyed her, caringly.

'I'll fetch you a nice cup of coffee, that'll help,' she offered. 'The men will be okay and you'll be happier when they return and it's all been for nothing.'

'It's that noticeable?' Sandy winced. 'It's being out of contact that worries me the most. I'm not used to it.'

Not used to caring this much about anyone other than her parents or Carlton, and nothing like the gnawing ache in her stomach she was unable to control. If she stayed she'd have to grow a harder skin, and that was the thing. What was she going to do about the ranch?

She'd already fallen in love with the freedom of the vast open space, the clean air, as if she was expanding to fit in. But falling for a man at last? She'd only been here a week and she couldn't even begin to grasp what was happening to her, her whole world was being turned upside down. From cutting herself away, wanting nothing to do with males, old or young, to feelings that were bewildering as her body tried to tell her it craved something she hardly understood. Unlike the boys at University, who she'd kept at arm's length, in Kyle's arms she'd felt safe, not even frightened by his advances.

Kate appearing through the door to hand her a mug made her jump, unaware that she'd been so into her thoughts she'd even lost track of where she was, thanking the older woman as she took the chair beside her.

'You're falling for Wyoming!' Not a question more of a statement.

'Yes I am,' she admitted with a soft sigh. 'It's only been a week, how has it done this.'

'Wyoming magic,' Kate looked at her, eyes twinkling. And Sandy laughed softly, for the first time in a very long time, she actually really laughed, the cares in her life seeming to fade away like the thistle heads that drifted in the winds during the fall.

She had inherited a beautiful home, she was already making friends, she even had someone strong enough to lean on, to help run the ranch if she allowed him to do that. And that was surprising considering how up to now she had never wanted to give up her hard won independence, those strengths that had enabled her to get over not knowing who her real parents were or why they hadn't wanted her. Getting over the rough time at University, to setting up her own enterprise. The strength needed to cope with the horses that came into her care, followed by the pleasure as they mended. Sipping from her mug she was surprised to find that it was empty.

'Oh, sorry, I was in a little world of my own,' she apologised as Kate allowed her expression to show sympathy.

'Wyoming magic,' Kate reiterated getting out of the chair to take Sandy's mug and go indoors, 'Lunch in five, if you're hungry!'

'Anything would be good but before you go, would you take

a photo of me in my western gear so I can send it to my friend!'

'Just show me which button to push but I can't guarantee it will be in focus.'

'I'll set it up, just push that white circle when you can see me in the screen, it's not a problem. If I can do it,' Sandy grinned, 'anyone can.'

With a lot of laughter as Kate tried to hold the phone still, and after several attempts while Sandy told her that she could take as many as she liked, the ones not right could easily be deleted, they finally decided on two. Following the woman inside to hang her coat and hat up, Sandy met with her in the kitchen.

'You don't have to keep running around after me,' but was interrupted by the phone ringing, heading to the office to answer it.

'Miss Carson? I'm Scott Scully, Willard's lawyer.' He waited for her to acknowledge who she was. 'I have your forms from the bank ready for you to look at and sign.' His voice was gravely as if from a throat problem.

'I have to be in Buffalo on Saturday around noon, could I see you then?'

'No problem I will be here. You can find my place in a side road behind the church hall in Wayne Street, three doors down on your left.'

'Thank you, see you then.'

Kate smiled as she returned to the kitchen. 'It's nice to have another woman to do things for,' she was assured. 'I miss my daughter so don't let me smother you.'

'I miss my mom, so smother away.'

Kate had made them a sliced beef and mustard sandwich

and they ate in comfortable silence something else that Sandy was beginning to appreciate, to her surprise. There wasn't much to do for dinner as there would only be the three of them so when Kate refused any help, Sandy went back out onto the porch to pick out various landmarks, trying to commit them to memory but giving them her own names to make it easier to remember. Then heading to the stables to see Satan, only to discover he'd been turned out with the others.

Entering the first corral and walking over to the far side, she stepped up on the lower rail to hook her elbows over the top. Instantly horses whistled and began to troop over, kicking and biting through nothing more than high spirits. Satan's lighter Palomino colour she immediately picked out, but mostly they were blacks and bays, even an Appaloosa that caught her eye. Light brown at the front, from the shoulders getting progressively whiter, his flanks and rump beautifully marked with brown and roan spots. Although his nostrils flared as he caught her scent, he had a kind eye that she liked and called to him.

It took him a while to decide, possibly he'd only been used to men so she'd smell strangely, before he began to inch his way towards her, the others having realised that there was no food having wandered off. Taking her eyes off him she held out her hand to be sniffed and when he threw his head up, took it away. That made him curious and after several goes she was finally able to rub his nose and run her hand down to his neck, snorting softly before beginning to enjoy her fingers gently circling there.

Pulling back, Sandy was able to look him over, good strong legs, the usual perfect small hard hooves, but unusual for this breed, a long mane and tail indicating a different ancestry somewhere. Suddenly his ears went up along with his head and Sandy knew someone was behind her.

'Miz Carson.' Buck appeared alongside her and the horse started back to the rest of the group. 'You like ol' Domino? He sure seems to like you.'

'Hi Buck, and please, can you make it Sandy.' She watched his expression change with slight discomfort. 'And yes, I think he's lovely. I'd love to ride him.'

'He can be a real handful, Miz Carson. Don't know if Kyle'd let you try.'

'Oh I think I can get round that,' she promised him, and herself. 'I have my ways with horses. I plan to bring what I do in Arizona up here.' She looked across at the large paddock. 'I would like to put up a round pen to work the horses in before they're saddled,' smiling at his confused look. 'Using techniques I've learned and taught myself, I could get a horse in off the range and have him saddled within an hour or two.'

Buck looked askance. 'What's a round pen?'

'Like a circular corral with room for the horse to run round free while we bond. No fights, no ropes, no cruelty. I can show you with Domino if you'll bring him into that small corral there.'

'I dunno, Miz Carson, Kyle might not like you messing on with Domino without him being here.'

'I'll take the responsibility, Buck. Just bring him in.'

Without another word, Sandy strode into the barn and on returning with a soft lariat, found that Buck had roped the Appaloosa and had him in the pen where he was prancing about, neighing at being apart from the other horses.

'You shore, Miz Carson!' He was alarmed when she came

into the corral.

'If you'll just wait outside, it'll be okay Buck,' she assured him.

As soon as the cowboy had reluctantly left the corral and she was in the centre, she snapped the end of the rope at him and Domino took off at speed, circling the corral away from her but after a while he started to calm so she made him turn and go in the other direction. Keeping him on the move for a while in both directions, she finally allowed him to stop and having got his full attention, his ears twitching and obviously trying to work out what it was she wanted, as she backed up, he began to follow until she reached out to pat and rub him all over, Buck nervously watching.

'See, I told you he'd be fine,' she told him. 'What do you think?'

'I don't believe it, Miz Carson. Er Miz Sandy!' Buck was dumbfounded as the horse continued to follow her round the corral like a big dog.

'Buck. Can you keep a secret?'

He stared at her for a moment before slowly, if reluctantly, nodding.

'That depends, Miz Sandy.'

'Don't tell Sheb or Kyle what you've seen and when they get back, I'll bring Domino in myself, he'll follow me anywhere.' She grinned. 'I learned to do this back home, it's never failed yet.'

'Miz Sandy, it's like magic. Yuh got no lead rope or halter and he'll do that all the time?'

'Yes.' She patted Domino, walked him to the far gate and turned him loose to go to the other horses. 'I'll saddle him next time and ride him. And if you're worried, I'll only do it in the paddock there. Right, it's close to dinner time and I don't want to upset Kate.'

'See you up there, Miz Sandy.'

Sandy grinned at him. At least Miz Sandy was less formal than Carson.

Back indoors she made her way through to the kitchen feeling decidedly hungry. She'd enjoyed herself and was definitely beginning to think about relocating here. But she wanted to know more about the ranch and how everything worked with the cattle before that. A twinge of guilt about the men broke into her thoughts, worried about them being so far away and especially now it was getting dark. She'd forgotten about them while playing with Domino. Perhaps they'd get a signal on their cells and could let her know that they were alright.

The evening seemed to drag out slowly even though she managed to link up with Blade on Skype. As she'd suspected he was highly amused at her using the medium but when she told him about her possible plans, he jumped at the chance to take over, either buying or running it for her.

'I'd have to see the bank about a loan to buy but if not I'd love to run it for you until I could,' he enthused. 'So you want to live there.'

'I'm not sure. It's early days, but yes I'm seriously thinking of it. Like with you, I could leave this place in the hands of the foreman, come back there, but I'd like to stay at least for a while longer.'

'Good for you, hope it comes off, you sound like you've really taken to the life. Meanwhile, Smoky and Danny are coming along real fine and it won't be long till they can leave, couple weeks at most I think. Callie is finally beginning to come round at last and I even managed to groom her today.'

'That's great, Blade. Thanks for keeping the place running, I really appreciate it.'

'No problem, I'm actually enjoying myself, hence the chance of running it appeals. Just keep me in the loop.'

'Will do, and thanks for all you're doing! Bye.'

Quickly she downloaded the two photos Kate had taken and emailed them to Mandy, giggling at what she suspected her friend would say, following that with a quick call to Alice before deciding to call it a night. A long laze in a warm bath and then she was in her PJs, curled up in bed. But her sleep was broken several times in the night, woken by her worries of where the men were and what could be happening so it was a relief to finally get up early and join Kate and Buck for breakfast.

'When do you think they'll be back?' she asked Buck who just shrugged, unconcerned.

'When yuh see them riding down the rise.'

And Sandy found herself trying to be as relaxed as him, getting Domino into the small corral and working him helped her nervousness, until she was confident that he was happy, knowing that Buck was keeping an eye on her. When she fetched a brush from the barn to clean him off, Domino obviously enjoyed it by dozing in the sun, even allowing her to pick up his feet and clean out his hoofs, showing no sign of being wary.

'Kin anyone do what you do, Miz Sandy?' Buck asked, leaning on the gate as she worked.

'Yes, once you understand how to communicate. It's mostly body language. Back home I train the horse and then train the people.'

Walking into the barn she turned to him. 'Which is his saddle, Buck?' looking pointedly at him when he hesitated. Flustered, he finally went and got a bridle, taking that and the saddle out to the corral. Domino immediately tensed but after she sent Buck out of the area and hearing the usual soft murmuring voice, stood as she slowly placed the blanket on his back, followed by the saddle, cinching it.

'You can breathe now, Buck,' she laughed without even looking round.

'How'd yuh know?'

'Because everyone does the same thing, I'm used to it.'

Fitting the bridle carefully as Domino appeared to flinch at the touch of the bit against his mouth, she was finally ready. Re-checking the cinch and tightening it, she walked round the corral with him following before patting him, leaning on the stirrup several times until he was aware she was going to climb on, and then stepped quickly up. Leaning forward to scratch his neck, happy to be on a horse again, she lifted the reins and urged him forward, doing simple turns, halts and roll backs, delighted at how well trained he had been, hardly needing to use the reins, and even better, found his gaits comfortable.

Finishing, grinning at Buck who'd obviously been nervous about her safety and making her wonder what had been wrong with the horse, she stepped down. With a quick pat, she removed the saddle, and putting him back out into the bigger corral, watched him relax in a dusty roll. Buck had already taken the saddle to the barn for her, so she retired to the house to sit on the porch in the sun with a coffee. On her second cup, Kate scolded her.

'You'll make yourself ill. They'll be in soon and you'll feel better.'

But it was late afternoon before the two horsemen rode in on tired horses, and with the quickening pulse thrumming throughout her body whenever Kyle appeared, Sandy watched them carefully to make sure no-one had been hurt. Fighting her anxiety, she forced herself to stay on the porch, biting her bottom lip in frustration at the delay in Kyle reporting, telling herself both men needed to relax first. Finally, near dinner time and with darkness closing in, all three men started up the track towards her.

All the time he'd been away Kyle had kept thinking of Sandy, couldn't wait to see her again. Remembering the kisses they'd shared, how the heat from her body made his heart pound, wondering where things could lead them. Trying, unsuccessfully to remind himself that she was Willard's niece, that technically he'd been relegated to being just the foreman, to work the ranch. That last thought had nearly thrown cold water on his feelings. Yes, she owned the ranch that should have been his. That she paid his wages. And several times a churning in his gut had settled like a rock making a return to the ranch harder than he'd thought. But the sight of her waiting on the veranda, a smile curving her lips, her eyes glittering from the porch light, waiting for him, changed that in an instant and his heart began to pound. He wanted to sweep her into his arms, to kiss her senseless, tell her how much he'd missed her. And then take her to bed.

'Miz Sandy.' He mounted the steps, leaving the two men to continue round to the dining room, seating himself in a chair next to her.

Sandy couldn't hide her relief and took a deep breath, unaware that she'd been holding it in. Hoped he wouldn't notice how tense she felt. Knew he would. They only had to catch sight of each other for the hot sparks to fly between them.

Kyle's eyes raked over her body, the usual aching need running through him at the sight of her. She'd been waiting for his return! In the gloom, he could only imagine the eyes that always seemed to look deep into his heart, into his soul, and made the blood run hot through his veins with want. His thoughts had immediately shifted from the report he should be giving to what they could be doing for each other! Images of what her body would be like under his until her voice snapped him out of it asking what they'd found out.

'Checked the shack, found no-one, the carcass of the steer was a little way off. Whoever had bin there had cut out a haunch, left the rest to the coyotes and bears, wasn't much left when we got there.'

'You think the person might be back?'

'Could, it's usually somebody stopping just for the night. That far off we can't keep checking unless we're out that way.'

He didn't say what he thought, that no-one would normally butcher a steer just for a night! It was the unwritten code of the range that the occasional vagrant or cowboy caught out by bad weather and needing shelter were welcome to stop in any of the different ranches' line-shacks to sleep and use some of the canned foods stocked for emergencies, but it never amounted to anything more than that. He had no wish to frighten her.

In the murky darkness, she heard his chair creak as he shifted and Sandy tried to see his darkened form but with no rising moon to wash over his features, had only her imagination visualising his outline. The sensations that seemed to wash from him to her was heating her body and she swallowed before keeping her voice as steady as she could.

'That's a relief. Dinner will be ready in a minute, you must be starving.'

'Heard you was worried, there was no need.'

'Naturally I was. Good staff are hard to get I believe!' She tried to keep it light, tried hard not to keep staring in his direction despite the urge to throw herself into his arms. Only to check he wasn't injured in any way she told herself. 'I'm not used to all this macho stuff, I'm used to calling the sheriff's department and letting them deal with things like that.'

She held up a hand as he moved, saw what she thought was a gleam in his eyes. Only from the porch light she told herself. He chuckled, that throaty sound that resonated inside her, turned her stomach upside down and her brain to a cotton bud. She couldn't think straight when he was so close. Wanting his arms round her. She'd so missed his kisses, needed him to kiss her until she was wilting and helpless, yearning for more. Felt the blood pounding in her ears drowning out the sounds of the night.

'Macho stuff?'

Sandy jerked back at the laughter in his voice. 'I'm a city girl, this is all new.'

She stood, started for the door but he rose and put his body in front of her. Don't look up, she told herself sternly, and failed, hardly breathing, drowning in the scent of him, manly, strong, overpowering her until she was trembling, begging inside for him to touch his mouth to hers.

'It's nice to think someone's worrying about me.'

'And Sheb,' she cut in quickly, softly, wondering if he could tell her face had heated, attempting to calm her wayward feelings before she threw herself at him, kissed him.

'Oh yes, don't let's forget Sheb.' He sounded amused. Oh he knew what she was feeling alright and it made his libido jump with longing.

Sandy was grateful that the door suddenly opened and Kate announced that if they didn't come and get it, she'd throw it to the hogs. As it shut, she couldn't resist, reaching up on tip-toe to put her hands round his neck and bring his lips down to hers, her skin tingling, burning with awkwardness. Would he mind, would he stop her? Would he prefer to be in charge? Now was the time to find out!

With a moan he hauled her into his arms, raising her feet from the floor, devouring her mouth before releasing her. She heard his breath rasping in his throat.

'Sandy,' he whispered. 'We have to go inside before anyone notices.' Felt her quiver and realised why. 'But any time you want to continue this I'll be more'n ready!'

He wheeled away leaving her struggling to control her breathing, watching him stalk off the porch to go round to the back door while she went into the hallway. How she hated that, the house had been his and Willard's before she'd come, now it was if he was deferring to just being a working cowboy.

'You okay, Miz Sandy?' asked Sheb, looking from Kyle to her as they took their seats and began to spoon food onto their plates, 'With what Kyle told you?'

'Yes, thanks Sheb. I feel better that whoever it was had gone. As I told Kyle, I'm a city girl not used to all this.'

They all suddenly looked at Kyle who'd mumbled something

no-one caught. He flushed guiltily.

'She said she's not used to macho men.'

Sandy's cheeks went pink and for a heartbeat in which she wished she'd never told Kyle that there was silence, until Buck spluttered, not sure what to do. Break their normal silence? But then everyone started chuckling, even Sheb while Kate began laughing so much she had to dry her eyes with her apron.

'Oh Sandy, that's so, so I don't know what.' She continued what she'd been doing, putting hers and Sandy's plates on the counter top. 'Macho! Oh. My!'

Kyle caught Sandy's eye for a second when he thought no-one was looking, his twinkling with merriment at her discomfort and she was just thankful that it had been taken so lightly. She really must be careful what she said in front of people but the laughter had helped her feel more now as if she belonged, a real friendship, as if they were all genuinely family. Not only that, it had made sure no-one had had time to wonder why they'd been on the porch for so long before coming in.

'Macho! I like it,' laughed Buck. 'I'm gonna tell the local girls thet next time I'm in town.'

Finished with their meal, waiting until Kyle and Buck had gone, Sheb looked at Sandy, and with uncharacteristic humour, said, 'You'll do tuh ride the range with, ma'am.'

Sandy smiled back, turning to clear the plates away only to notice Kate looking after him with a pensive expression, pausing to query her with a frown.

'Well I'll be,' the woman finally said obviously astounded, glancing at Sandy. 'You don't understand?' and at Sandy's shake of the head continued. 'That is the highest compliment any cowboy can give, or be given, and coming from Sheb after all these years I've known him is high praise indeed.'

'But what did I do?' Sandy started stacking the plates and cutlery bringing them round to the sink to rinse them off, suddenly self-conscious.

'Think about it, it'll come.' Kate filled the dishwasher and took off her apron. 'Honey, you have to understand men out here. They, well all of us, live with risks all the time, it's an acceptable part of life and they don't take kindly to being, what they'd consider to be, treated with kid gloves.'

Sandy sighed. 'I'll do my best, Kate.' She gave the older woman a hug. 'Thanks for all your advice!'

'I'll see you tomorrow.' She hugged Sandy back before going out the door leaving her to retire to the lounge, firing up her laptop.

Anyone there!

Sandy, thanks for the photos stunning and you look the part of rancher so what else is new up there in the wilds of Wyoming?

Sheb and Kyle came back safe no sign of anyone at the shack so it was probably what they said just a drifter but they laughed because I told Kyle I thought they were being macho men and he told them. After all I'm only a city girl.

Would have loved to have been there you still enjoying your vacation?

I've asked Blade if he wants to run the operation there IF I want to stay here.

You never! Sandy you're in love with the place I wish I could see your face so I can read it better. You're not coming back I know it :(it's that foreman I can "see" you blushing!

Mandy you see a romance everywhere go take a cold shower!

Oh, oh you were too quick to jump in there my friend I'm going to come up there and see what's going on and what about Buck would I like him or him me?

Come up and see he seems like a nice guy shame you can't make Saturday for the dance but there'll be others I expect. I can get you tickets to fly up pick you up at Cheyenne I guess that's the closest place and you can stay a week I need some girlie time.

Miss you too. You'd pay for the tickets?

I think the ranch could support it seems peculiar to think I don't have to scrimp for money makes me nervous.

Go you Sandy! I could learn to love having a rich friend :)

You're like all the rest only after me for my money.

Oh is that why the foreman is being so nice are you going to take my advice?

No and I'll say goodnight just let me know when you want to come because I'll be here for another week at least if I come back I need to sort out all sorts of paperwork.

Sleep well even if you're alone.

And the connection closed down before she could get in a quick reply.

Shutting the laptop she curled her legs up under her on the sofa and called her mom who sounded relieved to hear her voice.

'I'm fine, everything is running well, the foreman has everything under control and I feel a bit superfluous but it's fascinating. And the ranch and the views are spectacular. What did you think of the photos I sent?'

'Lovely. But I can hear in your voice that you are happy. When might you be coming back?' She sounded wistful and for moment Sandy felt guilty at having left, they'd been so close, and with Carlton far away too, she must be feeling a bit lonely.

'I'm not sure. If I come back I have to decide what to do with the ranch and if I decide to stay Blade has already agreed that he wants to either run or take over my yard for me. It's so beautiful here I couldn't bear to part with it so I would need to arrange for it to be left in Kyle's hands. He seems capable after all he ran it after Willard's death. I don't understand why it was left to me it seems more like Kyle was his family and I know he was shocked. There's a beautiful picture over the fire of Willard and his wife that I'm looking at but no-one seems to know anything about her.'

There was silence for a second then the reassuring, 'I'm sure you'll find out one day.' But Sandy had a feeling that something wasn't quite right.

'You okay mom? I know I'm far away but I do like it here, I'm quite safe.'

'I'm fine. Your father sends his love, just take care. It's so nice to hear your voice.'

'I miss you mom even though everyone is so friendly. And, I'm going to a dance on Saturday.' She almost felt the squeal all the way down the phone line.

'You are! Why that's wonderful, with the foreman?'

'What is it with this foreman with you and Mandy, no, the young man I met in the clothing store, Torrey. And no, I have no idea why I agreed, shook me, too.'

'I'm so happy for you, Sandy. You have a great time and I will quiz you on Sunday. My! My baby girl going on a date, I have to let your dad know.' She heard her mom call out to Ken.

'Not so baby mom, I'm nearly twenty-four,' but she couldn't help being delighted at her mom's reaction, or her dad's booming voice as he said, 'Have a nice time but I will want to vet this young man!'

'You'll both have to come up for a holiday, mom you'll love it. Okay you two. I'm off to bed. Sleep tight and don't let the bed bugs bite.' Sandy rattled the old saying off without thinking. It had been years since she'd heard her mom say it and it made tears well up, suddenly feeling homesick.

'Goodnight sweetheart.'

The line went dead leaving Sandy to wipe her cheeks from the damp of tears with the back of her hand. Checking the locks on the front door, climbing the stairs to her room, she plumped down on her bed feeling a bit lost after all the worry. She could have been at home, sleeping soundly with the knowledge that she was safe and wanted even though she felt safe here, too.

Snuggling beneath the covers the thought of who her real parents were popped unbidden into her head, every scenario from being too poor and unable to look after her, to corporate people too busy to want her. Had she been so unwanted? Or worse, had they now both died? She fell asleep with more tears on her pillow.

Kyle had hardly slept despite being very tired, his libido keeping him awake every time he remembered Sandy waiting for him on the porch, worried about him. Alright, so she'd said Sheb too, but only as an afterthought, and wondered at her coming on to him like she had. Did that mean she felt what he did for her? Standing there, wishing he'd had the nerve to wrap her in his arms, to kiss away her fears and hold her tight, and she had done it herself. Reached up and kissed him like she never wanted to stop. Even for the short space of time he'd been away from the ranch he'd so missed her, hoping that the older man hadn't picked up on it.

Rising to shave, splashing his face with cold water to try and clear his head, he knew he had a lot of work to do, organising the moving of the cattle to higher ground in the next few weeks. This would be the first time he'd do it without Willard and even the years of experience alongside him made this daunting, the weight of responsibility would now be firmly on his shoulders. Part of the old team was missing and it felt like a large part of his world had suddenly collapsed.

The 4x4 needed to be loaded with everything they'd need from extra tack in case of breakages, food them and the horses, eating utensils, firelighters, water, two tents if Sandy insisted on coming but he wasn't prepared to push that, hoped she would, wished she wouldn't as he'd need to concentrate. Along with nameless other things like ready-made shoes, nails, the blacksmiths tools. He also had to put out word for two new men so would head into Buffalo for that, go in on Saturday. Then there was the coming dance, could he ask Sandy if she'd go with him? Would people be curious about the lady ranch owner going with one of her cowboys, and even more, did he care?

Recited everything he'd need, already knew off by heart while he yanked his jeans, socks and thick shirt on. As it was overcast and threatening rain, he collected his slicker from the peg by the door, stamping into his boots. Acutely aware breakfast time was coming and therefore he'd soon be within range of Sandy's voice and presence. Without looking he always seemed to know when her eyes were on him. Would she be thinking of him the same way as he thought of her? Would she be worrying about having kissed him? He blinked trying to put her deliciously enticing body out of his mind, meeting up outside with Sheb and Buck!

Hiding his disappointment as they ate without her, perhaps she'd overslept, and having finished eating, giving Kate their thanks, they trooped out to get their horses. Sheb held back from Buck letting the younger man enter the barn ahead of them and Kyle frowned at the older man, studying the expression on his face.

'You look like you tangled with a bear this morning. You okay?'

'Yep,' he held his voice down the same as Sheb. 'Why?'

'You know why, just be very careful!'

Sheb walked off leaving Kyle stunned. Was that a warning note in the man's voice? Had he somehow given away his feelings for Sandy and if he had, what did it have to do with the older man? Felt a flicker of annoyance, following into the barn. As he saddled Precipice, he was giving Ranger a well-deserved rest, he couldn't help but wince at the appropriate name for he felt like he was on the edge of one! He'd wanted to snap back a denial but knew that he couldn't upset the man he'd grown up around, who he respected, had taught him about life and as much about ranching as Willard. Both men had been more like fathers to him than the man who'd ruined his boyhood and nearly wrecked his life.

Oh hell, Willard, what have you done, why have you left the ranch to this girl, what were you thinking! She obviously knew nothing about ranching, had lived in more civilised places than Wyoming. Was she planning on selling the ranch? Perhaps she'd go back home and leave him to carry on running the place. Meanwhile, all he could do was to carry on working as usual. He seemed to be in limbo at the moment, wondering just what was going to land on him next.

Mounted, slickers tied behind their saddles, this time they were headed west in the direction of the Grand Tetons although they didn't need to go that close. Out to where the range became rockier, needing a sure footed horse, looking for cattle who in their stupid way had decided to wander away from the easy grassland and the main herd. Whatever anyone said about bovines, to Kyle's mind, they had very little brains and were a pain in the neck to ranchers, seemingly getting into trouble wherever and whenever they could.

Sandy yawned and stretched glancing at her clock and getting a shock at the time, her eyes immediately looking towards the dark curtains, unlit by the usual early morning dawn and making her think it was still very early.

Leaping out of bed she drew them apart to look down at the bleak barn and corrals, the clouds lowering and overcast, the wind splattering rain against the window. Washed and dressed she raced down the stairs and into the kitchen where Kate looked up surprised at her rapid entrance.

'It's okay, I've kept your food warm, just grab a fork and I'll pour you a coffee.'

'It's so dark outside I thought it was still night. Up to now I haven't bothered putting my alarm on because daylight normally wakes me.'

'You needed the extra sleep obviously, worrying yourself the last two days it's not surprising you slept in. It doesn't matter.'

Sandy tucked into the meal while Kate went off to do the men's washing, coming back inside with droplets of rain sparkling in her hair and on her shoulders from the kitchen lights. Finished with eating, Sandy stacked her plate in the dishwasher.

'I'll be in the office if you need me. I'm still grappling with the more difficult aspects of the different paperwork, but winning! When do you need to go shopping, or can I do it for you on Saturday?'

'Thanks, but I can do what I need in Sweetwater, just fresh stuff, fruit and vegetables, the freezer's always stocked with meats.'

'Okay.'

Sandy turned her attention to the office, another scrutiny finally making everything fall into place, assuring herself that she could now deal with it all. Not forgetting the guiding hand in case of any problems she didn't know how to deal with, she mused. And was then struck by the thought that Kyle had always done this, she was virtually an interloper, literally trying to take over what he had been doing for years. How unfair was that! Attempting to see things from his perspective was as if some stranger had suddenly muscled in to take over her own business. Sitting pondering, she began to comprehend what it was doing to him.

'You look thoughtful.' Kate arrived in the doorway, startling her as a mug appeared on the desk in front of her. 'Can I help?'

Sandy couldn't hold back the sigh. 'It's all so complicated.'

'What is, exactly?' Kate sat down facing her.

'I was just thinking about Kyle. Some strange girl comes in, tells him she's taking over, and starts diving into what is effectively his job! Where does that leave him?'

'Have you spoken to him about it?'

'I'm ashamed to say that it's only just occurred to me.'

'Perhaps he'd prefer to be outside working the ranch and not have to sit at a desk doing accounts. You need to ask!'

'I will. He's been so good so far, like letting me into the accounts without him standing behind me to make sure I don't mess up!' She smiled at the housekeeper. 'Thanks Kate.'

'You're welcome.' Kate stood up, pointing to the mug. 'Don't let it get cold.'

Once Kate had left the room, she checked her emails, nothing on her personal ones but on the commercial side read that two new people wanted help with their horses, delighted that Blade had replied with details not covered on the web site. One of them had immediately booked their horse in. And if that didn't strengthen the feeling that she was cutting in on Kyle's life by being given the ranch, with Blade doing a good job without her nothing would, she mused. How would she feel if things were reversed?

Taking her beverage back into the lounge, she was again caught by the sight of Willard and Mary's picture. Who was he? What did he have to do with her? Why leave her the ranch instead of to Kyle? And Mary! She'd been a mother. Had they lost a child?

Something, a flash of light on the wall opposite the windows caught her attention for a second, and as it was immediately followed by another, she got up to look out the window. Expecting to see it was from a car window on the highway, the sun attempting to break through the veil of cloud in places. Another quick flash from the top of the rocky ridge a couple of miles away drew her attention. It wasn't repeated but had someone been watching the ranch?

Where were the men working today? Returning to the office to look at a big map on the wall that had been marked off in sections, she could see that they could be riding on the opposite side from the ridge, leaving her feeling slightly uneasy before deciding that whoever it was could have been looking out over the range for any number of reasons including as a hunter. Still, she waited for a while and when it wasn't repeated, decided she'd go and work Domino while the rain was holding off.

Leaving footprints in the damp dust crossing the corral she was immediately spotted by the horses and they came over, squealing and kicking to see who could get the closest in case food was in the offing, but once deciding that this human wasn't going to supply it, most wandered off leaving Domino begging for attention.

Sandy rubbed her fingers gently down his face and then in circles along his neck, allowing him through the gate and into the corral where he spun to face her, pushing his nose into her arm. The usual thrill of being able to get close to a horse ran through her. This was what made her life so enjoyable. She spent an enjoyable half hour just playing with him, getting him to move away from her hand, then following, backing up when she did, his full attention on her, ears and eyes working to understand what it was she wanted. And as the clouds gathered again and rain began to sweep over the range from the hills, she turned him back into the bigger corral. The men returned only just before dinner time, slickers wet, slapping against their legs, far off flashes of lightning making her recall the flashes of light she'd seen that morning.

Once the meal was over, she told Kyle she needed to see him in the office before he left and he nodded. Preceding him, at first she was unsure of where to sit but when he remained lounging against the frame, seemingly totally relaxed, she finally decided to stand. Her heart rate spiked and she tensed, hesitating as she tried to get her brain into gear. Just one glance at those glittering eyes and that kissable mouth along with the broad shoulders and the tight jeans hugging his narrow hips, had her almost lost for words.

'You wanted me!'

Was the insinuation deliberately made? It sounded so sexy that the overpowering sensual dominance radiating from him had her trying to get words past her dry lips. Unconsciously she licked them to find his eyes on her. He looked like the cat that wanted to taste the cream as she realised he'd deliberately meant to give his words double meaning. As he let his gaze rove from her head down to her feet she knew her nipples had peaked. Were they noticeable under her shirt? She refused to glance down but his look made her realise that he had already seen her reaction, as the muscles in her core tightened, felt the damp between her thighs that he always brought on when he was around, or when their eyes met. And often when he wasn't! She flushed. He should come with a health warning!

She had to act as if she was unaffected, and act now. Pointing to the chair beside him, she walked round the desk and sat down only to find that he had followed her and had again hitched a buttock on the side of the desk, lazily swinging his leg. A faint smile tweaked the corners of his mouth and she realised her mistake. Her shirt, the top two buttons undone because it had been so warm in the house, had opened. Her cheeks flushed knowing he was looking down, could see the valley between her breasts. That they were heaving as her breathing increased, that her skin was tingling with that familiar warm glow, permeating her blood until she thought she'd burst into flames.

'I think it would be best, wanted to ask your opinion actually… !' Why was she always so messed up when he was around? 'In case you're out on the range, if I, we needed you… to call you. In an emergency.' She tightened her resolve and her voice. 'As a backup to the cells you all carry, if there's no signal, whether those wireless radios would be useful.'

'Possibly!'

How could he make that one word sound so, so suggestive? Because his voice was molten, melting her muscles, and she knew that even if she had stayed standing, she would have had to find the nearest chair before her legs had given way.

'Can you find out?' She tried to hold his gaze without flinching but knew the battle on her side was being lost, finally looking down at the desk. Kyle chuckled, and she bit at her lip.

'I could, if you wanted me to but they might not work either.'

'Sandy, I'm just off home,' called Kate from the kitchen making her jump, annoyed that he didn't even seem to take any notice.

'OK, Kate, see you tomorrow.'

OMG, she was going to be alone with Kyle. Her mouth

went dry and she couldn't help licking her lips again to moisten them, unaware that he found it such a turn on but knowing he was watching her, playing her like a cat with a mouse. Just why he was she found perplexing, still convinced that there was nothing remotely pretty or even interesting about her.

'Are you saying you don't want them?'

'No.'

'Then I suggest you buy some and try them. I don't like you all being away from the house and out of range for help if Kate… We need one of you in an emergency. After the problems the other day, anyone might be around. It could be unsafe!' And who would I call to keep me safe from you! Could he hear her heart pounding? She felt sure that it would leap into her throat and strangle her.

'We have security lights and alarms, but it would be a good idea, if Kate, or even you, needed me, us, urgently! I'll ask tomorrow, I need to go to town to hire a couple of riders for the drive next week.'

He deliberately bent forward, drawn to those lips like filings to a magnet needing, wanting to kiss them again, watching her blue eyes darkening with a want that mirrored his own and pulling him ever deeper into their depths. Knowing full well she was feeling the same judging by the continued rise and fall of her breasts that he wanted to take into his mouth and suckle until she was like clay in his hands. His groin tightened. There was no way on God's earth he could keep his hands off her now. There was no-one else in the house, they were alone.

'So you think you might need me, us!' he softly, deliberately taunted, wanting her in his arms again, the flowery scent he associated with her now mixed with her femininity drifting up, increasing his arousal. Now they were alone his growing hardness was an ache he wanted desperately to itch. Preferably relieving it by burying himself deep into the tight clasp of her inner muscles, aware his breathing was becoming as laboured as hers.

Sandy couldn't breathe, her eyes taking in the stark beauty of his face, the faint darkness of new stubble showing around his firm jaw, the mesmerising hazel eyes with the flecks of gold that so intrigued her. His body so dominantly virile that she had no chance of fighting her feelings anymore, he'd been stirring her body into life since she'd first seen him, now wanting him to kiss her again. She had to fight against this before things went too far, but knew it was over for her.

Kyle dipped his head so that his lips lightly brushed hers, the sensual touch blindsiding him again. He wanted her so badly, the erection pulsing behind his zipper threatened to explode before he got what he wanted. What he needed. Understanding she was slowly giving in to her own body's wants, wanted him the same way. She might be trying to fight against it, but as her eyes darkened with desire, he knew he had to have her.

Standing up, reaching for her shoulders, lifting her to her feet, he increased the intensity of his mouth, and as she opened her mouth, gasped his name, he swirled his tongue inside to tangle with hers, tasting, revelling in it. Felt her arms lifting to his shoulders, her fingers curling on into his hair and with the blood pounding in his veins, knew that if she didn't stop him now, he would take her to bed. Had to divest her of her clothing then lay her down, taste every part of her body, bring her to an orgasm and then thrust his swollen hardness into her hot wet depths. He groaned with the thought.

Holding her head with one hand, the other wrapping around her waist, he pressed himself against her body to reinforce what he wanted. Felt her tense but continued to devour her mouth until she began to soften before she was kissing him as hard as he was, heard her soft whimper as she rubbed her body against his.

Sandy was confused, her mind telling her one thing, her body another, his fervour frightening yet compelling, the hardness of his body against hers intoxicating. Her breasts ached and as if aware, Kyle's hand began to tug her shirt free of her jeans, curling under to her bra, her non sexy bra as she fleetingly considered that she should have brought new and sexy lingerie underwear while in town. Wondered what he'd make of her boring cotton underwear as his warm hand cupped a breast.

His finger and thumb began rolling the blossoming nipple until she wanted to scream. Perhaps he knew she wanted more because his fingers forcefully pushed her bra up until his hard callused palm was caressing her flesh, moulding it to his hand while he continued to tease. She was only vaguely aware of the wetness between her legs, gripped by a deep longing that swept all fear away and she finally gave way to the inevitable.

Kyle drew back from her mouth to allow themselves time to breathe, opening her shirt and unhooking her bra, feasting his eyes on the full breasts peaked by hardening nipples, surrounded by deep pink aureoles, bent his head to fasten his mouth around one pebbled nipple. Shut his eyes to enjoy the feel as he lathered it with his tongue. Suckling, drawing it hard up into his mouth, heard a faint whimper that seemed to rise from the depths as her body reacted and she trembled, her hands gripping his hair to hold him tight against her. And as he swapped to suckle the other, her legs weakened. Running a hand down to cup her buttocks and hold her, Kyle heard another faint whimper in her throat. That was all he needed to know.

Without a word he swept her into his arms, expecting her to stop him because she was inexperienced, making his way up the stairs, pushing the door open to her bedroom, laying her down on the bed, staring along her length. But even with the hot desire to be inside her racing through his entire body, he caught the nervousness in her eyes.

'Stop me if you want to,' he growled, his erection straining against his zipper, 'Before I can't.' Praying she wouldn't say no or he'd need more than a cold shower to dowse his needs. More like cutting his manhood off altogether.

Sandy quivered at the rawness of his voice, she knew she needed to understand what she was doing, remember she was a virgin. But it was as if her blood had been replaced by hot molten lava raging through her veins, refusing to allow her to say no, looking at him as he leaned over to place his hands either side of her head. Could she do this? Could she not!

Mandy's voice seemed to shimmer in her head. You need to get laid at least once, you can't be a virgin the rest of your life you have no idea what you're missing! She nodded weakly, biting her bottom lip, seeing the devastating smile that revealed white teeth against his slightly swollen lips. She reached to touch them wonderingly. She'd done that to him? Were hers the same? Touching them with her tongue she realised they were, managed a faint smile back, her core hot and ready for that age old dance between a woman and her man.

Standing, he discarded his shirt revealing the hard muscles of his chest, the flat button nipples, his abdomen faintly covered by dark hair that thickened above his belt, the line leading downward like an arrow to disappear behind his zipper. He was mouth wateringly stunning, took her breath away. Unbuckling his belt, dropping it on the floor, he removed his jeans leaving him in just black boxers, and as her eyes fastened on his body, saw her tense at the sight of his arousal tenting the front, swallowing nervously.

He was every girls dream with his rock solid athletic body and she reached up wonderingly to touch his chest making Kyle think he'd go off like a rocket the second he entered her if she didn't stop. Knew he couldn't. If this was as he suspected going to be her first time he had to curb his fervour, control his passion and make it pleasurable. Then he was pulling her jeans off, leaving her in a pair of non-exciting plain panties that hid her femininity from him. Pulling her to her feet, he slowly removed her shirt and bra, his eyes feasting on her skin, pink with arousal, her firm nipples pebbling, cupped her breasts.

'You're exquisite,' he whispered, his voice throaty, hoarse as he looked at her. 'More beautiful than I even imagined.' Sandy felt her whole body flush.

She couldn't quite believe that he thought about her like that, she was just an ordinary girl who had never had anyone look at her the way he did. And it kicked her wanting him into a higher gear. She should have been embarrassed when he eased her panties down, his face at the apex of her thighs. but somehow wasn't. Perhaps because his eyes were burning into her as he dropped his gaze from her breasts to the soft hair of her femininity, he made her feel treasured, respected.

Laying her back on the bed, his eyes stared into hers,

darkening until they were almost black, mesmerising her as her heart rate spiked with the look of want in them. Kneeling inside her thighs, nudging them open, he bent to brush his lips against hers, pressing harder, his tongue sliding between hers to invite it in, tangling together as she did before trailing soft kisses to her nose, her cheeks, down her throat to where her life blood was beating under the skin. Felt her hands roving uncertainly over the sleek contours of his torso as she explored the ribbed abs and hard planes of his chest, her warm fingers burning his skin. When had a woman ever made him feel like this! She might have been innocent but it seemed she was willing to touch him.

Almost unable to wait any longer, he lay down alongside her, slowly massaging her quivering breasts, taking a nipple in his mouth, teasing the other until Sandy cried out with the exquisite sensations, whimpering, gripping his hair to hold his mouth against her, a tingling coursing through her whole body migrating deliciously deep into her core and lower. Knew she couldn't stop him now even if she wanted to! She wanted him desperately to touch her, where she needed to feel him.

He took his time suckling first one then the other while his hand ran down her stomach to her quivering belly, the tense shiver as he parted her legs further with his knee, felt the wetness on his skin to show her she was more than ready, the softness of her feminine folds inviting. Never had he wanted this moment to last. When she gave herself to him there would be no going back.

'Kyle…' she whispered, her voice quivering. 'I… !'

'I know darlin'.'

His voice, hoarse with want, tinged with understanding,

echoed in her head. He knew! But he still wanted her?

Then his fingers were sliding down to tangle in the soft curls of her mound, reaching under to cup her heat as his thumb played with her clit. Felt her shudder, her hips instinctively rising as he parted the soaked flesh, her legs widening instinctively to accept him. He kissed her wherever he could reach, his fingers toying, rubbing against her until she was shuddering with want, finally sliding a finger up into the silky smooth flesh. Felt her muscles tense around it, and her nails dig into his shoulders as he continued to tease. She began to arch and buck against his palm, crying out as the exquisite shock of her first orgasm threw her to the four corners of the world! He slowed until the quivering had slowed then began to circle the little sensitive bud, heard her breath catch in her throat. Her hand grabbed feverishly at his as if to try and stop the devastating swirl of an intense rapture that threatened to break her in two.

As he did such unexpected things to her body, it drove her wild, his finger pressing and circling before releasing until she came apart with a whimper, convulsing with each orgasm, her nails now gripping his waist as her back arched. Kyle held her until she came down off her high, astounded at how quickly and easily she had come for him, slipped two fingers inside to help stretch and ready her to receive him. He was big, and even in his frenzied need to be inside her, he knew he had to take his time. If he could! He gritted his teeth. Had no idea how he was managing to control his urgent need to bury himself inside her, her evident arousal making it even harder, but somehow he had to endure his throbbing need, knowing he had to take it slow, make her first experience the best.

'Please, please,' she whispered, afraid that she wouldn't be able to stand any more, her body on fire.

'Look at me,' he ordered softly and as her eyelids opened, wonderingly, trying to focus on his face. Divesting himself of his boxers, saw her eyes widen when she saw his size. He tried not to worry about entering her, but with his own body demanding its fulfilment, overcame it. Reaching for a condom, he opened the packet. Saw her staring as he rolled it over his hard manhood before pulling her legs further apart, lowering himself, his heart pounding in his chest. He kissed her gently, devouring her mouth.

'Sandy?' he whispered. Silently begging her not to stop him, that she'd kill him if she did! Saw her small nervous smile as she gave him permission, then the head of his shaft was poised at her entrance, nudging into her wetness inch by inch, withdrawing to give her a chance to relax, to adjust to his penetration, sliding in further until he couldn't take it any more, shattering the last remains of his control.

Grabbing her buttocks he tilted her pelvis then thrust, hard, felt her stiffen at the shock, the sharp gasp as he went deep, breaking her innocence while she pulsed around him, fingers clinging to his waist. Thrusting deeper still until he was fully enveloped, her muscles quivered and clenched, moulding themselves around him, along his length, until he saw stars. Couldn't stop, needed his gratification, kissing the pulse in her neck. Instinctively, Sandy pulled her knees up, jammed her heels against his buttocks, demanding he continue.

Staring into her eyes, Kyle started to move slowly, setting up a rhythm that her body responded to, joining in with him until they became as one, until his resolve wavered. He couldn't stop and gripping her tighter, drove deeper, faintly aware of her arching her back to give him better access, rocking her groin up to meet his. Her fluttering cries in his ear urging him on as he moved inside her tight, wet passage, awaiting his release as she met him thrust for thrust.

'Please, please,' she begged, her body numbed by his friction, needing fulfilment until, with a shattered cry of 'Kyle' as he swelled inside her, she convulsed around him, her knees clamped round his thighs as she broke apart. With three more hard thrusts, he was spilling himself deep inside her body, aftershocks enveloping them like bolts of lightning, scorching their bodies.

Kyle lay against her, ready to swear that he'd seen stars, had been to the moon and back, totally sated. He'd never come like this before, been so joined. Sandy's body had melded with his as if they were meant to be. And with that came the astounding knowledge that she had surrendered her innocence to him, had willingly trusted him with her body. It humbled him.

Sandy lay panting, adrift on a sea of exquisite fulfilment, her body knowing the shape of him inside her, his weight, listening to the sound of his harsh breathing until it slowed and realised that he was almost asleep, her arms still wrapped round his body, his chest rising and falling against her breasts. So this was what Mandy had been telling her to do, to have a fling, to be loved. She was astounded by what she'd felt, how she'd given herself to him, felt him pulse inside as her muscles had convulsed around his manhood, her body knowing what to do.

Kyle muttered something, rolling off to one side, moving himself gently from her body, throwing an arm across his eyes while she waited nervously. Waited for what, she had no idea. Would he dismiss her, get up and walk off now she'd lost her virginity to him, would she have been found wanting, was she just a one night stand. She froze, holding her eyes tight closed.

'I'd so like to do that again with you!'

There was that deep, smoky voice that excited her, stirring a body still aching from his lovemaking, still feel him inside her even though he'd removed himself.

'You would?' Her voice shook. Turning her face to look at him, she found he was staring at her as if he wasn't quite sure what she was saying. 'I didn't disappoint you, being... I was...!'

'Hell no, ma'am,' he drawled, pulling her against his chest, kissing her cheeks and along her jaw until reaching her trembling lips. He watched her carefully. 'Did I hurt you? Frighten you? I tried not to rush!'

Sandy thought back to that tiny pain as he'd taken her, it had been sudden and unexpected, almost frightening, but hurt?

'No to both,' she whispered, embarrassed.

Sitting up, he watched her expression change to one of wonder, as if she had expected to be rejected, wondered why. Slipping from the bed, he went to the bathroom to dispose of the condom, noticed her blushing as he returned, still naked, and began to feel into his jeans pocket to produce another packet. Her eyes widened, knowing from his reaction that he wanted her again.

'You are going to be a bit sore, need a long soak in a hot bath later,' he smiled. Lying beside her, ran his fingers through the silky blonde hair strewn across the pillow and over her shoulders, feeling his blood quickening, his erection hardening just at the thought of being inside her, and rolled on the new condom.

'But first, I want you again,' he growled, rolling her onto

her back. Took her lips, devoured her, his tongue demanding admittance as his hand slid down her belly to play with her curls, opening her legs with his knee to cup her wet folds, to slide his fingers inside as her hips bucked against his hand. Heard her tiny whimpers, felt her shiver as her muscles clasped them, her hands gripping his shoulders as he pressed upward against her most sensitive part, worked his fingers as deep as he could go until she cried out as she came against his hand, trembling.

'Kyle, please,' she softly pleaded wondering if she could take much more as he did things to her body that made her writhe and arch, pressing into his touch, yearning sobs forming in her throat. He took his time, bringing her to the tip of an orgasm again and again until she screamed his name, before he brought to another trembling orgasm that tore through her body. Clutching him frantically, she came apart with a cry of release.

'Please!' She drew his body between her legs, wrapped them around his thighs. Feeling the head of his erection nudging at the entrance to her body she couldn't stop bucking against it until he was sliding inside. Heard him groan as her muscles gripped his hardness and convulsed around it. Kyle cursed silently as she nearly forced him over the edge before he could make slow love to her, strengthening his determination to make her enjoyment last, thrusting and withdrawing until they both felt the searing aching need for release. The floodgates opened and he plunged deep releasing his seed as her body milked him, shouted her name as he came with her, felt her clutching him to her with fingers of steel, as if she never wanted to let him go. He had no idea how long they lay there, their bodies entwined and dampened with perspiration until she stirred, waking him, pushing him away to stand up. For a minute he was afraid he'd demanded too much of her.

'I need the bathroom,' she whispered.

His worries abated, he disposed of the condom into the basket beside the bed, lying on his side until she re-emerged, still shy about her nakedness even if his admiring look made her feel elated. She smiled and his world was reawakened, pulling her down beside him.

'Sandy, I'm going to have to leave. I don't want to be seen sneaking out the door. I don't want anyone finding out that I've stayed,' glancing at his wrist to stare at the time showing on his watch. 'It's gone eleven.'

'Are you ashamed?' he heard her whisper.

'Hell no,' he bit out, touching her lips with his. 'I wish I could stop and make love to you over and over, but I can't risk your reputation, it will be shot to hell an gone if anyone finds I'm still here in the morning. I won't, can't do that to you. I hate this, but it's better if no-one finds out.'

Sandy's emotions went into overload. He'd said he wanted to do it again and again! His lips met hers and he kissed her thoroughly before climbing off the bed, picking up his scattered clothes and dressing. With another kiss and a 'don't forget to get in a hot bath,' she was forced to listen to his footsteps going down the stairs, the front door opening and closing quietly, then a long silence before realising that he'd be going back to his cabin the long way round to avoid the bunkhouse.

Climbing out of bed to straighten the sheets, she was shocked to see a few tiny drops of blood, realising what it meant, her body feeling hot with embarrassment and set too stripping the sheets. Remaking the bed, bundling the offending sheet and its partner into her washing bin, she would see to putting them into the machine tomorrow.

Kyle had been right. She did feel a soreness inside, a soreness that seemed to sooth her with the knowledge of why. She could still feel him inside her while her inner thighs ached, a totally different ache that she'd never known before, her lips still swollen from his hard kisses when she touched them. Little shivers flickered across her sensitised skin, and it was bliss to run the bath and lower her body into the hot water, to slide down until she was totally immersed. To relive every second, to know it had been worth waiting for. She wished she could talk to Mandy, to scream out that she'd been right! That waiting for the first time to happen, with that special person, had been right, because Kyle had been that one. When the water had cooled, she finally emerged to dry herself. Not wanting to put on her PJs she slid straight under the sheet and curled up, arms hugging her waist.

Chapter Seven

Waking in the night, she found herself worrying if anyone would notice that she was different. Would she have changed? Would he? Deep down she had to acknowledge that they couldn't keep such a secret hidden but she'd try her hardest to treat him the same as she always had. Clambering out of bed in a panic, the inside of her thighs aching, she shot into the bathroom and under the light stared at her face, examining it closely to see if she looked guilty, but apart from perhaps her eyes were more sparkling than usual, she thought she could get away with it. With a sigh of relief she climbed back into bed and drifted back off to sleep.

Late getting downstairs, just as the men were about to leave the dining room, Kyle not even looking in her direction, for a second she paused, wondering if he would now ignore her, ignore what had happened between them, wouldn't want her any more. She spoke to Sheb, trying to calm her nerves.

'Hang on a moment, Sheb.' He looked round at her. 'I've been worried since that incident two days ago and I've asked Kyle to see if he can find some wireless radios so we can try and keep in contact with each other. Just in case Kate or I need you and the cells aren't working.'

He nodded his agreement, and then she blurted out that she'd thought somebody had been on the ridge across the road with binoculars as she'd seen flashes of sunlight yesterday. All three men spun to face her.

'I told yuh I thought I'd seed someone skulking about up there!' Buck sounded affronted.

'Could have bin anything, Buck. Mule deer, bison, but I don't go with coincidences.' Sheb looked at Kyle. 'Someone orta go up there for a look see.'

'I'll go.' Buck was enthusiastic, but not so much when Kyle told him he'd go too.

As the men turned to leave, Sandy drew a silent breath as she passed Kate to get her breakfast out of the warming oven, slowly relaxing now that she'd managed to divert any possible attention regarding the working relationship between herself and Kyle, ruefully acknowledging that it was perhaps because she felt as if guilt was written all over her face. Tucking into her breakfast, both women listened to the sound of the ranch pick-up scattering dust as it went down the ranch track towards the road.

'You didn't tell me.' Kate frowned at Sandy.

'I wasn't sure of what I'd seen I assumed it might be a hunter looking for something.'

'The men can figure that out, but I agree on the idea of being able to reach them in an emergency, cell phones often cut out between the hills and rocks, let alone a lack of towers in the area.'

Sandy checked that the washing machines were empty and returned to her room to get her washing, thrusting the sheets and other clothes into the machine, sighing with relief once they were hidden from view, her whole body hot. Well, she'd done it at last. She wanted to scream it from the roof tops! Almost mesmerised by the whirring of the machine she became lost in the memory of his burning kisses, the feel of his naked skin on hers, his calloused hands rubbing her nipples until she was drowning in ecstasy, his fingers deep inside as he coaxed her body into life and brought her to her first orgasm. The quick ache as he slid into her and the strange sensation of stretching to accommodate his size. The exquisite explosion of her own orgasm as he came with her… ! She shivered.

'You okay, honey?' The voice behind her made her start and blush guiltily, angry with herself because she was having trouble hiding her feelings, her secret. No-one must know what had gone on. She couldn't put Kyle in a bad position with everyone else. 'I'm sure it's nothing to worry about.'

'You're right.' Taking a deep breath and turning to face Kate, 'I'm just being silly.'

The housekeeper gave her a quick smile. 'It's so new to you, you've only been here a few days and you're still getting to know everything, give it time.'

'Thanks Kate.'

She fled to her bedroom only for the sight of her bed to draw her attention back what had happened, to remember every tiny little memory, her body craving more. It had been neglected for so long that she hadn't realised how she'd wanted to be a woman, to be loved, pleasured, closely followed by how could they meet again, did he want to? Did men lose interest once they'd got what they were after? Could her innocence be like a trophy! Was that really why he'd got up and left her straight after!

She sank onto the mattress her head in her hands. Oh Mandy, I so need you here. Because this is all your fault putting ideas in my head! No, not true, she'd so wanted to let herself go, to give in to her desires. She'd denied him twice so what had made last night so different! She didn't have to call him away from the kitchen and leave herself alone with him. Had she put herself in that position unknowingly wanting him so badly her fears had been pushed aside.

And what about the dance tonight! She'd promised to go with Torrey. She'd made love with Kyle, could she really go and dance with another man? She could plead a headache, she'd hurt her ankle, anything to get out of it. But then a promise was a promise, she couldn't not go. She had to try to get Kyle alone and explain her reasoning.

Climbing to her feet, she made her bed and almost dragged herself to the bathroom for another hot bath torn between what to do and unhappy at the thought of anyone's arms around her but Kyle's. He'd ruined her with any other man now he'd made love to her. Had she fallen for him when he'd stopped to check on her that first time? Was it in the diner? Or when he'd told her off for being late that first day?

She was having a chat with Kate about the dance, her stomach in knots, when Kyle knocked and came in, hat in hand. With the muscles clenching in her stomach at his sudden appearance, on instant alert, she steeled herself to do nothing but look up in anticipation of what he might have found.

'Someone's bin up there, from the tracks I'd say a couple of times, but no-one now, probably just a hunter or even a surveyor.' He smiled, keeping his eyes on the pair of them, damping down the fire that lit inside him at the sight of Sandy, to keep his expression blank. 'But we'll keep an eye open.'

'Thanks. I… !'

'You goin' to the dance in Buffalo tonight?' Kate cut in at the same time just as she opened her mouth to speak, and she cringed, staring down into her mug as if trying to magically disappear inside it.

'I might, why?'

'You two will bump into each other. Sandy's been invited by Torrey.'

Sandy watched as his body tensed. 'That would be nice!' his voice cool.

'Right, I've got to get on.' Kate finished her drink. 'There's more coffee if you want to help yourself, Kyle. And can you assure Sandy that it's not the Wild West out here, she's very nervous.'

'I think I will!'

Kyle poured himself a mug, leaning a hip seemingly innocently against the counter but his eyes were guarded. Sandy immediately bristled, from embarrassment or guilt she had no idea, but how dare he judge her before he knew the reason she was going. Let alone the battle she'd been having with herself about suddenly not dumping Torrey in front of the whole town. Anyway, he didn't own her, but he deserved an explanation, even this late.

'After what happened between us,' she whispered, trying to keep her voice from quivering, 'I was going to tell you when I could see you alone.'

'So you'll not go with him.'

'I have to. I promised last week. Do you have a date? Will you cancel?' Please say you have, to make me feel better about what was happening, she silently begged.

'Not yet. But there's usually someone without a partner,' he replied flatly. What did she expect? Was she going to cast him off as if nothing had happened between them, go straight into another man's arms! Well, he could do the same thing. He watched her eyes darken and flash a warning as she got up to dispose of her empty mug and despite his annoyance, shaken again by her attitude in standing up for herself. If he hadn't have been so incensed, her sassiness would have turned him on!

'So was I just a quickie for you!' she snapped, managing to hold her voice down.

'I could say the same thing,' his icy whisper as low as hers and sending a chill down her back. 'Didn't take you long to drop me for somebody else!'

'For your information, I haven't, but if that's what you think of me, judge me after only a week then be my guest!'

Furiously she went to slap him with her empty hand but he managed to catch her wrist, somehow holding onto his mug with the other, dragging her close up to him, his eyes glittering. Wrenching free before she could allow herself to fall for his charm, she stormed off out of the kitchen fleeing to her bedroom hoping that Kate hadn't seen her from where she was busy dusting in the big lounge, unaware of the drama unfolding. Sandy was so angry with him, and herself, she almost burst into tears but forced them back. If he wanted to be a jerk, let him, but couldn't resist watching from the window at his stiff and unyielding back as he stalked off towards the corrals.

Ranger was already tied waiting him to come, prodding Kyle with his nose, rubbing against him as if in commiseration at his owner's distress. Kyle drew a deep breath, furious at Sandy, furious at himself. She should have said something, explained, not just go into a temper tantrum. She was strong, been surprised at her tearing herself free of his hold, but the electric charge that had shot through his body had thrown him off kilter, the same response he always got when he touched her. He leaned his forehead against the horse's neck.

'Kyle?'

Shocked, he spun to see Sheb on the other side of Ranger not having heard the other man approaching. Found it strange as he should have been out with Buck.

'Miz Carson worried by what yuh found up on the ridge?'

Kyle drew on every reserve he could before replying, amazed at how steady his voice was, keeping his face down as he tightened his cinch.

'She's a bit upset, it's all so new and she found it a bit worrying. Told her it was probably just a hunter.'

'Humph!'

Sheb was studying him intently as if he could see right inside his guts, see them in turmoil, but then turned and walked off leaving Kyle drawing in the breath that he'd been holding back. How the hell had he managed to find himself in this situation? Swinging into the saddle, he passed through the barn and out the other side needing to get to Buck who had obviously gone off alone, checking that the strays they'd brought back yesterday hadn't decided to return.

What had Sheb been doing back at the barn? Had he been waiting to hear what Sandy had had to say about what little information they'd gleaned? But it smacked of him becoming protective of her, recalling the last remark made, the warning to be careful! Sheb shouldn't have seen Kyle returning late from the house last night, he'd been so careful getting back to his cabin.

Swiftly followed by Sandy's turning on him, of going to the dance with another man! Had last night meant nothing to her?

Yet she'd not denied him, her smile and her body had been welcoming, she'd given herself willingly. He was confused, so confused he almost overran the herd until Buck called to him.

'Everything good?' he asked, reining Ranger back to come alongside.

'Yep!' Buck, being young and still excited by life, was finding it all a bit of a game even if Kyle and Sheb were noticeably worried by what seemed to be happening around the ranch. He grinned, 'Yuh or Sheb going to the dance?' They'd been discussing that yesterday, Kyle reflected, Sheb having decided to stay behind.

'Not sure.' He was non-committal. Did he want to stay home and imagine what was happening there, or go, then find himself well out of his comfort zone. If another man touched her! But then he had no right to do that, she was new to the territory, didn't understand the way things were done around here. It was probably different where she came from. He should have explained himself instead of angrily rushing away. He'd hurt her, he knew that, should have listened to her explanation.

Sandy pulled her washing from the machine as it had finished its cycle, taking the warm clothing upstairs, getting herself ready to meet with the lawyer. Dressing in the new blue fringed shirt, jeans, and hat, in newly polished boots, she admired herself in the mirror as she knotted a blue bandana around her neck, pulling on her lightweight jacket to hide the shirt. Hands on hips she imagined sending Kyle wild with admiration, wanting her, but a little nervous about what she could be heading into. This was all too new for her. She didn't know the rules at home let alone here. What would happen at the dance, could all this turn into another argument? It would be so embarrassing for all of them, especially poor Torrey caught in the middle.

'Just off, Kate,' she called out, knowing that all the paperwork she needed was still locked in her SUV's glove box, that her purse and a warm coat were with her. She wasn't prepared to get caught out by a change in the weather. Receiving a reply, she headed out to the road for Buffalo.

Luckily she found just one parking space left, nosing into it, already aware of the state of excitement in the town, the streets half full of people as if everybody had turned up all at once to await the coming fun. Collecting her purse and holding the folder with the papers under her arm, she set off to find the lawyer's office.

It didn't take long to find the door, the bottom half in wood, the top frosted glass with Scott Scully, Attorney At Law in gold letters, and as it opened inwards from the narrow street, with a quick knock she was inside. Unlike the musty smell of the bank, the room was light and airy. A young, red haired girl, with more freckles than she had, looked up and smiled from behind her desk.

'Miss Carson?'

'Yes.'

'I'll tell Mr Scully that you're here, if you'd like to take a seat.'

Rising to tap on the frosted glass door behind her, also bearing the same name as at the front, when a male voice called to come in, the girl informed him that Miss Carson had arrived. A chair scraped back as the person inside rose.

'Please go in. Would you like anything to drink, coffee, soda or water?' the girl asked but Sandy shook her head.

'I'm fine, thanks.'

Scott Scully turned out to be tall and slim, almost skinny, with short slicked back grey hair, bushy eyebrows, pale washed out blue eyes, and thin lips. Judging him to be about sixty, he looked professional in a black suit and blue tie. As soon as he spoke Sandy recognised the gravely voice from his phone call.

'Please sit,' indicating an upright chair with dark red cushioning. 'I have the forms here for you to sign, Miss Carson. Please read them carefully before you do,' made an effort to lighten the mood, and smiled. 'Or it will take forever to sort out any problems, and I need my holiday before then.'

Sandy smiled back, pulled the forms towards her and took her time reading everything before nodding, signing where he had pencilled a cross.

'Thank you. I will file these for you. I hope you get to stay on at the ranch, we need young blood in town, Miss Carson. May I suggest that you change your Will to include the ranch unless of course, you already have made that proviso?'

Sandy nodded. 'My lawyer back home has already seen to that, but thank you for thinking of it. At the moment I'm still considering my options.' He raised an eyebrow. 'I've got a venture back in Lone Tree, but I have already fallen in love with Wyoming so it's a good possibility I'll stay on.' Make that fallen in love with a man in Wyoming, even if he was a jerk! 'Thank you for your help.'

When he stood, she rose and shook his hand, felt a slight tremor in his muscles, he didn't look that well, and allowed him to pass ahead of her to open the office door.

'Thank you for your business, Miss Carson.'

Acknowledging him, she let herself out the front door and back onto the street, making her way to her car to lock the paperwork safely away inside, unsure of what to do now. It was far too early to meet up with Torrey and anyway, he would be working. She could try for a seat in the diner but that had looked full and decided to go instead to the Walmart which she knew had a cafe area. Luckily she spotted some empty seats, ordered a coffee and a pastry, and slid in behind a table once she'd paid.

'Sandy!'

She looked up on hearing a familiar voice to find Torrey looking at her, and she smiled back, pleased to see him.

'Can I join you?'

'Sure, welcome.'

'I'll just get a coffee. I'm on my lunch break.'

As he walked away she couldn't help but compare him with Kyle. He was sweet, but without the rugged masculinity of Kyle whose raw physical appeal kept turning her world upside down.

When Torrey returned she knew that she couldn't have let him down for the dance, after all she had promised. It would have been embarrassing not to go with him, being a newcomer to the area and trying to be accepted into the community it probably wouldn't have gone down well. Especially when she stayed on at the ranch, her mind whispered treacherously. Oh! And just when did she decide on that?

'You look great. I'm really looking forward to tonight.'

'So am I.'

Actually she was, but not for the same reason he was thinking. A bit of her wondered if Kyle would turn up, praying that if he did he wouldn't cause a scene, then hoping that he'd dance with her, hold her close.

'Sorry!' She was shaken out of her thoughts. 'It's a bad trait of mine to let my brain wander off. Everything is so new, so different.'

'I was asking where you live.'

'I'm at the Boxed C at the moment.' Uncertain how much to tell him, she decided to leave out that Willard had been her uncle. 'I actually come from a place called Lone Tree. Arizona!'

'Wow, long way from home. No wonder you needed new clothes. I'm glad you decided on the fringed shirt, are you going to be wearing it tonight?'

Sandy realised that he couldn't see that she had it on already as it was covered by her lightweight jacket, the warmer thicker coat left in her car for later.

'I'll surprise you,' she teased.

Feeling slightly out of her depth, still unused to talking to men, even so she was pleased that as they chatted, she was enjoying his company. Back in Lone Tree or Phoenix, she'd have excused herself and fled home, so Mandy would be stunned to see what was happening. How she wished her friend was here, she was so unused to dating, didn't know the rules, worried about any fallout at the dance.

'I have to go, see you later.'

Rising to dispose of his polystyrene cup in the nearby bin, Torrey left, leaving Sandy to finish her drink. On a whim, deciding to wander round the store for a while, she browsed through the different departments. When did she ever have the time to do this? Never had she really had the desire to go to shops unless she needed something specific so she was bemused to find herself at the lingerie racks thoughtfully look-ing through the pretty bras and matching panties, refusing to give in to her inclination to look round in case anyone could see her cheeks going pink. Finally picking up two lacy, sexy sets, one in pink, one in blue, she paid for them at the till and left the store.

Making her way outside, she was surprised to find that the sun had slipped down behind the taller buildings leaving most of the square in shadow and now filled with people. Leaving her shopping and her purse securely locked away in the car, glancing around, Sandy wandered over to the bandstand, but with no seats available, had to lean over the railing to watch the activity.

Despite it all, the town appeared nowhere as overpowering as Phoenix or Lone Tree, just an air of calm with no pushing or shoving and people greeting each other with hugs or a handshake. A Peter Pan place sprang to mind. And then, there he was. Kyle. For no reason she could clearly think of, she ducked away before he could catch sight of her, licked her lips, her mouth suddenly dry. How was she going to be able to dance with Torrey knowing Kyle was close by? For a moment as she really considered running off and going back to the ranch rather than risk a meeting, felt a hand on her arm that almost made her stiffen despite knowing that Kyle was the other side of the square.

'Ready?' Torrey was beaming down at her, his black eyes sparkling in delight. 'You know everyone will be jealous that I have the prettiest girl in Buffalo on my arm!'

Little do you know, she thought as she responded. 'Thanks Torrey. You look good yourself.'

Somehow she managed to put one foot in front of the other as he steered her down to the meeting hall, joining the queue making their way inside. Old and young, men and women, all dressed in their finest country outfits, the riders sporting fancy bandanas, cleaned hats and shiny boots.

'Oh, it's fantastic.'

She couldn't help the gasp of delight at all the ribbons, streamers, and the colourful balloons, the small triangles of American flags strung round the walls, as well as the banner with Welcome emblazoned against the background of the American flag hanging over the stage where the three country and western men were getting their guitars ready.

'How often do you do this?'

'About three times a year unless we have a special occasion.'

He guided her over to the bar alongside which tables with the buffet were already filling the air with delightful smells, making her wonder if this sort of thing went on back in Lone Tree. Sadly she realised that she'd never been interested enough to find out, had been unwilling to join in anything there, how she had cut herself off since University. Had she allowed her time there to get embedded so far into her soul that she could now only interact with horses?

Torrey helped her to a glass of punch, laughing with friends, putting his arm round her waist as he fended off their friendly joking at having a girl with him. For a moment, the nervousness that had always washed over her and made her feel threatened being with strangers, began to subside. That remarks were actually complimentary about her, the welcoming acceptance that as she was with him, she was now part of the community. And she started to relax, looking round at the throng of happy people chatting and laughing, filling the hall with sound so that she hardly heard the band as they started up.

Finding a couple of chairs, she hung her jacket over the

back of one as Torrey swept her into the crowd of dancers. She hated to stop him, she'd never had the chance to learn to dance, but despite that, he led her so easily she began to pick up the rhythm and began to enjoy herself. He wasn't pushy she was glad to note, holding her gently but not close. She wasn't sure that she could do that yet, especially as she imagined about being with Kyle.

But a cold feeling began to sink into her bones as the tune changed and another dance began, as if something was chilling her. She knew! She knew he was here! Her steps faulted for a moment, refusing to look around to see where he was before picking up the beat again. Several people began calling for something different and she found herself one of three lines of dancers looking at Torrey in confusion. He smiled.

'Watch me.'

And as the music became more animated, she realised that they were going to start the line dancing. She'd only ever seen this on television and it hadn't looked too hard but watching Torrey and trying not to fall over her own feet, she didn't have the time to think of Kyle, swaying and turning while trying to mimic what he was doing, stamping her boot heels along with everyone else until she was giggling so hard she was out of breath. Just as she started to get the hang of it, a new tune began and everyone was off again, this time doing different steps, confusing her until she just had to pull out and sit down to avidly watch. Torrey was a natural, obviously being well used to it and she enjoyed keeping an eye on the movements, the excitement and fun everyone was having swaying with the music, slapping their boot heels with their hands, calling out yippee. Torrey grinned at her until he had to turn away but finishing up facing her again. Around her people were calling out encouragement to the dancers, and she began to feel a community spirit that she'd never known before, started to feel less like the odd one out. Somehow she would like to do this more often, learn the steps, come again. If she were to stay!

Kyle had watched her from the other side of the room his heart pounding, trying not to smile at her attempts to get to grips with the steps, her long blonde hair flying around her shoulders. Those same long tresses that had spilled across the pillow as she'd held him, accepting his swollen, eager shaft as he'd slid inside, heard in his mind her small cry as he'd taken her innocence. He forced his mind away but, as if they had connected ethereally, her eyes suddenly met his. Snidely he raised his glass to her, emptied it, turned back to the bar for another before he got good and mad. How could she be doing this to him!

'Hi, Kyle.' Buck slapped him on the shoulder, leaning forward to ask for two drinks, one for him and one for the young brunette he was with, one of the Dawlish twins who had recently moved into the area he realised. 'This is Diane. If you move quick Samantha's about somewhere.'

Kyle kept his mouth shut, irritated by the offer of another girl being available. The only girl he wanted was dancing with another man. A glance over towards where she'd been sitting, he felt a stab in his groin when he couldn't see her until he saw she had returned to the lines of dancers, joining in again. The sight of her was like fire in his veins and worse, she seemed to be picking up the steps as quickly as she'd learned to move her body under him. The punch was deliberately non-alcoholic but he felt like he was getting drunker by the minute and decided to get out of the building, especially as Buck was eyeing him nervously and beginning to back away.

The chilly air didn't do much to cool his blood as he sat under the bandstand, attempting to get himself under control. For God's sake he didn't own her, one roll in the hay, or on her bed, didn't mean she was his. So this was what jealousy was! He gripped his fists until they hurt. He couldn't go back to the ranch, Sheb would wonder why let alone the folks inside who knew that when he came to every dance, he'd always had a girl by his side. He had to get back and pretend to take it on the chin, pretend he didn't care. Keep an eye on Torrey and make sure he didn't get out of line.

Sandy was enjoying herself and as the band changed to slower music, was grateful to sit down, accepting Torrey's offer of food and drink.

'Both please. I'll let you choose.'

Where was Kyle? She couldn't see him in the throng of people or over at the bar, those that hadn't gone to sit down at the tables. Annoyed about his childish action in raising his glass to her. Eventually she spotted him chatting with a small group of men, his back to her, a young girl gazing up at him, affronted by him blatantly ignoring her and furious with herself for being affected. Grateful when Torrey returned and she could turn her attention back to him.

He'd also bought her some raffle tickets and just as they finished eating, was highly delighted when one of her numbers was called, going up to receive a big box of chocolates which he presented to her. Sandy didn't dare look round to see if Kyle had been looking.

At the next dance, Torrey was tapped on the shoulder and

replaced by one of his friends. This turned into a game as several others also cut in until she was laughing so hard she had to give up and sit down studiously keeping her face away from Kyle. But she missed him, wanted him to ask her to dance, to hold her close even if it upset Torrey. Glancing round the room looking for him, she suddenly caught sight of a scruffy looking man, and something about his hard glare in her direction made her nervous. On eye contact, he turned swiftly away and disappeared.

'Are you okay?' Torrey asked, 'you look a little pale.'

'I've never danced so much before, I'm either out of condition or you and your friends are very fit.' She couldn't admit that she'd never done this sort of thing before.

He laughed. 'I told you they'd be jealous of me. There's just one more dance before the end, would you care for it?'

'That would be lovely.'

They swayed gently to the slow music, Sandy guiltily looking around for Kyle but he didn't appear to be in sight. Why wouldn't he ask her to dance? She'd been hoping he'd come over to her at least once, Torrey's friends hadn't held back from cutting in. Reluctantly she had to come to the conclusion that what she'd been feeling for him, what she'd romantically thought he felt for her, had been all in her head. She'd been taken over by emotions she just hadn't been strong or experienced enough to hide, had given him her innocence because of what she'd felt.

As Torrey led her back to her chair, she realised that people were leaving, shouting their goodbyes across the room to each other. The evening had ended leaving her body and heart in turmoil. Holding her jacket so she could shrug into it, Torrey walked her outside. It was cold and she was grateful that she'd thought to bring the warmer coat, reaching her car to put it on.

'Thanks for a wonderful evening, Sandy. I hope you can come to another one.'

'I've really enjoyed myself, thank you for asking me, Torrey.'

He seemed to want to lean forward for a kiss, hesitated without her encouragement, and smiled, just as a soft cough the other side of her car made Sandy turn her head and Torrey to glance up. Wishing her a safe journey home, Torrey walked off along the street.

Sandy tensed. 'What are you doing here?'

'Was just passing, thought I'd see you were okay. Did I disturb you saying goodnight to lover boy!' His voice sounded hoarse, brittle.

'None of your business,' she snapped back. 'But I had a nice evening.'

'So I saw. You soon forgot our evening together.'

'Did I? So you were watching me!' She was as angry as him, glaring at him across the bonnet. 'Just what do you mean by that? I made a promise to come with Torrey, and whatever you think of me, I don't break promises! Who I see is none of your damn business, go back to your rotten cows!'

She leapt into her car, slamming the door hard and locking herself inside, furious that tears were beginning to brim in her eyes. Starting the engine, she shot out of her space not caring that he had to leap out of the way as she slammed it into drive and shot off down the road making a few remaining people chatting on the sidewalks look round in surprise.

All the way home she made up angry comments she could throw at him alternating with wanting his arms round her, kissing away her tears, so incensed that she was hardly aware of arriving back at the house. Having let herself in, she stomped up the stairs, grateful the place was empty, throwing herself on the bed. She was glad wasn't she that she'd never had any contact with men before if this was what they were like!

Climbing into bed, throwing the covers over her head like a spoiled kid, her rebellious mind and body began to remind her what had happened on this bed the night before but even those memories were unable to stop her from finally falling asleep through exhaustion, to dream of making love with Kyle, to wonder if it would ever happen again.

Sandy stretched, surprised to find that she'd actually slept all night, sitting up with a jerk on hearing noises outside from activity down at the barn. Peering around the curtains she could see the men already riding off. Her heart rose into her throat as if trying to choke her, felt the burn of tears, and suddenly felt drained, empty, slumping back to sit on the bed. They'd have been fed by now. She was late but then she didn't want to catch up with Kyle, the sparks between them would have alerted everyone to their attitude to each other, hopefully it was just an argument between employer and employee, not anything else. And now she would have to face Jilly. Could her day get any worse!

Dragging her feet, reluctant to face the girl with her own internal turmoil, having already decided not to rise to any bait, she nearly changed her mind at the mulish look on the girl's face but automatically set her body language to non-confrontational as she would with any horse that came on her yard with attitude. That usually came about through fear of the unknown and she suspected that that might be the case with

Jilly over Kyle.

'Morning, Jilly, it's nice to see you again.'

Jilly mumbled something, passing her a plate of food and a mug of fresh coffee, turning her back while she rinsed the plates and dishes to put them in the dishwasher.

'I didn't see you at the dance.' Sandy kept her voice neutral.

'I don't go!'

'Oh, I'm sorry. Don't you like them?'

'Don't have the time.'

Sandy was thoughtful, the girl had no time? 'Do you work Saturday's?'

'I got pa to help out.' Her posture stiffened. 'You did go, I heard.'

'Oh, word spreads quickly round here.' Sandy gave a small laugh trying to lighten the mood, hearing a faint mutter. Having forced the meal down and not wanting to upset the girl, she pushed her empty plate away with a 'thank you,' and deciding not to say anything, started to walk away.

'You come in here, pretty, and take all the men. It's not fair.'

'I don't take anyone, Jilly. Torrey asked me to go, I didn't ask him.'

'And you got Kyle!'

'I think you've got that wrong, Jilly. I'm his boss. I haven't got anyone.' Sandy swung to face her, crossed her fingers and prayed for forgiveness for the half lie. 'I'm just friendly. I have to be, I'm a long way from home, in a strange place and lonely, even if I could just chicken out and run back home if I had to.'

Jilly turned to look at her, and for a moment, without the tattoos, studs and rings, Sandy thought she could be quite pretty.

'You're lonely? But you have this place. You're rich.'

'Money isn't everything. I have my own business back in Arizona that I built up by myself. I've had to work hard for that. Being here doesn't make up for missing my mom, my dad and my friend.'

'You have a mom and dad?' She sounded wistful, twisting her hands in front of her.

'Yes. Well, sort of.'

Jilly stared at her, confused. Sandy took a deep breath and sat back down at the counter, deciding to open her heart to the one person she felt needed to understand.

'I was adopted when I was a tiny baby, but they're real to me. Actually I'm assuming that as I don't know who my real parents were, that they didn't want me, abandoned me for a reason I just don't know. I don't tell anyone, you're the first here that knows.'

'It's just me an pa now.'

It was if she and Jilly had become joined in sadness and for a moment wanted to give the girl a hug, decided that it might not be welcome even if they shared a common tragedy.

'I'm sorry, it must be hard. If you ever wanted to talk, I'm here.'

Jilly turned away. 'I gotta get on.'

Sandy went to speak, thought better of it now they seemed to be getting along better and left the kitchen. She still hadn't managed to talk to Kyle about setting up a place to work horses in the paddock but it wasn't until she was outside and heading towards the buildings that she began to wonder what the point of staying was if she and Kyle couldn't get along any more. What if he went out with other women! Knew she'd never find another man like him, once given, her heart could never belong to another.

The sound of horses calling from the far corral made her instinctively look up, recognising the noise as faint warning sounds to alert each other of something they didn't understand or like. Studying the area but not seeing anything out of the ordinary, she quickly ducked under the railings of the first corral to make for the second, heard hooves thudding on the hard ground and heads bobbing. Realising that it wasn't fright catching the animals' attention, she ruled out a bear or possibly even a cougar, anyway she couldn't have done anything as she didn't have a rifle or even her handgun, her familiar Colt, with her. She'd learned to shoot on a range with her father and was an expert shot with both while over the years he'd taken over being the President of the local gun club when the other man had retired.

Climbing onto the rails, she found the horses had settled, only one or two actually still wary. Toward the barns! Weren't the men out? Turning her head she carefully perused the ground between the corrals and the barns, scanning the rise behind them, but there was nothing. The shadow she'd seen last week came to mind and she began to suspect that more was going on than she'd first thought. A thief or thieves, or whoever had been staying in the line shack? But nothing had been taken or even moved around the ranch house, surely Kyle or Sheb would have told her. And if they hadn't, were they trying to protect her now she seemed so uneasy about things they took for granted. So far she hadn't shown much courage.

Deciding that it had been a herd of deer, it didn't take much to startle them so they in turn would have spooked the horses.

And possibly even a coyote was about, not that she thought the dog like creature would have worried them. Climbing down, she wandered back to the barn, wondering if she should fetch Domino in and ride him, but glancing about she caught sight of the dusty windows above the tack room and being inquisitive, decided to go and find out what was up there.

The wooden steps leading up were covered in dust and cobwebs as if no-one had been up there for a very long time, testing each one nervously in case they might have rotted, and as it grew darker the further up towards the roof, she clutched the handrail. Reaching the wide top step and taking a deep breath, unsure what she might find beyond, tried the door handle, disappointed to discover that it was locked. Rattling it didn't help so cleaning a circle in the glass with a tissue she had in her pocket and peering through, despite it being very dark in there, she could only just make out the faint outline of several metal boxes on the floor just inside, and behind them what she thought could be wood stacked against the back wall, nothing that she could see that would need to be locked away. With a last hopeless rattle of the handle she started back down, leaving the faint outline of her footsteps in the dust.

Once back on the ground, and having a last look round to see if anything seemed different or out of place, she decided to bring Domino in, give him a brush and work him, spending a relaxing hour in the corral. Neither he nor the other horses showed signs of being disturbed but that never really settled her.

Returning him to the big corral and going back to the house, she decided to pick up a book from her room, on an impulse swerving towards the office to see if she could find a key for the attic, spending some time going through draws and cupboards, finding nothing even remotely like it, not even in the safe. It would have been distinctive, the lock had looked very old so it would have been far bigger than a normal one, but if she couldn't find it she'd have to try and pick the lock. It looked easy enough when actors did it on the TV and it wasn't as if it was a newer, more secure one.

Giving up, collecting a cold glass of lemonade from the kitchen and a biscuit, with no sign of Jilly, she went out onto the porch to unwind. One of the chairs was a rocker and she settled herself in the sun to catch any warm rays coming through the clouds, sipping at the drink. Reading as usual made her doze off a couple of times especially being warmed by the sun, but on slowly opening her eyes, she had a shock, dragging herself upright in the chair.

'Kyle!' she breathed, keenly aware that her voice sounded soft and inviting. She was mad at him wasn't she! Pulling herself together, straightening her shoulders, she snapped angrily, 'How long have you been here?' A slight twitch of his mouth showed her how uncertain he was of his reception. The chair under him creaked as he adjusted his position carefully.

'Not long.'

His eyes travelled from her head to her toes as he'd been doing before she woke, he just couldn't get enough of her, saddened to see she had gone back into her dark clothes again, had he made her that forlorn? He'd been intently observing her from the other chair, keenly aware of his body's reaction to watching her breasts rising and falling under the shirt, the top couple of buttons undone showing the swell, the beginning of the valley between. The long legs that had been wrapped around him as he'd parted the folds of her femininity and

218

driven into her wetness had made his heart rate spike while the ache in his groin when she was close or in his thoughts was now becoming more than painful. If he could only get her alone and show her how sorry he was!

The pink in her cheeks that showed up the delightful freckles slowly turned to a dusky red as she flushed at his look, snapping her head away. But she hadn't been quick enough, he'd seen her eyes travel the length of his body, had lingered slightly at the bulge behind his zipper. Where his carnal thoughts had centred before she'd woken. His heart leapt. Would he be forgiven? She was still obviously angry but he was too nervous to ask, his throat almost too dry to speak. He'd felt guilty most of the day over the way he'd treated her last evening and had disturbed his sleep, lying in bed wondering how he could get into the house to beg her forgiveness, on his knees if necessary.

Finally, as the silence stretched into being more than uncomfortable, when she refused to look or even speak to him, he plucked up courage and said, 'I'm showing you where we've been today,' pointing past the barns, 'in case anyone is watching.'

Did she move? Her body still tense with anger?

'I wanted to say that I was an idiot yesterday, and to apologise.'

Nothing showed in her face although her lips tightened to a thin line and her outline stiffened, the only sign she gave that she'd heard him. Desperate, moving his hand, he went on, 'I'm still talking about the ranch!'

Did the side of her mouth twitch?

'Would you like to give your side of it?'

For a long, long silence that seemed to stretch into minutes then hours but more likely less, he watched as her arms wrapped around her waist as if for defence, trying not to stare as the movement pressed her breasts upward adding even further to his rising libido. How this girl, this woman could turn him on so. It staggered him.

'Over there?' She finally raised a hand, as if agreeing to something he'd said, and his sigh of relief was audible.

Sandy tried to stop the slight curve at the corner of her mouth before he noticed, still refusing to look at him, staring out over the range. She wanted her pound of flesh, and he couldn't blame her!

'Did you really want to hear? I thought you'd already made up your mind about me and my Arizona principles, found them somewhat lacking.'

Kyle leaned slightly forward, silently trying to prove that he wanted to listen, wanted to look into those deep sapphire-blue eyes, uncaring now about who might be looking their way. Grateful when she seemed to arrive at some sort of decision.

'Just in case you are interested, when I first came here I soon found out that I didn't have the right clothes for Wyoming weather. I went to buy some and for the first time since University,' he heard the slight check in her voice, wondered why, 'I was asked out and for the very first time in my life I accepted.'

She turned her head, glanced fleetingly into his face, before looking away out over the range, but not before he got a glimpse of hurt in her expression.

'I've had issues… since University, that made me insecure for years. It was the first time that I've ever wanted to accept. Then you and I, well got together. You gave me sensations I've never had before, but I was torn between what I felt for you and for

220

the feelings of a decent young man being let down, dumped, in front of the whole town and his friends.'

She sat up, folding her hands in her lap. Kyle looked everywhere but at her, ashamed of his behaviour. He hadn't even waited to see what she'd had to say yesterday morning, hadn't wanted to truth be told. But then he'd never felt this way for any other woman as he did for her. He dated, twice he'd thought he'd found the right one to be with before discovering that they hadn't been, and had just been drifting along until Sandy had arrived at the ranch and blown his mind. Let alone his body.

'I was jealous. I'm sorry.'

When Sandy nodded, he almost didn't catch it, it had been so slight, before she moved a hand to point as if to take in what he'd been telling her.

'I had a hard time making a decision, you don't know how hard it was, made even worse when Kate told you I was going to the dance before I could explain.' She turned and stared at him and he felt bad when he saw the shimmer of tears, wanted to take her in his arms and kiss them away.

'I'm sorry.'

Sandy took a slow breath before she finally whispered, 'Accepted, and now we've discussed the range can we go in for dinner?'

Kyle stood allowing her to reach the door behind them before walking along the veranda to go around to the back door. His faint words just caught her ear.

'Will you leave the door open tonight? Please!'

'I might!' She left him dangling as she'd meant to do, disappearing into the house, leaving just the faint enticing aroma of her warm body and the scent she used until the breeze swept it away.

Dinner went well, the men eating while Sandy and Jilly seemed to have reached some sort of silent pact following their talk that morning, making it easier on everyone, and as the men finally left, Sandy retired to the lounge to open her laptop and read her emails. But the whispered words from earlier had the fibres in her body in chaos, the blood pounding so much through her body that she almost didn't catch Jilly saying goodnight as she was about to leave, her father having turned up to collect her. Sandy looked across at the girl to smile and say, 'goodnight, hope to see you next weekend.'

A slow intense eagerness began to spread like molten liquid through her veins at the thought of Kyle appearing, her breasts reacting already to the thought of his roughened hands caressing them, teasing, his mouth drawing each taut nipple. The tingle deep inside her sex where she wanted to feel his fingers driving her mad with desire until her back arched and she could cry out her hunger. Before he moved between her legs with the promise of sweet fulfilment, his hard length buried deep.

Jerking back to reality, her heart pounding, her thoughts already making her wet between her thighs as if he was already there in the room, touching her. She forced herself to open her emails. No surprise that Mandy was already demanding to know how the dance had gone.

About time too I'm waiting in anticipation here Sandy.

Good things are worth waiting for. I enjoyed myself.

Was he a gentleman?

Actually yes he was very nice and taught me to line dance.

Shame :(Goodnight kiss after?

No that would be pushing me a little too far for a first time date.

Little do you know my friend about what has happened between me and Kyle, or might be happening tonight! Would he come? Do birds fly? A fine shimmer of damp began to creep over her skin in anticipation, her ears alerting to every creak, every tiny little noise in an otherwise deserted house.

SANDY!

What?

You stopped, what's going on there?

Nothing exciting I've spoken to Blade and he wants to run or buy my business IF I decide to set up here I've already sussed out a big paddock to work in. There's a lovely Appaloosa here I'm working after Buck said he would be a bit of a handful for me.

Ah Buck again I've got to come up there and see this man.

The invite is still open, choose your time friend so what's happening in Arizona?

Had she heard something? She froze for a moment, her fingers stilled, poised above the keyboard, swung her attention over to the doorway and out into the hall. Was there a shadow? As her heart pounded nervously in her chest she felt nothing and heard nothing, carried on typing.

Usual stuff but it's been hinted at that I could be in line for a promotion at work to probably manager.

Good for you, you deserve it it's been worth the wait.

Sandy's body suddenly went on high alert, responding. She just knew he was there without having heard a sound or even looking around, pure adrenalin sparking in electric shocks that set every nerve ending alight. How could they be so connected?

Phones going friend gotta run could be mom.

Keep in touch and remember what I said about going for it bye.

Her heart in her throat, mouth dry, she closed the lid to the laptop as with socked feet Kyle padded with into the lounge, the room going dark as he turned out the lights. As if she was going to go upstairs. He knew her routine? What did that say about him watching for her at night!

As he reached to pull her up, he thought how amazingly sexy she was, even her dark clothes couldn't quite hide the rounded breasts he would soon be feasting on as they rose and fell with the deep breaths she was taking, proving to him that she desired him as much as he wanted her. Her slim waist, the curvy hips, and those incredibly long legs that would soon be wrapped around him. The rising erection behind his zipper that had been plaguing him since their talk outside earlier demanding to bury itself in her slick tight wetness. The mind numbing ecstasy that had blown him apart as she'd come around him. Something he'd never felt so strongly before she'd come into his life.

'Hi!' she managed to stutter, already falling into a deep

chasm that made her legs weaken, unable to move a muscle until he grasped her shoulders and pulled her into his arms. Unresisting as his lips touched hers and fleetingly making her want more, dipping again more firmly, his tongue running the line of her mouth until she gave way and allowed it entry, to explore her mouth. He tasted deliciously of coffee and mint, more heady than wine and she tangled her hands in his hair, dragging him down, leaning into his hard body. And then he was devouring her, his mouth hard on hers and she could hardly draw breath.

Pulling back, without a word, he swept her into his arms and stalked up the stairs effortlessly, trying to hold back his body's immediate demands, wanting this to last a long, long time until once again he would be forced to flee her bedroom and her body. She made him crazy but not so crazy he wanted her to be the source of gossip. Switching the bedside light on like he knew she did every night, as he'd watched from his cabin window, imagining what she was doing behind the closed curtains. Allowed her form to slide down the length of his, to feel his hard manhood, gripping her buttocks to grind himself against her groin, rubbing where he wanted to be. He groaned, his mouth crushing down on hers, feeling her arms slip round his neck, running her fingers through his hair, tugging at it to hold him tighter.

Fingers shaking, he began to undo the buttons of her shirt, gazing down at the valley between her breasts, the swelling tops, sliding the material from her shoulders before reaching behind to undo her bra. The sight of such perfection had him on his knees, the dark red aureoles calling to him as he took a nipple into his mouth, laving it with his tongue, suckling as his hands went to her butt to hold her tight. He nearly lost his mind as her body arched back into his arms with a moan, forcing her breasts up to meet him. He swapped to the other and heard her whimper as he sucked harder.

Running his hands across the top of her pants, he eased them and her panties slowly down over her thighs to her ankles and as she stepped out of them, he released the nipple to bury his face into the hair of her mound, nipping with his teeth as he inhaled the aroused scent from her core. Heard her whisper his name as he laid her back on the bed, parted her thighs and took her into his mouth. Sandy shuddered at the strangeness, self-conscious that he could do such a thing until his tongue began to tease into her folds and she cried out, arching her back, gripping his hair as she bucked against him.

Sucking at her wetness, his tongue flicking her nub, heard her whimpers as the arousal he brought on swamped her body, felt her tremble. Her thighs tightening around his head as she came, waiting patiently for her to come down from her high. Beginning again, nipping her until her hands nearly tore the hair from his head as another orgasm hit.

'Kyle!' She couldn't hold back the throaty moan.

Couldn't take much more, she wanted, needed him inside her, but he took her legs over his shoulders, holding her wide to insert a finger, rocking it in and back, circling, then a second, pressing somewhere that sent sparks of white hot flames to suck the very air from her lungs. She throbbed, ached, writhed as he brought her to the brink again and again, one hand gripping her hips with fingers of steel when she tried to wriggle away. Sandy thought she would lose her mind if he kept this up, as he brought her so close towards orgasm before stopping and starting again, leaving her with a searing aching need, desperate to feel him inside her.

'Come, come for me Sandy,' he urged, desperate now for his own release, her back arching with the intense orgasm he now brought on, crying out his name, clutching him with rigid fingers and digging her nails into his flesh. He waited, letting her slowly relax, her body to stop quivering, pulling back to stare at her sweat slicked body, to memorise every part for when they couldn't be together. As he went to undress, with limpid eyes and shaking fingers, Sandy managed to sit up to undo his shirt, tugging the snaps open to run her palms over his taut abs, the soft dark hairs of his chest tickling her lips as she licked her tongue over his salty skin, tasting his flat button nipples. Pulling the shirt from his shoulders, she ran her fingers down the line of dark hair to his belt, her hungry lips following.

'Easy darlin' or you won't get me inside you before I come,' he warned hoarsely, pushing her onto her back on the bed, to gaze in reverence from her eyes molten with sexual need to the quivering lips. On to the breasts with their nipples swollen from his mouth, on down her delicious body to where the pink fleshy folds hid the delights to come, soaked from his mouth and her wetness. Staring into her eyes as he removed his jeans, he saw them widen at the evident erection behind his shorts, heard her deep groan as he revealed his body, removing them too. Kicking his clothing aside, he knelt between her thighs to nip her mound, licking her skin to taste the essence of her, trailing his tongue up to each nipple, on up to her throat and the pulse beating at her neck, suckling there as she bucked under the weight of his body. Running his mouth up along her jaw to an earlobe, nipping it while her hands wrapped themselves

227

round his waist, her strong fingers grabbing his butt, urging him down against her to give her the pleasure she badly wanted.

'Please, Kyle. Please,' she begged.

'Not yet, darlin',' he drawled.

He wanted more for her! He tamped down on his own needs, refusing his urges as his hand made its way slowly down her side, pressing the skin just above her mound, making her whimper, down until he could cup her damp warm flesh, widening her trembling thighs with his knees. Felt her arch up with a mewing sound as he slid his thumb into her depths, swirling in her wetness, rubbing against her clit, easing further and further inside until she was moaning, nails digging into him as he pushed upward to that special tender spot. Sandy's body and mind exploded with the intense hot pleasure of another orgasm that had her inner muscles clenching and unclenching around him with each convulsion as she came, sapping her strength with the exquisite ecstasy. Kyle held her, lying on her warm body until he felt her muscles unwind, staring into her stormy eyes until she could finally raise a smile.

'Was that good for you?' he whispered, now desperately wanting her, the head of his swollen and throbbing manhood nudging at her entrance.

'Yes. Please… !'

'Your word is my command,' his voice husky with need.

The sound of tearing paper surprised her given the state of her mind, felt his body rising as he sheathed himself. She hadn't given her safety a thought and was annoyed with herself for being so stupid. Felt him gripping her buttocks, lifting her pelvis so he could slide into the hot wetness of her passage, his breath halting as he eased out to thrust again and again, feeling her body align itself and pick up the rhythm of love as with each lunge he went deeper. She gave a quivering cry as she came, her silky tight wetness clamping onto his shaft until he exploded, heard himself shout her name as they crashed and burned together while he pumped his hips, spilling his seed deep. Her muscles clenched around him, throbbing, wringing every drop from him, they melted with a final release, sliding into a deep void of exquisite pleasure, wrapped in each other's arms.

Stirring, Kyle rolled off her body, heading for the bathroom to dispose of the condom, hearing her mumble as she dozed before climbing back into the bed, falling asleep with her spooned against his chest.

Waking, with Sandy's warmth against his chest, one hand enveloping a firm breast, he felt the heat rising in his groin, his libido awakening again. Had it ever stopped with her around? Even asleep it appeared that his body desired her, not helped when she stirred and mumbled, folding her hand over his to pull it against her. He obliged and rolled the nipple between his fingers, felt her tremble.

'You sure you want to do that?' he breathed, 'or we'll be here all night!'

She giggled softly, and as she pressed into him with her buttocks, couldn't stop his reaction, heard her soft gasp.

'Can you be quick?'

'Not a hope.' He glanced at the face of his luminous watch. 'It's already eleven.'

Sandy drew a deep breath, daring herself, turning to face him to timidly take hold of his shaft, to feel soft skin sliding over the inner hardness, feeling it jump in her hand. Holding it firmly, she tentatively began to move her hand like she'd felt him move inside her until he was rock hard and totally aroused, thrusting with her movement.

'Stop! Now,' he groaned through gritted teeth, pulling her hand away.

Reaching across to the cupboard top, he tore a packet open with his teeth, sheathed himself, opening her legs and rolling between them. Swiftly he buried himself as she arched up to meet him, her slick tight warmth claiming him, her muscles throbbing, clenching around him, driving him almost out of his mind. Plunging again and again into her willing body, as her legs wrapped around his waist, he heard her throaty cry as her nails bit into his buttocks driving him on. His balls tightening, he crashed into his release with a burst of stars behind his eyelids, his shaft pulsing as she came with him.

Sated, his head pounding, he collapsed onto her quivering body, her gasps in his ear as she held him tight in the last throes of her orgasm. How did she do this every time to him? He'd never experienced anything like this with any other women he'd been with. She hadn't been here long, how had she invaded his heart so totally. A strange flicker inside was insisting that he never wanted her to leave, to go back to Arizona. He had to make her stay somehow. And how the hell was he supposed to continue to work on the ranch knowing that she would be here waiting for him to join her, to bury himself again and again into her warmth?

'I've got to go,' he said, his reluctance showing in his voice, and Sandy turned on her side towards him, gently rubbing her fingers against his sweaty chest, breathing in his heavy musk odour. He pulled her hand away. 'Do that an they'll find us still in bed in the morning, darlin', cos I won't want to leave.'

'I know. I do appreciate your thinking of my honour.'

At the blissful look in her soft doe-like eyes, Kyle had to literally grit his teeth and force himself to roll out of the bed, to climb into his clothes before his will broke and he stayed. Leaning over, he gave her a chaste kiss, crossing the room in the darkness hoping he didn't fall and break his neck on the stairs. Sliding the lock so that it would re-lock securely, he slipped out into the night, a quick glance showing no lights in the bunkhouse, just the faint lone one in his cabin. For a moment he stood still, he felt uncomfortable about sneaking around, it just wasn't in his nature, but there was no way he could allow her to be talked about.

Like the first time, he made his way quietly round to the cabin, grateful he kept both lock and hinges well-oiled even if he was known to go out occasionally to check the barn and the horses. Luckily Sheb and Buck had got used to him doing it while the horses didn't kick up a fuss so if he was seen he still had a good excuse to be out. Falling into bed he thought he'd never get to sleep, his body still awash with desire, knowing that if this had been make-up sex he was all for waiting until their next argument, but he must have drifted off eventually because he awoke, startled, to a thundering knocking on his door.

Chapter Eight

'You okay, Kyle, day's awastin'.'

'Shoot,' staring at his watch he discovered it was half seven, unheard of for him.

'See you at the house,' he called back, swiftly jumping out of bed to get dressed, managing to shave without actually cutting himself even with the rush to leave, finally reaching the dining room halfway through the meal. Pouring himself a coffee, he drank too quickly, trying not to wince when he burnt his mouth.

He ignored looking to see where Sandy was, filling his plate as if he was starving. He was, but for a different reason. Starving for her! He could normally feel her presence without even looking, it was like his body vibrated every time she was near, but he also felt the emptiness when she wasn't. He was relieved when Sandy finally walked in looking somewhat embarrassed at Kate, taking the proffered plate from the housekeeper and sitting at the counter.

'Hi Kate, got distracted, I've been searching the office for a key.'

'What key would that be?' Kate asked curiously.

'The old store room in the barn.'

'Now why'd you want to go in there? It's dusty and dirty.'

'It looks interesting, there's boxes and other stuff, and looks like it hasn't been used in years!'

'Land sakes honey, if you want to, but I don't know about

any key.'

Sandy looked round at the men, Kyle and Buck weren't taking any interest, Sheb looked troubled, his body language tense as he kept his eyes on his plate. But he said nothing, following the other two outside when they'd finished their meal.

Sandy had to admire her own quick thinking, both her and Kyle being late she knew might look odd, and only while wandering reluctantly downstairs had she thought of saying about looking to get into the old room even if she'd already searched. Or did it only feel strange to her because she felt guilty! It had taken a lot of control not to keep glancing in Kyle's direction, knew if she did and he caught her eye, she'd never be able to keep her feelings under control. She was still worried that something would give them away.

'Oh well, I guess it'll turn up sometime if I keep looking.'

She headed back to the office glancing round to make sure she'd covered every conceivable hiding place then gave a start as the room darkened.

'Come to do some work, didn't know you were in here.' A slow smile spread over Kyle's face as he deliberately looked her up and down, and Sandy could have sworn her toes curled at the seductive sound of his voice. 'I can come back later if you're busy.'

'That's ok, I was just leaving.' If she could make her legs work.

She watched his smile deepen as if he knew what he was doing to her. Mentally shaking herself, she rose and walked round the desk, passing him, half of her praying he'd kiss her yet knowing they couldn't with Kate nearby, and with an irrational flash of annoyance, she forced herself to keep walking out of the office, heading for the staircase.

Having made her bed and tidied up, she spotted Sheb and Buck leaving. Recalling Sheb's strange behaviour, she decided to go out to the barn and see if she could find the key there. Just what was calling to her from that room, that she had to see inside, was puzzling.

The sun was warm when she went outside closing the door behind her, just a trace of a breeze with white clouds drifting across the blue sky hinting at the start of a late spring and good weather to come. Hearing the sound of horses calling and hooves thudding on the hard ground, she changed her mind, deciding instead she would ride Domino in the paddock before taking up her search. As if she intended to stay? When had that happened? Why was Arizona not calling her to go back home? For a moment it was a surprise to realise she didn't want to leave.

Sitting down suddenly on a chair to absorb the scenery and try to collect her scattered thoughts, a sense of belonging began to seep into her. The ranch had slowly taken her over without even realising, her heart telling her that this was where she should be. And it wasn't just falling in love with Kyle, it was something else, and with a flash she recalled something Kate had told her. Wyoming magic!

Wow, hang on a minute! For a moment it was if her breathing had stopped. In love! Not possible, why she hardly knew the man. Sex wasn't everything. What did she know of him, apart from that he was foreman of the ranch, loved what he did, worked tirelessly and was obviously trustworthy. But a creeping warmth began to slide over her as she tried to digest what her heart already knew, was telling her. When exactly she had fallen, she had no idea. When they'd first met on the road, first talked, first met him in his own surroundings, or after he'd taken her upstairs to her bed? And why had she given herself to him, it was so out of character, she'd sworn never to have a boyfriend and yet, here on the ranch, she'd not only been out on a date with a stranger but fallen into bed with one who she really didn't know anything about. What was his background? Did it matter, she had her instincts to go on, and what she had seen of him so far. That she was comfortable in his presence, felt safe.

Wyoming had crept into her soul while she wasn't looking, surrounded her with friendship and kindness, tried to tell herself she didn't believe in all that mumbo-jumbo about love at first sight. But then what was it that had called her to make such an epic journey? She could easily have sold the ranch unseen, never left what had been her comfort zone. And would have missed all this!

Leaping to her feet she headed for the barn, collected Domino's tack and went into the corrals. A quick whistle and when he came over let him into the smaller corral, giving him a quick brush down before saddling up. Taking him into the paddock, she swung easily up onto his back and began as she would have done at home, trying different gaits, swinging easily to his motion, finally attempting roll backs, stops, and turns. Domino turned out to be easy to teach and it was as if she and he were one and the same.

Just as she was comparing how she and Kyle had fitted together so well, Domino's ears shot up and she discovered the man himself had come into the field and was standing eyeing her, his body almost rigid. Confused, she rode over. What was wrong?

Kyle was first worried and then angry, he knew that horse, what the hell was she doing riding him! Domino had never been good with any of the other hands, including himself, doing the work reluctantly and only accepting people because he had to. So Kyle had been terrified to see her riding round even as he'd admired the way she sat him, how well the horse was responding to her. But as foreman he was responsible for everyone on the ranch, and that included her especially as there was no-one around if things had gone wrong. His heart would have been broken if anything happened to her.

'What are you doing on Domino and why are you doing it alone? That horse is untrustworthy.'

'Says who?' she snapped back. 'I've ridden him several times now and he's been the perfect gentleman. I do train horses for a living you know!'

'And you've never done it alone. I bet there's always been someone with you.'

'At the start, so what's the matter?' She caught herself in time, she couldn't tell on Buck or he'd be in trouble.

'I'm responsible for everyone on this ranch, including you. Suppose he'd thrown you!' His heart trembled for her, he wanted to snatch her out of the saddle and assure himself she was safe but one look in her eyes showed him that not only was she on the defensive but had a stubborn streak about her own capability. He softened his voice.

'You should have warned me what you were doing.'

'You know you'd have said no.'

Suddenly Sandy's annoyance began to retreat, beginning to

understand where he was coming from. Did this mean that she meant more to him than he was letting on? Domino shifted as her body began to react differently with her changing mood.

'You want to watch what we can do?'

She grinned and he couldn't help but smile back. To be honest after he'd nearly had a heart attack he'd enjoyed watching her, he'd never seen Domino so relaxed or known that he could be so willing. Perhaps she really did know what she was doing, or perhaps the horse preferred a woman's touch. Reluctantly, he nodded and Sandy set out to prove to him that her training methods worked.

Going through her repertoire and finishing with a short sliding stop in front of him, she slid from the saddle, scratching the Appaloosa's neck as he rubbed his face against her arm. Neither of them said a word as she led the horse into the corral and unsaddled, pleasure flooding her whole being at Kyle watching her every move. She needed him to approve of what she had done, had always wanted it for her methods. More than that, she wanted his arms round her, his lips crushing on hers, to feel the hardness of his need for her against her damp and aching sex. Setting Domino free with the other horses, she followed Kyle into the barn where he deposited her saddle on the wooden horse. Looking up at the attic, she frowned, still determined to look inside there somehow.

'I still want to look for the key to that door.'

'Never seen one, but then I haven't looked. Want some help?'

'Can you keep your mind on what you're looking for?' Sandy asked, sweetly.

'Long as you can, honey!'

Sandy flushed at the endearment, tearing her eyes away from

237

his lips. Not going to be very long then if the quiver he saw in her body had anything to do with it. He smirked.

'Do I get a reward if I find it?'

'What would you want?' Following the misery of their fight after the dance, she was beginning to enjoy the friendly by-play between them. Two could play at this game.

'I'm shore I can think of something, boss!'

He turned on the light and as she started combing through the hooks around the sides of the tack room that held bridles, ropes, and assorted straps, coming up empty, he checked the tops of cupboards and in draws. Sandy finally put her hands on her hips in frustration. Heading up the steps to the door, again she tried to look inside but without a switch to turn on a light, if there was one, everything was still hidden in darkness. She rattled the handle in the vague hopes that it would mysteriously open.

'You okay up there?'

'Yes, but no key. I guess it's been lost and long gone.'

It was strange, why had no-one been in there for so long, what could the room be hiding, or was she just letting her imagination run away with her. There was no reason that she should be this interested she just had a strange feeling that the room was calling to her, that she was being drawn in, had to go and look through everything. Had Willard stacked things away after his wife died to keep everything out of sight or was there things belonging to his own parents.

'Hang on.'

She heard Kyle rummaging about in the tool box followed by boot heels on the concrete floor before the loud creak of the dry wood steps as they complained under his heavier weight. And then his body was leaning against her back, his palms against the walls enclosing her, enveloping her with the tantalising smell of musk and warm male. Overpowering, breathtaking, it seemed to wash over her and she struggled to control herself, wondering if he could feel her quiver, straining to actually breathe.

'Not a lot of room up here.' His breath whispered against her ear as he seized the opportunity to brush his lips across the back of her neck and felt her shiver. Every nerve jumped into instant alert.

'Perhaps I should go down and give you room to work.' Her voice quivered as his arms tightened, his growing need of her very evident against her butt cheeks. 'Kyle... !'

'Yes, darlin',' he drawled. 'Don't move about or I won't be held responsible for the consequences.'

Sandy giggled and for a fleeting second or two, he was almost prepared to take her here and now but sense took over. There was a time and a place for everything and this wasn't it, although he nearly changed his mind as she wriggled.

'Sandy!' he warned.

'Sorry, I got an itch from all this dust.'

'It'll get scratched if you don't stop. Look, go downstairs and let me get on.' Reluctantly he stepped back.

'Spoilsport,' she teased, and he nearly dropped the screwdriver he'd brought. His blood began to boil and for a moment he couldn't even see the door as she squeezed past. Deliberately pressing her firm breasts against him? Damn, if he didn't have her soon he'd split his jeans! Trying to calm, to get his mind back on the job, and which one would that be he asked himself, he peered through the crack between the door and the frame, could just make out the metal lock, dull with age. Wondered why he'd never thought to ask Willard what was stored in its depths.

But then they'd both been busy working the ranch and with the room itself almost hidden from sight high in the roof he'd never taken any notice before Sandy had mentioned it. Easing the end of the screwdriver against the piece of metal it took a while before he could get purchase on it, splintering the wood, but it refused to budge. When was the last time it had been opened? And should he be helping her go inside? Supposing it was something that Willard hadn't wanted anyone else to see, it was personal, but then common sense reminded him that it was her ranch, she could do whatever she liked, and he wasn't sure that he liked that thought.

Again he felt that wrench to his gut. It should have been his, he'd worked hard, had given his affection and respect to his guardian and mentor, had thought he'd been given it back. Memories flooded back of the new life he'd been given, to all intent he'd become Willard's family, there had never been any mention of anyone else. So why had Willard done what he'd done? There had to be some reason why he'd been cut out of the will.

Kyle wasn't a blood relative but he'd been made to feel that he was, had always been supported even when in the early days he'd shrugged away from Willard when he'd tried to comfort him, had tried a couple of times to put a reassuring arm over his young shoulders. Willard had never said anything, hadn't shown any disappointment, but instead had respected his wishes and just been there until his anger and truculence had slowly dissipated. Along with the help of Sheb, he had learned to put his heart and soul into the ranch.

'Are you alright?'

Sandy's voice jerked him back to the present bringing the enjoyable knowledge that if Willard hadn't done what he had, he'd never have met Sandy and his life wouldn't have been turned upside down. Or become so pleasant! Deciding that his only option was going to be to dismantle the door frame and release the lock, could he do it without making too much damage?

'Yep!'

'Am I stopping you from doing your work on the ranch?'

'No, it's okay.' He took a deep breath and muttered to himself, darlin', you do that to me every single time I think of you!

Forcing his mind back to the problem of the door, it turned out that removing part of the old door frame was easier than he'd thought, the wood being so old and dry it pulled away but leaving nails protruding. He'd knock them in later, but Sandy would have to be careful going in and out.

'Done, you just got to watch out for nails!'

The door swung open and he heard her coming up, the steps only squeaking slightly under her lighter weight. Reaching round to feel for a switch and finding it, Kyle pushed it up, surprised when a light actually came on though the bulb was dim with dust. His automatic thought was to get the wiring checked out and a new bulb put in before she started working in here. Willard had seen to the barns and corrals when he'd had the security alarms and lights upgraded a few years back but had never mentioned this place. Sandy pushed under his arm to look and it naturally settled over her shoulders, instantly kicking his libido into life.

'Wow! And yuk!'

He felt her stiffen as she looked around to get a better sight of three dusty metal boxes laid on the floor haphazardly as if uncared for, unwanted. As if the person who had dumped them had lost interest or just wanted to be free of everything. Other paraphernalia stacked further on was still difficult to make out in the gloom, the dim bulb hardly able to penetrate into the corners but Sandy thought she could make out an old wardrobe and matching cupboard with draws, while a long mirror on a wooden stand reflected what appeared to be once white, painted framework among other bits of wood.

'Well, that should keep you busy for a couple of years.'

'Did you know of all this?'

'Nope, nothing, just that it was some sort of storeroom and Willard kept it locked. If you're going to come up here, I should get someone to check out the wiring but a change of bulb wouldn't be a problem. Perhaps an exterminator for any spiders or scorpions wintering here, snakes aren't likely to be although the warmer weather will be waking them around now.'

'I'll ask Kate if she has any rubber gloves and it looks like I'll need something over my nose.'

Closing the door he followed her back down the steps, turned on by the sight of her swaying hips in front of him, wanting to put his hands on her waist and pull her onto the re-awakening part that always wanted her, to bend her over and take her until she cried out his name as she came. As if she'd caught his thoughts or the warmth of his body as he closed the gap between them, she stopped so suddenly that he walked into her, automatically clutching at her waist to stop her stumbling.

'Sandy!' he breathed, his nose buried in her hair, smelling the freshness, went to wrap his arms round her. Aware of the state of his hands, not wanting to mess up her clothing in case she met up with anyone, he told her to stay where she was and went over to the sink to clean them. Returning to gather her in his arms, he latched onto her upturned lips with his while her hands reached up to his hair, twining into it to pull him close. Leaning in so her breasts pressed against his chest, urging him on, he thrust a knee between her legs to rub his thigh against her sex, hearing her moan into his mouth.

Gasping, seeing the knowing smile on her face that was driving him to distraction, Kyle turned her so his chest was against her back, wrapped his arms round her, pulling her tight against him, his throbbing manhood rammed against her backside. She wriggled and he groaned almost out of his mind with want. Lifting her shirt, pushing her bra up, his hands palmed her breasts, tweaking the hardening nipples, heard her whimper as her hands reached back to cup his buttocks pulling him harder against her.

'See what you do to me,' he whispered in her ear, nibbling her earlobe, feeling her tremble as his other hand reached down under the waistband of her jeans and on down under her panties, hearing the breath catch in her throat. Thrust his hard erection against her buttocks to show her he was more than ready.

'Kyle!' she breathed softly, her voice quivering with desire as he pushed further down between her legs, found her wet, sliding his palm to cup her heat, a finger rubbing between the soft fleshy labia before pressing up inside the silky tightness, shattering the last remnants of her control. She squirmed and gave a soft cry that made him desperate for release from the confines of his jeans. Finding her sensitive bud and pressing it, she reacted instantly, whimpering, circling her hips, reaching round to feel for his zipper, easing it down and taking the hard length of him in her hand. Sandy's head lolling back against his shoulder when he sucked at the beating pulse in her neck as she opened her legs as far as her jeans would allow.

Kyle's breathing grew harsher with the sweet agony of her touch and he groaned, nuzzling her neck, pulling her back against him into the shadows, his finger still pressing as far as he could reach until she unravelled as her orgasm crashed through her, leaving her floating on waves of ecstasy. God he was going to burst, aware of her fingers caressing him.

'I want you,' he whispered hoarsely against her ear, hearing her reply, begging for him.

Desperate for relief he undid her zipper, easing her jeans over her hips and thighs taking her lacy panties with them, leaning her against one of the saddles to press a second finger deep inside, circling, pushing into the sweet depths until she cried out and came against his palm, frantically moving with him. Felt her shake and her inner muscles clench on his fingers as her body exploded with another orgasm. Jeez she was so responsive. He'd taken to carrying protection with him in his jeans pocket in hope, pulled his hand free. Sandy heard the sound of cloth against skin as he released himself, then paper tearing. Felt him moving to sheath himself. Wondering when he'd turn her round. The head of his manhood prodded at her entrance and she froze for a second, realised what he proposed, and her whole skin damped with embarrassment and excitement. He couldn't be?

Felt his hands take hold of her hips, his whisper as he warned her to be ready, then his thumbs parted her folds, and he thrust the head of his hot shaft inside, stretching and widening her while she pressed back against him, wanting. He buried himself deep. Began to withdraw then thrust back in, taking up a gentle rhythm at first before speeding up, heard her breath catch in her throat. Felt her clutch at the leather under her as she absorbed him, pushing back, demanding as another orgasm threatened, her muscle spasms clamping round him, unaware of anything but the friction as he bucked against her. His groin banged against her buttocks as he forced himself deeper until she exploded around him. He closed a hand over her mouth before she could scream out, somehow withholding his own shout as he tensed, thrusting a few more times as her orgasm pulsed around him until, with a deep grunt, his groin in flames, he was emptying himself, her muscles milking him.

Kyle was reluctant to withdraw, leaning against her, panting, wanting to stay buried but as she wriggled he realised that his weight was bearing her down against the hard leather and pulled away, his heart still pounding in his chest. He couldn't get enough of her, she scattered his emotions to the winds leaving him sated but still wanting more. Slowly their gasps relaxed, slowing as they regained their breath. He eased her upright, kissing her ear, her neck, aware that he wanted to take her again, his manhood starting to thicken. Nothing like this had happened to him before, once sated, satisfied, he'd usually either slept or gone home. That had been enough. But now!

'Sandy?' His voice was hoarse.

'Wow!'

'Double wow!' He grinned, turning her to face him, aware

that both of them were still half naked, but he wanted her to know that he needed her again, holding her hips tight against him.

'I think we'd better get dressed,' she giggled, pressing herself against his body, breathing in his strong male scent now thickened by their sex. Looking down into her eyes, he could see them glowing with fulfilment, rounding as he pushed against her and she realised his growing condition. He smiled.

'Yes, or you could get a second helping,' he warned, removing the condom, tying the end and gently pushing it into the pocket of his vest to dispose of back in his cabin, yanking his pants and jeans back up to fasten his zipper and button. She did the same.

'My oh my, Mister Sherman, how romantic, and in a dusty old barn!'

'Yo'all complaining, Miz Carson?' His eyes twinkled as he bent to kiss her.

'Hell no,' she giggled.

'As the appropriate parts of my body still want you, we need to hurry. In case the others return early.'

Pushing past, he stood to look and listen until he was satisfied that all was well, indicating to her that she should go, and as she stepped away, the light scent he associated with her now mingling with her arousal, still swirling around them. Gazing after her as she walked towards the house, a rush of male pride filled him, knowing from the way she held herself that she'd been satisfied.

Collecting a new bulb from his cabin, as he replaced the light upstairs he couldn't help but bite back a feeling of discontent, a slow building of shame snaking into his mind and soul. He took pride in being a man. His liaison with Sandy should be an honest one, out in the open and above board. He needed to sort it. Perhaps this was why Sheb had given that hint of warning.

After a shower and a change of clothes, going to the kitchen, Sandy poured herself a coffee, taking it up to her room to relax and read more of her book, reflecting on Kyle and the over-powering feelings she had when she was with him. He made her feel feminine and sexy and for the first time in her life, she had to acknowledge that she liked it. A lot! The book didn't hold her attention for long and she fell asleep, curled up on top of the bed.

'Sandy! You awake?' Kate's shout woke her and she sat up, calling out that she'd be down, rushing to the bathroom to comb her hair and straighten her clothes before making her way downstairs.

'What have you been doing to get so tired?' asked Kate, putting a plate in front of her, the men sitting after she had to reach eagerly for the steaming dishes. Sandy couldn't help her body tensing, keeping her eyes firmly fixed on her plate with every nerve guiltily on edge at Kyle being so close.

'It's all this fresh air,' Sandy whispered.

No-one mentioned the storeroom or that Kyle had opened the door for her, but she had a feeling that it might not go down well with Sheb. Why, she had no idea, but once the men had gone, helping to clear the table, rinsing the plates and dishes, and stacking them in the washer, she told Kate that she had got in.

'I need some plastic gloves if you can spare them it's so dirty up there.'

'There's a box of them along with any other household

cleaning stuff by the washing machines, help yourself. What are you looking for out there?'

'Nothing really so let's just leave it that I'm nosy.' They both laughed. 'I'm just curious as to what's there. It looks like no-one's been inside for years.'

'You found the key?'

'No, not exactly, Kyle managed to open it for me.'

Kate frowned. 'Did you ask Sheb if he knew where it was, he's been here the longest, way before either me or Kyle?'

'I didn't get the chance, he was out on the range so when Kyle just happened to come into the barn, I asked him for help. The light bulb worked, sort of, but it was still so dark I couldn't get a good look at anything. Just boxes on the floor and things piled against the walls.'

'Well, you be careful, there's probably spiders and such.' The older lady shivered.

'I will but I don't think it will be unsafe, and I'll wear something over my nose in case I sneeze and disappear in a cloud of dust! I'll see you in the morning. And thanks for your dinners, I really enjoy them. To be honest cooking never has been my thing and it wasn't necessary, especially with a mom who does it all the time.'

Kate's face lit up at the praise. 'You're very welcome, nothing I like better than to see an empty plate.' She looked at Sandy. 'You'll never catch a man for yourself if you can't appeal to his stomach, you know!'

'I'm not interested in men.' Sandy felt her cheeks redden and crossed her fingers behind her back. It wasn't exactly a lie she told herself, she wasn't interested in men, just one man in particular.

'That's a real shame. Somebody hurt you, honey?' Kate asked sympathetically. 'You're too nice not to have someone in your life.' She sighed softly, so softly that Sandy almost missed it. 'We all need that special person even if it's cut shorter than we'd like.'

Sandy nodded, smiled back and quickly turned away in case her face gave away the secret that she kept close to her heart. Supposing that this all ended suddenly, too. What if she and Kyle decided they weren't made for each other! What if as time moved on, he came to resent her owning the ranch! What if she gave up and went back home before she got badly hurt! Everything seemed to close in, her life suddenly full of doubts and what ifs!

Retiring to the lounge, battling with her thoughts, she wondered if she should call her mom for a chat, needing a calming voice in what had become a sea of unrest that threatened to sweep her out of her depth. Knew she shouldn't or she might end up in tears. But in the end she did knowing her mom would love to hear from her, and that turned out to be easier than she'd thought by keeping to the attic room she'd found, and all about Domino.

'Oh dear, does that mean that you're not planning on coming home soon, Sandy? We miss you.' She heard her dad in the background shout out, 'Miss you, baby!'

'I miss you both, too. I haven't fully decided to stay it's just that while I'm sort of having a holiday and it's all so new and exciting, I want to stop a bit longer.'

'Oh!' Alice hesitated as if a thought had crossed her mind. 'That nice young man you went to the dance with? Are you seeing him again?'

Sandy laughed. 'Oh mom you're such a matchmaker, last time it was Blade. Oh, and before that the boy in the local Walgreen's. I'm looking for mister-right, someone for me like you found with dad.'

'You'll be looking a long time.' Her mom's voice faded as if she'd turned away, and she knew her and her dad were smiling at each other. 'Good ones don't come along very often.'

'You'll need a bigger net, baby,' her dad laughed.

Sandy felt a lump in her throat. Would Kyle fall in love with her? Could they have a love like her parents? Could they live together for the rest of their lives?

'Well, you know where we are when you want us.'

'I know, mom. Love you both. Goodnight!'

'Sleep tight, sweetheart!'

After a quick email to Mandy, Sandy went to bed and read a couple of chapters of her book before giving up and crawling under the covers, but sleep eluded her, tossing and turning, wondering if Kyle was thinking of her. Wishing he would magically appear, slide into the bed beside her, hold her in his arms and kiss away the doubts. She wanted to run her fingers across his ribbed abs, the hard planes of his chest, to taste the salty skin as she licked the button nipples. To experience again the honed muscles of his thighs between her legs as they opened for his entry, to wrap her arms around him, have him make love to her! Whisper that he loved her, that he never wanted to let her go.

It was so dark outside that Sandy had trouble waking up the next day, still groggy from lack of sleep, but she could hear the sound of the wind howling round the house making doors and windows creak eerily. Sliding out of bed to peer round the curtains, she could see lights on in the barn and the dark silhouettes of the men as they walked towards the house, slickers tightly snapped, hats pulled down over their eyes.

Quickly dressing, splashing her face with cold water, she made her way to the kitchen drawn by the smell of the strong coffee, the three men standing until she'd settled on her stool before helping themselves to breakfast. She went to ask a question, remembered that no-one chatted while eating and clamped her lips shut, catching sight of Kate trying hard not to express her amusement at her near breach of etiquette. Accepting her plate, she set about enjoying the food but anxious to ask about the weather, whether the men would go out in it, and was it safe? Better still, would she be able to go to the barn to look in the attic? She'd prefer to be alone when she did. Finally they had their fill and she could ask.

'Is this storm likely to last all day?'

'Yes ma'am.' Sheb answered, 'Probably just today.'

Sandy listened to the sound of the wind and rain. 'Will you be going out in this?'

They looked at her as if she'd grown two heads and while Kyle's eyes seemed to be trying to convey a message to her, for a moment she wondered if he'd slept as little as her, and her heart leapt at the thought of him thinking of her the same way she had of him.

'Work don't stop for weather lessen it's real bad, Miz Carson,' Buck told her, sounding proud, making Sandy feel as if she'd trodden on his toes, all their toes.

'I'm sorry.' She pulled a face and pretended to wipe a tear from her eyes. 'I'm just a townie. I forgot you're all macho men!'

For a split second there was silence and then everyone burst out laughing, even Sheb, and this time she felt as if she really belonged. Kyle stood.

'Need to talk to you, Miz Sandy.'

'Okay, here or the office?'

'Either. It's about the drive, into the hills to the summer pasture. I've got two men to help out. We'll be going tomorrow as the forecast is improving and packing the pick-up today.'

'Fine, I'll be ready.' Three pairs of eyes looked at her, shocked. 'I'm going.'

'Yuh, Miz Sandy?' spluttered Buck, red with embarrassment. Kate made a tut-tut sound with her tongue.

'And why not, I want to learn all I can about the ranch, I won't get in the way.' She stood and stuck her hands on her hips, her lips tightening. 'I can ride okay.'

Sheb regarded her with hooded eyes. 'Yuh shore yuh wanna do thet? It's no picnic.'

'I'm sure, Sheb.'

He looked at Kyle who just shrugged, not saying that he'd already known, and then they were heading for the door, donning hats and slickers before trudging out into the wind and wet. It slammed as a gust of wind caught it leaving Sandy bereft. She'd missed Kyle last night, he hadn't asked to come in, was he losing interest, had her inexperience turned him off, even if the lust yesterday in the barn should prove that it hadn't? That finally cheered her and she hurried to clear the plates in case her pink cheeks gave her secret away.

How could they have done that? How could she have wanted him so much that she'd allowed him to take her, in a barn, over a saddle? She'd been so willing. Just like that! What was happening to her brain and her body when he was around? Was she normal? Unaware she'd paused in clearing the table, she was brought back to reality when Kate asked her if she was alright.

'Are you really going, honey? I don't want to speak out of turn but the men won't want the worry of you on their hands, they'll have enough to do. Men and woman, especially one as pretty as you, sometimes can't mix, and you've got two strangers along.'

'I'll be fine, Kate. I've never had an adventure like this before, and I'd already told Kyle that when they went I'd be going too.'

Retiring to her room, looking out the window at the trees and grasses bending in the wind, at the horses huddled out under the trees, nipping each other to keep their place in the hierarchy in an endless movement of dulled colours, soaked by the rain. The big door to the barn was shut and there was no sign of life, the men must be sorting everything out for tomorrow and the next few days. As she watched, a strange pick-up drove past the house and down to the barn, two men stepping out. Staring round they went through the side door and inside making Sandy wonder if she'd made the right decision in going but she was desperate to do something different. Or was it the thought of Kyle not being around for three or four days! For the first time she began to realise just what it must have taken to carve out a living from this once raw land, the fight by men to conquer it, their women always worrying about them. Had she been seduced by the sun, the blue skies and the vast open spaces since she'd arrived, enhanced by her feelings for Kyle and that was why she wanted to stay?

The black scudding clouds looked ominous, the only sign that they were passing by the occasional line of a lighter grey between, the wind making the rain splatter against the windows. With a bit of luck the bad weather would be over by morning. She'd need to pack a bag with a couple of shirts, jeans, socks, underwear, toothbrush, and a wash-cloth. Would that be enough or too much? Boots and a winter coat she'd be wearing anyway.

Once they returned, she'd like to go for another ride on the ranch as according to the map in the office, two sections were fenced off for breeding herds, Angus and Herefords. Out of curiosity, she opened up the computer to investigate their history in the States. Not being a great meat eater, by choice as she wasn't a vegetarian, from the information she gleamed, she doubted she would be able to tell the difference in the quality of their meat. Turning to the files she finally found one referring to the sale of cattle and read that the ranch so far had been doing very well. The two year old steers were sold in the fall, and hoped she could go and see an auction, never having attended one.

Returning to the kitchen as the wonderful smell of baking began to seep through, she found Kate with flour halfway up her arms, pummelling the pastry before rolling it out to fit a big pie dish, the meat stew ready on the cooker.

'I came for a drink, drawn by that wonderful smell,' she said sniffing the delightful aroma, pouring out a mug for herself, asking, 'Do you want another?' having peered into Kate's one and found it almost empty.

'Not yet, just let me line the dish, turn the meat into it, and put the top on.' While she spoke, she neatly carried out making the pie before popping the whole thing into the oven, standing with a bit of a groan as she eased her back. Sandy rinsed her mug and refilled it with coffee, settling herself on a stool.

'Have you ever thought of getting a pastry maker?'

'Now why would I do that? Just makes for more washing up,' Kate laughed. 'Besides, I really enjoy cooking from scratch.'

'Can I make you a snack?'

'That would be nice anything you can find will do me.'

Laying a platter with cheese, pickles and slices of ham from the fridge along with chunks of buttered bread, they enjoyed chatting until Kate needed to prepare the vegetables, Sandy helping by chopping greens and the big beef tomatoes, making the afternoon fly by.

Everything was ready by the time the men were almost blown in the door, the two new men with them, Kyle quickly informing them that she was the owner of the ranch he'd told them about, and as they looked at her, Kyle introduced them.

Brad was the oldest, in his sixties Sandy thought, almost bald when he took off his hat, his skin weather beaten and craggy, eyes dark. She'd noticed his rolling gait, his legs bandy from long riding days. He nodded to her showing no real expression on his face. Drago was totally different, a brash twenty something, staring at her with undisguised pleasure from hawk like eyes. His nose was slim like a beak under which were thin lips, an equally thin moustache, and long dank hair. He grinned.

'Nice tuh meet yuh, ma'am.'

Sandy turned away, feeling uncomfortable, unwilling to look and see how Kyle was taking it, especially after his flare up over Torrey. Perhaps her adventure on the drive wouldn't be quite as nice as she'd have liked it to be! Kate told them to sit and eat, placing a plate in front of her and she set too with a will. The meat pie along with the rest of the food was followed by slices of peach tart and buttermilk.

Sandy thanked her, as did the men when they rose to leave the table, both Kyle and Sheb keeping an eagle-eye on Drago. He was obviously under express notice to behave while she was around.

'See you in the morning, Miz Sandy. Kate, we need to eat around seven.'

'It'll be on the table,' she replied, and with a smile, 'as usual.' He cheekily grinned.

'I know.'

Sandy retired to her bedroom to email Mandy and her parents, letting them know that she'd be away from the ranch for about four days, refusing to frighten any-one by saying where she'd be and what she'd be doing before climbing into her warm, comfortable bed.

Chapter Nine

The alarm woke her. It was still dark, and she scrambled up out of bed excited but nervous, enjoyed a quick hot shower that she knew she wouldn't get again until she came back home. Home! That thought resonated in her mind as she sat on the edge of the bed. Not Lone Tree, not even Arizona, but here in Wyoming and on the Boxed C. Dressed warmly, she rushed downstairs just as the men came in. Drago looked slightly sulky, refusing to look in her direction.

Once they'd eaten, Sandy hugged Kate who still looked apprehensive, heard Kyle saying, 'Daylights burning. Miz Sandy, leave your bag by the door and I'll pick it up. You'll be riding Bosco today.'

'No!' Everyone turned in surprise to look at her. 'I'm taking Domino!'

They might as well start off on the right foot in front of the other men. She was officially in charge. Kyle went to speak and she stopped him with a glare. For a moment their expressions mirrored each other's in a battle of wills but she knew he had no option but to back down.

'Your call, Miz Sandy,' he acknowledged.

The men went out into the growing daylight while she took her bag out onto the veranda, Kyle ready to take it down to the vehicle. For a moment his lips curled into a grin as she shrugged into her coat and boots, her slicker she would tie to the back of her saddle.

'Like being bossy, do you?'

'Sets the newcomers a drawn line, you might be in charge of them but I'm in charge of you.'

'Yes ma'am, Sheb's saddling Domino for you.'

Arriving at the vehicle that Buck would be driving, securing her slicker to the saddle and patting an excited Domino, she was quickly in the saddle knowing he'd calm once work was underway. As if to affirm his own line in front of them all before they set off, Kyle sternly told her to follow orders. She might be the ranch owner but her safety was his if she insisted on coming along. This was work not a picnic. If she disobeyed, she'd be free to return to the ranch house. Settling her hat firmly on her head, Sandy nodded in agreement. And in the brightening sunlight, the four riders began following Buck up the rise, Sandy beside Kyle.

The cattle had been slowly drifted north-west for the past week and were now more than twenty miles away and on reaching them, were easy to get pushed into a more compact herd, Kyle setting her back on drag until she became used to what they were doing. The two new men were assigned out on the flanks, turning back any cattle that decided they didn't want to move from their usual range while Sheb and Buck kept to the swing. As Kyle had made sure the herd was used to being hazed, everything went smoothly.

Domino had relaxed now he was able to get involved and Sandy began to enjoy herself despite finding that he was quicker at spotting the animals that weren't where he thought they should be and wheeling in anticipation. That sharpened her reflexes, she had to be more alert or she'd have been out the saddle and on the floor! Once everything was under way, Kyle rode back to check on her.

'How're you getting on with Domino?' He eyed the horse as if still unsure she should have brought him.

'He's teaching me a lot.' She sat into the saddle as the Appaloosa decided to chase a young steer back into the crowd, moving easily with his movements now she was beginning to learn to go with him, looking up at Kyle and laughing. So far she was having the time of her life. Kyle watched her face, flushed and excited, her bottom lip slightly puffy from where she'd been biting it as she concentrated, wishing he could kiss her. No chance till they were back at the ranch, and then she'd have to look out. Four days without taking her to bed was going to take its toll on him. He grinned and made his way back to the head of the herd only stopping for a quick talk to Brad.

By mid-day Sandy's muscles were beginning to tire, Domino's quickness had made her legs and body ache with the effort to stay with him but she refused to give in, she'd been given a job to do, gritting her teeth and getting on with it. The few times she'd ridden the horse had only been in the paddock, not enough time to get used to riding such a long distance, and with the herd slowly climbing towards the high hills, boulders became more prolific along with aspens and bushes, making manoeuvring round and through them even more difficult whenever a steer did decide to head out of line. Trying to curb Domino's continued enthusiasm, her only real relief was that most of the cattle had settled and were happy to continue upward.

Even so, she was grateful when the herd was allowed to slow and graze where Buck had stopped the pick-up to supply everyone with hot coffee. She refused to get out of the saddle, just taking the tin mug when it was offered, knowing that once off she might never climb back on again. Kyle had kept his eye on her as he'd had Sheb and Brad do, becoming aware of her gradually tiring, admiring her even more than he already did for her determination to go through with her decision to come. Then they were off again for another couple of hours until the sun began to go down behind the mountains, darkening the terrain and making travel through the trees even trickier, the cattle finally allowed to stop for the night.

Heading for the flames of the fire where Buck had stopped to cook, the delicious smell made her stomach growl as she became aware of how hungry she was. Slipping from the saddle, with her legs wobbly and aching but still loosing the saddle cinch to relieve Domino, she looked up as Kyle approached with rope hobbles.

'Want me to do them?' he asked quietly. Sandy nodded gratefully as he put them round Domino's forelegs, removing her saddle to stack it with the others while she took the bridle off. With a snort, Domino thumped his way into the dark to the other horses and began to graze.

'Come on.'

Reluctantly he didn't offer to assist her, knowing how independent she was, leading the way to logs rolled into place beside the fire for seats where she could really appreciate the warmth and light now that the sun had gone down. She sat carefully, wondering if she'd ever manage to get up again, gratefully taking the proffered plate of beef stew and beans along with a hot coffee.

'I've put your bag in the tent over there with a small bed to keep you off the ground, and if you want to freshen up, just beyond those rocks is a spring,' Kyle coming to sit beside her. 'I'll be night hawking with Drago till late then Sheb and Brad will take over till dawn.'

'Thanks.' Sandy managed a grin. 'I think this townie has almost bitten off more than she can chew, but I'm really enjoying this, Kyle. I won't hold you up.'

He sighed. 'I know, now go for a walk round camp to ease those muscles.' He bent his face down so no-one could see his lips moving and whispered, 'I can't wait to get you back to the ranch and give you a well-earned massage.'

Sandy hadn't thought she could move but knew she had to, and once Kyle and Drago had left, got up to stretch her legs with exercises she'd once used as a teenager when having lessons at the local stables.

'Yuh okay Miz Sandy?' Buck asked, concerned, looking up from cleaning the kitchen area and watching as she started a second circuit of the camp.

'I will be until I have to get back on Domino,' she managed to grin. 'I'll see you in the morning.'

Stamping her feet although at this altitude there was little fear of any night crawlers, she found the spring, cupping her hands into the cold water to wash her face before slipping into the dark tent. Lit only dimly by the faint glow from the fire, she fastened the ties, removed her hat and coat and gratefully crawled onto the bed to snuggle under a warm woolly cover. Before she knew it she was fast asleep until faint noises disturbed her in the night as the men changed shifts, but the next thing she knew was Kyle calling her.

'Miz Sandy, breakfast's ready, get up an' at it.'

'Okay.' Sandy swung her legs over the side of the bed

forgetting how low it was to the ground and stumbled onto shaky knees, relieved that no-one could see her. Managed a few stretching exercises in the small space to ease her aching muscles and warm herself in the chill of dawn, combing her hair before re-plaiting it with chilly fingers, and shrugging into her warm coat. Slapping her hat onto her head, and with a groan she almost suppressed, emerged to a camp that was surrounded by mist. Taking the proffered plate heaped with thick strips of bacon, scrambled eggs and two big biscuits offered by Buck, she seated herself as close to the fire as possible. Drago eyed her with interest until he caught Kyle looking at him, reddened, and went back to eating.

'Wow, chilly up here. How far have we got to go now?'

'Mid-afternoon on, yuh git too tired Buck'll take yuh in the pick-up,' Sheb answered. 'We'll be making camp fer the night then start back tuh the ranch. It'll be easier for yuh then without the cattle.'

Finishing her food, Brad came into camp leading his horse as well as a disgruntled Domino who was obviously unhappy with a stranger holding his bridle and quickly passing her now empty plate to Buck, she went to retrieve him, thanking Brad as she patted the Appaloosa to reassure him. Removing the hobbles, wondering if she could even throw the heavy saddle on him, Kyle had anticipated and came over to do it for her.

'Yuh good to go?'

'Sure.'

He smiled, waiting until she'd climbed awkwardly into the saddle, but once up Sandy felt better. Leaving Buck to clear the camp and drive on to the next campsite following a well-worn track through the trees, Kyle took her over to the back of the

262

herd where Brad and Drago were already chasing any animals who had spread out over a wider area during the night. Domino was immediately eager to start work.

'You gonna be alright?' He eyed the horse with trepidation, still unsure that she should have brought him, saw her nod and had to concede that she had him under control, still determined to get all but Drago to keep an eye on her while he was up-front riding point. It didn't take Sandy long to get warmed up as she hazed the slower of the cattle ahead of her. Brad and Drago had changed places around the herd with Sheb and him now being closest to her. She could only see part of the herd, the main animals hidden by rocks and trees but she could hear the men calling and whistling to keep them moving.

Finally the sun began warming her even more than riding, the cattle eager to follow those in front to get where they were going so there was less work to do, and with Domino moving about less she really began to enjoy herself as the aches and pains began to ease.

'I feel like a real cowboy,' she told Kyle on the first occasion he came back to check on her.

He took the time to look at her, taking in the pink cheeks, that bottom lip slightly swollen where she'd held it with her teeth in concentration again, and had to look away before he leaned in to snatch a kiss. Knew he couldn't get close anyway because not only Sheb or Brad might spot them but Domino and Ranger were not happy in each other's company, so he just grinned, riding back to the front, chivvying cattle back into line as he went.

And then to her relief, just before she was about ready to give in and get Buck to take her, she heard the cattle way ahead bawling, the whole herd began to speed up, and then they were spreading out. She gasped as she emerged into a beautiful valley that opened up in front of her, surrounded by high craggy cliffs with broken shale slides at the foot, checking Domino so she could take it in. The clear waters of a creek that crossed her path tinkled and splashed round boulders and stones, and she urged Domino across to where Buck had a fire going, and food cooking. Her now very tender muscles were more than aching, and had to admit to herself that she hurt.

While the men were pushing the cattle further into the valley, she slid from the saddle, grabbing the horn to hold herself up as she curbed Domino's desire to go with them, unsteady on her feet.

'Hep yuh, ma'am?'

Suddenly she realised that Drago had ridden over and shook her head, feeling Domino begin to shift, unhappy with anyone strange round him, his head rising. Sandy decided to carry on loosing her cinch, and ignore the man even if her muscles screamed with the ache running through them, preparing to take the saddle but Drago was off his horse and trying to push alongside as if to help. Sandy turned angrily.

'I can do it myself, Mister!' Mister said in that tone showed any man that he was disliked.

'I'm jest bein' friendly, Boss!' His eyes flashed as he stared at her making her feel uncomfortable. Domino swung his head aggressively, snorting, feeling the bad vibes, turning to face the man who instinctively backed up. Just as the thud of hooves came close and a rider dismounted on the run.

'Git away now,' Sheb forced his way between them, facing Drago who tensed.

'Wus only tryin' tuh help the lady!'

'She don't need none, git back tuh camp. Yuh bin told tuh keep yuh distance from the boss lady!'

Having spotted the commotion, Kyle rode over with Brad, unsure what was going on but eyeing both men, happy to leave Sheb to sort out anything that needed dealing with.

'Drago's jest goin back tuh camp.'

'Yeh!'

Drago led his horse towards the fire where Buck, having seen what had been happening, also looked angrily at him, saying nothing but his stance made it clear what his thoughts were.

'Miz Sandy?' Kyle asked.

'I'm fine thanks. He wasn't a problem but he would have got a knee where he wouldn't want it if he had been,' she smiled, even though admitting to herself that the chances of her actually being able to do it were slim to none with her tired legs. Kyle rode off to the fire where a somewhat terse conversation took place while Sheb took Domino's saddle off and hobbled him.

'Yuh're about beat, go set down, Buck's got coffee done I'll see tuh Domino.'

Sandy grinned at him, grateful, going over to take a steaming mug of coffee from Buck and settling down on a big log. Nothing else was said by anyone as they ate but Drago looked very uneasy the rest of the evening. Buck had already erected her tent, and as it got dark, she was happy to retire early to crawl onto her bed.

Voices woke her next morning and Sandy stretched very gingerly as her body rebelled at being asked to move, but at last she managed to get her outer clothes on, struggled with her boots but finally emerged to a bright, cold day. Going to the fire to get a hot drink, she noted that they were one man short and raised her eyebrows at Kyle. He smiled.

'He decided he needed to go to town.' And nothing else was said.

After a good breakfast, Kyle brought Domino in and saddled him, assisting Sandy into the saddle despite her wanting to refuse, having in the end to acknowledge that not only did she need help but also to have his strong grip round her waist. Apparently so did he, his eyes twinkled at hers, followed by a faint twitch at the corners of his mouth. Once settled, as she followed the men back down the trail her aches began to ease with the horse's movement, enjoying his easy gait now he didn't have any cattle to chase, so by the time they halted at midday for a hot drink, she was a lot happier. She knew that the men would probably have kept going had she not been along, that they'd only stopped to help her out on the pretext of needing refreshment.

By the time the lights from the ranch shone through the darkness, Sandy was ready to admit defeat, allowing Kyle to help her from the saddle after insisting on leading Domino right up to the veranda, greeted with concern by Kate.

'Landsakes girl, go get in a hot bath and tuck up into bed, I'll bring you up a tray,' shushing Sandy's effort to dissuade her.

Running the bath and adding salts, Sandy lowered herself very gingerly into the steaming water wincing at the pain in her joints, forcing herself to stay awake until the water began to chill. Donning her PJs she had just climbed under the covers when the older woman arrived with hot buttermilk and cookies, 'lighter on your stomach,' she said.

'Thanks Kate, you didn't have to.'

'You sleep in tomorrow, honey, I'll keep breakfast for you,' and with a big smile, Kate bustled out of the room leaving Sandy to drink the milk while fighting to stay awake, but she couldn't face the cookies and eventually succumbed to sleep.

She must have slept like a log because the next thing she knew, the sun was high and only a need to go to the bathroom made her crawl out of bed with a groan. Another hot bath eased her a bit more, so having combed her hair, she made her way down to the kitchen.

'You okay, honey?'

'I will be, guess I tried to do too much for my first adventure,' Sandy replied ruefully. 'But I wouldn't have missed it for the world.'

'Shouldn't tell you but the men were quite complimentary bout you, even that Brad before he left. But I never told you that,' she whispered, placing a plate of food in front of her.

'You mean I might just make it as a rancher?' Sandy laughed, blushing, tucking in with a will.

'You shore will!'

Sandy gulped as a familiar voice spoke behind her, sensations heating her skin, not having heard him, Sheb and Buck come in.

'I guess I might stay on then!'

'Hope so.' He reached past her, filled three mugs. 'Nothing much to do around the ranch now, we'll be doing jobs we couldn't do while the cattle were here.' He took the drinks to the big table.

'Before you left, Sandy's been on this Internet and looking up the cattle,' Kate mentioned when everyone had relaxed, the men turning curious eyes to her.

'Well, I saw the map and wanted to find out about the breeds we have. Perhaps when I feel a little more enthusiastic to get into the saddle again, I'm hoping I can go see them.'

'I shore could take yuh, Miz Sandy,' Buck offered with a sidelong glance at Kyle.

'You got work to do. Me, or Sheb'll take her!'

Buck clearly said, 'Dang it,' saw the glance from Kyle and grinned, so Sandy decided to ask Sheb first, and he immediately looked uncomfortable.

'Real sorry, Miz Sandy, I got a lot work tuh do.'

Sandy glanced at Kyle. 'I suppose you're going to be busy, too. How am I to learn about this ranch if no-one will take me out?'

He shrugged, looked from Sheb to her, and seemed to give in reluctantly.

'I guess I can find the time. You okay with that, Sheb?'

Sheb nodded, and as Buck gave a very loud sigh, the two older men turned to look at him. He threw his hands in the air.

'Okay, I shore know when I'm beaten. Sorry bout that, Miz Sandy, but yuh all is goin' tuh have to ride with the older hands.' He pulled a sorrowful face while saying older in a voice that clearly showed he was the younger.

'You'all could pull the mud hole up the river a ways,' threatened Kyle dryly as Sheb grinned.

'See, Miz Sandy, how they all gang up on poor me, being a sight younger and better lookin' they cain't take the competition.'

Sandy couldn't keep a straight face, and when she couldn't resist a giggle, Sheb and Kyle grinned. Reluctantly they stood to leave.

'I'll see you when you're better and if the weather holds out,' he promised.

'Thanks.'

With Kate's disapproving sigh, that she should be resting, Sandy cleared the table before going to the lounge, sinking onto the big sofa and opening up her laptop. Instantly several emails flashed up and she began to answer them knowing her mom and dad, and Mandy, would be working, and would receive them later. Occasionally getting up to walk around to stretch and ease her muscles, what was left of the morning and the rest of the afternoon soon flashed by as she concentrated, also checking on her web-site to see how Blade was doing.

Finished, closing the laptop, she went up to switch on the hot tub, waiting for it to warm before sinking slowly into the bubbling water. With this and the hot bath that morning, along with gently doing her exercises, she was already feeling the results as her sore muscles eased, so when dinner was called, going downstairs was a more pleasant experience.

Once the meal was over, she retired to her bedroom to answer her incoming emails, everyone eager to hear more, spending nearly an hour talking to both her mom and dad before opening Mandy's reply.

OK how you doing? Can't believe you went and did that Sandy. Amazing!

Been taking hot baths feeling better now want to go see the cattle we run once I can get back into the saddle.

Cattle WE run? Sounds like you are turning into a lady

rancher already so as if you and the foreman are hitting it off at last.

If I leave here I need to know what's going on nothing mysterious.

Ooh not going alone   : (

Course not Kyle won't let me ride alone and I wouldn't know where to go anyway.

Oh Kyle won't let you ride alone! I'm so jealous you riding off into the wilds with a handsome cowboy you both could get lost you know   :)

I don't think he'd get lost he's been here all his life.

Not a long ride then   : (

Can't you stop trying to match make my friend.

I have a feeling you're keeping something from me I'm coming up to check this all out you know.

Thought you might, you're like a limpet.

Guess that makes you a clam. Anyway things are going good down here your mom and dad are fine and Blade seems to be getting on without you.

He's doing great while I've been away I feel superfluous to the business.

You still got to come back sometime unless you already decided what you want to do.

Well I'm slightly undecided but it is lovely up here away from the rat-race the air so clear I can see for miles right over to the snow-capped Rockies. Come soon friend in case I stay you got to see this place it's unreal.

It's got you I can tell.

Kate the housekeeper calls it Wyoming magic.

Cute well got to go hope I see you soon sleep tight don't let the bed bugs bite, unless it's that handsome cowboy :)

And before Sandy could reply the connection closed down leaving her smiling, hoping that Mandy would come and visit her soon as she missed her.

Before climbing into bed, she peered through the curtains to the lights twinkling in the darkness from the barn and bunk-house. Felt a physical tug that almost overwhelmed her, to slip down to Kyle's cabin, to have his strong arms wrap round her, his lips on hers, his hard erection pressing where she was wet and aching. Knew it wasn't possible, she had no way of reaching him without making a noise in the dark, alerting Sheb and Buck. It certainly wouldn't be fair on Kyle who was trying to protect them both from talk. Falling into bed she was soon sound asleep.

Waking to a sunny day, stretching with a yawn, her body almost repaired, thoughts of going riding alone with Kyle soon quickened her pulse, thoughts that had her body reacting with a hunger for him that was drowning her core in exquisite sensations, memories ensuring she didn't want to climb out of bed too quickly. Trying to walk into the kitchen hoping her feelings weren't showing, the men also arrived at the same time as she came through the doorway, acknowledging her 'morning' with nods.

'Goin' to be a nice day, Miz Carson,' said Buck, quickly scooping into the dishes to fill his plate.

'That's good. Thanks, Kate.' She took her plate and there was quiet as everyone ate.

'I'll be at the corrals if you're up to a slow ride, Miz Sandy.'

Sandy nodded, looking up at Kyle. 'I'll be there.'

Once the men had left she cleared the table, heard Kate softly chuckle and looked up, confused.

'You seem to be anxious to get outside!' Kate tilted her head to one side. 'It wouldn't be because you're getting out into the fresh air? Or going riding with Kyle?'

Sandy couldn't help her face going pink. 'Oh!' She didn't know what to say. 'I, err… !'

'Landsakes, Sandy. Your face is almost an open book to anyone watching it.' Suddenly Kate reached out and hugged her. 'I've known for a while you have feelings for him.'

'Oh no, does anyone else suspect? I don't want to embarrass Kyle. I feel like a silly teenager!'

Kate's eyes twinkled and she laughed even more, wiping her eyes on her apron, sitting down on her stool.

'Dear girl, we all know, including Kyle! Not much is missed out here.'

'Oh. Poor man must be so mortified.'

Glancing at Kate, she began to have a suspicion that her words weren't going to throw Kate off-track, while the silence made her wonder if she knew that she wasn't going to be able to stop what was coming, her heart sinking into her stomach.

'I don't think so judging by what I can see, the way you two try to ignore each other is quite sweet.'

Sandy went beetroot from the tingle in the roots of her hair to the soles of her feet. 'I'd better go, don't want to be late.'

'Sandy, don't be ashamed, if you've nothing to be ashamed of. All sorts of people get together when they're thrown close. To be honest, I couldn't be more delighted if you two want to go, what we called in my day, courting.'

Somebody she could talk to with Mandy unavailable made Sandy want to open up and the housekeeper had always made her feel she could, almost, bare her soul.

'No-one here would mind? I've not been here very long. I've never felt like this before, it's kind of nice but kind of frightening.'

'You've never had a boyfriend? Someone must have asked you out?' Kate was amazed. 'You're pretty, and easy to get on with.'

'The first one ever, was Torrey.'

'Torrey. My word, you have led a sheltered life.' Her eyes were kindly, and Sandy blurted out what had happened to her in University. Why she was now so muddled by her feelings.

'Just go with what you know is right, child! What will be, will be!'

'More of your Wyoming magic, Kate?' Sandy asked, slyly.

'Could be, now get out and have a good time,' waving her hand to dismiss the younger girl. 'I've got things to do.'

Kyle had been left alone with two restless horses wondering what was holding Sandy up. Could she have changed her mind? The longer he waited the more he felt unnerved, finally walking up and down in frustration.

Finally, just when he was about to give up and go back out on the range, he heard the front door shut and looked up to see Sandy walking towards him. At the smile on her face as she saw him, he wanted nothing more than to fold her in his arms and kiss her until they were both senseless. He didn't.

'Everything alright?' his voice was gruff.

'Fine! Who's this?' She patted the black gelding's neck.

'Bosco, he's livelier than Satan.' He felt tongue tied, it felt like he was going on a date! When had that ever happened to him? Like never! What was she not saying! Her body almost radiated.

'Slow ride today?' Sandy found she couldn't look Kyle in the eyes.

'After seein' you on Domino I thought you might like a change instead of old Satan.'

'I would. Are we going far?'

Gathering the reins, checking her cinch, she swung up into the saddle and Bosco immediately became more animated although she found him responsive to the reins.

'Not far. You wanted to look over the other herds an they're kept close to home.'

'After my research, I'm looking forward to seeing them.'

Kyle stepped up into his saddle, curbing Precipice who wanted to get going, grateful for the questions, his mind churning with what Sandy wasn't saying. It seemed as if something had changed in her, why did he feel this sudden shyness, if that's what it was? Had he done something, said or not said something? His mind revolved round anything he could think of but nothing fit.

Leading the way through the gate, he turned left aiming for the open range with the snow glinting on the tops of the Rockies in the far distance, the warmth of the sun not quite reaching his heart. Perhaps she'd open up while they were out. He held back slightly so she could ride alongside him, easing Precipice into a gentle jog enjoying the sound of the hooves on the trail, the creak of the saddle. Every so often getting the slight fragrance that was uniquely her and never failed to put his senses on full alert.

'You enjoying being out, not sore from the drive?' he asked tentatively, trying to get through the minefield of quiet.

'I'm fine. I like Bosco, he's very easy-gaited.'

Kyle's slight apprehension loosened as she smiled at him, her long hair flowing out from under her hat making him want to tangle his fist into it, tilt her head and ravish the throat where a pulse faintly showed that she was also being affected by their close proximity.

'Not too fast?' he teased, relaxing. Her soft laugh made him look across at her. 'Faster?'

Sandy nodded and as the horses increased their stride to a comfortable lope, he couldn't help but admire her easy position in the saddle as she moved. At least the long drive hadn't left her too badly sore. His own pulse increased and he had to look away.

Half an hour later, they slowed to ford a wide creek, The Bear, Kyle told her, its melt waters less muddy than the deeper Little Sandy Creek on the opposite side of the ranch. Between tree-lined banks it was deep enough to reach the horses bellies as they splashed across but they seemed undaunted by the fast moving current. Sandy had never done this before and found it slightly unnerving after being told about quicksand even though Bosco proved both confident and sure footed, but even so she drew a deep breath once he'd clambered out onto the bank.

They resumed a slow jog until Kyle eased Precipice down to a walk and Sandy could make out a herd of black Angus cattle that fortunately were grazing this end of an enclosed thirty-acre field. The bull raised his head to study them warily before recognising the familiar horses with their riders, the newly born calves cavorting about, and Sandy became delighted at their antics. Coming to a halt, Kyle told her that they kept a regular check on them even though the cows didn't usually have a problem calving.

'Only thing we have to look out for are bears and wolves taking the calves if they can get through into the field.'

'They're stunning in the flesh. The pictures I found on the Internet don't do them justice.'

Kyle stopped to actually take a closer look at the herd. He was so used to seeing them just as a commodity that Sandy's words made him take more notice, made him look at them in a different light. Yes, they did look good.

'The bull's worth nearly $300,000, his lineage is the best Willard could buy at the time. Buy the best you get the best.'

Wheeling his horse back the way they'd come, he indicated to go right following another trail to reach another huge field. This time there wasn't any sign of cattle until he pointed to them down by a ford, their colour almost blending with the dry grasses.

'The Herefords,' and as he looked at them, noted her pleasure at the calves. Whatever affecting her earlier had obviously been alleviated by being out on the range, and the further they'd ridden the more he'd felt her mood lighten. 'Like the Angus, we bought the best bull around and he throws good stock.'

Leading the way back to the ford, he reined in, dismounting under a stand of trees to give themselves some relief from the sun and to give her a rest from the long ride. Sandy slid out of the saddle not feeling as sore as she thought she might have been but remembering that they had yet to go back. Removing her hat to hang it on the horn, she tucked her hair behind her ears. Knew that he loved to run his hands through it and had left it loose.

Kyle took a deep drink of water from his canteen, passing it over to her, took a deep breath. Heck she was so vibrant, so gorgeous.

'What do you think of the ranch so far?'

'Are you fishing for compliments, Mister Sherman?' she joked slyly, loosing the cinch and walking to the creek's edge for Bosco to drink. 'You know you're doing a great job.'

Kyle came alongside, her scent swirling around him, could feel the deep embers inside him fan into hot desire, tightening his groin like it always did when she was near. Or out of his sight. Turning his head, he found her staring at him with those wonderful sapphire-blue eyes rimmed with long dark lashes, felt his blood run south and tighten the flare of need. Knowing she wanted him. Dropping the reins he reached out and she immediately came into his arms, raising her lips. She was like a drug he couldn't resist, pulled her in close, his mouth devouring hers, tongues entwining. He slid his hands down from her waist to clutch her butt and drag her up against his swollen and aching manhood. What was it with this girl that he just couldn't leave her alone, so overpowered his senses that he couldn't think straight?

Running her hands under his open jacket, Sandy began to

pull his shirt from his jeans, to run her fingers along his solid muscles, on the warm skin, feeling him tense. Arched as he released her mouth to run kisses down her throat to her neck, nuzzling where the pulse beat under the skin. Pushing his hat off, she sank her fingers into his hair, gripping it, whimpering when his hand enveloped a breast to tease the nipple through her shirt and lacy bra, the abrasion sensitising it as it peaked between his finger and thumb. His breathing deepened as his fingers opened the snaps of her shirt, unhooking her bra, pushing both materials out of the way, bending his head, his mouth searching for and finding a nipple. Suckled it into his mouth while his tongue laved it, the scent of her arousal intoxicating. Felt relief when her hands went to his jeans and she unzipped him, her hand curling round his throbbing hardness as he groaned against her flesh.

'Sandy, I want you,' he whispered, undoing her jeans, sliding his hand inside to cup her slickness, his fingers finding her hot and soaked. She bent against him, begging for release, and never one to refuse a lady's wishes, Kyle slid two fingers inside, forcefully, demanding, thrusting until she screamed his name as she came against him, her inner muscles clenching with each spasm and almost sending him over the edge. He couldn't keep back the long drawn out groan as her hand tightened round him.

Looking into her eyes, darkening with desire, he knelt to ease her jeans down over her hips, yanking her boots off as she leaned over him. His jacket slipped down his arms and he shrugged out of it. Stepping out of her jeans and panties, Sandy moved into him as he caressed every inch of her, her skin rippling as the cool air touched it. His mouth closed on her wetness as he licked and suckled, hands tight around her buttocks to stop her from moving. With a cry she came, tangling her hands in his hair as she shook and shuddered. He couldn't hold himself back any longer. He had to be inside her.

'Wait!' He drew back, reached down to spread their coats on the ground, divesting himself of his boots and jeans. Only half aware of what he was doing, he fumbled for a condom, grateful that he kept some in his pocket and sheathed himself, taking them both to the ground and covering her with his body. Sandy wrapped her legs round his waist, feeling so wanton. How could she keep craving this man? Just what spell did he weave that allowed herself to be made love to out on the open range, needed him inside her so much that she was willing to have his body on hers? Whatever it was she prayed it would never end.

Hooking her heels behind his buttocks, as the head of his shaft nudged at her entrance, she raised her pelvis to give him access and as her hands dug into his back, he thrust deep into that delicious cavern that was slick and tight. Sliding deeper into her heat, her muscles tightened around him as they rocked together in a haze of desire and want, her whimpering cries urging him on. Her muscles pulsed as another intense and exquisite orgasm shook her and she couldn't hold back the long keening cry when he swelled, the pressure building until her moans gave him his own scorching release, pumping again and again until his thirst was slated. Gasping, he collapsed, both swept away on a tide of ecstasy that threatened to break her into pieces as she held him tight.

Putting his hands either side of her head, Kyle levered his upper body away from her, to stare into darkened eyes that were molten with deep embers he never wanted to stop seeing.

Finally, reluctantly, he withdrew, removing the condom, sitting up to take her with him and hold her across his lap.

'God, what you do to me,' he whispered hoarsely. 'I can't keep my hands off you.'

'I'll forgive you if you let me get dressed. It's chilly!' Sandy wriggled.

'Stop moving or be prepared for the consequences!' he warned.

Sandy smiled and straddled him, holding his face in her hands, gazing into his eyes as she rubbed her still aching folds over his rising manhood, pressing her lips to his. Her tongue slipped between and into his mouth, tangling it with his until they were panting.

'Wait, wait,' he gasped, dragged his jeans closer, scrabbled for another condom, tearing it free, pushing her away so he could cover himself.

Before he could do anything, she took him in her hand and guided the head to where she so craved him, lowered herself until he was deep inside and began to circle her hips. Lying back, Kyle gripped her waist and began to move while she went with him. If he'd thought she'd taken him to heaven before, as she rose and fell and continued to circle, clenching and unclenching her muscles around him, he'd been wrong. He'd become mindless, willingly conceded control, lost in her movement, rocking together until his seed began to rise. She felt him expanding, pulsing and filling her until there was only him in the whole universe. And as they climaxed together, cried out as he exploded.

Dragging her down to lay on him, gasping for breath, he tangled his hand in her hair, bringing her mouth to his and lightly kissing her, holding her waist, never wanting to let her go. And slowly they drifted, complete.

Sandy sat up and rolled off him, chilled in the light breeze, dragging her clothes closer while he rolled onto his side, head in his hand, elbow on the grass, taking in every curve of her body. The curly blonde hair at the apex of her thighs where the dampness of their love making showed, up to her rounded breasts with their delectable erect nipples encircled by the darker aureoles. She flushed and began dressing, and heard him sigh as the sight of her body began to disappear. Why she was suddenly embarrassed she had no idea especially after what they just done, twice! She couldn't help but ogle him, that gloriously strong muscular chest and abs down to his legs, and everything in between.

Kyle rose to his feet unashamed of his naked body, noting her eyes couldn't help but rove over him, and began reluctantly dressing, zipping himself up and shrugging into his coat.

'We really must stop meeting like this!' He lightened the mood, rewarded by her cheeks pinking, by the slow smile curving her lips still swollen by their kisses. He reached out to touch them reverently. 'You really are beautiful!'

'Kyle.' Her voice faltered and for a moment his heart sank as her mood began to change, terrified she'd tell him that after all this time she was planning on going home to Arizona. How could he stop her? There was no way he could live without her. His heart began to pound in his chest, saw her frown at his expression.

'Do you know that everyone knows how much we feel about each other?'

He froze. Sheb's words, 'you know why, just be very careful,' echoed in his mind. He turned away to stare off into the distance as the shock raced through his veins like ice. He hadn't been able to protect her from talk!

'They do?'

His voice seemed chipped, hard, even to himself as he tried to think of the consequences. Everyone knew about them? They had been that obvious? He had to take control somehow, what they had couldn't be sullied, he liked her a lot. Hell, he'd known for a while that he'd fallen in love with her but had no idea if she felt the same way. She could just decide to go anytime she wanted, leave him with his heart in tatters.

'It seems so.' She shivered as a touch of cold ran through her veins. He'd sounded so hard, as if he was horrified about being caught out. 'Not, well how far, just how much we like each other.'

Sandy waited for him to say something but he seemed remote, his back taut. When he didn't appear to want to reply, she turned away to walk to Bosco, both horses having moved away when they'd been frightened by their shouts, picking up the reins and tightening the cinch, keeping her back to him. Dread filled her with thoughts that he was ashamed of her, of everyone knowing about them. Please let him say it was okay, that he loved her, that they could now confess their love and be together.

As she swung up into her saddle Kyle turned, his face pale and devoid of expression. Without a word he stepped into his saddle, leading the way home at a slow jog, both buried in their own thoughts until the ranch came into view. Kyle reined in, Bosco stopping beside him, coughed to clear his throat.

'We should get married!'

Stunned Sandy stared at him. She'd expected something, but this? This was weird. Was he proposing?

'Why? You don't love me!' But I love you she wanted to cry out.

'To protect you, save your reputation!' Because I love you! The words caught in his throat.

'Kyle...I appreciate the offer but in this day and age isn't that a little extreme!' Saw anger flash in his eyes.

'I don't do, this day and age, Miz Carson. Sandy. I assume my responsibilities. And if you think I want to keep sneaking around in the dead of night to your bedroom or hide in barns to meet up with you, you've got another think coming!'

'You wanted to do just that,' Sandy pointed out, tense. 'Until we knew where we were headed.' Feeling her stiffen Bosco became restless, and she patted him, her heart beginning to freeze inside her.

'That was before you told me everyone knew about us!'

'But you still couldn't keep your hands off me back there!' she shot back angrily, 'A bit different to my bedroom, or the barn wasn't it!' Watched his face blanch and his jaw clench. 'So what you're saying is you will only marry me because you fear for my reputation. That's some reason for a marriage. We'd end up hating each other. Well, no thanks, when I marry it'll be for love.'

Without looking at him, kicking her heels into Bosco's sides, she rode fast down to the gate, throwing herself off to unlatch it, leading him through. Thankful no-one was around as she quickly unsaddled and turned him out into the corral. By that time there was still no sign of Kyle and resentment began as she brushed both angry and sad tears from her face, entering the house quietly, fleeing to her room before Kate heard her.

She was furious, pot boiling, the least he could have done was to follow her. Apologise! Propose properly, as if he really meant it. If he did it again without saying he loved her, she'd throw it back in his face! She was confused, how could he make love to her and not love her! She loved him. But then what did she know of men?

The sounds out by the barn woke her, making her aware that the men were back, refusing to look to see if Kyle was with them. She hated him, didn't she! Getting up, she washed her face with cold water, practising a smile into the mirror, knew it looked more like a grimace. Tough, it would have to do.

'Hi Sandy, have… ?'

Kate took one look at the younger girl's face and turned back to filling the dishes with food, and Sandy just had time to place them on the big table before taking her own seat. The door opened and the men filed in. From the chilly silence that followed them and descended like a shroud over the whole room, it was obvious that Kyle's attitude had affected the men like hers had affected Kate, so it turned into a very uncomfortable meal, everyone grateful when it was over. The men trooped out with their thanks to Kate, Sandy helped clear the table, along with her half eaten meal, and before anything could be said, left the room, collecting her laptop and retiring to her bedroom.

Wanting to go online she found she couldn't even think of what to put, too choked, ending up by soaking in a hot bath until the water was too cold to stay submerged, not even amused by her skin looking like a dried prune. Lying in bed, she tried to work out what had happened but ended up more upset and finally gave up, wrapping her arms round herself, sobbing softly and waiting for the hurt to go away. Naturally, it didn't and she had a bad night. She loved him, didn't he love her? Was it just sex for men?

Tossing and turning, getting up to make coffee through the night, going out to check the horses, wondering where he'd gone wrong, Kyle hadn't slept. He'd thought himself a gentleman, could have done no less than try to protect her, honour her by asking her to marry him. She wanted love. Why did she think that he couldn't stay away from her? She must have realised that the deep feelings, the electricity between them, the happiness they gave each other was love. Wasn't it?

Going for breakfast, still angry and frustrated, he was glad that Sandy didn't appear, ignoring the looks that Sheb and Buck, and even Kate kept giving him, finally heading gratefully out the door first to make his way down to the corrals.

'Kyle?'

'Not now, Sheb.'

He was ashamed at being short with the older man but there was no way he was baring his soul to another person, it was too raw. And anyway what could he say? Guess what, Sheb. I've been making love to the boss, to Willard's niece, proposed marriage, been turned down, and had no idea why.

He saddled Ranger who usually gave him a sense of peace but didn't today and rode out the gate, not waiting for the others, wanting to be alone knowing Sheb and Buck would be giving him a wide berth. His heart felt as if it was breaking, the hurt spreading throughout his body as he rode off across the range. He'd never been in love before, what if he had driven her away from the ranch, from him.

Sandy only nibbled at her breakfast, told Kate she wasn't

hungry she'd eat it later, refusing to acknowledge the older woman's sympathetic face. Donning her jacket, shoving her phone into an inner pocket with the sound off in case Kyle tried to contact her, made her way to the corrals deciding that she'd ride Domino. Out! By herself!

Slinging the saddle and bridle over the rails, he came eagerly when she called, shoving her with his nose once he was in the smaller corral, standing still enjoying the grooming, his ears swivelling to the sound of her murmuring voice. Being close to a horse, Sandy's frustration died down as she sat on the bottom rail thinking, wondering why she had flared up. She'd been walking about with her head in the clouds, telling herself she loved Kyle when it was obvious that he didn't love her. Why would he propose marriage only when he found out that their romance was known by everyone? She should have kept quiet then this would never have happened.

Angrily she brushed her tears away, saddled Domino who was as keen as her to do something, and was soon out on the range, allowing the horse to pick his own speed, which happened to be a long run along the trail down to the ford. With the sun on her face and the wind in her hair, her tears soon dried. Not stupid enough to try to enter, pulling him up, she turned in the opposite direction to where she and Kyle had ridden before.

A dusty trail led up to a flat plateau surrounded by rolling hills on one side, craggy rocks on the other, and wide clefts looking like they were run-offs from heavy rains. Following the trail, it finally led down to a sandy, sage covered flat with the wind blowing dust from under Domino's hooves, and here she found a relief from her thoughts, thoroughly enjoying the open air and a good horse under her.

After a few hours she decided to turn back but Domino insisted on continuing along to the right, halting at a small creek with rocky banks for a drink, making her feel foolish at not bringing any water with her. She allowed Domino to take his own way and as the ranch came back into sight, he speeded up, anxious to return. To her relief no-one was around, and after unsaddling, she turned the horse into the large corral where he lay down and had a good roll. Returning the saddle to the burro in the tack room, she made her way back to the house, defeat in her body now that the ride was over. She still had to face Kyle and everyone at dinner.

In the kitchen, Kate turned to look at her, pouring out a hot drink from the ever-ready coffee machine without a word, and Sandy took it into the lounge to wait for dinner. Finally, as dusk fell the men rode in, lights went on in the barn and the bunkhouse. Her stomach clenched and her heart lurched. She so didn't want to eat. Uncaring, she went to her room and stayed there, curled under the quilt until sleep finally caught up with her.

It was dark when she heard knocking at the bedroom door and groggily sat up.

'Yes.'

'You want anything, honey?'

'No, nothing thanks, Kate.'

'Can I come in, you should eat something.'

Sandy switched the light on by her bed. 'Okay.'

Kate came in with a tray, placing it on the table by the window. The scent of coffee and fresh baked biscuits made Sandy's stomach growl, and she stood up, seeing the concern on the older woman's face.

'I'm alright, I went out for a long ride, and fell asleep,' avoiding the woman's eyes and picking up the mug. 'I would have come down. I don't expect you to wait on me.'

'Sandy, if you don't mind me saying, you can't hide forever in your room. What ever has happened between you two, sitting up here brooding isn't going to do any good.'

Sandy bit into a biscuit to hide the dampness of her eyes, angrily refusing to give in to tears. She was a big girl now, could shoulder her problems.

'It's nothing.' She brushed the remark aside, staring through the window to the lights below. 'I guess I'm just homesick.'

There was silence and glancing up to see why, found Kate had a slight smile on her lips. Knew she wasn't believed. Refused to say anything, after all what could she say.

'I'm here for you, if you want to talk,' and she left, leaving the door ajar.

For a while, Sandy sat on the bed staring after her, longing to do just that, but with no idea what to say except that she was trying to decide to stay here or just pack up and go home. She hated to give up on something she'd started, and she had started to love the ranch, the people, everything about Wyoming but it was going to be too hard to continue knowing that her heart was shattered. She should never have come, should have sold the place without seeing it, but then Kyle deserved it more than her. She'd resolve it, that's what she would do, turn the ranch over to him and go back home before things became worse.

Chapter Ten

Kyle spent the night in despair. Whatever he'd done wrong he had no idea. The thought of talking things over with Sheb was like an anathema, talking to anyone was, he wasn't used to it. Sandy must have known he loved her because he had asked her to marry him. What would she do now? The thought terrified him that she would pack her bags and go, go back to Arizona, leave him here with his heart broken and his body shattered. How could he live knowing he wouldn't be able to hold her, to make love, to have her wrapped around him? No other woman would ever do for him. He'd have to get her alone, speak to her, explain what he had been thinking and why. Didn't the girl realise that's why he'd said what he did!

When he finally fell asleep, sometime after midnight, he was restless, waking tired and exhausted. Showered and dressed he joined the others, knowing that his mood was affecting everyone, hoping to see Sandy at breakfast. The mood in the room was sombre, and knew it was down to him.

Sheb stayed close, silently supporting him, trying to hide the fact that he was worried about the friend he'd seen grow from an angry frightened boy into manhood, solid and dependable, fitting into range work with him and Willard. Wondered if he should try and take him aside, get him to talk, knowing that men just didn't do that but willing to try. Tell him the secret that he'd kept hidden for so many years, had promised not to reveal. But with things the way they were, he knew the time was coming when he would have no choice.

Sandy appeared just as they were leaving and the atmosphere spiked, even Buck's normal cheeriness missing. Neither willing to look at the other, pretending all was well. As the door shut behind them, Sandy accepted her breakfast with a smile not meant. Picked at her meal just to please Kate, knowing the woman was waiting on her to open up. But she couldn't, just couldn't make the words come, to open herself up to more hurt, display her emotions to another person. Not even sure that she could take either her mom or Mandy into her confidence.

'Thanks Kate. I think I'll go for a ride again while the weather's holding.'

'Be careful.' Kate hesitated, softly adding, 'Think carefully before you act.' Their eyes met in sensitive friendship and Sandy nodded.

Once the men were out of the way, she hurried down to the barn, collecting her saddle, calling to Domino who was more than willing to come, giving a quick whinny of pleasure. Her heart began to melt with the thought of going off across the land by herself, do what she wanted without a care. Yes, without a care, she told herself firmly, and when she got back she'd pack and go, leave all this behind her. But before she went out, there was something tugging at her, something calling to her, something she needed to do that she couldn't put aside. Oh yes.

Leaving Domino, she crossed to the barn, mounting the steps to the attic room, opening the door and switching on the light. Once inside the room, now a lot brighter with the new, cleaner bulb, she skirted the boxes, taking note of things stacked against the far wall and with the faded framework leaning against the back wall.

Curious, pulling two pieces out, she discovered they were small head and backboards, both delicately carved, remnants of once colourful transfers still sticking in places. Pulling out three more frames, dust making her sneeze and forcing her to wrap her bandana over her nose, she recognised two as being the sides to a cot, the third with rusty metal grid work, any mattress long gone. She shivered, so there had been a baby here, on the ranch, once. Oh yes, she remembered the headstone, wife and mother. But what had happened to the baby, no-one here had said anything it.

Laying them back against the wall, she edged carefully over to the wardrobe, the doors opening with loud squeaks from dry hinges when she tugged hard on the handles, but it was empty. The cupboard draws yielded musty materials, torn up by pack-rats or squirrels for bedding, smelling so acrid of some animal that she stepped back quickly, closing them. And only then did it register that they could once have been baby clothes.

Turning back to the boxes and choosing one to open, she knelt down. Just browsing through old paperwork didn't stop her thoughts from wandering, about why she'd been so annoyed at Kyle's offer to marry her. Offer, she snorted, that's all it was. Not, I love you, will you marry me. A cold offer because he was worried about her reputation, nothing else. What was she looking for really? She'd been here just two weeks, that wasn't enough time to rush into marriage. She might think she loved him, it didn't mean that he felt the same.

So where did she go from here? Could she spend the next days, weeks, months ignoring him? Huh, as if that was possible.

Should she really just pack and drive home? And if she did how could she ever forget him, what they had meant to each other. Was she being unreasonable, irrational?

Sitting down on one box, she opened another to find crinkled and half-faded paperwork, bills and accounts neatly bundled by month, signed to say they'd been paid. Packed in age-old cloth and from where a musty odour arose. Down at the bottom were sketches for the house from way-back with how much everything had cost. So much detail that it could easily be duplicated even if the prices would be a lot, lot more these days.

A second box, packaged the same way contained the sale of cattle along with a record of which bull had produced which calf and how much they'd sold for. Kyle had been right, even she realised that the prices had been good at the time. Buying the best had seen the range prosper. How was the market now? Would they get a good price this year? Shocked at still considering going to an auction. Yes she was interested, had been interested, so why was she thinking of selling cattle, she wouldn't be here, would she!

She really should go up to the house and get herself a drink before she went out but the thought of seeing Kate made her change her mind, and a quick glance at her watch showed it was only mid-morning. She could probably do with a snack later although her stomach was still in turmoil. But it wasn't until she had started on the third box that something about a bundle of papers tied up with once pink ribbon down near the bottom caught her attention, made her throat and mouth go dry. Would this tell her something about the missing baby? Her hand shook. For a moment she paused, perhaps these were personal, something sad that had happened to the people living here. Should she be looking? But eventually an overwhelming curiosity overruled her.

Slowly, almost reverently, she undid them, reading the faded words slowly through each one and as she did her heart rose up into her throat, choking her. She swayed, everything seemed to go black, her thoughts scattering like leaves in the wind as she dropped them from nerveless fingers. They fluttered down into the box.

'No, no,' she cried out, slumping with her head in her hands, too stunned even to cry. It couldn't be true, it just couldn't. Her life was a lie, had been a lie! She had to run, to flee somewhere, anywhere.

Staggering down the stairs, grateful that she'd brought Domino into the corral, she threw a pad and saddle on his back, bridled him and went through the gate, somehow scrambling into the saddle and urging him into a gallop along the trail leading to the lake. Tears spilled down her face, drying in the wind, replaced by more as she tried to outrun her thoughts.

Domino, as if to try and please her, was more than willing to stretch out into a full gallop for a few miles and with no urging coming from his rider, slowed himself down to a lope, eased back to a jog, and then a walk as they approached the blue waters of the lake. Stopped of his own accord to regain his breath, sweat on his shoulders and flanks. Despite her mood, Sandy thought of his care, loosened the cinch and, leaving his reins trailing, knowing he wouldn't go far, dropped to the ground beside the bank, the waters ruffled by the wind lapping against the beach.

Willard wasn't her uncle, he was her father! Mary had been

her mother. Why had they got rid of her? Why hadn't they wanted her? But, what about Alice and Ken, how come they adopted her? She felt sick, it was all becoming too much to take in along with the argument with Kyle. She dropped her head into her hands, shaking.

Domino snorted and spooked, his hooves rolling the stones under the trees where he'd wandered for grass, just as a movement behind startled her as she looked up to see what had frightened him, but as she went to clamber to her feet, something hit the side of her head hard and she was stunned. Flung to the ground, tasting dust, hardly aware of what was happening. Her head swam, her limbs felt weighted as if she was trying to fight her way through clinging mud.

'Got yuh at last Miz Sandy Carson!'

Someone, a man with a deep voice was rolling her onto her back, tying her hands while she feebly struggled. She was dazed, her sight blurred, unable to think, heard Domino being brought over, snorting because he didn't like whoever it was and being told roughly to stand still. Bewildered, her head one mass of ache, Sandy couldn't do anything, although instinct tried to make her crawl away from the danger.

Yanked to her feet she was harshly told to get into the saddle, pushed up and over, leaning forward over Domino's neck, wanting to be ill, her head thudding agonisingly. Felt her hands being looped over the horn. Domino was moving about nervously, his every step increasing her sickness as he tried to pull back before reluctantly moving, pulled along by the reins. Whoever the man was, whatever he wanted, she mustn't allow herself to be intimidated. Showing fear only made kidnappers angry.

Kyle, where are you Kyle? She wanted him so desperately. He'd get back to the ranch near dark, find Domino missing, would think she'd gone for a ride. How long before he would realise she was missing, before wondering if she'd run away after their argument? Would he panic, worry she'd fallen off.

The sound of another horse, saddle leather creaking, the jingle of a bit and she knew the man had mounted, Domino being reluctantly dragged along beside it, unhappily jogging from time to time on softer ground, walking round obstacles, making her feel even sicker, her head pounding. The only thing she could hold onto while her brain was mush was who was he, where was he taking her, would he hurt her again?

Slowly her sight began to return and despite the pounding in her head, tried to sit up, whispering to Domino to calm him, unable to see the man's face. Turning her head even though that hurt even more, she tried to see where they were, had no idea, and even less as the narrow trail wound round rocks and boulders, through scrub, climbing ever higher. It gradually got colder as she realised that with the sun setting and the higher altitude, it would only get worse. Thankful that she'd worn her coat when she'd gone to the barn and that she'd kept it on, she knew that she had to endure whatever was happening. Grateful she'd put her cell on silent, had even shut off vibrate in case Kyle tried to contact her. If this man didn't find it too soon, somebody should be able to track it. Luckily she'd shoved it into a pocket in her jeans and not her coat.

'Who are you? What do you want with me?' she asked, her voice scratchy, throat dry from lack of water, eyes dry and prickly after all the tears she'd shed earlier. Trying to think was making her head hurt more, feeling sick again with every step

Domino took. 'Please, what do you want?'

Silence! And that was more frightening than him actually speaking. Fear of the unknown crept through her and she began to shake. She couldn't lose Kyle, she must see him again, tell him she loved him, should have told him even if he couldn't say it back. And still they wound further up into the mountains until she slumped over Domino's neck, exhausted by fear and the long awkward ride, the pain in her head having eased to a numbing throb. Even looking round she had no idea where they were, any landmarks that she might have remembered had long since disappeared behind them, not even a sign of the lake. What had taken her in that direction, an unconscious need to go back to where she and Kyle had first kissed?

Just as darkness was falling, the horses stopped. Before she could rouse, her hands were untied and she was dragged out the saddle. Trying to fight, he cuffed her round the head and she cried out with the pain as his hand caught the same place as he'd hit her before. Dragged into a cabin, she was pushed onto a bed where the stale smell of an unwashed body on the blankets nearly made her throw up, but terrified that the man would only get madder, she managed to choke it back.

'One peep outta you and I'll gag yer,' he snarled, starting a fire in the blackened grate that threw flickering light round the untidy room. He hung a battered, blackened old pot over the flames to boil. Whoever he was, he had to have been staying here for quite a while as she could see empty tin cans and old cellophane wrappers tossed into a corner. The smell of fresh coffee made Sandy's stomach growl and keenly aware she was starving even if the thought of food made her nauseous. She hadn't eaten since breakfast and then it hadn't been much. He stamped outside.

She heard him dealing with the horses, followed by the sound of one horse trotting off back down the track and she prayed it was Domino, hopefully he was now safe. Thank God, he'd head for home, before she thought of how frightened everyone would be when he arrived back at the ranch without her. But why had the man let him go? Had he escaped or was there some other reason, like a ransom note? Was it money he wanted? Trying to get a better look at the man as he came in slamming the door shut behind him was difficult, his face almost hidden behind a long unkempt beard and straggling hair. But there was something that made her think there was a familiarity about the only parts of the face she could see.

He flung her saddle bags onto the bed without a word. For a moment she didn't care, there wasn't much in there, dropped her head so the man didn't see a wave of relief that swept over her that he hadn't yet looked for a phone, and for a moment she thought she'd faint with the movement. Kyle would rescue her, somehow. Sandy avoided his penetrating glare, letting her shoulders slump with weariness, hoping he'd at least pity her distress. But he said nothing, clattering metal dishes, hanging a kettle to heat. Testing the coffee, he poured some into two tin cups.

'Keep mum an you kin have some. One wrong move and I'll tie yore hands an feet so tight you'll wish yuh wus dead.'

Sandy nodded, trying not to flinch from the smell of him as he placed the drink close to her feet, nudging it with a foot and swiftly stepping back. Not close enough to kick him, even if she had been in any condition to do that! She guessed that he'd been sleeping rough. Had he been the man in the line shack, or the shadow she'd thought she'd once seen by the barn, or had it been him when she'd seen the flash of light on the ridge overlooking the ranch? If it had been, had he been watching, waiting his chance for her to get within range. Well, she'd done a good job of that hadn't she!

Gratefully sipping the hot drink, unsweetened and with no milk, it was like ambrosia and though it made her feel sick, she drank it without complaint. She needed something in her stomach to help her cope with her predicament. What did he mean by keep mum, wasn't she going to be allowed to speak. She went to open her mouth until his angry look quelled the thought and she subsided. Ladling what smelt like stew onto a plate, he placed it on the floor with a spoon, nudging it warily over until she could bend down to reach, again swiftly stepping out of range. Grunted, returned to his chair and the table, eating while staring at her for any sign of a wrong move.

Sandy was thankful she was being fed, he was obviously anxious to keep her well for some reason. Finishing the food, she begged to be allowed outside to take care of business, totally exhausted, uncaring that he watched her while she went. Coming back into the warmth, she slowly eased herself onto the bed, trying to be indifferent to the smell. She just wanted to sleep, needed to recharge her batteries, almost unaware that he was retying her hands. She was still mentally shattered by the revelation that Willard and Mary had been her real parents. She still needed to know why they hadn't wanted her.

Back at the ranch, Kyle was tearing his hair out, stamping back and forth between his cabin and the house, demanding to know what the sheriff was doing, frustrated because he had no idea where Sandy might be. Domino had been missing. She'd obviously gone for a ride, Where to, and had she fallen? Even worse, had she run away after their row? Had he been to blame! Kate was silent, her eyes wet. Sheb had comforted her until he and Buck had both gone out with powerful torches, scouring the immediate vicinity of the ranch, Kyle torn between going out himself with Precipice who was a good night horse or remaining round the house, driving people to distraction as he stalked about. The townspeople had been told and several were driving the roads along with two police cars, coming back with nothing to show for their efforts but keeping Kate busy supplying everyone with hot drinks and food. Come morning, ranchers and cow-hands were going to saddle up and check the range, promising to do everything within their power to find her.

And then, in the early hours, came news from the sheriff's department in Cheyenne that they'd tracked a faint signal from Sandy's cell. Kyle wanted to go out immediately but they finally convinced him that they couldn't do anything in the darkness and that the helicopter would go up at first light. All they knew was that she was somewhere up in the Tetons, and he was forced to wait it out. Why was she up there? How did she get there? Had Domino bolted and thrown her? Every scenario rushed through his mind. She wouldn't be in good condition out in the still freezing nights especially up high, had she broken a leg, and arm, her back! What the hell was she doing up there? Why wasn't she using her cell to call for help? Was she unconscious?

'We have to get up there now,' he told them all, refusing to listen to anyone, stalking about.

'Kyle, we cain't do nothing at the moment. You gotta be patient.' Sheb tried to reason with him.

Kyle shook the hand off his shoulder. 'We've got to do something, can't just stand around and do nothing. She must be hurt. I should never have let her ride Domino he was too much for her!' For a moment he sank down onto a chair on the porch. 'We rowed, it was my fault. She was running away!'

'Why'd she go in the opposite direction to town, on a horse, and not in a car?' Sheb tried to get through to him with logic, his heart aching for the man who he loved as a son. 'See reason son! Come dawn we'll have lots a help, you ain't doing yourself or Sandy any good like this.'

He took a mug from Kate and thrust it into Kyle's hand, looking up as more cars began to come in from the road and men began piling out. A trailer turned up full of excited horses, stamping and whinnying, setting off the ranch animals.

'I love her, never told her. Told her I'd marry her. She refused! She thought I didn't.'

Sheb nodded, 'We all knowed bout yuh both son.'

For a moment, Kyle looked up at him as Sheb's words began to penetrate, gulping the last of the coffee, more for something to do as he wasn't really tasting it.

'What?'

Sheb put his hand back on Kyle's shoulder as the new men began to gather round having unloaded their horses, as dawn began to lighten the sky behind the ridge. Sheb leaned forward so no-one else could hear.

'Yuh two was like a book, we knowed how you felt bout each other.'

So Sandy had been right. They had known or guessed. He'd been in the wrong, should have made everything above board although how he could have done that he had no idea. Buck came up with Ranger, leading two others. He knew how Kyle felt about his horse, he would need the comfort.

'Got Ranger here for yuh, Kyle, Miz Sandy'll be ok, we'll find her.'

The shrill neigh of a horse in the distance alerted everyone something was happening and Kyle made it down to the barn and to the gate in record time, men crowding around the barn door anxious to know what was happening.

'Domino, where is she, what's happened?'

He led Domino inside, examining him closely for injury before Sheb spotted an envelope attached to the saddle rug up where it couldn't get torn off by brush, handing it to Kyle. He tore it open, read it quickly before folding it into a pocket. His heart leapt into his throat in anger, nearly choking him.

'It's from someone saying he's Willard's brother. Tom Parfitt needs to see this. Keep it under your hat for the moment,' he hissed, shoving his way through the small crowd. They turned to follow him, knowing something was going on. Pulling the sheriff aside and into the small lounge, Kyle showed him the letter.

'Willard's brother has got her. He's demanding the deeds to the ranch in exchange for her, or he'll do her harm!'

'How's that going to help him?' Tom said, frowning. 'Anything happens to her he won't inherit for years…! Ah that's it. He gets it immediately instead of waiting years for the law to sort everything out through the courts. Clever!'

'I'll kill him if he's hurt her,' Kyle threatened as he ran his fingers through his hair. Tom looked at him.

'No you won't, he'll be charged in the courts. This will mean prison for him, life at least if the community don't get him, but at least she's safe for the moment, he won't want anything to happen to her.'

They heard voices and swung to look at the door.

'Tom? Frank Price from Cheyenne, we've got a chopper ready to go up and track Miz Carson's cell.'

A well-built, grey haired man with a huge handlebar moustache appeared in the lounge doorway, his sheriff's badge sparkling in the light. Despite knowing the man, Kyle would have laughed at the sight if only he could have made one magically appear.

'You get the search party out and they can by guided in by the pilot.'

Within a short space of time that seemed to stretch for ever to Kyle, fretting at any delay, grim faced men were mounting up, many of them armed with rifles. Abduction was not taken lightly let alone of a woman. Kyle, Sheb and Buck rode swiftly ahead of the pack of riders, making for the Tetons as the rising sun behind them lit up the skyline, making everything glow pink.

Clattering pans woke Sandy, glad to feel warmth from the logs blazing in the hearth, struggled to rise but found that not only were her hands tied, that they had been attached to the leg of the bed. Her head didn't hurt so much, it had eased to a dull ache overnight and from what she could feel, she'd got a pretty good lump and a bruise there. Unaware of the extent of the search being taken for her but hopeful, Sandy clung to the only thing she knew in her heart, that Kyle would be doing his best to find her.

'What do you want of me?' she queried before she could stop herself, still half asleep. He scowled but this time left any threats out, heartening her. But he never said a word, bringing over a hot drink, just as wary as the night before but this time, left one wrist tied to the bed. The smell of the stew as he re-warmed it had her stomach rumbling. If he heard it he didn't even look round. She waited cagily until he'd shoved the plate over and had eaten it all before speaking again.

'Is it a ransom you want?' and was taken aback by the glittering eyes and grim smile turned in her direction as his hand lifted to spoon food into his mouth. But he kept quiet.

'I can give you money, enough to make your life easier,' cringing inside in case she might go too far, bring his wrath down on her. There was no way she wanted another slap to her head, setting off another headache. He said nothing coherent, just muttered angrily under his breath, taking her outside for relief when she asked, careful not to allow her any chance of escape.

It was cold. Through a few gaps between dark pine trees, she caught glimpses of snow covered rocky peaks now turning rosy in the rising sun while the cabin, being lower, was only just revealed in the faint light filtering through, surrounded by bushes and massive boulders. For those few minutes the smell of fresh air was like nectar and Sandy dragged it into her lungs while she could. Unfortunately that made the smell in the cabin more overpowering when she was taken back inside making her stomach rebel. She sat down, fighting the sensation to bring up everything she'd eaten. She needed it to keep her strength up.

What was happening at the ranch she could only imagine,

the worry, the turmoil, people milling about not knowing where she was or even where to begin looking. Had Domino made it back? Not that that would be of any help unless they could find anyone who could track him. And that, she knew, would be astronomically unlikely. Her only hope was that her cell phone was still working, the battery had been almost full.

It was strange. Why didn't he say anything? The silence was more nerve-wracking than threats. Any sound of his voice would have made her feel even slightly better, to keep her mind from revolving around and around as to what he wanted. He hadn't hurt her badly apart from the first time when she'd been struck, obviously only meant to subdue, the cuff to stop her fighting him. So what did he want?

During the course of the day he kept going outside to listen for something, was he expecting Domino to come back and bring her help? But by nightfall he gave up, angrily giving her water and a small plate of food. He was running out of supplies, hadn't expected it to take so long.

Although Sandy tried to keep listening out, she slept on and off, woken by the man moving about or the soft sounds of woodland animals scampering about outside the cabin, sitting up wearily as he put more logs on the fire, the cabin having chilled overnight. Apart from having to go outside, she'd been kept tied up and now hope was beginning to fade, her nerves shot to pieces with fear from the continued smells that had been dulled by her damaged senses for a while but now restarted her headache. She couldn't control her body from shaking, her eyes becoming slightly out of focus. If the man noticed, he never said a thing, but it was evident that he was strung out, stalking about outside the cabin door and making her even more scared for her safety.

Just as he shoved a mug of coffee towards her, three very faint shots rang out in the distance, so faint that for a moment she thought it was her imagination. She raised her head slowly trying to watch as the man stood very still, also startled, staring down the hill from the cabin entrance before edging his way down the trail, a gun in his hand, disappearing from sight. Was it a signal, had he been waiting for it? Was someone coming to rescue her, paid a ransom?

For what seemed like forever, with the smell of the coffee making her feel nauseous, couldn't touch it, there was the sound of footsteps outside the cabin. She wanted to scream but nothing more than a faint whimper forced its way through her lips, a faint scuffle of footsteps approached, he was back! The doorway darkened as something filled it. The man was back!

Sandy froze at the sight of a tall figure blotting out the light and tried to scream but nothing came out, she was frozen with terror. Before she could cower back against the wall, boots clattered across the cabin floor, and as she was enveloped by strong arms, caught the familiar smell that could only have belonged to Kyle. She nearly passed out.

'Sandy.' His voice sounded croaky with fear.

'Kyle!' Her voice came out as whisper. 'Ouch.'

He hadn't realised she was tied and she heard a burst of foul language as he untied the rope. Sandy couldn't hold back the shaking any longer, shivering so badly she would have fallen had he not picked her up in his arms, folding her into a blanket, appalled by the smell from it but having nothing else to use. With the movement her headache returned, blinding her.

The next few minutes, it could have been hours, she couldn't tell, were a blur of strange voices, the thundering sound of a machine, then everything went quiet and black as she passed out.

Carrying her limp body to a clearing back down the trail, aghast at the black bruise and cut on the side of her forehead, under his breath threatening to kill the man who'd done it, clasping her firmly to his chest, Kyle made his way through the throng of men who'd ridden with him. Was hardly aware of someone shouting inanely something about the ranch being his, struggling as he was held down by some of the angry posse of men, others around him asking how Miz Carson was.

He kissed her pale lips, whispering she was safe now, that she wouldn't be alone. Placing her gently into the rescue cradle lowered from the mountain rescue helicopter hovering overhead, gusts of wind from the down-draught of the rotors whipping him and the tree branches, leaves and debris swirling into the air, he stared upward, his heart in his mouth while she was slowly lifted high above to disappear into the dark interior of the helicopter. Terrified they'd forget to pick him up, that they wouldn't let him go with her, he raised his arms with relief as the cradle was finally lowered.

Climbing in, he was vaguely aware of strong hands slapping him on the shoulders, his back, wishing them both well. Refusing to waste time and wear the safety belt, anxious to get up with Sandy, he held on to the chains while it jerked its way up. Finally he was inside, trying to kneel beside her, uncaring that the doctor who was trying to check her vitals told him bluntly to get out of the way and let him do his job! The helicopter turned and started back towards the hospital at Cheyenne.

Kyle refused to let go, rubbing Sandy's hand, talking to her, he had no idea what he was saying, anything to try and let her know he was there, promising to propose to her properly, to love her forever, never let her go. He was terrified that she was so pale and almost lifeless, even when the doctor assured him that she had only gone into shock. That back in the hospital they could take proper care of her and check on the head wound. He suspected mild concussion.

An hour later it landed on the heliport at Cheyenne General where paramedics lifted the stretcher out, Sandy's still limp body transferred to a gurney and she was wheeled into the Emergency room. To Kyle's annoyance he was almost thrown out, never wanting to let her out of his sight again, threatened with Security before giving in. Taken to the waiting area he was bewildered by two people who tried to tell him that they were Sandy's parents, Alice and Ken, her mom in tears and being comforted by her husband. Beside them, a girl with auburn hair who informed him that she was Mandy, Sandy's best friend, crying, telling him they'd come from Lone Tree in Arizona.

But he was too tired and exhausted to take it all in. He'd had a sleepless night when the men in the posse had insisted the horses needed rest and the helicopter had had to return to base once it had got too dark to fly but promising they'd be return-ing in the morning to continue showing the way. A couple of draining hours later, a doctor finally appeared, unwilling to allow anyone in to see Sandy who wasn't immediate family despite Kyle's protests.

Sheb had turned up, a neighbour had contacted a friend

with a helicopter to pick him up from the rescue party on the mountain and bring him straight to the hospital, and he steered Kyle over to the couch, shoving a fresh cup of sweetened coffee into his hand, sitting on one side with Mandy on the other.

'So you're Kyle!'

'Do you know me?' Kyle stared at the girl's tear streaked face.

'I'm Mandy, Sandy and I go way back. We've been emailing each other since she came up to Wyoming and she's told me a bit about you.' She laughed softly, her voice unsteady. 'But to be honest I've only been reading between the lines, she hasn't actually said much.'

Kyle gulped down the hot liquid, feeling the bitter sweetness clearing his mind even if his battered body felt like he had been bull-riding. Not that he was stupid enough to do it but guessed how it would feel. Without a word, Sheb got up and went to get him another, pressing it into his hands.

'Get that down yuh! Everyone's down off the mountains, couple ranchers bin staying to check the ranch.'

'Thanks, Sheb.' He desperately wanted to talk to the man but not with people about. And then the door was opened by a man in white, a stethoscope handing round his neck.

'Kyle?' He looked around the room as everyone started to their feet, gulped the last half of his drink, stood unsteadily. 'Miss Carson wants to see you.'

Grabbing his arm as he went to go out the door, the doctor warned, 'She's sedated, I would advise you to make this short and sweet, and allow her to rest. There's no permanent damage, she's young and strong.' He smiled, for a moment confusing him. 'You are one lucky, lucky man,' slapped him on the shoulder and led him to a room across the hall.

Inside it was peaceful, just the soft beeping of a machine. Alice was sitting beside the bed, holding her daughter's hand and wiping away the occasional tear, but it was the pale face with the tragic eyes laid against the white of the pillows that burned down into his soul. How could he not have told her how much he loved her!

'Kyle, this is my mom, Alice.' Sandy's voice was faint as she looked past him, 'and my dad, Ken.'

'Hi son!'

Kyle turned to have his hand shaken, had no idea what to say or do until Alice stood and turned to face him. Now more composed, she held out her hand to grasp his, seeing the haggard look of a man in love and who had gone through hell.

'We'll be outside,' she told him softly, putting a hand on his arm.

'You don't have to go, you're her mom.'

'Sandy wants to see you, we'll be back.'

The door closed behind them, and Sandy held out her hand to encourage him closer. He took it and felt her grip surprisingly strong considering the drugs she'd been given. As he went to sit in the vacated chair, she pulled him closer.

'Sit beside me.' Her eyes burned brightly into his.

'How're you doing?' He sat carefully on the side of the bed.

'Okay. You look like death warmed up.' Her smile took the sting out of the words. 'So you're my hero.'

'How can you tell? I left my cape outside,' he joked, even though his face was serious. 'I think we have a lot to talk about.'

'Better late than never I guess! The bump on my head is not a problem, a touch of concussion. I guess with that and the strain it caught up with me and that's why I fainted, apparently.'

'You bumped your head? Did you fall off Domino?'

'Please don't blame poor Domino, it wasn't him.'

For some reason, she wanted to protect the man who'd kidnapped her, he'd obviously got mental issues especially after the death of his brother, and worried that Kyle would take out his own justice and end up in jail. Her eyes closed for a moment and just when he thought she'd fallen asleep, she pulled his hand to her lips and kissed his knuckles.

'Now go home, take my folks and my friend, have a party and then get some sleep. I believe that they might be sending me home tomorrow if I'm good.'

His heart nearly burst as he blurted out, 'Home?' To Arizona! She was leaving him!

'Silly boy,' she managed to whisper, her eyes closing. 'Home is where the heart is, didn't you know that!' Adding, 'Home is here now, in Wyoming.'

'Sandy.' He stood to kiss her gently, seeing her eyes close, the drugs taking affect. 'I've been so stupid. I should have told you how much I love you. That's the real reason I blurted out that I wanted to marry you.'

'I know,' she managed to get out. 'I didn't run from you. I have a lot to tell you.'

Kyle turned at the door to see that she'd fallen asleep, unwilling to leave the room but finally stepping out into the corridor to lean shakily against the wall. Ken and Sheb were instantly there, on either side, supporting him.

'Kate's gone home tuh cook since everyone's stayin' at the ranch, an yuh need sleep.'

Glad to be steered out to Sheb's station wagon, somehow putting one foot in front of the other, through a haze he heard

Sheb telling him that Alice, Ken and Mandy would be following them in their rental back to the ranch.

'So you knew about us!' he accused when he'd shakily belted himself in.

'Come on, Kyle, you wus both wearing yuh hearts on your sleeves. I ain't blind, only old. Anyhow, we bin talking, me and Sandy's parents an we all need to talk tomorrow. After a meal an a night's sleep!'

'Talk, what's there to talk about? I'm going to marry the girl.'

Sheb chuckled and Kyle looked at him. 'You never laugh, well very rarely, not till Sandy arrived at the ranch. What's with you?'

But Sheb stayed silent, and with Kyle too tired to continue, he was almost asleep when they arrived at the ranch, greeted by the sight of Buck standing on the porch waving his hat like mad, a big grin on his face.

'Hi Kyle, glad tuh hear Miz Sandy's gonna be okay,' and then his face changed. 'Who's thet?'

The other car had turned up and he was staring in awe as the passenger in the back got out.

'Uh, that's Mandy, Miz Sandy's friend, all the way from Arizona tuh meet up with a for real cowboy… !'

Sheb stopped because Buck had strolled over to the car with a swaggering gait, gallantly sweeping his hat off and obviously smitten. And from the look on Mandy's face, she was, too.

'I feel left out!' he muttered in disgust, following everyone.

Kate had laid the table in the small lounge with the best cutlery, and big tureens that hadn't seen the light of day for years filled to overflowing, everyone tucking in with a will, voices and relieved laughter echoing in the room as they hadn't since Willard had lost his wife. Sheb smiled to himself. It had been a long time since he'd seen such a scene. One of the two ranchers who'd looked after the ranch while the posse had been out, had also stayed for the meal, being a widower, glad of the food and the company.

Finally, everyone retired to their own rooms leaving Sheb and Buck to check the barns and head to the bunkhouse, Sheb keenly aware that the following day would bring everything to a head, something he had had trouble keeping to himself for years. Only a promise to an old friend had kept him silent.

Kyle woke feeling exhausted but better than he had done for some time, to find that he was still dressed having collapsed onto his bed the night before. Showered and freshly shaved, in clean clothes, he went up to the house to find everyone in the kitchen having breakfast. Embarrassed when Alice got up to throw her arms round him, to thank him for saving their daughter and Ken's eyes meeting his as he tilted his head with a smile towards his wife. Mandy had somehow found herself beside Buck and he was regaling her with tales of daring do, her eyes wide with excitement.

Alice had already phoned the hospital and been told that Sandy was being released that afternoon although she needed to be kept quiet and to rest, looking across at Kyle as she said it, but he excused himself by saying that the ranch wouldn't run itself. After all the problems there was a lot of work to do. He'd let them pick their daughter up. Buck groaned audibly, following Sheb and Kyle out, he'd promised to show Mandy round the ranch later.

'You ain't going far, Kyle. Me an you, and Sandy's parents,

got to talk if Miz Sandy is up to it. Buck kin entertain Miz Mandy.'

Buck perked up as Mandy giggled. 'It's gonna be hard but I'm up fer that there entertaining bit! Jest to help you out.'

Late afternoon, Ken and Alice turned up with Sandy who looked a lot better, her eyes immediately picking up on Kyle, and he wasn't sure who blushed the most, her or him. After a welcome snack and coffee, Sheb asked Alice, Ken and Kyle to come with him into the big lounge, Sandy between her parents.

'Sheb, I think I should say something first.' Sandy sat back in the settee, pale but determined.

'Before I rode off, I found out something, something that shook me and made me run away.' She held up a hand to stop him. 'Mom, dad, there's paperwork in the old storeroom that shows… shows… !' She floundered but Sheb smiled and told her to continue. She looked at him in confusion, then at her parents' faces, full of love and understanding. Kyle looked baffled.

'Willard wasn't my uncle. He was my real dad! And the lady in the picture up there was my real mom!'

There was a shocked silence before Sheb stood up to go to the fireplace, staring at the picture before turning to face them all. Kyle was silent, elbows on his knees, staring at the floor, bewildered at the statement.

'When Mary died of a brain aneurism, well thet's what they call it these days, Willard almost give up on life, he shore loved her so much, jest goin' through the motions. Having a tiny child in the house was jest too much for him, dang nigh broke his heart but he decided tuh hev her adopted. Sandy here is their daughter, their only child.'

'He found out through the adoption people thet Alice and Ken was lookin' to adopt, hed them checked out an after a word with them all, they agreed tuh let yuh hev her, the real reason he ast you to keep in touch.' He looked at Sandy. 'He never, ever stopped loving you lass!'

Sandy was silently crying on Alice's shoulder, Ken's arms stretching to encompass them both while Kyle sat staring at the floor, too shocked to speak. No wonder Willard had left his ranch to her, it made sense that only a really close relative would have inherited over him.

'I wus sworn to secrecy which was plumb hard, Kyle, but a promise is a promise. I knowed someone would find out eventually, knowed what you'd discover, Sandy. I think you wus bein' drawed there, why I wasn't surprised by you sayin' yuh wanted to go into the attic.'

'Something was, Sheb, and to the ranch that had been given to me. I'd never wanted to leave Arizona, but I just had to come.'

'Even iffn I'd told yuh the story, it wouldn't have stopped Elijah from trying to get the ranch, he wus always jealous of Willard's success an although I don't think he knew who yuh wus exactly, he would hev tried to get it anyways.'

Kyle stood up and walked out the room, his footsteps echoing down the hall. Alice looked at Sandy and gently squeezed her hand.

'Don't lose him, sweetheart. He's been through enough and obviously loves you very much.'

She smiled, and Ken looked at her with love in his eyes, a love Sandy had known they'd always had for each other, she'd always wanted for herself. She hugged the lady who she'd always called her now mom.

'You've been the best parents ever, Willard couldn't have chosen better. Thank you for all you've done.'

'We didn't always know what to say, but we did our best.' Ken grinned slyly and kissed Alice resoundingly, making her blush. 'Go talk to Kyle. Men always find it hard to say, I love you. Your mom had to drag it out of me but it gets easier with the years.'

Sandy laughed softly, really laughed for the first time in days, looking across at Sheb whose eyes were twinkling.

'Something to do with being macho men I bin told!'

And then she was walking quickly to the door, ignoring the warning shouts to take it easy, and out to stand on the veranda.

'Kyle Sherman you just wait right there,' she called out.

Having stopped just to take a deep breath and try to collect his scattered thoughts, Kyle turned and as Sandy ran right into his arms, he scooped her up, his lips finding hers, pressing her willing body against his, dismayed that there wasn't anywhere he could take her, to show her again and again, how much he loved her. Not having seen either Buck or Mandy for some time, he had a strong suspicion that the barn was already occupied.

'Don't you dare walk off and leave me.'

'Never,' he assured her.

'Have you got something to tell me?' Staring deep into his eyes, seeing them darken, his lips drawing back in that breathtaking smile that always made her heart beat faster.

'That I love you, fell in love with you the first time we met out on the road, will love you for ever and ever? You mean like that?'

'Perfect.' She pulled his head down and let their lips meet gently, at first. They had so much to tell each other that would take more than words.

Sitting on the porch later, holding her hand, he told her all about Willard taking him under his wing as a youngster. About how his father used to beat him whenever he got drunk, how at the age of nine the man had seen him sitting in the street with new and old bruises on the side of his face. Asked his name and got him to tell why he was hurt. How after Willard had stalked into the house, he'd heard a lot of shouting and a crash and when Willard had returned, urged Kyle to get into his car to go for a hospital check-up. There it had been discovered that not only was he limping from a kick, there were more bruises on his body, old and new. The police had been called to investigate but he hadn't really understood why his father had been arrested and taken into custody.

He'd been brought back here, to the Boxed C and sometime after that his father had been charged with assault. A quiet word by his lawyer and the man hadn't pressed charges against Willard. But he had been imprisoned for child abuse. When his mother couldn't be found, she'd left years before and he couldn't even remember her, his father had willingly signed Kyle over to Willard's care. Taken under Willard's wing, as well as the many cowboys who'd drifted through and especially by Sheb, he'd learned to ride and work cattle, also learning how to run the ranch.

Going back indoors, smiling mysteriously, he left Sandy chatting to her mom for a while before coming back to take her hand tightly, leading her into the big lounge where, to her surprise she found everyone waiting. Kyle turned to face her, went down on one knee and asked a blushing Sandy if she would do him the honour of marrying him. Even though he hadn't got a ring yet, they could go into Cheyenne to the big jewellers and she could choose what she liked.

To cheers and claps, she accepted. How could she not, didn't she know how much she loved him and, daringly, told him. Her mom and dad, Mandy who was still holding Buck's hand, and Kate, were all hugging her, crying, Mandy telling her that she'd love to be a bridesmaid. With congratulations all round, Kate brought out a few bottles of wine and they held an impromptu party.

Epilogue

After a few days stay, when Alice and Ken had decided to go back home taking a reluctant Mandy with them, flying out of Cheyenne, Sandy and Kyle also travelled with them leaving Sheb and Buck in charge of the ranch.

Sandy proudly showed him her stables and he chatted with Blade over the work he and Sandy had been doing, even more proud of what she'd achieved. Blade had eagerly accepted taking over the business, with an option to buy whenever he wanted.

They'd also met up several times with Mandy in Lone Tree and Phoenix, and to Sandy's obvious amusement, Kyle had admitted that he had been uncomfortable with the crowded sidewalks and the busy streets of Phoenix, happy to retreat back to Lone Tree. He couldn't understand how on earth she could have grown up with all the confusion and noise, and no wonder that she'd been a little intimidated when she'd turned up in the wilds of Wyoming.

Luckily, she didn't have to go to court to testify against Willard's brother, he had been assessed and already taken to the psychiatric ward of a prison. She tried hard to feel sorry for him, but suffered nightmares for weeks after, waking in the night, when Kyle would hold her tightly in his arms and whisper that she was safe, and slowly they began to abate.

A few months later, Sandy and Kyle were married in the grounds of the ranch on the front porch, attended by her mom and dad, her brother, Carlton and his girlfriend Dana, who were now blissfully planning their own wedding. Sheb had been proud to be Kyle's best man but refused to get into a suit instead wearing brand new western clothing, while Mandy, who now came and stayed at the ranch as often as possible to Buck's evident pleasure, was her bridesmaid. Along with what appeared to be everyone in Sweetwater, Torrey and his mom from Buffalo had also been invited. Somehow, to her amazement and delight, Kyle had arranged for Domino, following a lot of training to accept the noisy occasion, to present the rings tied to his browband.

Before the party and dancing had finished, and before they changed and saddled up to ride to the lake to watch the sunset because, after all, as Kyle told her, that's where it had all begun, Sandy gave him her wedding present, half the deeds to the ranch. They were now partners. Kyle, lost for words, scooped her into his arms and kissed her until they were both breathless.

Riding to the lake hand in hand, snuggling into Kyle's arms, she whispered, 'I'd like to have two babies, a boy and a girl.'

'Would you now?' he grinned. 'Will it take a lot of practice?'

'Oh lots and lots of practice.'

'Then we should get started right away.'

He bent his head to let his lips lightly touch hers, slowly increasing the pressure, gathering her body tight against his hardening body, her hands winding round his neck, sending delicious shock waves of pleasure skittering through their bodies at the promise to each other of a lifetime of love. He drew her down onto a blanket, covering her body with his,

his hands and lips melding them together, her core already pulsing.

'Wyoming magic,' she finally managed to whisper before she wasn't allowed to speak again.

THE END